Inches away. Her breath caught. Only then did she realize what she had done. Her hands were clutching his arms and her body was pressed against his. Intimately. Chest to chest and hip to hip. She could feel every hard inch of his chest and legs. She could feel something else as well. Something that made her mouth go dry, her heart drop, and her stomach flip all at the same time.

Oh, my.

The shock of it startled her. It was as if every nerve-ending in her body had been struck by a lightning bolt of awareness. She opened her mouth to gasp, but the sound strangled in her throat when their eyes met.

Heaven help her! Despite the rain and the cold, her body filled with heat.

If she hadn't felt the proof of his desire, she could see it now in his eyes. He wanted her, and the force of it seemed to be radiating under her fingertips, making her tremble with unfamiliar sensations. Her heart seemed to be racing too fast, her breath to be short and uneven, and her limbs too heavy.

She couldn't seem to move. She was caught up in something she didn't understand but couldn't resist. Didn't *want* to resist.

By Monica McCarty

The Hunter
The Recruit
The Saint
The Viper
The Ranger
The Hawk
The Chief

Highland Warrior
Highland Outlaw
Highland Scoundrel

Highlander Untamed
Highlander Unmasked
Highlander Unchained

The Hunter

A HIGHLAND GUARD NOVEL

MONICA McCARTY

BALLANTINE BOOKS • NEW YORK

The Hunter is a work of fiction. Names, characters, places, and incidents are the products of the author's imagination or are used fictitiously. Any resemblance to actual events, locales, or persons, living or dead, is entirely coincidental.

A Ballantine Books Mass Market Original

Published in the United States by Ballantine Books, an imprint of The Random House Publishing Group, a division of Random House, Inc., New York.

BALLANTINE and colophon are trademarks of Random House, Inc.

ISBN 978-0-345-54391-2
eBook ISBN 978-0-345-54392-9

Cover design: Lynn Andreozzi
Cover illustration: Franco Accornero

Printed in the United States of America

www.ballantinebooks.com

9 8 7 6 5 4 3 2 1

Ballantine mass market edition: July 2013

To Kate,
for being editor extraordinare of nine books
in five years, for your support and enthusiasm,
for making me forget this is supposed to be work,
and for always knowing exactly what I *meant* to write.
Our last book together is for you! Sláinte!

THE HIGHLAND GUARD

Tor "Chief" MacLeod: Team Leader and Expert
   Swordsman
Erik "Hawk" MacSorley: Seafarer and Swimmer
Lachlan "Viper" MacRuairi: Stealth, Infiltration, and
   Extraction
Arthur "Ranger" Campbell: Scouting and
   Reconnaissance
Gregor "Arrow" MacGregor: Marksman and Archer
Magnus "Saint" MacKay: Survivalist and Weapon
   Forging
Kenneth "Ice" Sutherland: Explosives and Versatility
Eoin "Striker" MacLean: Strategist in "Pirate" Warfare
Ewen "Hunter" Lamont: Tracker and Hunter of Men
Robert "Raider" Boyd: Physical Strength and
   Hand-to-Hand Combat
Alex "Dragon" Seton: Dirk and Close Combat

   Also:
Helen "Angel" MacKay (née Sutherland): Healer

FOREWORD

The year of our lord thirteen hundred and ten. Four years ago, Robert the Bruce's bid for the Scottish throne seemed doomed to failure, when he was forced to flee his kingdom an outlaw. But with the help of his secret band of elite warriors known as the Highland Guard, Bruce has waged a miraculous resurgence, defeating the countrymen who stood against him to retake his kingdom north of the Tay.

With the Borders and most of Scotland's major strongholds still occupied by English garrisons, however, the war is only half won. The biggest challenge to the Bruce's fledgling kingship—the might of the greatest army in Christendom—is yet to come.

After a brief respite from warfare, the truce with England comes to an end when Edward II marches on the rebel Scots. From his headquarters in the heather, Bruce launches his new "pirate" warfare, harrying the English with surprise attacks and skirmishes but refusing to meet them in an open field, eventually sending King Edward and his men scurrying back to the Borders for the winter. Delaying, not deciding, the final battle to come.

But there is no peace for treachery. And this time, it will be not the warriors of the Highland Guard who come to his aid, but another powerful ally that has been by the Bruce's side from the first: the church. The support of men such as William Lamberton, the Bishop of St. Andrews, has proven invaluable, with his network of spies and "couriers of the cloth" providing much needed intelligence—intelligence that just may end up saving the Bruce's life.

Prologue

❧

Dundonald Castle, Ayrshire, Scotland, late June 1297

Fynlay Lamont was drunk again. Ewen Lamont sat in the back corner of the Great Hall of Dundonald Castle with the other young warriors and tried to ignore his father. But every raucous burst of laughter and belligerent boast that filtered back from Fynlay's table near the front of the hall made Ewen want to slide deeper and deeper into his bench.

"That's your father?" one of the Earl of Menteith's squires asked. "No wonder you don't talk much. He does enough for both of you."

The other young warriors around him laughed. Ewen wanted to bury his head in shame, but he forced himself to smile at the jest and act as if it didn't bother him. He was a man now—nearly seven and ten—not a boy. He couldn't run away the way he'd done as a child every time his father drank too much or did something outrageous.

But his father's lack of control—his lack of discipline—was going to ruin everything. As it was, this meeting was like a bed of dry leaves next to a fire just waiting for a spark to ignite.

Though the great lords gathered in secret here today were kinsmen, all descendants of Walter Stewart, the 3rd High Steward of Scotland, they didn't always see eye-to-eye. They had come to see whether they could put aside those differences long enough to fight the English rather than each other. Adding Wild Fynlay to the already volatile mix of men in the room was like holding up a blacksmith's bellows to fan the flames with hot air—lots of hot air.

But like Ewen, Fynlay Lamont of Ardlamont was Sir James Stewart's man, and as one of Stewart's chief battle commanders, his father had a right to be here. If there was one thing Wild Fynlay knew how to do it was fight. It was keeping the fighting contained to the battlefield that was the problem.

Wild Fynlay's epitaph had been well earned. He was quick to fight, quick to argue, and quick to take offense. Rules, law—nothing could bind him. He did what he wanted, when and where he wanted. He'd seen Ewen's mother thirty years ago at a local fair, decided he wanted her, and had taken her. It didn't matter that she was betrothed to his cousin and chief, Malcolm Lamont. It didn't matter if those choices nearly cost him—and their clan— everything.

His father hadn't changed at all in the year since Ewen had seen him last—except for the missing finger. While Ewen had been in the Borders in the service of Sir James Stewart, the 5th Steward of Scotland, his father had gotten so drunk, he'd bet one of their kinsmen that he could pull his hand away from the table faster than the other man could draw his blade. The top joint of the middle finger on his right hand proved Fynlay wrong.

Ewen's reckless, more-savage-than-civilized father was always getting into trouble. He spoke with his sword and his fists—usually in a whisky-induced slur. Fighting and drinking were sports of which he never tired. And wagering. Fynlay Lamont had never met a challenge too crazy or dangerous for him to like. The last time Ewen had been home, his father had wagered that he could fight a pack of wolves with his hands—bare-arsed naked.

He had, and won. Although he'd suffered a serious injury to his leg when one of the wolves had managed to get his teeth on him.

Instead of returning to Rothesay Castle for his training as he was supposed to that winter, Ewen had stayed at Ardlamont to act as chieftain to his clan while his father recovered. It had been six months before Ewen could return to Sir James's household. He'd missed every minute of it. But if there was one thing he'd learned from Sir James, it was the importance of doing his duty.

He sure as Hades hadn't learned it from his father. Duty and responsibility were an anathema to Fynlay Lamont. He left everyone else to clean up his mess. First Sir James, and now, if he got his wish, Ewen.

But Ewen wasn't going to back to Ardlamont. He didn't care what his father wanted. He was going to earn a place in Stewart's retinue and hopefully, if the men in this room could be persuaded, join the uprisings started last month by a man named William Wallace.

King Edward of England had ordered the Scottish lords to appear in Irvine on July 7. The question was whether they would march the five miles to Irvine to submit to the English or march to do battle with them.

Sir William Douglas, Lord of Douglas, had already joined Wallace and was trying to recruit his kinsmen, Stewart, Menteith, and Robert Bruce, the young Earl of Carrick to do the same. Sir James was inclined to join the fight; it was the others who would need convincing that following the rebellion of a man who wasn't even a knight, against the most powerful king in Christendom, made sense.

With any luck, Ewen would be marching off to his first battle in a few days. He couldn't wait. Like every other young warrior around this table, he dreamed of greatness, of distinguishing himself on the battlefield. Then maybe everyone would stop talking about his "wild" father and the wolves he'd fought, the ships he'd nearly run aground in some half-crazed race around the Isles, or the bride he'd stolen from his own chief.

His father's voice stopped him cold. "When it's complete, my castle will be the greatest stronghold in all of damned Cowal—no disrespect, Stewart."

Oh God, not the castle. This time, Ewen couldn't prevent the heat from crawling up his face.

"Where are you going to find the gold?" one of the men laughed. "Under your pillow?"

It was well known that Fynlay couldn't hold a coin longer than it took to gamble it away. It was also well known that his infamous castle had stood half-built for sixteen years, ever since the day Ewen's mother had died in childbirth, when Ewen was barely a year old.

Ewen had had enough. He couldn't listen to his father any longer. He pushed back from the trestle table and stood.

"Where are you going?" one of his friends asked. "The feast is just getting started. They'll be coming around with Sir James's special whisky soon."

"Don't bother, Robby," another of the lads said. "You know Lamont—he doesn't believe in fun. He's probably off to polish Sir James's armor or sharpen his blade or stare at the dirt looking for tracks for a few hours."

He was right. But Ewen was used to their jesting about how seriously he took his duties, so it didn't bother him.

"You might try staring at dirt a little longer, Thom," Robby said. "From what I hear you couldn't find a fish in a barrel."

The others laughed, and Ewen used the opportunity to escape.

A blast of cool, wet air hit him the moment he stepped outside the Hall. It had been raining most of the day, and though it was only late afternoon, the skies were near dark against the backdrop of the magnificent new stone keep perched high on the castle motte. Like Stewart's castle of Rothesay on the Isle of Bute in Cowal, his Dundonald Castle in Ayrshire was one of the most impressive strongholds in Scotland, reflecting the importance of the Stewarts to the crown.

Making his way down the hill to the castle bailey, Ewen stopped first at the armory to check Sir James's armor and weapons, and then, having seen to them, went to the stables to make sure his favorite mount had been exercised. It had, so he pulled a bale of grass over and sat to, as Thom had said, stare at dirt.

It was a game he'd played since he was a boy whenever he needed to get away, to see how many tracks he could find or details he could pick up. In the stable, he liked to see if he could match the tracks with the horses.

"What do you see?"

He turned, surprised to see Sir James in the doorway. The sky was dark behind him, casting him in the shadows. Tall and lean, his dark red hair starting to streak with gray, the hereditary High Steward of Scotland exuded nobility and authority. He was a knight, and as all knights he was good with a sword, but Stewart's true brilliance was as a leader. He was a man whom other men would willingly follow into war—and, if necessary death.

Immediately, Ewen jumped to his feet. How long had he been in here? "I'm sorry, my lord. Were you looking for me? Is the meeting over? What has been decided?"

The older man shook his head and sat on the bale, motioning for him to sit beside him. "Nothing, I'm afraid. I grew tired of the squabbling and decided I needed a breath of fresh air. I assume you needed the same?"

Ewen bowed his head and concentrated on a long piece of dried grass, not wanting him to see his shame.

"You're looking at the tracks?" Sir James asked.

Ewen nodded, pointing to the hoofprints in the dirt. "I'm trying to find distinguishing marks."

"I hear you bested all my knights at a tracking challenge yesterday. Good work, lad. Keep this up, and you'll be the best tracker in the Highlands."

Sir James's praise meant everything to him, and Ewen was pretty sure it showed. He swelled with pride, not knowing what to say. Unlike Fynlay, words didn't come easily for him.

The silence stretched for a few moments.

"You are not your father, son," Sir James said.

Son. If only it were true! Sir James was everything Fynlay was not: honorable, disciplined, controlled, and thoughtful.

"I hate him," Ewen blurted fiercely, instantly ashamed of the childish sentiment and yet unable to take it back.

One of the best things about Sir James was that he didn't condescend to any of his men—no matter how young. He considered what Ewen said. "I wish you could have known him when he was young. He was different then. Before your mother died and the drink took over."

Ewen's jaw clenched belligerently. "You mean when he abducted my mother from his chief?"

Sir James frowned. "Who told you that?"

He shrugged. "Everyone. My father. It's well known."

"Whatever your father's sins, do not lay that one at his feet. Your mother went with him willingly."

Ewen stared at the other man in shock, but if there was anyone who would know, it was Sir James. Ewen's mother had been his favorite cousin, and he was the man they'd gone to for help when the reprisal for his father's rash actions had come from Malcolm Lamont.

"That is why you helped them," Ewen said. Suddenly it made sense. Ewen had never understood why Sir James had come to his father's rescue and prevented his ruin after he'd started a war by stealing his chief's bride.

"Among other reasons," Sir James said. "Your father's sword, for one. He was—still is—one of the best warriors in the Highlands. You will be like him in that respect, I think. But aye, I wanted your mother to be happy."

Bride abduction was perhaps one less sin to lay at his father's feet, but Fynlay still had plenty of them left. It didn't change the reckless, disloyal act that had broken him from his clan and nearly seen the destruction of the Lamonts of Ardlamont. Nor did it change everything that had come after.

"You shouldn't have allowed him to come," Ewen said. "Not with Malcolm here."

Malcolm Lamont wasn't his chief anymore. His father's actions had caused the Ardlamont Lamonts to break from their chief. They were Stewart's men now.

"There was no choice. Malcolm is my cousin Menteith's man, as your father is mine. Your father has given me his oath he will not break the truce, no matter how hard Malcolm presses him. God knows there is enough disagreement among my kinsmen without the old feud between your father and Malcolm getting in the way."

It was hardly right for Ewen to be questioning his lord, but he asked anyway. "And you trust him?"

Sir James nodded. "I do." He stood. "But come, we should get back. The feast should be dying down by now."

It was, but not for the reason they'd anticipated. They stepped out into the dark rain and heard a loud ruckus coming from the opposite side of the *barmkin*. It was the sound of cheering, followed by a gasp, and then an eerie dead silence.

"I wonder what that is all about?" Sir James asked.

Ewen felt a flicker of premonition.

All of a sudden men started pouring into the *barmkin*, racing toward the keep. He could tell by their expressions that something was wrong. "What is it?" Sir James asked the first man to approach. "What has happened?"

Ewen recognized the man as one of Carrick's. "The Lamont chief claimed that no one could climb the cliffs in the rain. Wild Fynlay bet him twenty pounds that he could. He made it to the top, but slipped on the way down and fell onto the rocks below."

Ewen froze.

Sir James swore. His father had kept his word not to fight, but the challenge had served the same purpose. Tempers were bound to get hot as men would take sides. "Is he dead?" Sir James asked.

"Not yet," the man answered.

A few seconds later, Fynlay's guardsmen entered the *barmkin*, carrying the body of their chieftain.

At first, Ewen refused to believe this was any different from the hundreds of other times his father had been hurt. But the moment his father's men laid him on a table in the laird's solar behind a wooden partition in the Great Hall, Ewen knew this was the end.

His father's reckless wish for death had come to fruition.

Ewen stood off in the far corner of the room as first Fynlay's men, and then Sir James said goodbye.

He could feel his eyes grow hot and hated himself for the weakness, rubbing the back of his hand across them angrily. Fynlay didn't deserve his emotion or his loyalty.

But Fynlay was his father. No matter how wild, irresponsible, and brash, he was his father.

Guilt for his earlier words made Ewen's chest burn. He hadn't meant that he hated him. Not really. He just wanted him to be different.

He would have stayed in the corner, but Sir James called him forward. "Your father wishes to say something to you."

Slowly, Ewen approached the table. The giant warrior whose face so resembled his own looked as if he'd been mashed between two rocks. His body was mangled, broken and crushed. Blood was everywhere. Ewen couldn't believe he was still alive.

He felt his throat grow tighter, anger and frustration washing over him at the prodigious waste.

"You'll make a good chieftain, lad," his father said softly, the deep, booming voice now raspy and weak. "God knows, better than I ever was."

Ewen didn't say anything. What could he say? It was the truth, damn the man for it. He wiped the back of his hand across his eyes again, even angrier.

"Sir James sees great things for you. He will help you. Look to him for guidance and never forget what he has done for us."

As if he could. He and his father didn't agree on much, but on the subject of Sir James they were of one mind: they owed him everything.

Fynlay's voice was growing weaker and weaker, and still Ewen could not speak. Even knowing time was running out, he couldn't find the right words. He'd never known how to give voice to his feelings.

"The best thing I ever did was steal your mother."

"Why do you say that?" Ewen lashed out, the emotion erupting all at once. "Why do you say you took her when you didn't? She came with you willingly."

Fynlay could only manage to lift one side of his mouth; the other side of his face had been bashed in by the rocks. "I don't know what she saw in me." Neither did Ewen. "I think the only irresponsible thing she ever did in her life was fall in love with a barbarian." He coughed uncontrollably, emitting a sickly wet sound as his lungs filled with blood. "She would have been proud of you. You might look like a brute like me, but you are much like her. It tore her apart to disobey her father."

Ewen knew so little of his mother. His father rarely mentioned her. Now, suddenly, when time had run out, he wanted to know everything.

But it was too late. His father was all but gone. The light flickered in Fynlay's eyes. A wild look came over him, and in a final burst of life, he grabbed Ewen's arm. "Promise me you'll finish it for her, lad." Ewen stiffened. He wanted to pretend he didn't understand, but he could not hide the truth from death. "Promise me," his father repeated.

Ewen should have refused. Every time he returned home and saw that half-finished pile of rocks, he wanted to die of shame. It was the reminder of everything his father had done wrong. It was a reminder of everything Ewen didn't want to be.

But somehow he found himself nodding. Duty and loyalty meant something to him, even if they never had to his father.

A moment later, Wild Fynlay Lamont breathed his last breath.

With his father's death, Ewen's time in Sir James's service came to an end. Instead of marching off to Irvine to join Wallace and fight the English, Ewen returned to Ardlamont to bury his father and take over his duties as chieftain.

Sir James told him to be patient. To practice his warrior's skills and make himself ready. When the time came, he would be called upon.

Eight years later, when Robert Bruce made his bid for the throne and handpicked a team of elite warriors for his secret army, Ewen Lamont was the greatest tracker in the Highlands and ready to answer the call.

One

❧

Coldingham Priory, near Berwick-upon-Tweed, English Marches
Ides of April, 1310

Ewen didn't hold his tongue, which more often than not, caused him problems. "You sent a woman? Why the hell would you do that?"

William Lamberton, Bishop of St. Andrews, bristled, his face red with anger. It wasn't the blasphemy, Ewen knew, but the not-so-subtly implied criticism.

Erik MacSorley, the West Highland chieftain and greatest seafarer south of the land of his Viking ancestors, shot Ewen an impatient glare. "What Lamont meant to say," MacSorley said, attempting to mollify the important prelate, "is that with the English tightening their watch on the local churches, it could be dangerous for the lass."

Not only could MacSorley sail his way through a maelstrom of shite, he could also talk his way out of one *and* come out smelling like a rose. They couldn't have been more different in that regard. Ewen seemed to step in it wherever he walked. Not that he cared. He was a warrior. He was used to wallowing in muck.

Lamberton gave him a look to suggest that muck was exactly where he thought Ewen belonged—preferably under his heel. The churchman addressed MacSorley, ignoring Ewen altogether. "Sister Genna is more than capable of taking care of herself."

She was a woman—and a nun at that. How in Hades did Lamberton think a sweet, docile innocent could defend herself against English knights bent on uncovering the pro-Scot "couriers of the cloth," as they'd been dubbed?

The church had provided a key communication network for the Scots through the first phase of the war, as Bruce had fought to retake his kingdom. With war on the horizon again, the English were doing their best to shut down those communication routes. Any person of the cloth—priest, friar, or nun—crossing the borders into Scotland had been subject to increased scrutiny by the English patrols. Even pilgrims were being harassed.

Perhaps sensing the direction of his thoughts, Lachlan MacRuairi interjected before Ewen could open his mouth and make it worse with Lamberton. "I thought you knew we were coming?"

The thin, nondescript bishop might look weak, especially compared to the four imposing warriors who were taking up much of the small vestry of the priory, but Lamberton had not defied the greatest king in Christendom to put Robert the Bruce on the throne without considerable strength and courage. He straightened to his full height—a good half-foot under the shortest of the four Guardsmen (Eoin MacLean, at only a few inches over six feet)—and looked down his long, thin nose at one of the most feared men in Scotland, as MacRuairi's war name of Viper attested. "I was told to look for you at the new moon. That was over a week ago."

"We were delayed," MacRuairi said without further explanation.

The bishop didn't ask, probably assuming—correctly—that it had to do with a secret mission for the Highland Guard, the elite group of warriors handpicked by Bruce to form the greatest fighting force ever seen, each warrior the best of the best in his discipline of warfare. "I could not wait any longer. It is imperative that the king receive this message as soon as possible."

Though they were in England, it was not Edward Plantagenet, the English king, of whom Lamberton spoke, but the Scottish one, Robert Bruce. For Lamberton's efforts in helping Bruce to that throne, the bishop had been imprisoned in England for two years, and then released and confined to the diocese of Durham for two more. Although recently the bishop had been permitted to travel to Scotland, he was back in England under English authority. It was where Bruce needed him. The bishop was the central source for most of the information winding its way to Scotland through the complex roadway of churches, monasteries, and convents.

"Where did she go?" MacLean asked, speaking for the first time.

"Melrose Abbey by way of Kelso. She left a week ago, joining a small group of pilgrims seeking the healing powers of Whithorn Abbey. Even if the English do stop them, they will let her on her way once they hear her accent. What cause would they have to suspect an Italian nun? She is probably already on her way back by now."

The four members of the Highland Guard exchanged glances. If the message was as important as the bishop said, they'd best make sure.

MacSorley, who had command of the small team for this mission, held Ewen's gaze. "Find her."

Ewen nodded, not surprised the task had fallen to him. It was what he did best. He might not be able to sail or talk his way out of a maelstrom like MacSorley, but he could track his way through one. He could hunt almost anything or anyone. MacSorley liked to say Ewen could find a ghost in a snowstorm. One wee nun shouldn't give him too much trouble.

Sister Genna was used to finding trouble, so initially she wasn't alarmed when the four English soldiers stopped them on the outskirts of town. It wasn't the first time she'd been questioned by one of the English patrols that roamed the Borders from one of the castles they occupied nearby, and she was confident of her ability to talk her way out of any difficulties.

But she hadn't factored in her companion. Why, oh why, had she let Sister Marguerite come along with her? She knew better than to involve someone else. Hadn't she learned her lesson four years ago?

But the young nun with the sickly disposition and big, dark eyes so full of loneliness at being so far from her home had penetrated Genna's resolve to avoid attachments. Over the past nine days on the journey from Berwick-upon-Tweed to Melrose, Genna had found herself watching over the girl who'd just recently taken her vows, making sure she had enough to eat and that the walking wasn't tiring her overmuch. The girl—at barely ten and eight, Genna couldn't think of her as anything else—had already suffered one breathing spell since leaving Berwick. Sister Marguerite suffered from what the Greeks called "asthma." The lung ailment had taken her from her home in Calais in a pilgrimage to seek the healing powers of St. Ninian's shrine at Whithorn Abbey.

But Genna's journey had come to an end at Melrose, and when the time had come for them to part ways this morning, she'd found her throat growing suspiciously tight. Marguerite had looked at her with those soulful brown eyes and begged Genna to let her walk with her part of the way. And God forgive her, Genna had relented. "Just as far as Gallows Brae," she'd told her, referring to the small foothill not far beyond the market cross where the church used to hang its criminals. What harm could come to the girl in the middle of the day, a stone's throw from the abbey?

Plenty, it seemed.

Marguerite gave a startled cry as the soldiers surrounded

them, and Genna cast her a reassuring glance. *It will be all right,* she told her silently. *Let me handle it.*

Genna turned to the thickset soldier with a tinge of red in his beard, whom she took for the leader. Seated on his horse with the sun behind him, she found herself squinting at the gleam from his mail. What little she could see of his face under the steel helm and mail coif looked blunt, coarse, and none-too-friendly.

She spoke at first in Italian, with its roots in Vulgar Latin, which it was clear he didn't understand, and then in the heavily accented French that she used with Sister Marguerite and was more commonly understood in the area, which he did. Looking him straight in the eye and giving him her most reverent smile, she told him the truth. "We carry no messages. We are only visitors to your country. How do you say . . . p-p," she feigned, looking for the right word.

He stared at her dumbly. God, the man was thick—even for a soldier! Over the past few years she'd run into her share. Giving up, she pointed to her pilgrim's staff and the copper scallop-shell badge of St. James that she wore on her cloak.

"Pilgrims?" he filled in helpfully.

"Yes, pilgrims!" She beamed at him as if he were the most brilliant man in the world.

The man might be thick but he wasn't easily put off. His gaze sharpened first on her and then on Marguerite. Genna felt her pulse jump, not liking the way his gaze turned assessing. "Why do you not speak, sister? What are you doing out here on the road alone?" he asked Marguerite.

Genna tried to answer for her, but he cut her off. "I will hear from this one myself. How can I be sure you are foreigners as you say?" He said something in English to one of his companions, and Genna was careful not to react. She didn't want him to realize that she understood English. Not even Marguertite knew. "Look at those tits," he said, pointing to Marguerite. "Bet they're half her weight."

Marguerite shot her a terrified look, but Genna nodded her head in encouragement, glad for Marguerite's ignorance of their words. Still, Genna's heartbeat quickened.

"We were saying goodbye, *monsieur*," Marguerite explained in her native French.

His eyes sparked. "Goodbye? I thought you were on a pilgrimage?"

Fearing what Marguerite might unintentionally reveal, Genna interrupted again. "My destination was Melrose. Sister Marguerite seeks the healing powers of Whithorn Abbey."

His eyes narrowed on the young nun, taking in her thin face and pale complexion. For once, Genna was grateful that the fragile state of Marguerite's health was reflected in her delicate appearance.

"Is that so?" he asked slowly. "I did not realize Melrose Abbey was a popular pilgrimage destination."

"Perhaps not as popular as Whithorn or Iona, but popular enough for those who revere the lady," she said, crossing herself reverently, and he frowned. Melrose, like all Cistercian abbeys, was dedicated to the Virgin Mary.

"And you travel by yourself? That is quite unusual."

Genna had had a dog like him once. Once he got hold of a bone, he wouldn't let it go. She just needed to find a way to get him to drop it. But first she had to make sure Marguerite was safely away. "In my country, no. Only someone possessed by the devil would harm a bride of Christ." She paused innocently, letting him contemplate that. His face darkened, and she continued, "There is a group of pilgrims we passed on their way to Dryburgh Abbey," which was only a few miles away. "I hope to join them for the rest of the journey. Perhaps you will be so kind as to show me the way?" Without waiting for him to answer, she pulled Marguerite into a hug. With any luck, Marguerite would be gone before he realized what she'd done. "Goodbye, Sister. Godspeed on your journey," she said loudly, then whispered in her ear so that only she could hear, "Go . . . quickly . . . please."

The girl opened her mouth to argue, but Genna's hands tightened on her shoulders to stave off her protests.

Marguerite gave her a long anxious look, but she did as she was bid and started to walk away. She tried to slip through a gap between two of the horses, but the leader stopped her. "Wait there, Sister. We have not finished our questions yet. Have we, lads?"

The way the men looked at each other made Genna's pulse take an anxious leap. They were enjoying this, and it was clear that it was not the first time they'd been in this position. Could these soldiers have something to do with the group of nuns who'd gone missing late last year?

She looked around for help. It was the middle of the day—mid-morning, actually. Surely someone would pass along this way soon. However, although the village was just behind them, the thick trees that shrouded the road like a leafy tunnel prevented anyone from seeing them. And even if they were seen, would anyone interfere? It would take a brave soul to stand up to four mail-clad English soldiers.

Nay, it was up to her to get them out of this. She'd tried appealing to the leader's vanity and that hadn't worked. Nor had appealing to his honor, which appeared distinctly lacking. The man was a bully, who liked to prey on the weak and vulnerable—which, fortunately, she was not. But he'd shown discomfort when she reminded him of her holy status, so she would concentrate on that.

A quick glance at Marguerite made her heart sink with dread. God help them, fear was bringing on one of Marguerite's attacks! Though it had happened only once before, Genna recognized the telltale quick gasping of breath.

Genna didn't have much time. Having lost patience with the soldier's game, she rushed over to the girl and pulled her under her arm protectively. She murmured soothing words, trying to calm her down, all the while glaring up at the captain. "Look what you have done. You have upset her. She is having an attack."

But the words seem to have no effect on the man. "This won't take long," he said. "Bring them," he said to his men in English, presumably so she wouldn't understand.

Before Genna could react, she and Marguerite were being dragged deeper into the forest, her staff lying useless in the leaves behind them. Marguerite was clutching at her frantically and let out a desperate cry when the soldiers finally managed to separate them.

Genna tried to appear calm though her heart was racing. "Don't worry, Sister," she said confidently, "this will all be sorted out quickly. I'm sure these good Christian men mean us no harm."

It was a sin to lie, but in some cases, she was certain it would be excused. Genna didn't need to understand the soldiers' words to guess what they planned. But unfortunately, she understood every one of them, so she heard the chilling details.

"The old one is prettier," the captain said, switching again to English to speak to his men. "But we'd better start with the sickly one in case she doesn't last. I want to see those tits."

Genna forced herself not to show any reaction to his words, but anger, and perhaps a twinge of fear at hearing them talk so matter-of-factly about rape and the death of her friend, surged through her. She had no intention of allowing that to happen. And seven and twenty was mature, not *old*!

The situation was deteriorating, but Genna had been in lots of sticky situations before. This might be stickier than most, but it wasn't over yet.

The soldiers didn't bother taking them very far, almost as if they knew no one would dare interfere. Bruce might control the north of Scotland, but the English reign of terror was still in full force in the Scottish Marches. The English operated with impunity—except for the occasional raid or ambush from Bruce's men. The English were no more than brigands with authority, Genna thought. But soon Bruce would send them running back to England. She had put herself in this position to help ensure that happened.

They entered a small clearing in the trees, and the men released them with a hard push. Both women stumbled forward, Genna barely catching herself before falling to her knees. Marguerite wasn't so fortunate, and Genna watched in horror as her gasping intensified. She couldn't seem to get off her hands and knees, as if the effort was too much for her.

"I see she's ready for us," one of the soldiers snickered.

Genna bowed her head, muttering a prayer in Latin so the men wouldn't see the heat rise to her cheeks in anger. She might be innocent, but she'd been in enough barns with rutting beasts to understand their meaning. Apparently, men were no different.

The captain was eyeing Marguerite's raised bottom. When his hand reached under his habergeon mail shirt to loosen the ties at his waist, Genna knew she had to act fast.

She stepped between them, trying to turn him from his foul intent—or at least turn it to her. "My sister is ill, sir. Perhaps if you tell me what you are looking for I can clear up this misunderstanding, and we can all get on with our duties. Ours to God," she reminded him, "and yours to your king."

It was clear he'd forgotten the original purpose for which he'd stopped them. "Messages," he said, his gaze drifting impatiently to Marguerite behind her. "Being carried north to the rebels by churchmen—and women," he added. "But treason will not hide under holy vestments any longer. We've had reports that many of these messages have passed through Melrose Abbey. King Edward intends to put a stop to it."

"Ah," she said, as if in sudden understanding. "Now, I see the reason for your suspicion, sir. You were certainly justified in stopping us, but as I told you, neither Sister Marguerite nor I carry any of these messages." She held out the leather bag she carried with her belongings for him to inspect. Bending down, she reached for Marguerite's small purse, trying to ignore the frantic gasping of her friend's breathing. Comfort would have to wait. Untying it, she held it up to him. He barely glanced inside before tossing it away.

"See?" she said. "Nothing to hide. Now that we have proved to you our innocence, you have no cause to detain us."

He was angry; she could see that. But the longer she delayed him, the more time he had to think about his actions—his *unjustified* actions. He seemed to be hesitating when one of the men suggested, "What if it's hidden someplace else, Captain?"

She pretended not to understand him, but a cold chill ran down her spine as a slow smile spread up the captain's mouth. He reached down and tore off her veil. She cried out as the pins were ripped free, and her hair tumbled down her back in a heavy silken mass. Her hands immediately went to her head, but there was no way to hide it.

She swore under her breath at the reaction it provoked, hearing the exclamations and oaths. The long golden tresses were her one vanity—her one connection to her past identity. Janet of Mar was dead; it was silly to hold on to what she'd been. But she couldn't bear to cut her hair as most of the nuns did. And now that vanity might cost her.

The captain let out a slow whistle. "Would you look at that, lads," he said in English. "We found ourselves a real beauty. Wonder what else the lass is hiding under those robes?"

No amount of training could have prevented her from flinching at the words she was not supposed to understand, knowing what he meant to do. Fortunately, he was too caught up to notice her reaction. He pulled her to her feet, put his gauntleted hands at her neck, and ripped the coarse wool fabric of her scapula and habit to the waist.

Marguerite screamed.

Genna might have too. She struggled, but he was too strong. He tore the cloak from her neck and tugged the damaged gown past her shoulders. All that prevented her from nakedness was a thin chemise that was far too fine for a nun—another indulgence—but he didn't notice. And after a few more tears, that was gone too. Wool and linen had been reduced to strips of fabric hanging off her shoulders. She tried to cover herself, but he pulled her arms away.

The captain's eyes grew dark with lust as his gaze locked on her naked breasts.

Her heart froze in terror. For one moment her confidence faltered.

"What does she have on her back, Captain?" one of the men said from behind her. Genna wanted to thank him. His words—his reminder—struck the fear from heart, replacing it with fiery determination. She would get them out of this.

She spun on him, not bothering to cover herself. "They are the marks of my devotion. Have you never seen the mark of whips and a hair shirt?"

The men startled. Genna knew what they saw: the horrible lines of pink puckered flesh that marked her pale back. But she didn't see them that way. The scars were a reminder, a badge she wore to remind her of a day she could never be allowed to forget. Of a man who'd been like a father to her whose death was on her soul. These scars had made her stronger. They'd given her a purpose.

"I've never seen scars like that on a woman before."

"I'm not a woman," she snapped at the man who'd spoken. He was younger and not as certain as the others of the course his captain had set upon. "I'm a nun. A bride of Christ." She hoped this was another one of those times that a lie wouldn't be considered a sin. She pulled down the shreds of cloth that remained, turning slowly so each man could see. "Touch either of us and you will suffer eternal hellfire. God will punish you for your transgressions."

The younger man went white.

She looked back to the captain, her eyes blazing with the fury of her conviction, daring him to come near her. "Our innocence is meant for God. Take it and you will suffer." The captain started to back away and Genna knew she had won. She stepped toward him, unrelenting and uncowering. "Your body will burn with the fire of your sin. Your manhood will shrivel to black, your bollocks to the size of raisins, and you will never know another woman. You will be damned for eternity."

Ewen and MacLean were approaching the abbey from Eildon Hill through the Old Wood when they heard the woman scream. Not knowing what they'd find, they approached cautiously, on foot, using the trees for cover.

Ewen heard her voice first and shot a look at his partner. MacLean had heard it too. His mouth fell in a hard line, and he nodded. The words might be in French but the accent was Italian—Roman, unless he'd missed his mark.

It seemed they'd just found their nun. He peered through the trees to confirm it and stilled at what he saw, momentarily stunned.

Holy hell! His mouth went dry and heat settled low in his groin as he beheld the half-naked woman with the tumbling, wild mane of golden hair. It caught the light in a shimmering cascade of gold and silver. But it was the bare skin it curled against that jolted him with a hard bolt of lust. Admittedly, he'd yet to see a pair of breasts that he didn't like, but these . . .

He didn't think he'd ever seen any so fine. They weren't overlarge, but a pleasant handful in keeping with her slim waist and flat stomach. Soft and round, high with a youthful pertness, the milk-white skin was so creamy and flawless, he didn't need to touch it to know how velvety soft it would be.

But he wanted to touch it. He wanted to run his hands over those soft mounds and bury his face in the deep cleft between them. He wanted to caress his thumbs over the delicate pink tips until they were hard, and then circle the hard points with his tongue right before he put them in his mouth and sucked.

Jesus!

A frown gathered between his brows when he noticed the odd smattering of scars on her back. Vaguely, he wondered about them, but his attention was too focused on the mouthwatering perfection of her chest.

Apparently wondering what had caught his attention, MacLean leaned forward to take a look.

His low curse snapped Ewen from his momentary stupor.

This was a nun, for Christ's sake!

Something the English soldiers seemed to have forgotten. It wasn't just her shredded gown and chemise—a rather fine one for a nun, Ewen noticed from the intricate embroidery—but the soldiers' lecherous expressions that made it clear what they intended, and Ewen felt the surge of anger race through him. Raping a nun took a special kind of evil.

He nudged MacLean, who seemed as stunned as he, and the two men readied to attack. Typically, Ewen favored a pike—the weapon of the infantryman—but as they'd been riding, it was a sword he drew from the scabbard at his back.

He was just about to give the signal when *she* went on the attack. He paused. It was magnificent. One of the bravest things he'd ever seen. He wanted to put down his sword and cheer. She might be a nun, but she had the heart of a Valkyrie. Every impassioned word rang with the voice of authority and conviction as she defended her chastity. Her *holy* chastity.

He winced, the reminder striking a little too close. But any remaining lust he might be feeling was tamped harshly down by her words extolling the litany of horrors that would befall them for touching her. *Shrivel? Raisins?* He shuddered and adjusted himself. For a woman of the cloth, she sure as hell didn't lack for imagination.

But surely it was some kind of sin to give breasts like that to a nun?

He gave the signal.

With the fierce battle cry of the Highland Guard, *"Airson an Leòmhann,"* he and MacLean shot into the clearing.

Two

❧

Janet—or rather, Genna—knew she'd won when the English captain's gaze shifted. He was no longer staring at her breasts with anything resembling lust. Actually, he seemed to be doing anything to avoid looking at her at all.

But barely had she tasted her victory when two men emerged from the trees and assured it.

At first, the sound of their battle cry sent a chill racing down her spine. Though it had been a long time since she'd used her native tongue, she translated the Gaelic words easily enough: *For the Lion*. The cry was unfamiliar to her, and she could not immediately reconcile it with a clan. But they were Highlanders—that much she understood—and thus, friends.

She bit her lip. At least she hoped they were friends.

The cold efficiency with which they dispensed with the soldiers gave her pause. She didn't relish having to talk her way out of yet another dangerous situation. And everything about these men bespoke danger.

She'd had little contact over the past few years with the men of her birthplace, and she'd forgotten how big and intimidating they were. Tall, broad-shouldered, and heavily muscled, Highlanders were every bit as tough, rugged, and untamed as the wild and forbidding countryside that spawned them. They were also exceptional warriors, their no-holds-barred fighting style a legacy of the Norse raiders who'd invaded their shores generations ago.

She shivered. These two were no different—except perhaps even more skilled at killing than most. She cringed and turned away as one of the men stuck his blade in the throat of the young English soldier. She hated the sight of bloodshed, even when warranted.

She barely had time to pick up her cloak, throw it around her shoulders to cover her nakedness, and help Marguerite to her feet before the fighting ended. The four mail-clad Englishmen lay in bloody heaps on the grassy moor.

The threat was over. Although when she noticed the man walking toward them, as she did her best to calm a sobbing Marguerite, she reconsidered. A strange prickle spread over her skin when the warrior's gaze met hers. She gasped and her heart took an odd little stumble, as if it started and stopped in quick succession.

She could see little of his face beneath the steel nasal helm. Goodness gracious, did Highlanders still wear those? His jaw was covered in a good quarter inch of scruff, but it looked strong and imposing just like the rest of him.

Indeed everything about his outward appearance was threatening, from the menacing helm, to the dust- and blood-spattered black leather *cotun* studded with bits of steel, to the plethora of weapons strapped across his muscular physique (it seemed to be the second time she'd noticed that). Yet looking into the steel blue of his eyes, she knew he was not a threat. To her at least. The dead soldiers behind him might disagree.

She let out a breath she didn't realize she'd been holding.

He was just a regular Highland warrior. Perhaps a bit more physically dominant than most, but nothing she couldn't handle. She'd crossed paths with hundreds of fighting men over the years, and they'd never given her problems.

Still, something about him made her uneasy. Perhaps it was the way he held her gaze the entire time he walked toward her with an inscrutable expression on his face. She was good at reading people, sizing them up, but he gave nothing away.

How much had he seen? From the way he glanced at her cloak when he came to stop in front of her, she suspected enough. An ill-timed blush stained her cheeks. Feeling as if he suddenly had the advantage over her, she decided that the quicker this was over with the better.

She released Marguerite and sank to her knees, grabbing his leather-gauntleted hand and rattling off a quick succession of thank-yous in French interspersed with prayers in Italian. With any luck, like most common Highlanders (and nothing about his appearance suggested otherwise), he would not speak Italian or French, and this would be a quick conversation indeed.

If she could have managed it, she would have shed a tear or two, but some things were beyond her acting abilities. The look of reverent gratitude she'd adopted might have worked, but when he looked at her hair and frowned, she remembered that she wasn't wearing her veil. Without it, she felt . . . exposed. It had been a long time since she'd felt like a woman in a man's eyes, and it made her feel strangely vulnerable. She'd been pretending to be a nun for so long, she'd almost forgotten that she wasn't one. Not yet at least.

Without stopping to let him get a word in, she stood and thanked him again before letting his hand go. She snatched her fallen veil off the ground to drape it over her head, linked Sister Marguerite's arm in hers, and started to move away. She would return her to the abbey, make sure the young nun was all right, and then leave as soon as possible—this time, alone.

But it seemed her penchant for finding trouble wasn't over.

"Sister Genna," the Highlander said in perfectly accented Norman French. "We aren't done yet."

She muffled an oath, realizing this wasn't going to be over as fast as she'd hoped.

And how did he know her name?

What in Hades was going on? Was this simpering creature who'd just babbled all over his gauntlet the same bold Valkyrie who'd bravely defended herself and her companion against four English soldiers?

Ewen was having a hard time reconciling the two, when he realized she was walking away. When he stopped her, he could have sworn he heard her mutter an oath before she turned around. "You speak French?"

Though she said it with a smile on her face, he suspected she was anything but pleased.

He nodded, not bothering to answer the obvious question.

"You know my name?"

Again, he saw no cause to answer. He glanced at the young woman beside her, whose sobbing had abated and who now seemed almost too quiet. "The lass," he bit off sharply. "Is she ill?"

"Sister Marguerite suffers from a lung ailment," Sister Genna said in the pious and subservient manner she'd adopted. But he didn't miss the subtle way she tucked the younger woman behind her, as if putting herself between her charge and any threat he might present. He admired the impulse, no matter how ridiculous.

The younger nun rallied enough to explain. "Asthma," she said in a wavering voice. "I feel much better now, but if Sister Genna hadn't stopped them when she did . . ." Her voice fell off and her eyes filled once again with tears.

Her fierce protector shot him a reproachful glare, showing a flash of the spirit she'd masked behind the reverent exterior. He was glad she'd covered herself and put on her veil, but even the memory of what lay underneath was distracting.

"You are upsetting her. As you can see, she is unwell, and I need to get her back to the abbey right away. So while I thank you for your assistance, I'm sure you don't wish to delay us any longer. Nor do I imagine you will want to be here when these men are found. There are bound to be others in the area."

It was clear the lass was trying to be rid of him, and he didn't think it was concern for their welfare that motivated her. Did she think to frighten him away with Englishmen? He almost laughed. "I'll keep that in mind," he said dryly. "But you aren't going anywhere."

MacLean had finished disposing of the bodies as best he could and came up beside him. "Christ, Hunter," he said under his breath in Gaelic. "You might try explaining rather than issuing edicts."

Given that MacLean was only marginally less blunt and possessed at best incrementally more finesse when it came to communication, the criticism was somewhat ironic.

"My name is Eoin MacLean, and this is Ewen Lamont," MacLean said in broken French. Unlike Ewen, MacLean wasn't quick with languages. Normally they used their war names for Highland Guard missions, but as this mission wasn't in the dark and the nuns would be able to see their faces to identify them, they'd decided it was safer to use their clan names. "We were sent to find you," he added.

Ewen didn't miss the instant look of wariness she shot in his direction at the mention of his clan. A look that unfortunately he was used to among Bruce supporters. Like the MacDougalls, Comyns, and MacDowells, the name Lamont was not a trusted one.

The long feud between the two branches of Lamonts had not ended with Fynlay's death at Dundonald. Ewen's cousin John, the current Chief of Lamont, had chosen to fight with his mother's clan, the MacDougalls, against Bruce. When the MacDougalls had been chased from Scotland after the Battle of Brander, his cousin had gone into exile with the MacDougalls, and the vast lordship of *Mac Laomian mor Chomhail uilethe,* The Great Lamont of all of Cowal, had been forfeited to the crown, including the important clan strongholds of Dunoon and Carrick.

Distancing himself from his cousin's rebellion and his father's "wild" legacy was a constant battle. But he was surprised an Italian nun was that apprised of clan politics.

"Who sent—" She stopped herself, obviously remembering her companion. Slowly, she nodded. "I see."

She'd realized that it must have been Lamberton who'd led them to her.

"With such an important undertaking as your, uh . . . pilgrimage," MacLean added, "your superiors were concerned that nothing go wrong and wanted to make sure you reached your destination safely. As you have discovered, there are many enemies to the church these days."

Ewen hadn't realized MacLean was so adept at speaking with double meaning—especially in a language he wasn't exactly fluent in—but it was clear that Sister Genna understood what he was trying to say: they were here to make sure the message to Bruce did not go astray.

He was studying her while MacLean spoke and didn't miss the flash of what might be deemed annoyance in her eyes. They were sea blue, he realized. A very pretty, very crystal shade of bluish green. And what kind of nun had long, feathery eyelashes like that?

Whatever pique he'd detected was quickly smothered behind the pious facade. "I fear your journey was unnecessary. I reached my destination two days ago without any problems. Indeed, I was on my way back to Berwick this morning. Sister Marguerite was simply walking me to the hill to say goodbye."

"You were planning to travel by yourself?" Ewen said.

He hadn't bothered to keep the incredulity from his voice, and the face she turned to him was serene enough, but he could swear her eyes were shooting tiny greenish-blue darts at him. Damn, she was pretty! Not too old and not too young. He'd guess she was in her mid-twenties—a handful of years younger than his thirty. The other one was pretty too, in a frail, helpless manner Sister Genna was trying to adopt, but she didn't look much older than a child.

"I hoped to catch up with another group of pilgrims at Dryburgh Abbey, a few miles away. We in the service of God are used to walking long distances. I walk much farther to sell our embroidery at market. Most people I encounter on the road are not like these."

"But some are," he pointed out.

She shrugged with far less concern than she should have. Even after what had just happened, she seemed oblivious to the danger she was in. Which only reinforced his belief that women had no part in war—even nuns acting as couriers. Women were too fragile. Too trusting. Too innocent of the ugly side of the world. How could she expect to defend herself against an armed knight?

Though he admired the bravery and spirit he'd just witnessed, the next group of soldiers she came upon might not be so easily persuaded by her threats. What the hell was Lamberton thinking? The good bishop was sending his pretty lamb out to the slaughter with no idea of the danger she faced. And without protection, damn it.

He should be glad to hear she'd passed the missive along and leave it at that. Escorting pretty nuns who didn't know enough to realize that they were out of their element wasn't what he'd joined the Highland Guard to do.

As the only Lamont not in exile, it was up to Ewen to restore the good name of his clan and reclaim the clan lands lost by his cousin, ensuring that one of the greatest lordships in the Highlands did not fade away into the mist like those of the MacDougalls and Comyns.

All he had to do was keep his head down, do his job, and

not do anything to anger Bruce. When the war ended, he would be rewarded with land and coin.

It was a simple equation. He sure as Hades didn't need any complications from unknown variables—unknown variables like pretty little Italian nuns. As much as he liked Arthur "Ranger" Campbell's eldest brother, Neil, he didn't want to see any more Lamont land in Campbell hands.

But he couldn't very well leave her out here to fend for herself. Not after what he'd seen.

She made an attempt to explain. "A few, perhaps. Though even these men, I think, were realizing the error of their ways." Realizing that might sound ungrateful, she added, "Although, of course, we are grateful for your help. You were magnificent! Your sword skills were most impressive; I will make sure to pass along our praise to my superiors."

Though it was said with the perfect balance of feminine flattery and sincerity, Ewen had been around MacSorley long enough to recognize when he was being humored.

Perhaps detecting his skepticism, she added, "Truly I do not know what we would have done had you not appeared when you did."

If he hadn't seen her display earlier, the meek, helpless act might have fooled him. His eyes narrowed. Why the act at all? What game was she playing?

She gave them a solemn smile, as if she were blessing them. But he was distracted by the small heart-shaped mole she had above her lip. God's blood, a mole like that belonged on the mouth of a jade!

"You have our deepest gratitude. Sister Marguerite and I will keep you both in our prayers. Goodbye."

Jesus! Ewen frowned and came to a sudden stop. How the hell had she done that? She'd been walking, and they'd been following her without even realizing it. They were almost back to the road.

He felt like bloody Odysseus with the sirens. "Not so

fast, Sister." He had no intention of letting her walk off alone. MacLean could take the missive to Bruce, and he'd see their courier safely back to Lamberton. And when he was finished, he and the bishop were going to have a nice, long talk about using nuns as couriers. "Say your good-byes if you wish, but you are coming with me."

Genna tried not to let her discomposure show, but it had been a long time since a man had tried to order her around. Not since . . . Duncan. Her chest pinched thinking of her brother. It was still hard to believe he was gone. Her big, strong, seemingly indestructible brother had been killed by the MacDowells at Loch Ryan not long after her disappearance.

She turned around calmly and met his gaze—the disarming one whom, as he'd not seen fit to do so himself, MacLean had introduced as Lamont. Odd, as she thought the clan had stood with the MacDougalls against Bruce and had been exiled to Ireland. The Lamont clan was located in Cowal, she recalled, near Argyll in the Western Highlands. Their name was thought to be derived from the Norse "Logmaor," or lawman. Which was especially ironic given that this man seemed to have the communication skills of a rock.

He wasn't responding in the way she expected, and it was mildly disconcerting. He also had a disarming way of looking at her. Hard. Intense. As if he could see all her secrets. Thinking of the scars, she realized that he had—some of them, at least. But she had plenty more waiting to be discovered.

The sooner she rid herself of this unnerving man, the better.

Feigning a patience she certainly didn't feel, she bestowed one of her most nunly smiles on him. Calm. Serene. Understanding. With that slightly mysterious and hallowed detachment that set the nuns apart. How Mary would laugh to see her affect such a countenance! Her chest pinched, and she pushed the thought away. Her twin sister was safer without her around. But she hated not being able to see her and tell her she was all right. Soon, she hoped. The war couldn't go on forever . . . could it?

"I don't understand. I believe I explained that there was no cause for you to come." She'd delivered the missive, blast it. Why would the bishop send them after her? Lamberton had never displayed such a lack of faith in her before. She didn't need an escort; he would only interfere with her plans. "Was there something else?"

The smile had no effect on him. His face was as impenetrable as the steel that hid his brow and nose. She frowned. She had to admit, she was curious to see the entirety of his face. He had a nice mouth and jaw—

She stopped with a startled jerk, wondering what in perdition had come over her.

"I will return you to Berwick. You don't need to worry about your friend. MacLean will see her safely back to the abbey. He will make sure *everything* reaches its intended destination."

The man wasn't as adept at hidden meanings as his friend, but she understood well enough. Apparently, MacLean would take the missive she'd left with their contact at the abbey directly to Bruce himself.

"You are so kind. Although I appreciate your gallant offer, it isn't necessary. Why don't we all return to the abbey, and you and your friend can both see that everything arrives safely."

She turned to leave, but he stopped her with that deep, lilting voice of his that despite the curtness of his words seemed to seep right through her like warm caramel.

"It wasn't an offer, Sister."

The man was like a rock all right. Utterly immovable! She felt a spark of temper but tamped it down. Her smile this time might have been a little forced. "It isn't necessary—"

"Yes, it is." He motioned with his head to his friend, and MacLean came toward her. "Take the girl to the abbey and then see that our friend receives the message," he added in Gaelic. "I'll deal with our little holy warrior."

Good thing she had plenty of experience pretending not to understand. But still his comment managed to get a small rise out of her. Little holy warrior, indeed! He made her sound like a bairn playing some game.

"Sister," MacLean said, holding out his hand to Marguerite.

The girl looked back and forth between Genna and MacLean. Genna held tightly to her arm, not wanting to relinquish her. But she knew Marguerite needed to get back to attend to her lungs with the butcher's broom sweetened with honey that she used, and as it was clear that it was going to take a little more time to reason with this infuriating man, she had to let her go. "It's all right," she said. "Go with him. I will be along soon enough."

"Say *goodbye,* Sister," Lamont instructed from behind her.

Genna shot him a glare, and then turned to Marguerite to give her an encouraging squeeze. "Take care, *ma petite.*"

Sister Marguerite glanced at Lamont uncertainly, and then back to her. "Are you sure? I don't want to leave you . . ."

"Perfectly sure. This man will do me no harm." She hoped that wasn't her third lie of the hour. "Don't worry about me; just promise me you will rest before you continue your journey."

The girl nodded.

Genna bit her lip. "It is probably best if you don't say anything about what happened here. I do not wish to put these men who helped us in any danger."

Marguerite nodded again, and then after one last hug, Genna let her go. She watched as MacLean led her away through the tunnel of trees. They were almost out of sight when Lamont shouted something at his friend in Gaelic. It sounded like, "Striker, *Bàs roimh Gèill!*"

She translated the last as Death before Surrender, but what did "striker" mean?

MacLean nodded and repeated the phrase, adding something she did understand: "hunter." Strange . . . "What did you say to him?"

"It isn't important."

"And yet you chose to speak it in a language that I could not understand?"

He shook his head. She thought it quite remarkable that he had the same exasperated look on his face that her brother and father used to have, which had taken them years to perfect. He'd managed it with her in minutes. "Yes."

The man had also perfected the non-answer. "Your friend," she said. "Won't it be dangerous for him?"

He dismissed her concern with a shrug. "He'll be careful. He knows how to blend in."

Genna couldn't imagine how either of them would blend in anywhere. They stood out. They were so big, for one thing. Standing next to him she couldn't help notice just how big. He stood nearly a foot taller than she—he must be at least a hand over six feet—and his shoulders were nearly twice as wide. With all the weapons and armor, he was a bulky man. Not fat, but with far too many muscles for her taste. He was a man built to remind women of their vulnerability, something she tried not to think about. But she couldn't ignore it with him, which made her all the more eager to be rid of him.

Genna had noticed that he liked the direct approach—or in his case, the stunted approach—so she decided to take it herself. "Why are you insisting on escorting me back to Berwick? Did my superior instruct you to do so?"

"Nay."

"Then why?"

"That should be obvious: it isn't safe."

"And you think I'll be safer with you? You are wrong. The English are far more likely to stop a warrior on the road than they are a group of pilgrims. I will be far safer with them."

"Then it's a good thing we won't be traveling on the road."

"Do you proposed to fly to Berwick?" The sarcastic words were out of her mouth before she could snatch them back.

He smiled, and some of that irritation she was feeling squeezed strangely in her chest. He was handsome, she realized. Sinfully handsome. She didn't need to see the rest of his face to know it. It was right there in that crooked smile. A strange shudder passed through her, prickly and warm, as if someone had just spread a thick plaid over her naked skin.

"Not quite," he said. "We'll keep to the trees and stay off the main roads."

He took a step closer to her, and she caught a faint whiff of leather and pine that she wished she could say was unpleasant. Instead she felt the nearly irresistible urge to inhale. She shook it off, wondering why she was acting like this. She had never been the type to be made silly by a man—not even when she was young. In fact, it had been the other way around.

She had to tilt her head back just to look at him. "What if we get lost?"

The harsh sound out of his mouth was almost a laugh. "We won't get lost."

He glanced down, and their eyes met. Something locked

in her chest. Her breath, she realized. It seemed to have become stuck. Something strange passed between them. Something hot and intense. Something that made the skin beneath her cloak prickle. She was suddenly very aware of her naked skin beneath the wool.

Almost as if he knew what she was thinking, his gaze dropped to her chest. A strange warm flush spread over her, and she gasped. The small sound was enough to break the connection. He jerked his gaze away, a dark look crossing his face.

He took a step back and she tried to cover the moment of awkwardness, but her voice sounded unusually breathy. "I'm afraid it's impossible. You may escort me to Dryburgh if you insist, but it isn't proper for me to travel alone with a man." Jerusalem's temples, they'd have to spend at least one night together!

His mouth twisted. "There is nothing improper; you are a nun. Your chastity is safe with me."

There was something about that little smile and the way he said it that didn't sit well with her. Had she misread what had just happened? Was he telling her he wasn't attracted to her? Though that was exactly the way she *should* want it, she had just enough vanity left to discover that it bothered her.

She needed to change into a new chemise and put her veil in order. Then she was sure she would feel like herself again. *After* she got rid of him. "I did not mean to impugn your honor. You are a man of honor, are you not?"

"Usually."

She frowned. Not exactly the answer she was hoping for, but it would have to do.

"And as an honorable man you would not force your person on an unwilling woman?"

For a chivalrous man there was only one answer. He, of course, gave her another.

"Well, I guess it depends upon the circumstances, because I have every intention of forcing my person on you, Sister. So if you are done trying to talk circles around me until I do what you want, you can change while I find my horse, and then we can be on our way."

And without waiting for her to respond, he turned on his heel and left her there, gasping. Or perhaps sputtering was more accurate. It had been a long time since she'd lost a war of words.

It seemed she wasn't going to be rid of him as easily as she'd hoped. Actually, it seemed as if she wasn't going to be rid of him at all.

Three

❧

Something about her expression when he walked away made Ewen want to laugh. He'd wager it wasn't often the wee nun heard the word "no." He was less amused, however, upon his return. For a woman of God, she sure as hell had a way of rousing the devil in him.

He stared down at her from atop his horse, his hand extended. "I said, give me your hand."

She shook her head, the hideous black veil back in place, completely hiding the golden beauty that lay underneath. But he knew it was there, and if he looked hard enough— which he did—he could just see the silky-fine strands of gold curls escaping from beneath the tight wrapping at her temples. The softness, however, was at distinct odds with the stubborn set of her mouth. "I thank you for your kind offer, but I prefer to walk."

It was the third time he'd asked, which was already the second time too many. His jaw tightened, but it didn't help to moderate his words. His patience had run out. "It wasn't kind, it wasn't an offer, and I don't give a rat's arse about what you prefer. You'll get up on this horse voluntarily or I'll put you there myself, but be assured that one way or the other you will ride with me."

Her eyes widened just a little, but to her credit her gaze did not falter from his. "You have an unusual way with words."

This from the woman who'd threatened a shriveling manhood and bollocks like raisins?

"So I've been told."

Ewen had never been very good at conversing with ladies. He was too rough around the edges—hell, he was too rough all around. MacSorley had enough charm for all of them put together. Which was fine by him. Ewen was a warrior, not a troubadour. He had neither the time nor the inclination to charm. His plain speaking might be off-putting, and maybe even harsh at times, but it was effective. In battle and in the other life-and-death situations that faced the Highland Guard, being clear and concise was what mattered. There was no room for subtlety. Besides, the kind of communication he enjoyed with women didn't require much conversing.

Immediately his mind slipped to places it shouldn't go. His gaze dropped for an instant to the woman's well-covered chest before he snapped it harshly back.

Jesus, he needed to stop doing that! *Nun,* he reminded himself. *Belongs to God.*

But he suspected it was going to be a long time before he forgot the sight of the perfect, soft feminine flesh hidden under the habit.

He clenched his jaw. "Well, what's it to be, Sister?"

After a long pause, she gave a loud harrumph and put her hand in his. Apparently, Sister Genna had decided not to test him. It was a wise decision. She would learn very quickly that he didn't make threats; he did what he said.

He lifted her effortlessly into the seat before him—she weighed next to nothing—and they started off. By his estimation, they should reach Berwick the following evening. It was only a distance of about forty miles, but with two on a horse and keeping to the countryside to avoid the roads in difficult terrain, it would take twice as long.

Having ridden in and out of the Borders more times than he wanted to remember over the past two years on Highland Guard missions to wreak as much havoc as possible with the English garrisons who held the castles, Ewen was intimately familiar with the landscape. He knew every forest, every patch of trees, every contour of every hillside, every mask that nature provided to pass in and out unseen.

Because it was instinctive, not because he thought there was any real threat of being followed, he did what he could to avoid leaving tracks, but with the recent spate of spring thunderstorms, the soft ground made it nearly impossible. However, the rain would hide what he could not. In the time it had taken to retrieve his horse and "persuade" Sister Genna to ride with him, dark clouds had gathered across the sky, the wind had started to ruffle the leaves, and the temperature had dropped a few degrees.

But it wasn't the brewing storm that made him dread the miles ahead. No sooner had he settled her in the seat in front of him, and slid his arms around her slim waist to take the reins, than he realized he might have been too hasty to dismiss her plea to walk. Having her body nestled against his was making it difficult—bloody difficult—to remember that she was a woman of the cloth.

Now admittedly, he didn't have much experience holding a nun in his arms, but he couldn't recall ever coming across a nun that smelled like the bluebells that blanketed the hillside near his home in Ardlamont. The soft floral fragrance infused his senses, teasing him and making him draw her closer, lean down, and inhale.

Damn it, he needed to do something. Perhaps say a prayer. "*Lead us not into temptation and deliver us from evil*" seemed appropriate.

He bit back a groan, the prayer forgotten, when her body slammed into his again.

God, it felt good. *She* felt good. And his body was noticing.

He tried to keep some distance between them, but the movement of the horse over the difficult, uneven terrain made it impossible. It seemed as if with each clop of the hooves, her bottom slid back into his groin, her back into to his chest, and the soft weight of those breasts that he couldn't forget bounced against his arm.

No amount of prayers, no amount of saying "nun" over and over in his mind, could prevent his body from responding to the intimate contact. He was hard as a rock, though thankfully, due to the thick leather of his armor, he didn't think she was aware of the big column of flesh riding against her.

But God sure as hell knew that every time that softly curved bottom slid against him, Ewen thought about swiving. He thought about it until he could almost imagine what it would be like to wrap his hands around her hips and sink in and out. The sensual rhythm was driving him half-crazed with lust. He was hot, bothered, and so distracted that he nearly missed the turn he'd been looking for.

He cursed, furious with himself. Control and discipline were seldom a problem for him—especially regarding women who were off limits. Lately, it seemed like every other member of the Highland Guard was marrying a beautiful woman, and not once had his appreciation for their beauty veered into an inappropriate flash of lust.

Hell, Christina MacLeod was one of the most beautiful women he'd ever seen, with just the sort of lush, well-curved body he liked—the nun was a little on the slender side—but he'd never had one impure thought about her. Of course, having the greatest swordsman in Christendom watching every man who came within a hundred yards of her served as a rather effective deterrent. But if there was anyone who could strike fear in the heart more than the chief of the Highland Guard, it was God.

He felt her shift against him as she turned her head to glance back. "Is something wrong?"

Other than the slow, torturous descent into hell that was

the soft curve of her bottom pressing against his turgid cock? He gritted his teeth together. "Nay, why do you ask?"

"You cursed."

His eyes narrowed. "I thought you didn't understand our language."

"I don't. But I didn't need to understand Gaelic to know that it was a word I should not wish to hear."

His mouth twitched with amusement. He supposed that was true enough. Sometimes tone said it all. "There is nothing wrong."

"I thought you might have been confused about which way to go. Are you sure you know where you are going?"

This time he couldn't resist the full smile, even though she had no idea how amusing her question was. He was the best tracker in the Highlands; he didn't get lost. He'd built his reputation by focusing on every detail of his surroundings. A reputation that had led to Bruce selecting him for his team of elite warriors. "Don't worry, I know where I'm going. We aren't going to get lost."

A little furrow appeared between her brows. No doubt she'd sensed his amusement but didn't understand the source. "You seem quite confident."

"I am."

"It's just that it looks like it's going to rain, and with the mist—"

"We'll be fine."

She tilted her head back a little to study him for a moment. Their faces were so close, it was hard for him to resist doing the same.

She really was quite pretty—for a woman of God, he reminded himself. The lines of her face were simply but classically drawn. Wide-set almond-shaped eyes framed by delicately arched brows. High cheekbones, a small, straight nose, and a tiny pointed chin. The only extravagances were those ridiculously long lashes, the brilliant sea-blue of her eyes, and that sensually curved mouth. Her lips were too pink, too lush, and too damned tempting—especially with that wanton freckle distracting him.

He shifted his gaze back to the road ahead of them, where it was safe.

He was relieved when she did the same. Until she shivered a little and settled back against him. He nearly groaned, and his voice came out a tad gruffer than usual. "Are you cold?"

"A little."

With one hand holding the reins, he reached back and unfastened a plaid from the roll on the saddle. "You can use this," he said, handing it to her.

The smile she gave him was almost girlish in its delight and so out of keeping with the serene nun, his heart jogged a beat or two.

"Thank you." She wrapped it around her and sighed contentedly, sinking back against him again.

At least one of them was comfortable. Ewen had the feeling that the next twenty-four hours were going to be some of the most uncomfortable of his life.

The plaid smelled like him, cozy and warm with a faint hint of the outdoors, and the soft blues and grays reminded her of his eyes. Steel-blue, she would call them—with an emphasis on the steel.

Steel rather summed him up quite nicely, from his eyes, to his intractable temperament, to the solid shield of his chest behind her and the hard strength of the arms that had lifted her from the ground. She'd never felt arms like that in her life. She'd reached out to brace herself in surprise as he'd lifted her, and she might as well have been trying to grip rock. A strange shudder had stolen through her, and her stomach had taken the oddest little dip.

Actually, her stomach seemed to be doing that quite a lot

around him. And she would feel flush at the oddest times. She hoped she wasn't becoming ill.

But for such a hard-edged man, she had to admit he was surprisingly comfortable to ride with. It was nice. Quite nice, she realized. Perhaps she'd been worried for naught? It was infinitely more comfortable riding with the warmth and protection of his big body behind her, especially as the weather grew more ominous. That wind was cold, and he was like a bread oven, radiating heat. She shivered, burrowing deeper under the plaid when a powerful gust tore through the trees.

She thought he made a pained sound, but when she glanced over her shoulder he was looking straight ahead with that masculine square jaw set at the same uncompromising angle.

It wasn't often that she didn't get her way, but Genna could accept defeat graciously, particularly when it was proving to be to her benefit. She would just have to ensure he didn't interfere with her plans. When the time came she would find a way to make a quick stop in Roxburgh, which shouldn't be too difficult, as they would pass in that direction anyway. Until then, there was no reason not to make the best of it and try to pass the time pleasantly. At least as pleasantly as they could until the rain started.

She eyed him curiously. She wasn't sure what it was about him, but he wasn't like anyone she'd met before. Her first impression hadn't changed much in the short time they'd been riding. He was hard to read—which strangely intrigued her.

"You don't talk much, do you?"

He gave her a sidelong glance from under that terrifying-looking helm that she wondered if he'd ever remove and said dryly, "I didn't think you noticed."

She laughed. "Are you suggesting I talk too much?"

"I'm suggesting you talk until you hear what you want to hear."

She lifted a brow in surprise. The comment was insightful. She'd never been very good at hearing "no." Mary used to say she was like a big boulder rolling down the hill, and heaven help whoever was in her path when she wanted something.

Apparently, he was a big enough wall to get in her way. She bit back a smile at the appropriateness of the comparison. "As you can see, it doesn't always work," she said wryly.

That elicited a smile from him. Well, at least one corner of his mouth lifted, which from him she supposed was good enough to be characterized as a smile. "Just most of the time?"

She shrugged noncommittally. "Let's just say it has come in handy more than once."

His face darkened. "You've been damned lucky, then."

She suspected she wasn't going to like what he had to say, yet she felt compelled to ask, "What do you mean?"

"I mean that what you are doing is dangerous, and you've been lucky to have avoided trouble, but believe me, Sister, not all men are susceptible to manipulation. Women don't belong in war, even as couriers—a fact I intend to impart at the first opportunity to the good bishop."

Perhaps it had been a bad idea to get him to talk. Genna was so outraged, it took her a moment to know where to start. She didn't manipulate anyone; she argued her point. And how dare he try to tell her what she could or could not do! She might have taken a different name, but she was still the daughter of an earl. Her sister had been Robert the Bruce's first wife. She had more right than anyone to help his cause. And she had reasons of her own for wanting to do her part that weren't his to question.

She took pride in what she did. She *liked* it. And she was good at it, woman or not! "I serve the king, just as you do. He needs everyone to help—man and woman—if he is going to have a chance to defeat Edward. What you do is dangerous, is it not?"

He didn't say anything in response. An annoying tendency of his, she was learning.

She took his silence as agreement. "And yet you choose to fight for what you believe. Why should I not be able to make the same choice?"

"It isn't a woman's place."

Was that an answer? Genna tried to control her temper, but the flames were snapping. "And where exactly is a woman's 'place'?"

"Somewhere safe, running the household and keeping watch over the bairns."

Genna stiffened. "A place that is hardly fitting for me, sir." She paused. "And your wife? She is content to stay at home and watch you ride off into battle?"

"I'm not married."

"What a shock," she muttered under her breath, but from the way his eyes narrowed, she knew he'd heard her.

She didn't care. She knew that most men felt the way he did about the traditional roles for women (which probably explained why she intended to take the veil!). Perhaps it would have been different if either of her two betrothals had ended in marriage. But now that she'd experienced freedom, she couldn't go back to being ordered about as if she had a pea for a brain and being treated like chattel. For that's what marriage did to women. God, hadn't she seen enough of it when she was growing up?

She lifted her chin and met his gaze. "Not all women desire to be coddled and protected. Some of us can take quite good care of ourselves."

"A silvery tongue is no match for a blade."

She flushed, and before she could think better of it, she reached down, slid her *sgian-dubh,* her hidden knife, from the scabbard near the top of her boot, and had it pressed against the inside of his thigh where it met his hips. "Then it's a good thing that I'm good with both."

The expression on his face was one Janet—Genna, she reminded herself—would remember with satisfaction for a long time.

The lass moved so quickly, Ewen had no idea what she intended until the blade was pressed against the soft leather of his thigh. Like most members of the Highland Guard, he did not wear mail to protect his legs—or his upper body, for that matter (it was too heavy)—and the five-inch-long blade was pointed right at the place where a deep enough cut would kill him. He didn't think it was a coincidence. The lass knew one of the few places he was vulnerable.

Jesus! One slip of that knife and he'd be dead—or gelded. Neither option of which was very appealing.

All of his attention should be on that blade, yet he was achingly aware of the placement of her other hand. To brace herself—and give herself better leverage to wield the blade—she'd put her left hand on his right thigh. *High* on his right thigh. And too damned close to the part of him that had been made half-crazed by their ride.

So even while he watched the right hand with the blade, he couldn't stop thinking about the left, and how good it would feel if she moved it a few inches and took him in her hand. He wouldn't have thought it possible to be aroused with a knife a few inches from his cock. He now knew differently.

Slowly—very slowly, so as not to jar her into sudden movement—he drew the horse to a halt. Outwardly he kept calm, but his heart was pounding. He kept his eyes pinned to hers, but she didn't flinch. She was as cool and calm as any of his fellow Guardsmen would be, and he knew without a doubt that she would use the knife if she had to.

What the hell kind of nun was she, anyway? He stilled when she pressed the knife a little harder, the tip of the blade digging deeper into the leather. A bloodthirsty one, apparently, who knew how to wield a dagger.

"You've made your point," he said.

She quirked a well-formed brow. Like her lashes, her eyebrows were thick and dark, framing her blue eyes to perfection and providing a striking contrast to her fair hair and skin . . .

He stopped himself, furious. There he went, doing it again. Noticing details was part of his job, but he shouldn't be noticing those kind of details about her.

Knife, he reminded himself.

"Have I?" she said. "Somehow I think not. Men like you only respect in others what they see in themselves. In your case, physical strength." She looked him over in a way that might have made his blood heat had she not added, "Of which you appear to have an over-abundance." She gave him a taunting smile, digging in the knife a little more. "But as you can see, physical strength isn't always enough."

There it was again. Ewen had a gift for languages, and every now and then he caught something in her accent. At times it didn't seem quite so strong. Like now, when she was angry. Given the current circumstances, he supposed it was safe to say that she'd dropped her pretense of being meek and serene.

Holding her gaze, he reached down and circled the wrist holding the knife with his hand. He felt shock run through him at the touch. The baby softness of her skin and delicacy of her bones took him aback, but he felt the determination in the firmness of her grip. Slowly, he moved her hand—and the blade—to the side so he could breathe again.

But he didn't let her go. She was practically turned around on the saddle now, facing him, eyes flashing and chest heaving with the fury of the confrontation. *Damn it!*

He *really* shouldn't think about her chest, because despite the black wool that almost covered her from head to toe, he could remember every luscious inch of naked flesh, and a very sinful part of him wanted to reach down and scoop it up in his hands.

And then there was the placement of that other hand. Perhaps he should have moved it instead because now that the blade was at a safe distance, his focus wasn't split anymore, and all he could think of was the soft pressure so near to the place he really wanted it.

Almost as if she could read his mind, her face flushed, and she removed her hand from his thigh, while tightening the one holding the *sgian-dubh* defensively. He knew plenty of warriors who carried a hidden blade—usually under their arm—but she was the first woman.

Men like him. Was she correct in her characterization? He didn't want to think so, but then again, she'd managed to surprise him. He'd underestimated her because she was a woman—not to mention a nun.

He couldn't remember the last time someone had been able to get a blade close enough to him to do real harm. It was probably Viper. Lachlan MacRuairi had earned his war name for his silent, deadly strike. He'd snuck up on Ewen once in training and managed to get a blade to his neck.

Obviously, she'd had training, too. But unless the recently disbanded Templars had opened their ranks to include nuns, it hadn't been at a convent.

"Where the hell did you learn to do that?"

She glared back at him. "My sister-in-law."

His brows drew together; it wasn't the answer he was expecting. Another woman? "Unusual family you have. Or do they teach knife skills to all little girls in Italy along with needlework?"

He was watching her closely and saw something flicker

in her gaze. She seemed to shake something off, and then her mouth curved in a smile. "Was that a joke, *monsieur*?"

To his surprise, he realized it was. It was the kind of wry jest he would make to MacLean or MacKay. But he didn't jest with women. Actually, he couldn't recall the last time he'd had this long of a conversation with a woman. Hell, this was the longest conversation he'd had with *anyone* in a long time.

He was staring at her, trying to make sense of it, when she gave a flick of her head in the direction of her hand.

"If you let go of my wrist, I'll put the knife back where it belongs."

He released her with all the subtlety of a hot iron. But he watched her hand carefully this time as she slowly returned the dirk to her boot. He caught a quick glimpse of the scrollwork on the handle and stopped her. "May I see that?"

The hesitation was brief, but it was there. She handed it to him. He looked at the intricate scrollwork on the horn handle, knowing that he'd seen something similar before. Though the design on the grip was Norse, he suspected the blade was from Germany and very fine. It had probably been a large eating knife for an important man, but it made a perfectly sized weapon for a woman. "Where did you get this?"

"My sister by marriage." She held her hand out, and he gave it back to her. He didn't think he was imagining it when her shoulders relaxed after slipping it back in the scabbard above her boot, which must have been made for her. "Her family is Norse."

That explained it, but something still bothered him. He knew he'd seen it before. "What is her name?"

She laughed. "I hardly think you would know her. Do you know many Italian ladies?" She paused expectantly, and when he didn't respond added, "Her family came to my village many years ago. The knife was passed down from her grandfather to her father."

"And she gave it to you?"

"She did."

"You must have been very important to her. It's an exceptional knife."

A shadow of sadness crossed her face. "I was. And she to me."

"You miss her?"

"I do."

"But you will return home soon?"

Though he'd been trying to make her feel better, he sensed his words had the opposite effect. She shrugged as if indifferent, but he knew she was not. "Perhaps when the war is over."

"But it is not your war. Why do you involve yourself in the problems of a country not your own?"

"My reasons are my own." She turned back around to face forward. "We should proceed? If we hope to reach Roxburgh before the rain."

He took her cue and snapped the reins, urging the horse forward. She was right: they were making abysmally slow progress. But she was wrong about their direction. "We aren't going to Roxburgh. We'll stay north of the Tweed on the way to Berwick—it will be safer."

His pronouncement was met with a quick snapping around of her head. "No! We can't. We must go to Roxburgh!"

Four

❧

Ewen Lamont was having a bad influence on her. Apparently, Janet's oratory skills were deserting her, and she was blurting out whatever came into her head just like he did. First she'd mentioned her sister-in-law without thinking, then had the near disaster with the blade, and now she was showing a lack of finesse in handling the news of his plan to cross the river.

She could tell by the way those steely blue eyes fixed on hers that he had questions. She shouldn't have pulled the knife on him, but he'd stung her pride, and she'd wanted to prove to him that she could protect herself. Instead, she'd made him suspicious. Nuns didn't wield weapons like that. Most women didn't. But her sister by marriage wasn't like most women.

Christina MacRuairi, the Lady of the Isles, was the heir to one of the greatest lordships in Western Scotland and a force to be reckoned with, much to her brother's frustration. Christina had learned how to defend herself from her pirate scourge of a brother, the disreputable brigand Lachlan MacRuairi.

Christina had passed on those skills to Janet when one of Duncan's men in a drunken stupor had tried to force himself on her. He might have succeeded if Christina hadn't come to her rescue. The cut her sister-in-law had given him in the back of his leg had hobbled him for life, but it was nothing to the punishment her brother Duncan had exacted. She shivered, recalling the brutal flogging Janet had been forced to witness, as was her duty.

In many ways, Duncan would have made a better chief to the clan than her eldest brother, Gartnait. Duncan, like Ewen Lamont, possessed the firm authority and unyielding attitude that was necessary for a leader that her fun-loving elder brother had not. But now both her brothers were gone, and the earldom rested on the young shoulders of her eight-year-old nephew Donald, who was under King Edward's authority.

War had stripped her of most of her family. She'd learned of Duncan's death at Loch Ryan only upon her return to England last year. Of the powerful family of Mar, all that remained were her, Mary, and Donald.

The last thing she wanted to do was to make Lamont suspicious about her true identity. Not only would her ability to do her job be compromised if it became known that Janet of Mar was alive, but her safety would be at issue as well. Edward of England already had her twin sister in his control; he would be only too happy to have her as well.

Nay, it was better that Janet of Mar stay dead—exactly as she would have been had the fisherman and his son not fished her out of the river, after her disastrous attempt to secret her sister out of England three and a half years ago.

Had she really thought she could simply ride into England and sneak Mary out from right under Edward's nose? That was the problem: she *had* thought she could do it. She hadn't wanted to listen to Duncan's warning that it would only make things worse. She hadn't wanted to wait for a better opportunity. She hadn't wanted to hear "no."

So she'd gone to her sister-in-law Christina, persuaded her to let her borrow some of her men, and gone after her sister on her own. But something had gone wrong. Or rather, *everything* had gone wrong. Christina's men had been discovered, and Mary, her son David, Janet, and their loyal servant Cailin had all been caught up in the ensuing battle. Janet would never forget seeing Cailin felled by that arrow on the bridge. She'd tried to help him, but suddenly the world had exploded in thunder and lightning—the most terrible she'd ever heard.

Janet remembered little of what happened after the bridge had seemingly burst into flames. She'd woken up a day later in a convent surrounded by a sea of nuns, thinking she'd died and gone to heaven. She'd been quite relieved on that point, actually, the alternative having been threatened by her father and brother often enough.

She been confused at first, stricken and unable to remember anything, so when the nuns assumed she was one of them (which wasn't surprising given her attire at the time), she hadn't protested. After a day or so her memories returned, but by then the abbess of the convent where the fishermen had taken her had connected their found "sister" with the Scottish lady the English were looking for.

Later she learned that Cailin, the man who'd been more of a father to her than her own, had lost his life, along with many of Christina's men; Mary had barely escaped imprisonment, and David had been taken away from her again.

All because of her.

The abbess had taken a great risk in protecting Janet and smuggling her out of England to Italy with a group of pilgrims where she could recover in safety. But perhaps it was understandable, as the abbess's husband before she'd taken the cloth had been one of the thousands slaughtered by the first Edward of England in the sacking of Berwick ten years before.

By the time Janet had left for Italy, the plan for her to act as a courier for the Scots had already been hatched and "Sister Genna" was born. Only three people knew of her true identity: the abbess, the Bishop of St. Andrews, and later—when Lamberton had been able to tell him personally—Robert the Bruce. Not even her twin sister, Mary, knew she was alive.

It was safer for all of them that way. She'd hurt her sister enough by what she'd done. She would not put Mary in more danger were it to be discovered that Janet of Mar was alive and a "traitor" to England.

The scars from that horrible night held no shame for her, though she wished she could say the same for the actions that had led to them. But she wasn't the same impetuous girl who thought she knew what was best for everyone around her. Who didn't take no for an answer.

She bit her lip. Well, perhaps she hadn't changed in that regard, but at least she didn't embroil others in her trouble. Usually. Which was what made her lapse earlier with Sister Marguerite all that much worse. Janet knew she was better off alone. Fortune seemed to disfavor those near her. Which was one of the reasons she'd decided to become a nun.

Though Ewen Lamont seemed like a man who could be trusted, she could not take the chance in revealing her identity to him. What she was doing was too important.

Although admittedly, he did not seem to share her belief. His feelings about a woman's place still rankled. If she ever met a man who thought of her as an equal, she might have to put aside her plans to take the veil and marry him! But she might as well pray for wings to fly. Not even her formidable sister-in-law had managed that task. She could still hear the terrible rows Christina and Duncan would have before disappearing together into their chamber for hours.

Nay, Janet was happy with the path she'd chosen. Marriage meant strife or serfdom, and she was glad to escape those particular chains.

Why was she even thinking about this? Her immediate concern was Roxburgh. The imperious Highlander had interfered with her plans enough.

He was studying her in his off-putting silent manner

with those too-intent steely eyes of his. She knew her outburst had given away too much. She tried to explain—
calmly this time. "The English are watching the bridges. It
will not be safe to attempt to cross."

She couldn't repress the small shudder that ran through
her. It wasn't just an excuse. Since that night with her sister, she hated bridges.

"We aren't taking one of the main bridges. I know of a
place where we will be able to cross that the English won't
be watching." His eyes held hers—another unnerving
habit of his. "Why are you so eager to go to Roxburgh?"

Janet cursed her outburst again. She'd meant to persuade
him gently—when the time came—to make a quick stop in
Roxburgh. But she hadn't anticipated him having to change
course.

Having heard his opinion about her job, she knew better
than to mention it. Instead, she feigned embarrassment.
"There is a merchant in the village I wish to see."

"For what purpose?"

She untied the buckles of the large leather bag she still
wore over her shoulder and retrieved a small bundle. "For
these." She held it up to his nose so he could smell the fra-
grant spices.

"What are they?"

"Chestnuts roasted in honey and spices. They're my favorite, and I promised to bring some back with me for the
other nuns."

She tried not to shirk under the intensity of his gaze, but
he seemed to see right through her deception. "You're sure
this isn't another errand for the bishop?"

She hoped the flush of heat to her cheeks didn't show on
her face. "Has anyone ever told you that you have an
overly suspicious mind?'

"Has anyone ever told you nuns aren't supposed to lie?"

She lifted her chin. "It isn't a lie. The nuts *are* my favorite."

"Well, you can ask the bishop to pick them up for you

when he runs his own errand. We aren't going to Roxburgh. The area will be crawling with English. In case you haven't noticed, we're in the middle of a war."

She bristled at his patronizing sarcasm, but the subject of her involvement was not one she wanted to reopen. He was suspicious enough already, and heaven only knew what she'd say if he got her angry again.

So she bit her tongue and bided her time. But she hadn't given up. The bishop had received word from an important source at the castle and had asked Janet to make contact. He didn't trust anyone else. She would just have to find a way to convince the stubborn Highlander (a redundancy, in her experience) to reconsider. But she knew she'd better do it before he found that crossing.

Something was wrong, Ewen thought. The lass was too quiet. She'd given up too easily. He'd wager half his earnings for the month that she was up to something. Hell, he'd wager it all—if he wagered. But he wasn't his father, and he needed whatever coin he earned to finish that damned castle.

He just hoped she didn't have any more hidden daggers. Now that the rain had begun he needed to keep all his attention on the path ahead of them through the forest. The slippery mud and uneven ground was bad enough, but the thick mist that had descended around them was disorienting. Nor did it help his concentration any that the harder the rain came down, the deeper she seemed to burrow into his chest. His bollocks were probably a deep shade of blue by now after having her bottom wedged against him for God-knows-how-many hours.

She shivered dramatically. He didn't blame her. For an April day, it felt as cold as the dark of winter. "Please, may we not find a place to stop to wait out the storm?"

He felt a prickle of guilt. They'd been riding for hours

now. In addition to wet and cold, she was probably tired as well. "As soon as we cross the river."

"And when will that be?"

"Soon."

She glanced back at him from over her shoulder. She'd wrapped the plaid around her head, but water still streamed down her pale face. Her lashes were damp and clumped as if she'd been crying. Guilt pricked him again. She was only a lass. Women were delicate creatures—a fact he had to remind himself of in her case. What would make her want to put herself in such danger?

"I thought you knew—"

He cut her off. "I know exactly where we are." Mostly. They should be reaching the ford in the river soon. He hadn't gone too far. It was just the rain that was making it look so unfamiliar. He wasn't lost.

"I just thought that with the mist, it might be difficult—"

"We aren't lost, damn it."

She gasped, drawing back a little in the face of his temper. "I did not mean to slight your navigation skills. Of course, we are not lost." He felt a moment of satisfaction until she ruined it with, "If you say it is so."

Guilt forgotten, he fumed as he looked around for any sign that the path he'd taken was the right one. Women of the cloth weren't supposed to be so damned irritating. What happened to meek and serene?

He fought through the trees and brush for another twenty minutes or so. The rain was coming down harder and the wind . . . the wind seemed to be blowing straight off the North Sea. Bone-chilling was putting it mildly.

Finally he saw it—the gap he'd been looking for. "There it is," he said, as if there had never been any doubt.

He steered the horse toward the bank, but the sight that met him there was not what he expected.

* * *

Whatever blood Janet had left that wasn't frozen from the cold drained from her face. "You can't mean for us to cross here!"

She didn't need to feign horror; it was real enough. She looked at the twenty-foot-wide spans of the River Tweed and felt her stomach heave and ho like a ship upon storm-tossed seas. The normally slow-moving waters of the river were rushing by in a torrential fury, swollen from the winter runoff and the recent spate of storms.

The waves—waves!—were almost cresting the three big trees that had been set across the banks to form a make-shift bridge. How long would those trees stay in place against the powerful force of the river?

She shook her head, fear slamming around in her chest. "I can't."

He spoke to her gently—more gently than he ever had before. "It will hold."

He dismounted and held up his hand to help her down. She slipped her hand in his, and when she leaned forward, he caught her around the waist and lowered her gently to the ground. It was nothing that should have made her breath catch. She'd been helped down from a horse count-less time before. But never had she been aware of a man's hands around her waist, of the soft press of his thumbs against her rib cage, or of the strength of the arms that she gripped to keep her steady.

And never had she wanted to inhale so deeply. He smelled of leather, rain, and the forest, but also of some-thing warm and undeniably masculine.

Their eyes held for a long heartbeat, and she knew he felt it too. He shifted his gaze and released her so quickly her legs wobbled.

Confused by her reaction and more than a little embar-rassed, Janet avoided his gaze as he tied the horse to a nearby tree while he inspected the "bridge." She watched as he pushed a few of the trees to make sure they were solid and tested the muddy bank with his boot. As usual, it was impossible to read anything from his expression. There was a grim set to his mouth, but she couldn't say it was any more grim than usual.

He returned to where she waited under the shelter of a large tree to collect the horse. "It looks fine. I'll take the horse over first and come back for you."

The air seemed to be expanding in her chest and her heart pounded frantically. She looked up at him and shook her head. "I can't. I d-don't like bridges. Please, can't we go a different way?"

He gave her an encouraging smile that broke through her moment of panic. "It looks much worse than it is. You don't need to worry—I won't let anything happen to you."

She believed him enough to follow him to the bank of the river. But with what she saw next, nothing would have possessed her to go across. A big surge in the current caused the water to break over the trees. The force was so powerful, the entire structure seemed to rattle.

He started to lead the horse (who seemed just about as eager as she was) forward, but she stopped him. "Please, you must reconsider. The current is too strong. The trees are thick with moss and slippery. It is too easy to fall in, and I don't know how to swim. Isn't there someplace we could stay nearby until morning? Perhaps by then the rain will stop and the water will have subsided?"

As if to punctuate her words another surge crashed over the bridge, sending a spray of water bursting into the air.

She turned to him with a cry. "Please," she begged, looking up into his eyes.

His gaze fell into hers. "You really are scared?"

There was a strange note in his voice. A slight huskiness that penetrated through the haze of panic and sent a twinge of heated awareness racing through her.

She nodded, her face tilted toward his only inches away. *Inches away.* Her breath caught. Only then did she realize what she had done. Her hands were clutching his arms and her body was pressed against his. Intimately. Chest to chest and hip to hip. She could feel every hard inch of his chest and legs. She could feel something else as well. Something that made her mouth go dry, her heart drop, and her stomach flip all at the same time.

Oh, my.

The shock of it startled her. It was as if every nerve-ending in her body had been struck by a lightning bolt of awareness. She opened her mouth to gasp, but the sound strangled in her throat when their eyes met.

Heaven help her! Despite the rain and the cold, her body filled with heat.

If she hadn't felt the proof of his desire, she could see it now in his eyes. He wanted her, and the force of it seemed to be radiating under her fingertips, making her tremble with unfamiliar sensations. Her heart seemed to be racing too fast, her breath to be short and uneven, and her limbs too heavy.

She couldn't seem to move. She was caught up in something she didn't understand but couldn't resist. Didn't *want* to resist.

When his gaze dropped to her mouth, she knew what he was going to do. And she would have let him had he not found enough sense for both of them.

His jaw locked, and the tiny muscle below his chest began to tic. He looked away.

She let her hands drop and took a sudden step back, as if she were a bairn who'd just been caught by the cook with her hand on a tart and was trying to distance herself from the scene of her crime.

She didn't know what had come over her. She'd never touched a man so freely before, let alone tried to persuade one in such a manner.

His voice sounded more curt than normal. "There is an

inn not too far away in Trows that should be safe to stop at for the night."

Janet couldn't hide her relief. "Thank you."

Trows! She realized suddenly what that meant. Not only had she avoided the bridge, she'd also managed to find a way—unconsciously, as it happened—to get to Roxburgh. Trows was only a short distance away.

He gave her a hard look, and not for the first time, she wondered if he knew what she was thinking. "We cannot go as we are. A nun and a warrior traveling alone will draw too much comment."

Since he was being agreeable for once, she refrained from pointing out that she'd told him that same thing when he insisted on accompanying her. "What do you suggest?"

"I'll remove some of my armor, and you'll have to take off your veil and the white scapular."

Her eyes widened as she realized what he intended. "You mean to pretend we are married?"

Why did the idea frighten her more than pretending to be a nun? If she were going to parse her sins, the latter was infinitely more damning.

"Do you have any other suggestions?"

"Aren't there any other places we could take shelter? A cave? An abandoned shieling? A hut?"

"Yes, on the other side of that river." He pointed to the bridge just as another rush of water poured over it. "It's up to you."

The choice was obvious. There wasn't any reason she should have hesitated, but she did. Why did the idea of pretending to be his wife terrify her almost as much as the bridge did? "The inn."

He gave her a curt nod. "I will leave you a minute to tend to your needs and remove your habit." He pointed to the wooden cross on her neck that she'd worn since the night she tried to free her sister. "Hide that as well."

She was grateful for the moment of privacy. She tended

to her most pressing need, and then quickly removed the veil and scapular, which wasn't easy in the rain with everything sopping wet. She tried not to think that right now had he not insisted on accompanying her, she would be warm and dry in the abbey. When she was done, she wrapped the plaid around her again and packed the clothing in her bag. Without the protection of her habit she felt . . . vulnerable.

But to what?

She'd just finished tucking the cross under the plain black gown she still wore, when he returned and she knew exactly *what*.

Oh God.

Her stomach dropped. He'd removed the ghastly helm, and for the first time she could see his face in full.

She was wrong. He wasn't just handsome, he was *brutally* handsome. Handsome in the dark-haired, blue-eyed, rough-hewn kind of way that made every primitive female instinct in her stand up and take notice. His mouth . . . that jaw . . . those eyes.

She sighed in a way that she never had as a young girl. What a time to start acting like one!

His hair hung in sopping-wet clumps across his forehead, the stubble of his beard was a day or two too long, and rain was pouring down his face, yet it only seemed to add a rugged edge to his attractiveness. She felt something grip her chest and squeeze.

The horror of realization hit her. She knew why she was acting like this and why he'd made her feel so uneasy from the start.

Jerusalem's Temples, I'm attracted to him!

Instinctively, like the hare who sees the hunter for the first time, Janet felt the urge to run. She may have persuaded him to do her bidding, but part of her wondered whether crossing the bridge was any less dangerous than spending the night with him.

Five

❧

It wasn't until the innkeeper opened the door to the room that Ewen realized exactly how big of a mistake he'd made in letting her persuade him not to cross that river.

His eyes scanned the second-floor chamber, which didn't take long, as it wasn't much bigger than the solitary bed that had been pushed up against the far wall. Aside from a small table and wooden stool, nothing else was in the room. There wasn't room for anything.

Alarm hit him like a poleaxe in the chest. There was no way in hell they could stay here. Jesus, they would be right on top of one another!

He was just about to ask for another room—a much larger one—when the plump, matronly-looking innkeeper turned to him with a proud smile. "It's our largest room, and I think our best. You can see right down to the court-yard from that window," she said cheerfully, pointing to the shutter above the bed. "The roof is tight and will keep you nice and dry. Of course, we can't have a fire in here with the thatched roof, but it is warm and cozy from the fire in the hall below, and if you give me your wet things, I'll hang them by the fire downstairs, and they should be nice and dry by morning."

Neither he nor Sister Genna seemed to know what to say. For him that wasn't uncommon, but he suspected it was a rare occurrence for the silver-tongued nun.

The innkeeper set down the stack of bed linens she was

carrying and placed them on the bed. Then she turned to Sister Genna and said with a wink and meaningful glance toward the bed, "If you need another blanket, let me know. But your husband is a braw laddie, he should keep you plenty warm."

Sister Genna seemed to turn even paler and her eyes widened to such enormous proportions, Ewen would have laughed if he wasn't feeling exactly the same way. Apprehension was an understatement. This room was beginning to look like his very own personal torture chamber.

He was tempted to thank the innkeeper for her trouble and go right back down the stairs, but that might provoke exactly the type of attention he was trying to avoid. So far everything had gone well, and they had not seemed to attract any undue notice. He didn't want to do anything to jeopardize that.

Besides, part of him knew Sister Genna was right: it would have been dangerous to attempt to cross the bridge in the storm. They were both cold and soaked to the bone. He might have been able to build a makeshift shelter, but it would be a long, torturous night outside in the cold and rain. In here it would be a different kind of long, torturous night for him, but at least she would be warm and dry. He couldn't stand watching her shiver anymore; it made him feel . . . odd. Like he would do just about anything to make her stop.

With grim acceptance he took pity on his horror-struck "wife," who couldn't seem to find her tongue for once, and answered for her.

"The room will do," he said with his usual brevity. He spoke in English, the tongue spoken by the ordinary people in the border towns. He was surprised to discover that Sister Genna spoke it quite well—albeit with a heavy accent—something she'd neglected to tell him until now. The lass was full of surprises.

He realized he'd said something wrong when the older woman's face fell. But Sister Genna immediately moved to make it right. "It's the perfect refuge from the storm," she said to the innkeeper with a grateful smile. "I'm sure we will be quite comfortable." She gave a gasp of delight that hit him hard in a place it shouldn't. "Is that a feather pillow?"

The innkeeper beamed. "It is indeed, m'lady."

"How wonderful! I will be asleep as soon as my head hits those feathers. I suspect my . . ." He hoped he was the only one who noticed her slight hesitation. "My husband might have to pry me out of bed in the morning. But we have a long journey ahead of us."

Much mollified, the innkeeper patted the sister's arm as if she were a young girl. "Where did you say you were traveling to?"

"We didn't," Ewen said.

Sister Genna shot him a glare and gave the innkeeper a roll of the eyes as if to apologize for his poor manners. "My mother is very ill," she said in low tones. "I only hope that we will make it to London in time."

"You poor child," she said, patting her again. "And all the way to London? But you are . . ."

"Flemish, Madame," Genna filled in. They'd decided to be careful in case anyone was looking for an Italian nun. "My father is a merchant."

He had to admit she was good at this. For a nun, she certainly lied well. He was almost believing her himself.

"How did you and your husband meet?"

Ewen was forced to stand in the doorway for another ten minutes as Genna regaled the innkeeper with the story of their chance meeting at a market in Berwick before "Bruce had caused all this trouble by taking the throne." He hardly thought he looked like the type to leave wildflowers on her doorstep for a fortnight, but the innkeeper was charmed by his "romance," and he found himself blushing like a fool (as was no doubt the little minx's intent!) under her approving gaze.

Sister Genna was a natural, Ewen realized. If he'd

wanted to deflect suspicion, she'd succeeded for him. But finally, after promises to send them up some food, the woman left them alone.

The moment the door closed behind her, all his trepidation returned full force. The room seemed to grow thick with it. The sudden silence made him wonder if Sister Genna had been keeping the other woman there to delay this very moment.

Trying to break the moment of awkwardness, he took the two steps to the table and put down the leather bag he kept tied to his saddle. After taking off the plaid he wore around his shoulders, he turned to face her. She'd inched her way to the foot of the bed at the opposite side of the room—about as far away from him as she could manage.

He cursed silently, seeing the wariness on her pale face. She was looking at him as if he were a wolf and she were a juicy lamb. Worse, he knew it wasn't unwarranted. She must have realized how close he'd been to kissing her out there earlier.

What could he have been thinking? She was a nun, for Christ's sake! He didn't consider himself a particularly devout man, but the church was a part of his life, as it was for every man and woman in Christendom. His lust for a woman he'd been taught since childhood to revere as holy and sacrosanct was shameful.

If the fate of his immortal soul wasn't enough, the possible damage he could do to Bruce's cause—and thus his own—were he to touch her should be all the reminder he needed. Bruce needed the support of the church to win his war, and Ewen needed Bruce's if his clan was going to survive. He could only imagine what Lamberton's reaction would be if it became known that he'd despoiled one of his anointed.

But she sure as hell wasn't making it easy on him. She didn't act like any nun he'd ever met—or any woman, for that matter. And it might have been easier to ignore his feelings if he wasn't pretty damned sure she was feeling them, too.

His mouth fell in a grim line when he saw her shiver. She'd lowered the hood from around her head and the golden locks that had been plastered to her head had begun to dry. *Damn it, not the hair again!* He felt a tug in his groin and bit off another curse. "You should do as she says and get out of those clothes before you catch cold." With the innkeeper gone, he went back to speaking French.

Wide-eyed, she shook her head. "I'll be fine. It's warm in here. They'll dry soon enough."

"Don't be ridiculous. I'll turn my back while you change; your modesty will be protected."

Two bright spots of pink appeared on her cheeks. She'd obviously taken umbrage at his tone. "It's not my modesty I'm worried about. I only brought two gowns with me, and if you'll recall, the soldier destroyed the other."

He untied the strap of his bag and pulled out an extra *leine*. "You can wear this." Anticipating her refusal given the transparency of the fabric he added, "Wrap the plaid she brought for the bed around you."

She debated for a minute or two before comfort won out. "Very well. But don't turn back around until I tell you."

"As long as you promise the same. I'll be changing as well."

He watched her fight the smile around her mouth and lose. "You might have used some of that charm with the innkeeper. If the English come looking for us, she would have happily turned you in after that less-than-complimentary comment about the room. And not telling her our destination? You'll only make people suspicious by refusing to answer their questions."

Charm? He'd never been associated with that before. But talking with Sister Genna was different—easier. It was almost like talking to one of the Guard. His brusqueness and rough edges didn't seem to bother her.

"Does the same hold true for you, Sister? Can I trust you not to peek?"

She flushed. "Of course."

He held her stare. She did not back down from the challenge in his gaze, but he knew she was hiding something. Something about her wasn't right, and he intended to find out what it was.

"Change," he said gruffly, turning around.

He'd taken his clothes off in the same room as a woman countless times before, but he'd never been so achingly aware of it. Though they stood well over five feet apart, he swore he could feel every one of her movements. He made quick work of his own wet clothes, exchanging them for a clean tunic and breeches.

And then he waited. She seemed to be taking an infinitely long amount of time. He started to turn his head . . .

"Are you looking?"

His head snapped back. "Are you done yet?"

"Almost."

A few minutes later, thinking that she must be finished by now, he glanced over his shoulder again, catching sight of her slim back right before the *leine* dropped over it.

He sucked in a groan, going as hard as a spike. Lust pounded through him and the painful ache returned. It was his own damned fault. This was what he got for looking.

Now he had the image of a smooth, shapely, creamy bottom to go along with the smooth, shapely, creamy breasts. The walls of the torture room seemed to be drawing in tighter.

But not all of her had been smooth. He frowned, recalling the scars that he'd noticed earlier. A hair shirt and whip? He didn't think so. They looked like some kind of burn marks.

The lass was going to start answering some of his questions.

"You can turn around," she said.

The frown was still on his face. "How did you get the scars on your back?"

Janet stiffened instinctively. It wasn't shame but the natural defensiveness that the subject aroused. Though they'd faded, she knew the scars were unsightly. But somehow that seemed fitting. She wanted the reminder. She didn't want to lose sight of her purpose. She might not be able to change what her interference that day at the bridge had wrought—or bring back Cailin—but she could ensure that something good came from it.

She must be getting used to Ewen's blunt manner of speaking, because neither his question nor his appalling lack of manners in bringing up such a personal subject surprised her. He was lucky that she wasn't self-conscious.

All of a sudden, she stopped. Her eyes narrowed. What had made him think of the scars? "You looked!"

He shrugged without apology. "It was unintentional. You were taking too long."

"Is that supposed to be an excuse?"

"If you wish it to be."

Janet fumed at him.

"You've nothing to worry about," he said. "You don't have anything I haven't seen hundreds of times."

If he was trying to make her feel better, he'd failed. Her eyes widened with outrage. "Hundreds of times?"

He shrugged, and for some reason the careless indifference infuriated her all the more. She shouldn't care how many women he'd been with or whether he thought her unremarkable in comparison, but hearing him so blandly state it rankled.

"How nice to know that you have such a breadth of comparison to call upon."

"You didn't answer my question. How did you get the scars? And before you think about telling me what you told the soldiers today, I know they aren't from a whip and hair shirt."

"Have you 'hundreds' of scar comparisons as well?"

He grinned; obviously her irritation amused him. "More."

"You've been fighting the war for some years, then?"

"Aye. Now tell me about the scars."

Janet pursed her mouth. He was just like Duncan. She'd never been able to distract him either. He'd been positively intractable when it had come to questioning her about some perceived issue or problem. If only Ewen Lamont reminded her of her brother in other ways. But the feelings Ewen aroused in her were definitely *un*-brotherly.

As it seemed he would not be turned from his course without an answer, she decided to tell him the truth. Well, part of it, anyway. "I was on a bridge when it was struck by lightning. I don't remember exactly what happened, but there was a fire, and some of the wood splintered and ended up in my back. The sisters did their best to remove them, but some were buried deeply."

He held her gaze as if he knew there was more that she wasn't saying. But that was all she intended to tell him. How she ended up on the bridge was none of his business.

"So that's why you didn't wish to cross. When did this happen?"

It was her turn to shrug. "Some time ago." Hoping to put an end to the subject, she added, "I do not like to talk about it."

"The scars are no cause for shame. They are a mark of your strength. You survived."

She bristled. "I know that. It is not the scars that cause me pain, but the memories they bring."

This time, he took the hint and changed the subject— though unfortunately, this one was no better than the last. "You have an unusual accent. Where are you from?"

She hoped he hadn't seen the slight stiffening of her

shoulders, but she'd already learned that little escaped him. "My father was a merchant," she said, staying with the same story she told the innkeeper. "We moved around quite a bit."

"And that is why you speak so many languages?"

"Yes." But it hadn't been easy. She'd always been horrible with languages. Deciding that they'd talked about her long enough, she asked, "And what about you? I have not met many Highlanders who speak such fluent French who aren't noblemen—" She stopped, blushing.

"And you have figured out that I do not qualify?"

"I did not mean to offend you."

"You didn't. I was fostered with a local nobleman and had some tutoring. Languages come easily for me." She made a face, and he laughed. "I take it that it is not the same for you?"

She shook her head. "Latin was the worst."

The words were out before she could take them back. She hoped he wouldn't notice, but, of course, he did.

"I would have thought with Italian being so closely related, it would have been easy."

"For most people it is," she said. She feigned a yawn. "If you don't mind, I think I should like to go to bed. I'm very tired."

And talking to him was dangerous. It was easy to forget herself, in more ways than one. For a few moments, she'd forgotten that she was a nun—or planned to be soon—that they should remain strangers, and that they were alone in this room. For a few minutes, she'd felt as comfortable with him as if they were truly man and wife. For a few minutes, the intimacy had seemed . . . natural.

But suddenly being alone with him felt awkward again. She was deeply conscious of him as a man. And as much as she wanted to pretend that she was a nun, her body seemed to know differently. Being alone with a too-tall, too-handsome, too-virile warrior made her feel very feminine and very aware of that femininity in a way that she never had been before.

She pulled the plaid around her shoulders more tightly, even though the room suddenly felt too warm. It *was* the room, wasn't it? But that didn't explain the heat in places she had never felt warm before. Warning beacons seemed to flare all around her. She needed to get away from him.

He must have picked up on the charge in the atmosphere as well, because he suddenly seemed very eager to leave. "If you give me your clothes, I will take them down to the innkeeper to hang by the fire. You don't need to leave the candle burning for me; I will be able to find the floor when I return."

She bit her lip, wanting to ask how long he'd be but not wanting to make him suspicious. Because she had no intention of being here when he woke up.

With his father's penchant for drink, Ewen wasn't much for whisky, but at times he could appreciate the dulling effects of the fiery brew. The last time he'd drunk too much was after one of his friends and fellow Highland Guardsmen, William Gordon, was killed in an explosion in Galloway. Before that, it had been when he and MacLean had finally made it to safety after surviving the slaughter that had befallen Bruce's men at Loch Ryan at the hands of the MacDowells. Eighteen galleys, and only two had survived.

But tonight, it wasn't the pain of losing friends that had driven him to drink, but another kind of pain—the lustful kind. Knowing that he'd lie awake all night hard as a rock if he didn't do something, he spent a good hour draining a flagon of very peaty whisky, trying to cool his heated blood. He was tempted when an alternative method of dulling his lust presented itself in the form of a comely barmaid, but the whisky must have already been having an effect, as her flirtatious grazes and bold glances didn't get the barest rise out of him.

By the time he returned to the room, he was good and relaxed, and the source of his trouble was fast asleep and bundled up safely out of eyesight under the blankets. He threw his plaid on the floor, barely noticing how hard it was before passing out in a whisky-induced haze.

But the drink didn't penetrate his sleep. He dreamed of her. Hot, restless dreams of high, round breasts and a curvy bottom. He imagined touching her, cupping her, running his hands over every naked inch of baby-soft flesh. His body was hot, his blood rushing, his nose filled with her soft scent. The sensations were so strong, they tore him from his sleep. Or at least he thought they had. But when he opened his eyes, his hand was wrapped around her wrist and she was looming over him, her eyes wide with shock.

Then he knew he had to be dreaming because he could feel the soft stroke of her hands on his hair and hear the soft, soothing tones of her voice as she filled his dreams with the lulling sounds of song. He felt his body relax. Felt the tension that had been teeming through his limbs release under the gentle, calming strokes. It was nice. He'd never had a mother to put him to bed when he was young, but he suspected it would have been something like this. The last thing he remembered before she left was the soft brush of her lips on his cheek.

He woke to a cold room and the first rays of dawn streaming through the cracks in the shutters. Though weak, the sunlight sent shards of pain piercing through his drink-thickened head like daggers. He closed his eyes, listening instead to the peaceful sounds of . . . silence. *Absolute* silence.

His eyes snapped open again. Ignoring the pain, his gaze went to the woman sleeping on the bed. Or the woman who *should* be sleeping on the bed. But even before he jumped to his feet and tore back the bunched-up plaid, he knew.

It hadn't been a dream. His damned "wife" was gone.

Six

❦

Janet didn't think her heart started beating again until she was halfway to Roxburgh.

After she'd managed to get him back to sleep, she'd retrieved her belongings from the hearth downstairs and slipped past the sleeping occupants of the inn to escape into the cool morning darkness with little trouble. But her heart had jumped straight through her throat earlier, when she'd tried to step over him to get to the door and he'd opened his eyes and grabbed her by the wrist.

Whether he'd been awake or half-asleep, she didn't know, but for one long heartbeat she'd thought he meant to pull her down on top of him. The knowledge of how badly she wanted him to made her panic. She needed to do something.

Without thinking, she reached out and touched him, trying to calm him back to sleep as she had her sister Mary after a nightmare when they were young. But touching him was nothing like touching her sister.

Even as Janet hurried along the road through the forest that connected Trows to Roxburgh, she could still feel the silky thickness of his hair running through her fingers. Surely a man—particularly a soldier who looked like he was born on the battlefield—shouldn't have such soft hair? But the dark, glossy waves slid through her fingers like the finest silk. She could still feel the solid thickness of his back and arm muscles as she'd tried to soothe the tension from his limbs and ease him back to sleep. But most of all, she could still feel the scratch of his whiskers against her mouth as she'd brushed her lips over his stubble-roughened jaw.

What in heaven's gates could have possessed her to kiss him? She still couldn't believe it. But she'd been singing in his ear, and his cheek had been so close and irresistible.

He'd smelled like whisky and pine, and his skin had tasted so . . . good. Dark and sweet, with a faint trace of spice. A rush of strange sensations washed over her. Her pulse raced, her skin felt flush and prickly, her limbs felt heavy and her breasts full. Her nipples tightened, and she suddenly felt the restless urge to rub her body against his.

For one treacherous moment, there in the darkness, she'd wanted to crawl in beside him. She'd wanted him to take her into his arms and show her what a man did to a woman. She wasn't ignorant about the act, but until that moment she hadn't though herself capable of wanting to experience it.

No man had ever made her feel like this. Confused, half-crazed, and scared all at the same time.

Her feet quickened as she sped up her pace, racing as much away from him as she was toward Roxburgh and the future she had all planned out. A future that didn't include lustful thoughts or being distracted by a man. She was going to be a nun, for goodness' sake!

It was what she wanted, wasn't it? She felt a small squeeze in her chest before she brushed it away. Of course, it was. Taking the veil made sense. How else could she continue what she was doing? As a nun, she had freedom. A purpose. She liked working for Lamberton and was proud of all she'd done to help Robert.

What other options did she have? For a noblewoman there were two: marriage or the veil, and she knew marriage wasn't for her. She'd been engaged twice before, and both times the engagement had ended in the death of her fiancé. War had killed many of Scotland's young noblemen, but to Janet their deaths had seemed like an omen that marriage was not meant for her.

Besides, she was happy, and in her experience happiness and marriage did not go together. Her father had ordered her mother around like a serf, her sister Mary's girlish love for the Earl of Atholl had turned to misery, and Duncan and Christina had spent most of their time arguing.

Why was she even thinking about this? Even were she to decide she wanted to marry, it would never be to an ordinary soldier, even if he didn't *seem* ordinary. She frowned. She was a daughter of Mar, the former sister-in-law of a king and aunt to his only heir. Her choice of husband wouldn't be hers at all. It would be a political match brokered by Robert.

For more reasons than one, the gruff Highlander with the silky hair and irresistibly kissable jaw wasn't for her.

She was practically running now, breathing hard, and despite the chill of the morning mist, a sheen of perspiration appeared on her brow. She couldn't seem to get away fast enough. She figured she had at least an hour's lead on him, which even if he tried to follow her would give her plenty of time to reach Roxburgh on foot—it was only a mile or so away. But just to make sure, she veered off the road as she drew near the town and took a roundabout route to the castle through the forest.

She'd thought about absconding with the horse but hadn't wanted to risk waking the stable lads. In hindsight, perhaps it was a risk she should have taken. Too late, she heard the sound of hoofbeats. She gazed around like a startled hare, frantically looking for a place to hide. But he was on her before she could dart into a hole—or in this case, the brush.

Her heart was beating like a drum, but she hoped she managed to appear cool and serene when she turned to face him. "How did you find me?"

He didn't bother to answer her question. His face, half-hidden by the helm again, was a mask of icy rage. He leapt off the horse and grabbed her roughly by the arm. "You little fool, are you trying to get yourself killed?"

She might have felt the urge to cower—having six-foot-plus of solid muscle and angry male bellowing at her wasn't exactly unintimidating—if he hadn't riled her own anger. "If anyone is acting foolish, it is you for chasing after me! I've told you before, I don't need or want an escort. I didn't ask for you to accompany me, and I don't need your permission to leave without you."

"The hell you don't."

She had to admit, she felt a little shiver of fear when he growled and pulled her even harder against him. But then she wondered whether it was something else when her heart took a sharp dive and heat coursed through her. A reaction that she was becoming used to where he was concerned.

Good Lord, she loved the way he smelled—the mix of the wind in his hair, the pine of the forest on his skin, and the leather of his *cotun*.

His face lowered to hers, and she sucked in her breath, wishing that helm covered the steely blue-gray eyes that were flashing at her with as much danger as the sword he had strapped to his back once again. "Did you stop to think that my 'wife's' sudden disappearance from our bed before dawn might be a little suspicious?"

Janet bit her lip, fighting back the flush. She hadn't. All she'd been thinking of was getting out of there. "I'm sure you thought of something to appease her."

"Not everyone is as clever at lying as you."

There was no stopping the flush this time. He didn't know the half of it. She lifted her chin stubbornly. "Even if the innkeeper is curious, I'm sure it will come to nothing."

"Is that so? I'm not sure the party of English soldiers I saw approaching the inn as I was leaving will agree with you. But let's hope the excuse I made will suffice."

English soldiers? The first prickles of guilt started to form. "What did you say to her?"

"That you'd gone to the local church to pray for your mother's recovery before we started out on our journey."

Air eased out of her lungs, and she nodded. "It's a good excuse." She was surprised he'd come up with it.

His eyes narrowed as if he could read her mind. "The innkeeper might have believed me, but the English sure as hell won't if they decide to follow up on us at the church."

"*If* they are indeed looking for us, and *if* they make the connection, perhaps. But there is no reason to suspect either. It was probably just an English scouting party from the castle." She wrenched her arm out of his hold and took a step back. This was all his fault. If he hadn't insisted on accompanying her, she wouldn't be feeling so . . . *confused*, and she wouldn't have felt the need to run away. "I'm sorry for leaving you with an explanation to make to the innkeeper, but there is something I have to do in Roxburgh, and you aren't going to stop me."

Janet saw the flash in his eyes and knew she'd made a mistake. Whether it was the challenge of her words or something else, she didn't know. But before she could take another breath, he'd jerked off his helm, pulled her into arms, and fitted her tightly to his body, giving her no doubt of his intent.

This time the thrill that shuddered through her was unmistakable. It was as if a wave of molten heat had been poured over every limb. She couldn't move. She couldn't push him away.

She didn't want to push him away.

"The hell I'm not," he said, right before his mouth covered hers.

So this was what it felt like to lose control. Ewen didn't know what possessed him to take her in his arms, but the moment his lips touched hers he no longer gave a damn.

Her lips were so silky soft and sweet, he groaned at the first taste of her. The blood and anger roaring through him urged him to go fast and hard, to take and plunder, to lose himself in the sweet, enveloping heat. But something stronger quieted the primitive urge and made him slow down.

Innocent. She was so damned innocent, and suddenly that was all that mattered. As much as he wanted to ravish her senseless, he didn't want to scare her. So he loosened the hold he had around her, lightened the pressure of his lips, and kissed her gently. Tenderly. Reverently.

He couldn't recall ever wooing a lass with his mouth, but he did so now. With each deft caress he beckoned her to him, showing her—teaching her—what he wanted from her.

Slowly, he could feel the shock slip away and her body begin to relax. He wanted to roar with masculine satisfaction, but he settled for a soft growl.

But then she nestled in closer against him with a sound that went straight to his cock and nearly wiped away all his good intentions.

Take it slow, he told himself. *You can do this. It's nothing you haven't done hundreds of times before.*

He nearly chuckled at the exaggeration, recalling her reaction—oddly, it had seemed more like jealousy than religious condemnation—but he didn't feel much like laughing when he realized that this was not like anything he'd done before. Kissing her was an entirely *different* experience, and he didn't like it.

Except he did like it. Too damned much.

Slow.

But she wasn't making it easy, the way her fingers were digging into his shoulders as she gripped him harder and harder, and he felt her own pleasure building.

He cradled her face in his hand, stroking his thumb over the soft curve of her cheek, feeling his chest squeezing tighter and tighter with each caress. Her lips were like velvet, her breath like honey, and she smelled . . . God, she smelled like a fistful of bluebells that had been sitting in the sun. He wanted to sink into her and let that scent swallow him up.

His fingers slid around her neck, plunging through the soft waves of her hair. She'd been wearing a hooded cloak, but the hood had slid back to reveal the magnificent golden mane, loose, no doubt, because of the haste of her departure.

He didn't want to think about that now—but it was a good thing tracking her had been so appallingly easy. All he wanted to think about was how incredible her lips felt on his, how good it felt to have her breasts crushed against his chest and her hips nestled to his groin, how silky soft her hair was on his fingers as he gripped the back of her head and held her mouth to his, and how much longer could he stand to take it slow when every fiber, every instinct, every drop of blood and bone in his body wanted to slide his tongue into her mouth and taste her deeper.

He groaned, anticipating the feeling of her tongue circling his. It was going to feel so good . . .

His head, his heart, every part of his body was pounding. He couldn't wait any longer.

He brushed his mouth over hers again and urged her lips apart. Then he filled her mouth with his, swallowing her gasp of surprise when his tongue licked into the honey-sweet cavern.

Oh God, that was good! Even better than he'd anticipated. Hotter. Sweeter. Darker and more erotic.

He pulled her closer, needing to feel the friction of her body against his as his tongue plunged deeper and deeper in her mouth. He bent her to him, feeling himself drowning, feeling his body being dragged into a vortex of pleasure so acute he wasn't going to be able to pull himself out.

He could feel her heart hammering against his, feel her shock, and then her discovery as her body awakened to the passion that ignited like wildfire between them—hot, devastating, and uncontrollable. He'd never felt anything like it. But it was nothing to the sensations that exploded inside him when he felt the first circle of her tongue against his. It sent a wave of heat to his groin so strong that it nearly made his knees buckle.

She might be innocent, but there was nothing innocent about her response or the sensations it incited. Going slow was forgotten as he pushed her back against a tree, wrapped her leg around his waist, and descended into the madness of passion, their tongues gliding and sparring in a wicked dance.

His cock was throbbing, positioned at the sweet juncture between her legs. He couldn't resist. He started to rock, needing the friction of her body moving against his.

He wasn't thinking now—had he ever been?—instinct had set in. He was kissing her harder, dragging his hands over her body with a possessiveness that said they were meant to be there. He cupped her incredible breasts, and then her bottom as he lifted her more tightly against him.

Oh God, right there. That was it. He clenched, his buttocks tight against the pressure. It felt so good, he had to fight the urge to come.

He couldn't wait to be inside her.

He dragged his mouth from her lips to her neck, covering the frantic pulse beneath her jaw with his mouth and sucking until she squirmed and moaned against him.

Hot. It was so damned hot he couldn't breathe.

He could hear the quickness of her breath, and the soft little gasping sounds she was making were driving him wild. He felt her body shudder with surrender and knew she was his.

Mine. The knowledge pounded through him like the hammer of a drum. He tore his mouth away and looked down at her. Her face was flushed, her lips swollen and her eyes half-lidded with passion. He didn't think he'd ever seen anything more beautiful.

Something strange stirred in his chest. A feeling—an emotion—he'd never felt before. It was more than lust and more than possessiveness, it was softer . . . sweeter . . . more significant.

But then his gaze dropped and all the desire, all the passion, all the strange emotions he was feeling tore out of him in one horrified breath. Dangling across the breast that he'd just held in his hand was a wooden cross.

Shame rose inside him, as bitter and nauseating as bile.

What the hell was he doing? She was a nun, for Christ's sake! The immensity of his sin took him aback.

He released her so suddenly, she swayed, and he had to reach out to catch her before she fell to the ground.

One moment Janet was climbing the gates of heaven toward a beautiful sea of light, and the next she was flailing in darkness, trying to catch herself from falling on the cold, hard ground of reality.

The swift curtailment of the most incredible sensations she'd ever experienced left her yearning, aching, and confused. When the arms that had been holding her so tightly suddenly closed around her again, she gasped with relief and clutched him like a lifeline.

Don't stop, she wanted to say. *Please don't stop. It feels so good.*

But then she looked into his eyes and the coldness—the disgust—was like a drench of icy water, shocking her back to reality.

She jerked away from him, but she couldn't seem to tear her gaze away from his. Why was he looking at her like that? What had she done?

And then she remembered. The look wasn't directed at her.

They stared at each other in a moment of mute horror.

Hers for how easily she'd succumbed, and his with the shame and guilt of what he'd done. Or rather, what he *thought* he'd done.

Were she really a nun, kissing her would be a grave sin indeed, and from the sickened look on his face, the realization was hitting him hard. Seeing the depth of his torment, Janet felt something in her chest grow tight and hot.

She wanted to tell him the truth—and for one moment she almost did—but then sanity returned. Right now, her habit was the only thing that was keeping them apart. Were she to remove it—figuratively—it could very well lead to having it removed literally.

After that kiss, she didn't trust herself.

She'd never imagined . . .

Never thought . . .

Never realized it could be like *that*.

She'd never thought she could be capable of such madness. For surely it was madness when the feeling of his mouth moving over hers, the wicked sensation of his tongue flicking against hers, the heat of his hands on her body, could obliterate all rational thought and make her forget everything that was important to her?

She didn't want anything to interfere with her work for Bruce and Lamberton, and instinctively she realized that this man could threaten that.

Her gaze slid to his mouth. For lips that were often thinned and pulled in a rather grim line, they were certainly soft and smooth as honey when he wanted them to be. For that matter, she would never have expected such a rough and uncouth warrior to kiss with such skill and tenderness.

Obviously, those "hundreds" had not been without effect.

Why did that realization make her chest ache?

It wasn't that she cared who he'd been with, she told herself, it was just that she didn't like surprises. Especially ones that were so devastating. And that kiss certainly qualified.

Mother Mary, she'd nearly let him take her innocence! Indeed, she'd practically handed it to him with no more inducement than a skilled kiss and a few heated caresses.

Her cheeks burned. Well, maybe more than a few. She had to force herself not to drop her gaze further, remembering the incredible sensation of the thick column of his manhood riding against her. She'd wanted him even closer. She'd wanted him—her cheeks burned—*inside* her. Wanted it so intensely that she would have thrown away everything— her virtue, her morals, her honor. She'd been brought up a lady, never allowed either of her betrotheds even a chaste kiss, but with one press of his lips he'd turned her into a wanton.

The charged silence stretched on until finally, he broke it. "That should never have happened."

For once they were in agreement.

His gaze had shuttered, and once again she found herself looking at the hard, implacable warrior.

"I hope you will accept my apology, but"—he should have stopped there—"you made me angry."

Janet was aghast. "So this is my fault for not meekly following along and doing your bidding?"

His eyes narrowed at her sarcasm. "Meek and biddable might help to remind me that you are a nun. And pious and serene, for that matter. You don't act like any woman of the cloth I've ever met."

"And have you had 'hundreds' of them with whom to compare me as well?"

He stilled, his gaze turning as hard and penetrating as a steel dagger. "What happened to your accent?"

Janet hoped she hadn't gone as pale as it felt like she had. "What are you talking about?" she replied in her Italian accented French, careful not to overdo it.

But he was like a hunter who'd just trapped a hare and

wasn't about to let go. He took her by the elbow. "What are you hiding, Sister? Who the hell are you?"

Fear rose inside her as those penetrating steel-blue eyes locked on hers. She felt exposed and wanted to run, but had no place to hide. Her heart fluttered wildly in her chest as the veil she'd erected between them threatened to dissolve. She just wanted him to let her go.

"I'm an innocent maid in the service of the Bishop of St. Andrews whom you almost seduced. That's all you need to know, and all that matters. Do not attempt to absolve your own guilt by seeing things that aren't there and making excuses for your own actions."

Her dagger had drawn blood. He dropped her arm and stepped back. "You are right."

Janet felt a twist of guilt in her chest, seeing the shame once again on his face, and wanted to reach for him. But she kept her hand firmly planted at her side. *It's better this way*, she told herself.

"There is no excuse, and I will not attempt to make one. You have every right to blame me for what happened. You can be assured I will confess my sins at the next opportunity." His mouth fell in that grim line that she was beginning to find strangely attractive. He gave her a pleading look, which she suspected was rare and didn't appear to sit very comfortably on his face.

He reached his hand to his head as if he meant to rake his fingers through his hair, but then let it drop. "Look, can't we just try to forget about this and pretend it never happened? I don't want there to be any difficulties when we reach Berwick."

She would like nothing better. But Janet suspected forgetting about it and pretending it had never happened was going to be impossible. Even now, just looking at him, her skin flushed with a new awareness. Passion, desire . . . lust. Like Pandora, she'd opened the lid and was now tasked with finding a way to put away all those feelings again. But once released, would they ever go back?

She had to try.

Difficulties, he'd said. He was obviously concerned that she'd tell Lamberton what had happened. Janet was about to assure him that she'd rather swallow nails than speak of what had occurred here, when she stopped, considering what else he'd said: Berwick. She hated using his torment against him, but in this case, she told herself it was warranted. She had a job to do.

She nodded. "Confession will ease my mind a great deal. There is a small church in Roxburgh where you can go while I attend to my business in the castle."

"We aren't going to Roxburgh. Berwick will be soon enough."

"Not for me. Besides, if I return to Berwick having failed to bring back those sugared nuts, the bishop might wonder why, and I will have to give him an explanation." They both knew she wasn't talking about nuts. "It is no more than a half-mile away. Please, I will be careful, and there is no cause to think there will be any danger. I've done this *hundreds* of times."

Her gentle teasing and attempt to ease the tension between them elicited nary a flicker of a smile. Ewen wasn't in the mood for teasing.

He knew what she was trying to do—use his guilt against him—but was too damned angry with himself and wracked with shame to find the energy to put up a fight. Or maybe he just didn't trust himself to have another argument with her. He was still reeling after what had just happened. By how thoroughly he'd lost control, and how quickly a kiss had dissolved into so much more.

How could he have forgotten himself like that? His father was the one who took what he wanted. Ewen had much more discipline than that—usually.

It had been easy, he realized. She'd responded with an openness and eagerness that made it easy to forget she was untouchable.

He wasn't the only one who'd sinned. She might not want to admit it—and he was (just) gallant enough not to point it out—but she'd wanted him as badly as he'd wanted her.

"Please," she repeated. "It won't take any more than an hour, and then we can be on our way."

Ewen stared down at that pale upturned face, at the wide blue-green eyes, the pink lips still swollen from his kiss, and the classically arranged delicate features, and felt something shift in his chest.

He was going to give in, damn her. They would go to Roxburgh. It was his guilt, he told himself. It wasn't that he would give her anything she wanted when she looked at him like that.

"I think you missed your calling, Sister."

She blinked at him in confusion, her long, feathery lashes fluttering like a raven's wing. He had to steel himself against the sudden gripping in his chest, but she was so damned beautiful it hurt. "What do you mean?"

"You should have been a lawman."

He watched as understanding that she'd won dawned on her features, and thought that no morning, no glint of sun upon the land, could have been as beautiful. "Thank you."

Ewen held her gaze for a moment, but then forced himself to turn away with a gruff nod.

Guilt might have given her what she wanted this time, but he wasn't going to let her manipulate him again. He needed to finish this and get back to the business of winning this war and seeing to his clan's future. Getting as far away as possible from Sister Genna had become his first priority. To Ewen's mind, they couldn't reach Berwick soon enough.

Seven

Janet had been right. The quick detour into Roxburgh had been easy. No hue and cry had been raised, no one had noticed them; indeed, it had all been accomplished with little risk to either of them.

She'd slipped in and out of the castle, making contact with a potentially war-changing source of information, and returned to Ewen at the church in less than an hour. The importance of this contact could not be understated; and Janet would be right in the thick of it.

Yet it was hard to be excited. She may have won the battle in getting him to agree to take her, but victory was proving cold and lonely.

They rode in virtual silence the rest of the way from Roxburgh to Berwick-upon-Tweed. The ease of conversation they'd shared had disappeared. His curt, blunt responses returned tenfold, making him seem almost chatty in comparison before. He rode so stiffly behind her, she couldn't relax. After hours of riding together, her body ached with the effort to keep distance between them. Snuggling against the comfortable shield of his chest was a distant memory.

During their brief stops to eat or water the horse, he barely looked at her.

Something had changed between them, and Janet knew it was her fault. She felt guilty for what she'd done but didn't know what to say. Worse, she knew it was better this way. She had a job to do and so did he. Apologizing, telling him the truth, would only make things more complicated.

But every time she looked, his implacable features set in such cold repose that something inside her cried out. She wanted to reach for him, to draw him back from the remote place to which he'd removed himself. But what purpose would it serve?

Though she told herself over and over that she was doing the right thing, it didn't help to calm the restlessness and anxiety teeming inside her. It wasn't until they stood outside the gates of Coldingham Priory, however, that Janet felt the first stirrings of what could only be described as panic.

"We're here to see the bishop," Ewen said to the monk who answered the bell. "Tell him it is Sister Genna and her escort."

He dismounted and helped her down while they waited for the man to return.

It wasn't quite dark yet, leaving plenty of light for her to see the rigid set of his jaw. She bit her lower lip, her hands twisting in the folds of her gown, as she contemplated what to say. "Ewen, I . . ."

He turned his face to hers, his expression a mask of indifference. "Yes?"

Her heart fluttered wildly as she searched for . . . *what*? "I . . . Thank you."

Why she was thanking him, she didn't know. She hadn't wanted his protection or his company, indeed she'd fought against it. But he'd given it, and that demanded something, didn't it?

He nodded, and for one minute she saw some of the warmth in his eyes that she hadn't realized had been missing until it was gone. Whatever he intended to say, however, was lost when the monk returned and opened the gate to take them to the bishop.

They were led across the courtyard and into the small chapter house that was attached to the priory. As it was dark inside, the monk lit a few candles before leaving them alone again.

While they waited for the bishop to appear, Janet suddenly found herself wondering what Ewen might say. As happy as Lamberton would be about the contact she'd made in Berwick, she didn't think he'd be pleased to learn what had happened with the English soldiers near Melrose. She knew better than to think that Ewen would agree not to tell him, but there was no telling how he would make it sound if she let him be the one to relate it.

"I would appreciate it if you would let me explain to the bishop about what happened in the forest."

The shrewd quirk of his brow told her how easily he'd guessed her thoughts. "I'm sure you would."

She gritted her teeth. Whatever had changed between them, he still managed to rile her temper easily enough. "Perhaps you will tell him *everything*, then?"

His blue-gray eyes hardened to slate. "I think you've already used that bargaining marker, Sister."

Janet felt her cheeks grow hot, knowing he was right. "I don't know why you must be so difficult about everything. It's not as if I'm not going to tell him."

"Aye, but it's *how* you'll tell him that concerns me. I suspect you could make Armageddon sound like a day at the fair."

Janet pursed her mouth. "You give me too much credit. I assure you, the bishop will understand the danger."

"Aye, but do *you*?" His gaze held hers. "Promise me that you'll leave the fighting to the men and stay out of it, and I'll let you explain to the good bishop any way you want."

With some effort, Janet bit back her angry retort. But inwardly, she fumed. Whatever confusing emotions she'd been feeling earlier disappeared. *Leave the fighting to the men.* Ewen Lamont saw women as nothing more than helpless, silly creatures who needed a big, strong man to protect them. Although he certainly qualified, she wanted nothing to do with a man who thought like that. Physical attraction—no matter how powerful—wasn't enough. She should thank him for reminding her.

"You'd better decide quickly," he said. "The bishop is coming."

She didn't hear anything. But she frowned a few moments later when she heard the unmistakable sound of footsteps approaching.

"Very well, I agree," she said, not feeling the least bit guilty about the lie. Although technically, it wasn't a lie. She would let the men do the *fighting*, but that didn't mean she wouldn't continue doing exactly what she'd been doing.

His eyes narrowed as if he didn't believe her, but she was saved from further enquiry by the arrival of the bishop.

Lamberton gave her a smile of greeting, but it fell from his face when he saw Ewen. Janet didn't need to have much insight to see that the bishop didn't like him. "You were expected back earlier," he said to Ewen. "Your friends have been looking for you."

Janet sensed Ewen's immediate alertness. It was as if every muscle in his body flared to life. She tried not to remember all those muscles, or how good they felt—

She stopped before she could finish the thought. Heaven help her, he'd turned her into a wanton!

"When?" he asked.

"Immediately." Lamberton handed him a missive, which Ewen quickly unfolded and read.

Her frown deepened. In addition to fluency in multiple languages, it seemed her ordinary soldier could also read.

But she would not get the chance to question him. He turned to her with a curt bow of his head. "My lady."

My God, this was it. He was leaving. She would probably never see him again. It was what she wanted, wasn't it?

Then why did it feel as if someone was pulling the strings of her heart in opposite directions?

"*Monsieur*," she managed in a whisper, returning his nod.

He hesitated as if he wanted to say something, but like her, struggled for the right words. He found the wrong ones. "Remember your promise."

When the door closed behind him with a slam, Janet told herself it was good riddance. A stubborn, patronizing, women-are-the-weaker-vessel kind of man wasn't for her. She'd had enough of that attitude from her father and brothers to last a lifetime. The past few years had proved what she'd already known: she was better off alone.

Ewen didn't believe her for an instant. Although he had no intention of telling Lamberton what had happened, he intended to give Bruce a good earful of his opinion on letting nuns be involved as couriers.

But it would have to wait. The missive he'd received was from Hawk. Apparently, Sutherland was in trouble, and they needed to extract him and his wife from England as soon as possible. Ewen raced to the coast north of Berwick Castle and caught up with his fellow Guardsmen as they rode to Huntlywood, where Mary of Mar, Sutherland's wife, was residing, in hopes of executing a rescue.

As it turned out, Sutherland didn't need them. Their new "recruit" had proved himself worthy of his place in the Highland Guard by rigging a bridge with black powder to ensure his wife's safety, and then by defeating a score of Englishmen to ensure his own.

But the journey back to Dunstaffnage Castle on Hawk's *birlinn* had been twenty-four hours of sheer hell. Sutherland's wife had gone into labor a short time before she'd arrived at the ship, and the sounds of her pained cries were not something Ewen would forget anytime soon.

Bloody hell, there was a reason men were not allowed anywhere near the birthing chamber. Hearing a lass in pain and not being able to do anything about it went against every primitive bone in the male body. Apparently he had a lot of them.

Sutherland, who'd been known for his hot temper, surprised them all by being the calmest man on board. Were the woman giving birth his wife, Ewen might have jumped overboard.

When an image of Sister Genna's face sprang to mind, he pushed it away. Ewen knew he would have to marry sometime, but this was the first time he'd ever thought of "his wife." He didn't miss the irony in a nun being the source of his inspiration.

Fortunately, Sutherland's heir had waited to make his appearance until they were safely arrived at Dunstaffnage and Angel—Sutherland's sister Helen, who was the Highland Guard's healer—could attend the birthing. By all accounts, both mother and child were doing well, but even two days later Sutherland—or Ice, as he'd been dubbed after that hellish journey—had the stunned look of a man who'd been through a long, savage battle and somehow walked out alive.

It wasn't just the flurry of excitement over a new child that Sutherland had brought to the castle, however; he'd also managed to uncover some important information about Edward's battle plans when the truce expired at the end of the month. Once again war with England loomed on the horizon, and every member of the Highland Guard was eager to get back to the work of solidifying Bruce's kingship and defeating the English—this time for good.

But Ewen hadn't forgotten about Sister Genna (hell if he knew why), or his intention to speak with Bruce about the increasing dangers faced by his female "couriers of the cloth." Usually, Ewen did his best to stay in the background, but for this he would make an exception.

A few days after their arrival, he entered the Great Hall, which was already burgeoning with activity as the midday meal was well underway, and approached the dais, intending on requesting a private meeting with the king in his solar.

He was making his way around the crowded trestle tables on the east side of the Hall, dodging serving lasses with platters stacked high with food, when he glanced toward the head table and noticed a woman seated next to the king.

He stilled, a strange buzz radiating down his spine and spreading over his skin. Her head was bent toward the king, but there was something about the deep, golden blond of her hair that reminded him of another. It was the way the light caught the different-colored strands, from silvery blond, to golden brown, to rich copper. He'd never seen the like—until he'd met Sister Genna.

A quick glance at the man on her other side identified the woman as Mary of Mar, Sutherland's new bride, who was making her first appearance after the birth of the child. It was also the first time he'd had a good look at her in the light, Ewen realized. God knew he'd stayed as far away from her as possible on the *birlinn*.

His heart was beating strangely as he walked closer, almost as if he sensed something momentous was about to happen.

He was about ten feet away when she looked up, and he stopped dead in his tracks, as if he'd run into a stone wall. *Christ!* The color slid from his face. It was her. Sister Genna. She was Sutherland's wife? He felt an unfamiliar pain in his chest, as if a hot dagger had just been plunged inside and twisted.

Nay. The shock cleared from his head, and he realized she couldn't be the same woman. Sutherland's wife had been pregnant a few days ago, and Sister Genna hadn't. He ought to know, he thought with a hard clench of his jaw; he'd had his hands all over her.

A closer study of the woman's smiling face as she re-

sponded to something Bruce said revealed further differences. Mary of Mar's face was fuller, the lines around her
mouth and eyes were etched a tad deeper, and her hair was
a few inches longer. She had the same unusual blue-green
eyes of Sister Genna, but Mary's leaned toward the blue
whereas Sister Genna's favored the green.

Yet they had the same pale skin—albeit Sister Genna's
had a few more freckles, including the one strategically
placed above her lip—slender noses, high cheekbones,
dark, sooty lashes, and full pink lips. Hell, even the delicate arch of their brows was the same.

How could there be two . . . ?

The truth slapped him. Mary of Mar had had a twin
sister. Everyone had heard the story of how the lass had
disappeared a few years ago after an ill-advised and failed
attempt to rescue her sister from Edward the First's
clutches. She had been presumed dead. A presumption that
apparently was wrong.

The bridge! Of course. The lass had disappeared when a
bridge had collapsed. Sister Genna had told him as much,
but he hadn't put the two together.

His mouth fell in a hard line as the full import of his
discovery hit him. The wee nun had lied to him. Sister
Genna wasn't Italian; she was Janet of Mar, Mary's lost
sister, and, he realized, Robert the Bruce's former sister-in-
law. Bruce's first wife, Isabella, had been her sister. Ewen
clenched his fists as anger surged through every vein in his
body.

Suddenly some of the inconsistencies that he'd noticed
made sense. The accent that had faded in and out with
anger. The too-fine chemise he'd glimpsed during the attack.

The dagger.

Bloody hell, now he remembered where he'd seen something similar! Viper had a dagger that was nearly identical.

Obviously the sister-in-law Janet had been talking about

was Christina of the Isles, one of the most powerful women in the Highlands, and Lachlan MacRuairi's half-sister. Christina had been married to Duncan of Mar. Sister Janet's brother was well known to him; Ewen had considered him a friend. He'd fought beside the fierce warrior and witnessed his beheading at the hands of the MacDowells at Loch Ryan.

Did Bruce know Janet was alive? Ewen intended to find out. He closed the distance to the dais in a few steps. Though his attention was on the king, he caught the frown on the newest member of the Highland Guard's face and suspected that Sutherland had noticed his reaction to his wife. But he would deal with him later.

The king glanced up as he approached, his brows furrowing as he took in Ewen's dark expression. "Is something wrong?"

"I need to speak to you," Ewen snapped; then, remembering to whom he was speaking he added, "Sire."

"I haven't finished my meal."

"It's important," Ewen replied stiffly, though it should have been obvious. Ewen could count on one hand the times he'd asked anything of the king. He put his head down, did his job, and tried to avoid conflict. Ironic for a soldier perhaps, but making trouble had been his father's way, not his. Another reason to avoid Sister Genna, he thought. She was nothing but conflict. And not the way to distance himself from his wild father and rebel cousin.

Bruce shot him a dark glare. "It had better be."

Tor MacLeod, the leader of the Highland Guard, must have been watching from the other end of the table. When the king rose, he did as well.

"Alone," Ewen said.

Bruce didn't hide his annoyance but waved off the fierce Highland chief.

Ewen followed the king into the laird's solar, the small room located just off the Hall, and waited for the king to take his seat in the throne-like chair. The MacDougall chief had forfeited both his chair and his castle to Bruce after his loss at the key Battle of the Pass of Brander two summers past.

"Well, what is it that couldn't wait, Hunter?"

The king preferred to address him by his war name, even when there was no danger of his identity being discovered. The name Lamont was nearly as reviled as that of Comyn, MacDougall, or MacDowell, and it was almost as if Bruce didn't want to remind himself of the connection.

Ewen didn't waste any time. "Does Mary of Mar know that her sister is alive and working as a courier for Lamberton?"

The king's lack of reaction answered Ewen's first question: Bruce knew. "Lady Janet has been missing for over three years. How can you be so sure she is alive?"

Ewen put his palms flat on the table and leaned toward the king. "Because I spent two days escorting her to Berwick after she narrowly escaped rape at the hands of some English soldiers near Melrose Abbey."

The king's expression cracked at the word *rape*, but Robert the Bruce was every bit as fierce as his elite band of warriors, and he hadn't dared to wrest a crown from Edward of England's hands by showing emotion. Only someone who knew him as well as Ewen would have detected the reaction. He quickly schooled the concern from his features and drummed his fingers idly on the table. "How can you be certain it was Janet? Did she identify herself as such?"

Because Ewen could still see her damned face in his dreams. Still feel the curve of the baby-soft cheek that he'd held in his hand. Still taste the sensual mouth that had moved under his.

He was angry enough to tell Bruce exactly how he knew, but for once he curbed his tongue—albeit not completely. "You know damned well Sister 'Genna' is hiding her identity and pretending to be Italian. What the hell are you thinking, allowing your former sister-in-law to put herself in such danger?"

Bruce's eyes turned flinty black. "Have care, Hunter. I'm used to your blunt manner of speaking, but I'm your king. I don't care how good of a tracker you are, or how much Stewart believed in you; you'll control your anger when you are talking to me or find another army to take your chances with."

Ewen sobered at the sharp reminder—and at how thoroughly he'd forgotten himself.

Angering the king probably wasn't the best way of going about seeing the Lamonts restored to their former glory. Discretion intervened, and although it wasn't without some effort, Ewen managed to get a hold on his anger. "I apologize, Sire."

Bruce stared at him intently, dark eyes hard as onyx as his fingers continued to drum ominously on the table. Another man might have started to shift, but Ewen stood perfectly still while the king decided whether to accept his apology and, apparently, weighed how much to tell him. "If you've met my former sister-in-law, you can probably guess that I was not consulted. She came up with the idea all on her own. I was only made aware of her survival and the part she was playing with Lamberton about a year ago when she returned from Italy, where she'd taken refuge after her attempt to rescue her sister went awry."

That explained the Italian.

Bruce shook his head. "You have to admire the lass— she does not lack for courage in going after her sister at such a time. We were being hunted like dogs. There was no place to hide. Edward's reign of terror was in full force; he had eyes and ears everywhere. Not even Atholl dared to attempt to reach his wife before he fled north, but Janet commandeered some of her sister-in-law Christina's Mac-Ruairi clansmen and sailed halfway around Scotland, riding into England bold-as-brass, to pluck her sister right out from under Edward's nose." One corner of his mouth lifted wryly. "It almost worked, too."

That sounded like her all right. But the story that instilled admiration in the king only made Ewen more irate. Then, like now, the lass didn't seem to have any concept of danger. He said as much to the king, who didn't disagree with him.

"Tell me what happened," Bruce said.

Ewen gave him a brief but concise report of how he and MacLean had arrived to discover the two nuns surrounded by soldiers, and how "Sister Genna" had protected her young charge and fended the soldiers off with her threats. He described how MacLean had gone after the note to ensure it reached Bruce (which it had) and how Ewen had insisted on escorting Janet back to Lamberton.

The king's expression, which had been very grave as Ewen described the attack, lightened with a wry smile at the last. "I'm sure she wasn't happy about that. Janet was headstrong even as a girl and never liked following orders. I suspect that streak of independence has only grown worse in the intervening years. I'm surprised she did not try to talk you out of it."

"She did."

The king lifted a brow. "And you didn't fall for her honeyed tongue?" He laughed. "I should like to have seen it. After her father died, the lass lived with Isabella and me for a time. I can't tell you how many times I started out trying to punish her for some mischief she'd gotten into and ended up sending her away feeling as if I were the one who deserved to be sent to the nearest priest to repent."

Ewen had no interest in rehashing old memories of Janet's youthful follies; he was more interested in her recent ones. "The English are tightening their noose all across the Borders in an attempt to break our communication routes through the church. It has become increasingly dangerous for all of our couriers, but the women are particularly vulnerable."

Recalling his earlier gaffe, Ewen was careful not to imply any criticism, but Bruce heard it all the same. "We cannot win the war without the support of the church—both the men of the cloth and the women. They know the risk when they agree to undertake their mission, and I will not second-guess them. Nor will I refuse help simply because it comes from a woman. Janet is the only person I can trust for this."

Ewen clenched his mouth to prevent himself from arguing. But he didn't see what could possibly be so important as to endanger her life.

"Have you forgotten what Bella did for me?" Bruce asked, referring to MacRuairi's wife, the former Countess of Buchan, who'd suffered years of English imprisonment for her part in crowning the king, part of it in a cage. "Or how my wife, daughter, and sisters are still suffering for my cause?"

"That's exactly my point," Ewen said. "Women don't belong in prison or cages. It's our duty to—"

He stopped before he said the offending words, but it was too late.

"It's our duty to protect them," the king finished his thought.

Ewen winced. Damn it, he'd stepped in it again! The king was haunted by what had happened to his women and blamed himself for the fate that had befallen them. He didn't need Ewen to remind him.

"It isn't always possible," the king said softly. He paused a moment before clearing his throat and continuing in a harder voice, "Your fears about my former sister-in-law are not unwarranted, but do not let it concern you. I've already started to make preparations for her return, as soon as I can arrange an alternative, which won't be easy."

Ewen didn't bother to hide his relief. "I'm glad to hear it, Sire."

"Sutherland was making it difficult with his enquiries on behalf of his wife, renewing interest in the lass, and with what you have said . . ." He shrugged. "Janet will have to understand."

He didn't sound any more convinced than Ewen.

"Lady Mary doesn't know she is alive?"

Bruce shook his head. "We thought it was safer for all involved to keep it secret. Until recently, I wasn't sure in which direction Mary's loyalty lay. She was in England for many years."

"I'm sure she will be relieved."

"She'll be furious," Bruce quipped dryly. He laughed. "But I hope to appease her with wedding plans."

Ewen frowned. "Wedding plans? But I thought Sutherland and Mary were already married."

"They are. It's her sister's wedding I speak of."

"But Janet is a . . ." Even before Ewen could say the word, he realized the truth. He stared at Bruce, feeling as if he'd been kicked in the chest. Or maybe a little lower.

Bruce smiled. "She hasn't taken any vows."

A dam burst as anger rose dangerously inside him. It felt like his whole damned body was shaking. "She is *pretending* to be a nun?"

He was going to kill her, or kiss her until he earned the sins he'd been paying for and she begged forgiveness for the torture she'd put him through—he didn't know which. But one way or another, his too tempting little *non*-nun was going to pay.

Bruce stared at him with a frown, but Ewen was too angry to hide his reaction. "It started as an innocent mistake," the king explained, "but ended up being the best way to protect her. Who would think Janet of Mar was an Italian nun?" *Who indeed?* Ewen fumed, feeling as if his head were about to explode. How long would it take him to reach Berwick? He was counting down the hours. "Sister Genna" wasn't going to talk her way out of this one. "Lamberton said the lass has some ideas to take the veil in truth, but when she hears the husband I have picked out for her, I'm sure she will change her mind."

Ewen thought the knowledge of how she'd lied to him, let him wallow in his guilt for kissing her, and then used it against him was bad enough. He was wrong.

Married? Every instinct in his body recoiled at the idea.

"Who?" he asked in a flat voice.

The king looked at him oddly. "Young Walter."

The blow could have felled him in two. "Stewart?"

The king nodded.

Ewen's liege lord and the son of the man to whom he owed everything. The door that had cracked open for a moment slammed shut. If Ewen had harbored any thoughts of something more with Janet of Mar—even for an instant—the knowledge that she was meant for Walter Stewart erected a wall in his mind that was far more powerful than any veil.

Everything Ewen had he owed to James Stewart—his home, his land, his education, his place in Bruce's guard—and now that loyalty belonged to his son. Moreover, any hope he had of restoring his clan's good name rested not just with Bruce, but also with the Stewarts.

Pursuing his liege lord's intended wasn't likely to endear him to either. He wasn't going to jeopardize everything he'd been fighting for for a woman, especially one who infuriated him half the time. *More* than half the time.

No matter how hot she fired his blood.

No matter that she was the first woman he'd ever talked to that didn't make him feel as if every word out of his mouth was wrong.

No matter that every time he closed his eyes he saw her face.

A ridiculous thought stole through his mind: What if

Stewart could be persuaded to step aside? Hell, one could even argue that Ewen would be doing him a favor. Janet was probably a good half-dozen years older than the eighteen-year-old Walter, and infinitely wiser. The lass would eat the poor lad up alive.

But Ewen stomped on the flicker of hope before it could flame. Who the hell was he fooling? She was the former sister-in-law of a king. The daughter, sister, and aunt of an earl. He was a Highland chieftain with one finger of land in Cowal, a holding that was a pittance compared to Stewart's—or even his cousin's before the Lamont lands were dispossessed.

Even if he wanted her—which he sure as hell wasn't saying he did—Janet of Mar was not for him.

Or so he would keep telling himself over the long months ahead.

Eight

❧

An eerie prickle raced down her spine. Janet turned anxiously, scanning the area behind her, but nothing seemed amiss. No one was paying her any mind. It had to be the weather.

It was a hot autumn day, and the sun beat down mercilessly on the heavy black wool of her habit as she waited for the group of ladies from the castle to appear from among the throng that had descended on the high street for market day. The ladies were late, but as they had been delayed before, it did not give her undue cause for alarm.

She passed the time exchanging *brief* conversations with the people who stopped to enquire about her goods (a benefit of supposedly speaking only Italian and French) and the other nuns and friars who brought their goods to market, as well as listening to the talk of the villagers around her while pretending not to understand their words.

As usual, the talk was of war. Since Edward had marched his troops north into Scotland late last spring, the talk had been of little else.

"Another supply train was lost," one of the merchants in a stall behind her said.

Her ears pricked up.

"Bruce's phantoms again?" another replied in an almost reverent whisper.

"Aye," the first answered. "Like wraiths they appear out of the mist to slay all in their wake, with their swords forged in the fires of Valhalla, and fade back into the darkness again. It's the Devil's magic," he whispered. "How else could they know where King Edward's men will be?"

The stories about the mysterious band of warriors— "Bruce's phantoms"—spread across the Borders like wildfire. They were either devils or heroes, depending on which side you were on. But even among their enemies, there was a certain amount of awe and admiration when speaking of their exploits. Like all good legends, the stories were getting better with each retelling. If the warriors had managed even a quarter of the feats attributed to them, it would have been impressive.

The common folk might think them phantoms, but King Edward's commanders were keenly aware that they were only men—exceptional ones perhaps, but men all the same. The rewards being offered for any of "Bruce's secret army" were staggering. But it was hard to capture men whose identities were shrouded in secrecy.

Except for one. Janet still couldn't believe that her sister-in-law's disreputable bastard brother, Lachlan MacRuairi, was one of Robert's chosen few. Janet had met the brigand only once—at Duncan's wedding, before Lachlan had been accused of murdering his wife—but that was enough. The big, mean-looking warrior with a temperament as black as his hair had terrified her. Since John MacDougall, Lord of Lorn, had unmasked him, Lachlan had a price on his head nearly as high as Bruce's.

Janet enjoyed the stories as much as anyone else, but she was curious about the real men behind the myths.

"How many?" the other merchant asked. She didn't want to look, but she guessed by his voice that he was only a lad.

"Four, against nearly a score of English soldiers." She could almost hear the older merchant shake his head.

"How can King Edward expect to compete with such magic?"

Janet bit back a smile. It wasn't magic, it was her messages—or at least the ones she passed back and forth. But she could hardly tell them that. Over the past few months, she'd become the intermediary for Robert's most important—and secret—informant in the enemy camp. Only a handful of people knew of their informant's identity. Indeed, Robert was so protective of their source that Janet didn't think he would have agreed to risk using her had she not been available to act as an intermediary. It had to be a woman—to lessen the chance of discovery for their informant—and someone he could trust. Like a former sister-in-law.

On the first Saturday of every month, Sister Genna brought embroidery from the good sisters of Mont Carmel Nunnery outside of Berwick to sell at the market here in Roxburgh, one of Edward's key command posts in the Borders. The finely stitched pieces were a favorite of the ladies in the castle, and they were always excited to see the Italian nun. If Janet occasionally found a folded piece of parchment in one of the purses they examined (or left one to be found as she did today), she knew it wouldn't be long before there was another sighting of "Bruce's phantoms."

"It's not right," the older merchant continued. "Bruce is a knight, yet he hides in the forest and countryside like a craven mouse while he sends his phantom brigands to harry our valiant and chivalrous soldiers. Edward will be forced to return to England for the winter, having never taken the field against the traitor."

Janet would not argue with the mouse analogy—with Edward playing the part of the cat—but Robert the Bruce was no coward. However, she understood what these men did not: the battle could be won by evasion as easily as it could by taking up arms—with much less risk.

Why should Robert take the field? He had nothing to gain by meeting Edward on the battlefield right now. The quick, surprise attacks from the heather that were meant to harry and discourage the enemy might not be "knightly," but they were giving him all the victories he needed. When he was ready, Robert would take the field against the powerful English army, with their knights, mail, and destriers.

But until then, the war would go on.

Janet sighed, sadness and resolve rolling over her in a wistful wave. If she'd harbored a secret hope that the war would end soon, she knew it was not to be. Scotland, her sister, and what remained of her family would have to wait a little longer.

The talk around her continued, but Janet's interest waned as the morning dragged on and the sun climbed higher in the sky. Jerusalem's Temples, it was like midsummer during a heat wave! She dabbed a damp cloth at her forehead, not for the first time wishing she could tear off the blasted veil and gown.

The vehemence of her reaction took her aback. It seemed that more and more, Janet was growing uncomfortable in the garments that had protected and kept her hidden for so long.

Her mouth pursed, knowing exactly who was to blame for her discontent. Before Ewen Lamont had burst into her life and ruined everything with his confusing, bone-melting kiss, she'd barely noticed the clothes she wore. But now, every morning after she washed, she dressed with a feeling of wrongness. It felt wrong to pretend to be a nun when her thoughts—her dreams—were filled with such wickedness. And her intention to be a nun . . . that felt wrong, too. It had never been a calling to her, not in the way it should, but had seemed the practical solution to enable her to continue doing what she did enjoy.

It was the only way; blast him for making her question it!

It was ridiculous. All these months, and she was still thinking of a man she would probably never see again, who'd probably forgotten all about her. Who was utterly wrong for her. Who saw only one place for women in this modern world, and that was behind castle walls.

Why couldn't she stop thinking about him? Why did the short time they'd spent together play on her mind even all this time later? And why did she feel so guilty for lying to him?

Lies in war were necessary. If she needed any proof that she'd done the right thing, all she had to do was think about today. Her role in Robert's network had become more important than she'd dreamed. Robert needed her.

It was for the best. Of course, it was. She was glad Ewen had never come back. Truly. He'd confused her enough already.

For the second time that morning, Janet felt a prickle at the back of her neck and turned. She scanned the crowd of villagers, looking closely at the soldier who stood in their midst, but no one seemed to be paying her any mind.

The long wait was making her antsy. Fortunately, when she looked back up the hill toward the castle, she could see that her wait was over. A group of about ten ladies were making their way down the hill toward the village. They were easy to pick out by the bright colors and finery of their gowns and jewels. They sparkled like diamonds in a sea of dreary gray.

Janet was unable to suppress the pang of longing that stole through her chest. At one time, she'd looked just like them. As a girl, she'd driven her father half-crazed with her penchant for spending "a bloody fortune" on the latest fashions from France and England.

But now . . .

She gazed down at the hot, black homespun gown that she wore, which had no more shape than a sackcloth. Her chest squeezed. Was it wrong to want to be pretty again?

She pursed her mouth, telling herself to stop being so silly. But she knew exactly who was to blame for the errant thoughts.

The ladies from the castle were only two stalls away when she felt someone at her side.

"Don't turn around," a man's voice whispered in French. "You are being watched."

Janet did her best not to react, but the heat that had spread over her skin from the sun turned to ice. She cast a sidelong glance at the man who'd voiced the warning, recognizing one of the friars from the Friary of St. Peter's, located just across the river from the castle. They'd crossed paths many times before at market, and he'd been the one to arrange for her stall among the other religious houses' offerings, but she'd never paid the nondescript young churchman much mind.

Perhaps that was the point. He was easy to overlook. Friar Thom was of average height and build, with a circle of straight brown hair around his tonsure. He was neither handsome nor ugly, with brown eyes and unremarkable features. Nothing stood out. Which probably made him the perfect spy or courier—she hoped, for Bruce.

He moved away as quickly as he'd approached. If someone was indeed watching her, it would have seemed as if he'd passed right by after a quick glance at her table.

But the brief contact had sent her heart racing. Whether friend or foe, she could not take the chance in meeting her source with him near.

Her pulse took another anxious spike when she glanced over and saw the ladies from the castle at the very next stall.

She tried to make eye contact, but one of the ladies was blocking the person she was looking for. If someone was watching her, perhaps that wasn't the best thing to do anyway. She needed a distraction, something to keep the women away.

All of a sudden, she had an idea. *"Mais non!"* she cried out in despair. She began tearing through the items she had laid out on the table.

"What is it, Sister Genna?" one of the nuns at the next table asked, continuing in French.

"The alms purse made by the Reverend Mother," she said, twisting her hands. "I cannot find it. Someone must have stolen it from the table when I was not looking."

She'd spoken loud enough for those around her to hear, and the use of the word "stolen" had the desired effect in creating a disturbance. A number of the nearby churchmen and women came forward to help her.

"What does it look like?" the first nun, Sister Winifred, asked.

"It was an image of Our Lady embroidered in gold thread," Janet answered about the nonexistent item.

"When did you notice it missing?" another one of the nuns asked in English—this one she didn't recognize.

Janet pretended not to understand, and Sister Winifred, who knew she was Italian (or at least pretending to be), translated for her in French.

Janet shook her head, hoping her eyes looked as if they were filling with tears. "I don't know."

"Someone should send for the constable," one of the friars said, outraged.

Janet glanced at the ladies and nearly sighed with relief to see them being urged away by her contact, who'd obviously figured that something must be wrong.

She shook her head at the friar who'd spoken. "It is no use. I did not see who took it. I'm sure the thief is long gone."

"What seems to be the problem?"

Even before Janet turned, she felt a chill sweep across the back of her neck and knew without a doubt that this was the person who'd been watching her. He wore the robes of a priest, including a finely embroidered cope that spoke of his importance, but there was nothing about this man that was holy. He seemed to exude danger and animosity. For a moment she felt like one of the hunted Templars under the inquisitor's gaze.

As he'd spoken in French, she could not feign ignorance. "A purse, Father. It seems someone has stolen it."

"Is that so," he said carefully, eyes narrowing. "And how is it that this thief made off with your purse and no one noticed?"

Janet's eyes widened innocently. "What a wonderful suggestion, Father. Perhaps I should ask around. Did you see something, by chance?"

"Of course, I didn't see something."

"I only thought since you were watching—"

"What are you talking about? I wasn't watching you!"

She blinked a few times in confusion, hoping she wasn't overdoing it. "You weren't? But I thought I saw you standing over there gazing in this direction." She pointed to the area where she'd felt someone watching her.

"You were mistaken."

"That is too bad. I was hoping you might have seen something."

"That isn't possible, as there was nothing to see."

She tilted her head. "But I thought you were not watching."

His face flushed. "I wasn't."

"Oh! Pardon me! I must have misunderstood." She shrugged. "My French is not perfect."

"Where are you from?"

"Sister Genna is from Italy, Father Simon," Sister Winifred interceded on her behalf. "But she comes to us from the Sisters of St. Mary's Priory at Coldstream."

His eyes lit up. "That's in Berwick-upon-Tweed, is it not?" he said in perfect Italian.

Janet nodded with a silent curse. Her heart raced even harder. She'd become fluent in the language, but she prayed she didn't make any mistakes. "It is, Father. But I will be returning to Italy soon."

Very soon, she suspected. "Sister Genna" had probably just served her last mission. She would not take the chance in leading this man back to Berwick. She was going to have to change her identity again.

"The Reverend Mother is going to be most displeased with me. The purse was worth a great deal of money." She wrung her hands in despair.

Sister Winifred moved to comfort her.

Janet hoped that would be the end of it, but the man's next words turned her blood to ice. "May I see the missive you removed from the purse at your waist and slid into the edge of your scapular?"

Dunstaffnage Castle, Scotland, late autumn, 1310

"What the hell do you mean you don't know where she is?"

Sutherland shot Ewen a glare, interrupting before the king—to whom the comment had been directed—could respond, and no doubt saving Ewen from a scathing setdown. "Janet hasn't been seen since a week after Michaelmas. She left for a mission in Roxburgh and never returned."

But if Sutherland meant to calm him down, his comment only infuriated Ewen further. "October? Bloody hell, that was weeks ago. Why didn't someone go after her right away?"

Ewen had apparently forgotten that he was supposed to be not angering the king.

"That's exactly what I'd like to know," Mary added, coming to stand beside him in front of the table opposite the king. If there was anyone in the room more outraged than he, it was Janet's twin. From the moment Mary of Mar had learned of her sister's survival (not long after Ewen discovered the truth), she'd hounded the king incessantly to bring her sister back. "I thought you said Janet was handling a few more things, and then you would call her back home?"

If Robert the Bruce had a weakness, it was for the women in his life. His fondness for his former sister-in-law was evident by the contrite look on his face and the effort he took to mollify the obviously distraught female. He might chastise Ewen for speaking out of turn, but the pretty former Countess of Atholl and future Countess of Sutherland would enjoy far more leeway.

"We were not concerned until recently." He paused. "It isn't uncommon for Janet to be delayed or take a couple of weeks longer than expected."

Ewen knew there was something he was leaving out.

"But wouldn't she find some way of letting you know?" Mary asked.

Bruce looked decidedly uncomfortable. He may have even shifted in his chair. "We can't check up on all the people we have working for us. It isn't possible."

"You mean you let her out on her own without protection?" Mary accused, tears glistening in her eyes. "And Janet isn't 'people,' she's *our* sister."

Bruce appeared to wince. As Mary was doing such a good job, Ewen saw no reason to intervene. He simply stood to the side with his arms folded across his chest and watched the king squirm.

Sutherland had taken his wife under his arm and was making some attempt to console her. "Of course, she is, love," he murmured softly.

Not long ago the display of affection would have made Ewen do a little squirming of his own, but in the past few weeks since he and Sutherland had returned to Dunstaffnage after Edward's retreat to England for the winter, he'd grown used to such displays. He'd grown surprisingly close to Sutherland's bride. The unusual ease he'd felt around Janet apparently extended to her sister. Actually, being around Lady Mary was easier. Despite their similarity in appearance, Sutherland's wife didn't set every one of his nerve-endings on edge, heat his blood, or make him harden like a lad at a Roman orgy.

Once Mary had learned that he'd spent time with her sister, she'd asked him hundreds of questions about what he could remember. He was sure that was why every detail about Janet of Mar was so fresh in his mind even after all these months. Her sister had kept her that way.

"I am sure there is nothing wrong," the king said, but it sounded as if he was trying to assure himself as much as them. "But you don't have to worry, Mary. I'm sending my best man after her. Hunter will find her."

Although an attempt had been made to keep the wives ignorant of the Highland Guardsmen's identities, it had proved impossible. Of the men who were married, only MacLean's wife was unaware of her husband's role in the king's secret army. But as his wife was a MacDowell that was hardly surprising. To Ewen's knowledge, MacLean hadn't seen his wife in years. If he hadn't disavowed her formally, he'd done so de facto.

Ewen was tempted to refuse. If he were smart, he probably would. But he couldn't do that with Mary looking up at him. For a moment she looked so much like her sister, his chest ached. "Will you?"

He nodded. "I will leave as soon as it can be arranged."

"Wonderful. I'm going with you," Mary said.

The four male occupants of the room went silent, showing varying degrees of alarm. Bruce had an "oh no" look on his face, Sutherland an "over my dead body" one, and Chief a "you'd better do something about this" look directed at Sutherland. Ewen supposed his was a combination of all three.

It was Sutherland who made the first attempt to get his wife to see reason. "Now, Mary, you know how dangerous it would be for you to go to England. I'm sure the king will see fit to allow me to accompany Hunter—"

"Don't 'now, Mary' me! It's just as dangerous for you to go to England as it is for me. Even more so with Felton recovered and looking for blood—*your* blood. Besides, a man and a woman traveling together will draw much less attention than you two."

Sutherland's jaw was clenched so tight, Ewen was surprised he could still talk. "If you think I'm going to allow you to travel with Hunter alone—"

Mary waved her hand dismissively. "Then come along if you must."

Apparently the lass had more of her sister in her than Ewen had realized. She may have tricked her husband into conceding the point, but Ewen wasn't falling for it. "I will travel much faster alone, my lady. If you come, you will only make my job more difficult."

The blunt, matter-of-fact assessment (rather than worrying about her tender feelings) worked. Mary's demeanor changed from bound and determined to chastised. "I did not think about that. I do not wish to be a burden."

"Then let me do my job. You can trust me—I will not let anything happen to your sister."

Mary nodded. Sutherland and Bruce eyed him as if he'd just accomplished some kind of miracle.

In the end, it was decided that Sutherland and MacKay would accompany Ewen and MacLean in the event they came across any English patrols. The war might have come to a standstill while Edward retreated to the comfort of Berwick for the winter, but the hunt for the "rebels"— Bruce's phantoms in particular—had not diminished. If anything, their reputation had only grown after the past few months of fighting. The surprise attacks for which they'd become known had taken on a prescient edge. No matter what the English did, the Highland Guard "magically" knew where to find them.

Of course it wasn't magic; it was exceptional intelligence. Whoever this new informant of Bruce's was (the king had refused to say), he hadn't been wrong yet. Some of the other Guardsmen were speculating that it must be someone high up in Edward's command. The best guess was Ralph de Monthermer, who was married to a sister of both the king's and Hawk's wives. Ewen didn't care who it was, as long as the information continued.

But for the next few months, while Edward rested and tried to bolster the spirits of his demoralized troops, the fighting would be reserved for the local skirmishes in the Borders. There were talks of peace—even now, Bruce was negotiating for a parley at Selkirk before Christmas—but the Borders had been and still were a war zone, and venturing into the English Marches near any of the English strongholds had grown increasingly perilous for the much hunted "phantoms."

The Highland Guard might be the best, but they weren't invincible—or invisible for that matter, though Ewen did his damnedest to make them so. This mission would not be without its risks, and Ewen would be glad for the extra sword arms in the event they drew any unwanted attention.

It was decided that they would leave at first light. Sutherland led his wife from the room, but not before exchanging a glance with Ewen. He nodded in acknowledgment of the silent communication. Ewen would fill him in on the rest later, when Mary wasn't around to hear it. Like Ewen, Sutherland had sensed that there was something else going on.

"What aren't you telling us?" Ewen asked as soon as the door closed behind them.

The king's expression turned grim, sending a flicker of unease racing down Ewen's spine. Hell, it wasn't a flicker, it was more of a deluge. If Ewen didn't know better, he'd think the anxious feeling twisting around in his chest was fear.

"One of our couriers—a friar—was found dead a few weeks ago."

His chest squeezed like a fist. Bloody hell, it *was* fear.

"What connection did he have to Janet?" Ewen managed.

"Very little, but he was our main contact in Roxburgh when Janet's, uh, work took her there."

Ewen hoped his annoyance didn't show. The king knew what he thought of Janet's "work." A lass had no part in any of this. "Why was she in Roxburgh?"

Bruce seemed to be debating how much to tell him. "Selling embroidery and exchanging messages with someone in the castle. The friar helped facilitate her place at the market."

"Is there a chance she could have been discovered?"

"Possibly, but our person inside is safe."

"Might he have betrayed her?"

Bruce gave him a strange look and shook his head. "No."

"How can you be so sure?"

"I am; that's all you need to know."

"But the friar's death bothers you."

Bruce nodded. "It seems too much of a coincidence."

Ewen agreed. But he wouldn't let himself consider that something had happened to her. He had to keep his mind clear for the search that lay ahead.

"Find her," Bruce said, "and bring her home."

Ewen nodded. "I will."

The king gave him a long, measured look. "I trust this mission won't be a problem for you?"

He stiffened. "Why should it?"

"My former sisters by marriage have always been pretty little things, as I suspect you noticed. But I'll remind you that while she might not be a nun, she is meant for another."

Ewen's mouth hardened. "I'm aware of that, Sire." And he sure as hell didn't need the reminder. But obviously, Bruce had sensed something from before and was letting him know in no uncertain terms to steer clear of her. Ewen didn't need it spelled out.

"Good." The king bowed his head, dismissing him. Ewen turned on his heel to leave, but Bruce stopped him with a sharp laugh. "Although when you do find her, you may not want to tell her that I have a husband waiting for her—she's liable to get it in her mind to disappear again."

The reminder of her betrothal set Ewen's teeth on edge. But he managed a smile, as it seemed to be expected of him.

He would find Janet and bring her back to her betrothed. But he wasn't looking forward to it.

Nine

❧

Janet's self-imposed exile had begun to chafe. An excess of caution did not sit well with her, especially when anyone would be hard pressed to connect the Italian "Sister Genna" with "Novice Eleanor," the English widow from Cumberland. She might not be able to change her face, but she'd done her best to change everything else—her name, her nationality, even the color of her veil.

Not much longer, she told herself. Friar Thom would come for her when it was safe, he'd told her as much.

But what was taking him so long?

The leaves had been thick on the trees and the grass still green when he'd delivered her to the nuns at Rutherford's priory, the small convent of Cistercian nuns located a few miles west of Roxburgh, after her unfortunate confrontation with Father Simon.

She had to admit her heart had been beating fast there for a minute. Knowing she couldn't deny the missive, which the priest had obviously seen, she'd slid the folded piece of parchment out of the hem of her scapular. "This?" She smiled. "It isn't a missive, it's a list."

The priest's eyes had narrowed to hard beads. "What kind of list?"

It had been her idea to use an inventory as a kind of code when passing messages about troops and supplies, and never had she been so glad of it. The priest had already unfolded the paper and scanned it when she replied, "As you can see, it's a list of items for my next journey."

She hoped her heart wasn't pounding as loudly as it sounded in her ears and prayed he didn't ask her where, as she had no idea of the specific contents of the letter.

"Why would a nun from Berwick travel to Carlisle? I thought you were returning to Italy."

She heaved a silent sigh of relief. *Carlisle!* "I am. After next month's market in Carlisle. As for why, our embroidery is much sought after, and surely a few miles isn't too far in the name of the Lord's work?"

He didn't bother answering her. "Surcotes, purses—why are only two items written on this list?"

Men and horses. Those were the numbers the king was requesting for the English at Carlisle, if the information could be obtained.

Janet shrugged as if she were puzzled by his question. "Those are the only items of which I am short." Her face fell, and she forced tears to well in her eyes. "Which makes the loss of the alms purse so much worse. It took Reverend Mother nearly six months to make. The level of detail was exquisite. It would have fetched a goodly sum that would have helped to feed the unfortunates—"

"You cannot remember two things?" he asked, cutting off her verbal detour.

"I am very forgetful, Father. It is a terrible sin," she bowed her head for a moment as if shamed by the admission. "But the Sisters are helping me work on it. Lists help."

"Is something wrong, Father Simon? Why are you questioning Sister Genna like this? She has done nothing wrong. It is she who is a victim of a crime."

Janet had never noticed how formidable Sister Winifred could be, but she did so now.

Father Simon sniffed as if at something unpleasant. It

was clear he and the older nun did not like each other. "She was acting suspiciously."

"By possessing a folded piece of paper?" She laughed, and the priest's face flushed an angry red. He looked foolish and knew it.

Fortunately someone had indeed gone for the constable, and he chose that minute to arrive. Janet held out her hand to Father Simon. Reluctantly, he handed her back the note. She knew the priest was suspicious but could think of no reason to question her further. No legitimate reason, at least.

Thankfully, that was the end of the unfortunate incident. It had been a closer call than most, but Janet had escaped unscathed—or relatively unscathed. Initially, she'd resisted Father Thom's suggestion that she remove herself from Roxburgh for a while. But at his urging, she'd decided to take precautions.

Friar Thom had seen what had happened and had intercepted Janet as soon as she left the market. He'd told her that Father Simon, the priest who'd questioned her, was thought to be trying to earn himself a bishopric by ferreting out suspected rebels in the clergy for Edward. The priest from the castle church of St. John's was much hated and feared in Roxburgh.

With Friar Thom's help—and that of a handful of nuns who'd provided a distraction in case she was still being watched—Janet slipped away from the market and didn't return to the Priory of Roxburgh, where she'd been staying at the convent. Instead, she changed her veil from black to white and made her way to Rutherford. There, Sister Genna had disappeared and Novice Eleanor had emerged. She'd given the friar a message for Lamberton, explaining her change of identity and where to find her, and Janet went about the long, tedious process of biding her time and waiting for his return.

She used her time to read, pray (mostly for patience), indulge to her heart's content in enjoying her favorite nuts (which the nuns were kind enough to buy for her when they went into town), and try to think of a way to get a message to her source at the castle that didn't involve going to the market and potentially coming face-to-face with Father Simon again.

After four weeks the friar still hadn't returned, but Janet had a way to make contact, which proved far easier than she'd anticipated.

Her informant had come to her.

The next time the Sisters left to tend the sick and needy at the nearby Hospital of Saint Magdalene, "Eleanor" accompanied them. The important hospital along the Abbey Road—linking the four great abbeys of the area—served not only as a sojourn for travelers and a place for the poor and infirm, but also as a charity for many of the ladies of the castle. When the next saint's day arrived, Janet knew they would arrive to give alms to the sick and the poor who'd taken refuge there.

Every day for the next two weeks, Janet accompanied the nuns to the hospital. Surprisingly, she took to the work of nursing. When some of the other Sisters shied from the lazar house, the separate cottages housing the lepers, Janet took over the task of bringing them their daily loaf and, three times a week, their salt meat.

Finally, on St. Andrew's Day, which also happened to be the first Sunday of Advent, Janet's efforts were rewarded. The informant had been surprised but greatly relieved to see her. In the one moment they'd had to exchange a private word, her source told her that something important was brewing, and they hoped to have more information by St. Drostan's Day, about a fortnight hence.

The following morning there was still an excited spring in Janet's step as she took the lepers their bread. As she left the last cottage to walk back to the hospital on that chilly first of December morning, she was feeling so pleased, she didn't notice the shadow that moved behind her until it was too late.

Fear leapt to her throat, cutting off the scream that might have sounded before his hand covered her mouth as he dragged her behind one of the cottages. A green sleeve. Her abductor wore the cloak of a leper!

He captured her hard against him, pinning her arms so that when she tried to lash out to free herself, she couldn't move. His hold was like a steel vise, cold and unyielding. Yet while his body was solid as a rock wall, it was warm—achingly warm—and smelled of pine and leather. By the time he'd lowered his mouth to whisper in her ear, her heart was racing not with fear but with something else.

Her captor was no leper. It was Ewen. He'd come back!

"You seemed to have forgotten your promise to stay out of trouble, *Lady Janet*."

She was so happy to realize it was he that it took her a moment to realize what he'd said—in Gaelic, no less. Her heart started to pound all over again, this time with trepidation. He knew her name. Her *real* name.

And he hadn't called her Sister.

Tending lepers? *Christ!* The lass couldn't seem to avoid danger; she only jumped from one fire to another. Speaking of fire, his body was getting too damned hot just from having her pressed against him.

Ewen released her as soon as they were safely out of eyesight behind the farthest cottage, spinning her around to look at her.

The bottom dropped out of his stomach. He'd forgotten how pretty she was. Glimpses from afar hadn't prepared him for seeing her face-to-face again. With her bright eyes and cheeks rosy from the cold, Lady Janet of Mar was the picture of country vivacity and health. His mouth hardened. Far healthier than someone who'd caused him so much damned . . . trouble (not fear, damn it!) had a right to look.

This mission had been plagued from the start. No sooner had he and his three Highland Guard brethren left the ship at the coast in Ayr than they'd run into an English patrol in Douglasdale. Normally a single patrol of a dozen men wouldn't be of much concern for four members of the Highland Guard, but after months of fighting Edward's army, they were all a little battered and bruised. Ewen was no exception. He'd suffered an arrow wound in the leg while on a mission to track down some of Bruce's men who'd been taken in a skirmish near Rutherford Castle, and even with Angel's help, it had yet to fully heal.

Arrow wounds, cuts from swords, broken bones from war hammers and maces, and stabs from pikes were nothing they weren't used to, but the various injuries had hampered them in their efforts against the patrol. There was no other explanation for how one of the Englishmen had been able to escape and find safety behind the walls of Douglas Castle before Ewen, MacLean, Sutherland, and MacKay could catch up to him.

The unfortunate result was that reports of Bruce's phantoms in the area had spread, and their presence was no longer a secret. With God-knew-how-many soldiers looking for them, they would have to be very careful.

Then, as if the English hunting them weren't enough, they'd arrived at Roxburgh to retrace Lady Janet's last steps and heard from one of their loyal clergymen about the confrontation at the market with the priest. Worse, no one had seen her since. The lass had seemed to disappear without a trace at about the same time as the dead friar.

Ewen would not soon forget the gut-wrenching fear he'd experienced when the trail seemed to have come to a dead end. For days they'd scoured every road leading out of Roxburgh, hoping to find something—anything—except for the one thing he would not consider: a body.

Damn it, why hadn't she listened to him? She had no business being out here doing this. Bruce should have brought her back earlier. Ewen should have done more to convince him. But he hadn't wanted to stir up trouble.

He knew what could happen to women who were thought to be helping Bruce. Not a day went by that he didn't see the faces of the slaughtered villagers near Lochmaben Castle in his mind. All those women and children. His stomach turned. He probably should have done more then, too. But it had been just after Bruce had returned to Scotland, and Ewen had still been reeling from the disaster that had befallen them at Loch Ryan.

They hadn't realized the danger they were putting the villagers in when they'd sought their help. But weeks later, when some member of the Highland Guard had returned, they'd learned the horrible truth. The entire village had been decimated by the English for helping them. The only survivor had been a young girl who'd been tossed in the pit prison and forgotten. Arrow's wee ward, they called her, after MacGregor had taken pity on the poor orphaned lass—who obviously worshiped him (which wasn't unusual for lasses with MacGregor)—and taken her back to his home.

Had the same thing happened to Janet? He'd about given up hope of tracking her—the trail was just too cold—when he had an idea. Thank God for her love of those damned nuts. It had taken a while to locate the merchant, and then to track down every nun who'd purchased from him in the past few weeks, but eventually their hunt led them to the priory at Rutherford.

He would never forget the relief he felt yesterday when he'd seen her stroll out of the convent with a devil-may-care smile on her face. It was only later, while he waited for the right opportunity to intercept her, that anger settled in. How dare she look so happy and carefree when her disappearance had caused such turmoil!

He caught the flash of alarm in her eyes as she realized what he'd said, but it didn't take her long to collect herself. She gave him a long once-over, taking in the green cloak and hood. "You are missing your alms cup and bell so that I might hear you coming."

His mouth thinned. "There wasn't time."

"To steal them?"

"To borrow them," he corrected, returning the scrutiny. As long as they were talking disguises, the nun's costume had been more believable. "Aren't you a little old to be a novice?"

She gasped, her eyes flashing with outrage. "I'm not old! And I'm a widow."

He lifted his brow at that. "Who is the unfortunate groom?"

Her eyes narrowed as if she were trying to figure out whether he'd meant it as "unfortunate dead" or "unfortunate married to her."

He hadn't decided.

"An Englishman. He was a soldier who died in the war. And hasn't anyone ever told you that it's rude to comment on a woman's age? I'm seven and twenty—younger than you." She bit her lip uncertainly, and he nearly swore at the swell of heat it provoked in his groin. "How old *are* you?"

He frowned. "One and thirty." He'd just celebrated his Saint's Day last week.

She nodded, pleased to have made her point. "What do you want? Do you have a message for me?"

Ewen fought to keep his temper in check, but after nearly a week of looking under every rock between Roxburgh and Berwick for the lass, he was having a difficult time.

"Bloody right I have a message! Where the hell have you been? No one has had sight or sound of you in over a month."

He didn't know what he'd expected, but damn it, perhaps to find her in a little more peril? And a little more gratitude on her part to see him, rather than this feeling that he was somehow interrupting her.

Ignoring the voice that warned him not to touch her, he took her by the arm again and hauled her up against him.

The wall he'd erected in his mind was proving a little thin. Instead of thinking that she belonged to Walter Stewart, he couldn't help thinking how good she felt against him.

Janet of Mar, damn it.

"Did it occur to you that people might be concerned?" He may have growled the last.

Her eyes widened. "Of course, it didn't. I'm not missing."

His jaw locked. "So I see. But it might have been nice for you to tell the rest of us."

"Did no one receive my message? I sent word of my change in plans to our friend in Berwick."

Ewen grimaced, guessing how she'd sent her message. "With a local friar?"

She nodded, and he swore, letting her go. Some of his anger dissipated. It wasn't all her fault. Messages failing to reach their destination was a common occurrence in war.

Part of him hoped she wouldn't ask, but she was too smart not to have figured it out. "What happened? Did something happen to the friar?"

He didn't make an attempt to soften the blow. Perhaps this would make her understand the risks she took. "He was killed. Tortured, by the look of it, and his body was dumped on the road to Berwick about a month ago."

She recoiled from the shock. "No!" Her eyes filled with tears, and he had to steel himself from reaching out to give her . . . what? Comfort? Bloody hell! He was furious with her; what in Hades was wrong with him?

He nodded, giving her a moment to come to terms with what he'd told her. "No one knew what had happened to you."

She gazed up at him, tears dampening her lashes. Her eyes shimmered like a sunlit sea. His chest squeezed so tightly he had to look away.

There was long stretch of silence, but finally she said, "Thank you for coming to find me. I'm sorry to have caused so much trouble, but as you can see, I'm perfectly safe."

Safe? The lass wouldn't be safe until she was locked up high in some bloody tower in . . . *Bute*. The only tower she'd be going to would belong to Walter Stewart.

Not your problem. But the knowledge didn't seem to calm him down any. He held his temper in check—barely. "I think you and I have a very different definition of 'safe.' I heard you were nearly discovered in Roxburgh by one of Edward's priests."

"I wasn't nearly discovered at all. He asked me a few questions, that's all." While he clenched his fists so he wouldn't grab her again, she frowned. "How did you find me, anyway? We were very careful."

He sure as hell wasn't going to tell her how difficult it had been. "There was one thing you told me that wasn't a lie."

She paled and eyed him warily, as if this were the moment she'd been expecting and was bracing herself for it. And God's blood, he wanted to give it to her. He wanted to show her exactly how angry he was.

But he wasn't going to. It was better to pretend it had never happened and never mattered. It was better to pretend he didn't care. Because something told him that if he touched her again, if he vented the dangerous maelstrom of emotions twisting inside him, she would end up in his arms once more with that too soft, too sensual, too tempting pink mouth melting under his.

He shouldn't be thinking of how good she'd tasted. He shouldn't remember it at all after this long, blast it. She wasn't going to affect him; he wouldn't let her.

"The nuts," he said, taking a step back to clear his head. "They *are* your favorite."

She blinked at him, obviously surprised that was all he had to say. Did she expect him to rail at her for lying to him about her identity and letting him believe that he'd committed a grievous sin? Did she expect him to be angry that she hadn't kept her promise to stay out of danger? She bloody well should.

She had a puzzled look on her face, as if she was trying to figure him out. "You found me through the merchant?"

He'd found her; now he just wanted to be rid of her. The sooner the better, if the heat pounding in his body was any indication. He shrugged with an indifference he didn't feel. "We should go."

"Go where?"

"I'm taking you back to the Highlands."

She shook her head as if she had a say in the matter. "I'm not done yet. There is something important—"

"I didn't ask, my lady." She stiffened again, and that wary look returned. He supposed he did get some satisfaction in that. Keeping her on her toes, waiting for the axe to fall, gave him an advantage.

"You can't order me—"

"I'm not the one doing the ordering, it's the king."

"Why is he calling me back?"

"I'm just following orders. You'll have to ask him." He sure as hell wasn't going to tell her. The last thing he wanted to do was get involved in *that* battle.

She bit her lip.

Bloody hell, stop that!

Only when she frowned did he realize he'd spoken aloud. "Stop what?"

A few minutes in her presence and he was already losing his mind—and other parts of him were having a little trouble, too, with her nearness. "We need to leave."

She shook her head. "Tell Robert that I'll return as soon as I can, but there is something important I have to do first."

"You can tell him yourself."

"You don't understand, this is very important. I have to be here when—" She stopped, as if uncertain how much to say. She lifted her chin defiantly. "Robert will understand."

He could have guessed she was going to be difficult

about this. "If you are so certain of that, tell him yourself. I thought you were good at explaining things."

He knew she wouldn't be able to resist that.

Her eyes narrowed, and he suspected she'd guessed his intent. "I am. But it will take too long. I told you there is something I must do." She put her hand on his arm, and he froze. She stood so close he could practically feel the press of her body against his. Heat washed through him in a hot, pulsing wave. "I don't see why a week or two will make a difference. Please, can't you just tell him I'll be back as soon as I am able?"

Staring down into her eyes, Ewen felt something inside him tug. The soft imploring look pounded against the wall he'd erected in his mind like a battering ram. He leaned down for a minute, inhaling her sweetness, wanting to give in—

He came back to reality with a jerk. "No." He didn't know whether he was talking to her or to himself. "We leave now."

He could see her try to control her temper. Her lips were pursed tight. "I know you are only trying to do your duty, but I'm sure if you come back—"

"Don't bother with one of your roundabout attempts to change my mind. It won't work."

"Why do you have to be so unreasonable!"

She looked so infuriated, he nearly laughed. Fearing a full-fledged rebellion and wanting to avoid having to drag her back, he said, "We have a ship at the coast in Ayr. If the king agrees to let you return, you can be back in ten days or so."

She looked uncertain. "Ten days? You are sure? I have to be back by St. Drostan's Day."

He shrugged. It was feasible. Not that he thought she'd be in the position to find out, but he sure as hell wasn't going to tell her that. If she wanted to think she'd be permitted to return to Roxburgh, that was fine by him. As soon as he returned her to Dunstaffnage, she was Bruce's problem. And Stewart's, he reminded himself, his teeth gnashing together so hard his jaw hurt.

It's up to you. Keep your head down, do your job, don't do anything to anger the king. That was all he had to do. Simple. He couldn't let her make it complicated.

Her eyes narrowed. "What are you not telling me?"

He gritted his teeth. "Look, my lady, my job is to bring you back. A job I have every intention of fulfilling. But how I do that is up to you. We can make this as difficult or as easy as you want. The king has given you a direct order to leave the Borders and appear before him at Dunstaffnage. Refuse and you aren't defying me, you're defying the king."

"Eleanor!"

Her head turned toward the sound of the cry, and then back to him. "They're looking for me."

She would have moved toward the voice, but he clasped her arm. "So what's it to be, *Eleanor*?"

Her mouth pursed with annoyance. "What choice have you left me? I will go, but I can't just disappear without word. Give me an hour and then come for me at the priory. I will say you are my brother come to fetch me home for an emergency."

He nodded. They wouldn't be able to leave until it was dark anyway.

"I'm here, Sister!" she yelled back, starting around the building.

"Janet."

She turned, her big sea-green eyes looking up at him expectantly. "Don't make me come after you." He'd meant it as a warning, but his voice sounded oddly gruff.

Their eyes held for a long moment, almost as if she were waiting for him to say more. But he couldn't.

Finally, she gave him a short nod, and then she was gone.

Ten

꧂

Janet was furious. Leaving now was a mistake. What if it took too long? What if her informant came to her with something important, and she wasn't here?

If Ewen would just *listen* to her. But the man was utterly impervious to reason! She might as well have been trying to bend iron or dent stone. He had to be the most infuriating man she'd ever met.

All these months. All the time she'd wasted wondering about him. Thinking about him. She must have been daft.

In her memories—all right, in her fantasies—Janet had forgotten just how unreasonable Ewen Lamont could be. How could she have thought there could ever be something between them? The man was perfectly immovable. Utterly recalcitrant. Rigid and uncompromising. Who cared if he could take her breath away with his kiss and was so heart-stoppingly handsome that seeing him again after all this time made her knees turn to jelly? She could never care about someone so totally *unreasonable* and indifferent to her wishes.

Talking with him was an exercise in frustration.

But it was also exhilarating.

Janet's heart was still beating hard as she stomped her way up the hill to the priory with the other nuns.

Of course, he wasn't here because he had feelings for her. How could she have been so foolish as to let herself be disappointed even for a moment? The only reason he was here was because the king had ordered him to come fetch her. He'd probably forgotten all about the kiss. He didn't even seem to care that she'd lied to him about her identity. She'd thought he'd be furious to discover she wasn't a nun.

Heaven's gates, of all the time to start acting like a lovesick girl. He wasn't the man for her. There wasn't a man for her. She was going to be a nun, wasn't she? Of course, she was. How could she have let him make her lose sight of her plans for even a minute?

"Is something wrong, Eleanor?"

It took Janet a moment to realize Beth was talking to her.

She smiled at the young novice, whose big, dark eyes reminded her so much of Sister Marguerite. "Nay, why do you ask?"

The girl looked puzzled. "You were muttering." She blushed. "I thought I heard you say 'stubborn oaf.'"

It was Janet's turn for hot cheeks. "I was thinking about my brother. He'll be here to fetch me soon. I've had some distressing news from home and must return to Cumberland for a few days. My mother is ill."

Beth appeared so distressed, Janet almost reached out to offer *her* comfort. Lying was part of the job—and she was good at it—but recently it had begun to chafe.

"How horrible!" the girl said. "Is there anything I can do?"

Janet started to shake her head, but then she thought of something. "If anyone asks for me at the hospital, will you tell them I will return soon?"

Beth nodded solemnly. "The patients will miss you. As will I."

Janet felt a soft tug in her chest. As with Sister Marguerite, it was hard to keep herself distant from the young novice. But as Sister Marguerite had proved, a connection with her could be dangerous. Janet almost regretted making the simple request of Beth, but just in case she took longer than expected, she wanted their informant to know she would be back.

The abbess accepted without comment the story of her needing to leave. Friar Thom—the horror of his death still weighed heavily on Janet—had told her the abbess was a friend. How much she knew, Janet didn't ask, but she suspected the older nun had guessed most of it.

When Ewen arrived to collect her at the gate at the appointed hour—thankfully, dressed in the plain clothing of a farmer rather than his leper's cloak and hood—she was ready to go. He grunted some kind of greeting, took her bag, and led her (or rather, he stalked away and she hurried after him) down the path to where he'd tied the horses. She was pleased to see two. Of course, she was. The last thing she wanted to do was ride with him again.

It wasn't as if the memory of his arms around her, the big, hard wall of his chest behind her, or the gentle warmth and feeling of contentment was something she dreamed about. Nor was the thought of spending a few days with him something that should be making her pulse race, blast it.

She noticed that he did a surreptitious scan of the countryside around the convent before he turned and helped lift her onto the horse. But other than a few nuns working in the garden, and a young lad fishing by the river, there was no one else about. Janet supposed he was just being cautious, but she did sense an unusual watchfulness about him.

No doubt any warrior in Bruce's army would feel a bit anxious being in the Borders, but the convent was in a quiet part of the village, at least a quarter-mile away from any other abode. He had no cause for concern.

She might have told him so, but the moment his hands wrapped around her waist to lift her, she jolted. There was no other way to describe the blast of sensation that surged through her at the moment of contact. She could feel the imprint of every one of those big fingers splayed over her ribs.

Good heavens, she'd forgotten how strong he was. He lifted her as if she weighed no more than a child. She reached out to steady herself by grabbing the solid muscle of his arms, and the jolt was followed by a heavy rush of heat. Heat that poured through her body in deep, molten waves.

Oh God, it was just like she remembered. She'd wondered if she'd imagined it—exaggerated it in her mind. But she hadn't. One brief touch and she was falling to pieces.

Yet one glance at his stony expression and she felt a pang. Obviously he was not similarly affected. He wore that same grim look on his face that she remembered so well, except that his mouth was even a tad tighter than before. Little white lines were etched around his lips and the muscle below his jaw seemed to tic a few times.

He set her down so harshly on the saddle, she gasped. "Ouch!" she said, rubbing her affected backside. "That hurt." He didn't bother to offer an apology but glared at her as if it were her fault. She lifted one eyebrow. "I can see you've been perfecting your gallantry skills since last we met."

His eyes glinted and her insides did a little tossing about at their steely intensity. He gave her a mock bow. "Forgive me, *my lady*. I'd forgotten who I was serving."

Janet bit her lip, regretting the sarcasm that had reminded him of her wee deception. Apparently, he wasn't as indifferent as he appeared about learning her true identity. She half-expected him to start bellowing at her, but instead, he turned sharply away and mounted his own horse.

Janet wasn't the best judge of horseflesh, but even she could see that the horses were better suited to plow animals and certainly weren't going to be able to carry them far from Roxburgh. They rode a few minutes before she asked, "Did you borrow the horses the same place you borrowed those clothes?"

He shot her a glare. "You didn't leave me much time to

plan for something grander, *my lady*. I thought the farmer better than the leper or wearing my armor to collect you."

He had a way of saying "my lady" that made her want to cringe. "Stop calling me that."

His gaze bit into her and she shuddered, seeing the anger simmering there. But his voice was deceptively even. "What would you prefer I call you? Sister? Genna? Eleanor?"

"Janet. You know that's my name. Stop pretending you've forgotten."

"Oh, I haven't forgotten."

With that ominous bit of warning that made her stomach feel as if a rock were bouncing up and down inside, he turned away.

They rode in silence for a while, each mile more and more uncomfortable. Why didn't he just get it over with? Waiting for the axe to fall was making her anxious.

He was tense, too, although not for the same reason. The alertness she'd noticed had only increased the longer they rode—south, she realized suddenly.

"Why are we riding in this direction? Shouldn't we be riding away from England?"

He ignored her sarcasm. "I'm making sure no one is following us."

"Why would they be?"

She wasn't surprised when he didn't answer her, as it seemed she had about a one-in-two chance of that occurring. If he was trying to deter her from questions, however, it wasn't going to work.

He seemed to be making an effort to cover their tracks. At least that was what she assumed he was doing, when he occasionally led them off the path into rocky ground or obscured their direction at junctures by riding back and forth a few times and varying the speed—and thus the stride—of their horses.

"*Is* anyone following us?" she asked.

"I don't think so, but we'll go a few more miles before we circle back to meet the others."

"Others?"

"You did not think I would come alone? Your former brother-in-law sent four of his best men to find you, including your new brother-in-law."

"Mary's husband?"

She'd heard from Lamberton about Sutherland's defection from the English and knew that her sister was safely returned to Scotland. If there was one good thing about being dragged back to Scotland like this, it was that she would finally be able to see her sister.

But beneath the excitement was also nervousness. Would Mary feel the same? Janet had caused her sister so much grief. She'd made a mess of everything, and Mary had been the one to suffer for it. She'd only narrowly escaped imprisonment and her son, Davey, had been taken from her again. Mary had every right to blame her for it.

Did she?

God knows, Janet did. Because of her, the man who'd picked her up and wiped her tears when she'd skinned her knee, who'd taught her how to ride a horse, who'd told her stories on his knee, was dead. The old servant had loved her like a father—better than a father and much better than her actual father. And what had he gotten for it? An arrow in the back.

Ewen must have been watching her face. When he spoke, it was in a far gentler voice than he'd used before. "Aye. Kenneth Sutherland, heir to the Earl of Sutherland."

Janet nodded, having learned as much from the bishop. "Is . . . is she happy?"

He nodded, and for a moment she saw a glimmer of the softness in his eyes that she remembered. "Aye, lass. Very happy."

Janet smiled. "I'm glad. No one deserves it more."

He looked as though he wanted to say something. But

when he turned away instead, Janet told herself not to be disappointed.

It didn't work.

They followed the road south for a few more miles, encountering no one, before veering off the path near a small loch, where they stopped to water the horses. Not having ridden a horse for some time, Janet was grateful for the short reprieve to stretch her legs.

She tended to her needs, and then walked to the edge of the water. It was a small loch, no bigger than a mile in diameter, but pretty, with the trees shrouding it in shades of green and brown.

The light was beginning to fade, and she guessed it must be a few hours after midday. With winter approaching, the days were growing shorter. It would be dark before long. They would barely be back to where they'd started, when it would be time to stop for the night.

Ewen came up beside her, seemingly reading her thoughts. "We will travel at night."

"Won't that be dangerous?"

His gaze hardened. "Aye. But that shouldn't bother you."

Janet couldn't stand it anymore. His not-so-subtle barbs were driving her mad. "I know you are angry about what happened before. Why don't you just say what you have to say and get it over with?"

Then maybe he would stop acting like a stranger. Like nothing had happened between them. And then maybe they could . . . what?

Janet didn't know, but it wasn't this.

Not giving in to his anger was a hell of a lot harder than Ewen expected. Every time he thought of what she'd been doing—of what she'd done—he went a little crazed with it.

"Angry?" he repeated. "Why should I be angry? Because you let me kiss you, and then let me believe I'd committed a grave sin, or because you gave me your word you would stay out of this?"

She stiffened, pursing her mouth the way she did when she found something distasteful. In other words, when someone pointed out something she didn't want to hear. "I didn't say that. I said I would leave the fighting to the men—which I have."

It took everything he had not to put his hands on her. No woman had ever riled his temper so easily. Hell, he hadn't even known he had a temper. The muscles in his arms flexed at his side, shaking with the effort not to touch her. Not to take her by the arms and haul her up against him, where he was damned sure she would have to listen to him. "Don't try that shite with me, Janet. You know bloody well what I meant!"

Not heeding the warning of his crass language, she gave a careless shrug of her shoulders and batted those big sea-blue eyes at him innocently. "Do I?"

He wasn't aware that he'd moved until she gasped and took a step back—right into a tree. He loomed over her, a flurry of dangerous emotions firing inside him. Anger, frustration, and something that went far deeper. Something extreme and uncontrollable. Something wild. Something that roused every primitive and base instinct left over from his barbarian ancestors. Something that made him want to push her up against that tree, rip her clothes off, wrap one of her legs around his hips—what the hell was there about a woman wrapping her legs around him?—and ravish her until she vowed never to put herself in danger again. He could almost feel her shuddering against him. Feel the softness of her breasts crushed against his chest. Feel the heat of her. The taste of her.

God, he wanted her, and restraint hurt. He was hot and hard, and pounding with need.

How did she do this to him? How could she strip him

bare in a matter of minutes? Make him as out of control as . . .

As his father.

A sudden chill penetrated the heat.

Rather than be intimidated—as any lass in her right mind *should* be—the lass only looked more outraged. Stretching to her full height, a good foot shorter than he, she stood toe-to-toe with him and dotted her tiny finger into his chest to emphasize her words. "You have no right to order me to do anything. What I do is none of your business."

Whether it was her words or the thought of his father, he didn't know. But as quickly as the anger had stoked inside him, it was doused. Ewen was nothing like his father. *Nothing.*

His father had been rash and undisciplined, wild and irresponsible. He had no concept of duty and loyalty.

Ewen knew exactly where his duty lay, and it wasn't in laying with her.

He stepped back. "You're right."

He should thank her for reminding him. He wasn't going to have this conversation because it didn't matter. *She* didn't matter. Janet of Mar was not for him.

It didn't matter that no other woman had ever affected him like this. It didn't matter that he took one look at her and felt every inch, every bone, every ounce of blood in his body heat with desire so fierce and raw that it took his breath away. It didn't matter that she made him angry. It didn't matter that she was the first woman he could talk to without having to worry about whether he'd said something wrong.

Hell, it didn't even matter that he *liked* her. So what? Marriage wasn't based on likes and dislikes. It was based on duty, and people did their duty and ignored their personal desires every day.

Civilized men—responsible men—didn't simply take a

woman because they wanted her. His father might have done that, but he wasn't his damned father. He didn't get impassioned about anything, damn it. And sure as hell not about a woman.

Except her.

He swore. It was only a few days. He could handle a few days of almost anything—including being aroused to the point of pain.

His physical discomfort was almost worth the expression on her face. His sudden retreat had discombobulated her.

She blinked up at him. "I am?"

He nodded. "Aye. It's not any of my business. But you'd think after what happened with your sister at the bridge, you would be more cautious." She flinched, and Ewen sensed that his barb had struck deeper than he'd intended. But maybe it would make her think. "Now, if you are ready, we should go." And with that, he turned on his heel and left before the hurt in her eyes made him do something stupid.

Stung by the reminder of her sister, Janet watched him walk away. What had just happened? One minute he was looking at her as if he didn't know whether to throttle her or kiss her (she was rather hoping for the latter), and the next he was walking away as if he didn't care one whit about her.

Perhaps he didn't.

The realization stabbed. Why was he acting like this, so cold and indifferent? Good heavens, he'd seemed more attracted to her when he'd thought she was a nun!

Something had changed between them, and it wasn't just a veil. She'd thought . . .

What? That he felt something for her? That there had been some kind of special connection between them? Had her own feelings made her see something that wasn't there?

It wasn't often that Janet felt unsure of herself, but it was becoming an all-too-frequent occurrence around Ewen Lamont. How a rough, uncouth soldier with limited communication skills (which sounded better than "spares words but not feelings") and abysmal manners could leave her so unbalanced and confused defied comprehension. She'd come across a thousand men like him (although admittedly not many who were built like a stone wall and handsome enough to make her knees weak).

She didn't know what she wanted from him. He wasn't right for her—she knew that. He was too opinionated, too rigid, too much like her patronizing "lasses-can't-do-that" brothers and father. But she couldn't deny that seeing him again made her heart flutter as if she were a thirteen-year-old lass who'd just met her first handsome knight. She felt silly and woozy and flushed all at the same time.

Jerusalem's temples, she couldn't even breathe right! All he had to do was stand next to her and the wild fluttering of her heart took over her lungs, making her breath quicken into short little gasps.

And heaven forbid he touch her! If he touched her, she would turn into a horrible soupy mess. All melty and hot, and unable to think straight.

She was too old to be acting like this. Surely these kind of feelings were the province of lovesick young girls, and not a woman of seven and twenty who was basically a nun?

Except there was no "basically" when it came to being a nun. He'd made her remember that she was a woman. A woman who was no longer young, but who knew exactly what she was going to do, until he'd come along and confused her with his no-nonsense, say-whatever-is-on-his mind and won't-be-gainsaid manner, his ruggedly handsome face, that broad chest and distracting display of muscle, and most of all, the fierce taste of passion that had shown her just how far from nunhood she really was.

Instead of trying to remember every facet of a kiss that should never have happened, she should be focusing on her job. And instead of feeling excited at the prospect of spending time with him over the next few days on the journey north, she should be angry at him for insisting that she leave the Borders and interfering with her mission yet again.

Winter might have brought a temporary lull in the fighting, but the war was not over. Her job was not yet finished. She had to be back by St. Drostan's. Janet was confident that once she explained everything to Robert, and he could see that she was perfectly safe, she would return to her post in Roxburgh. The king needed her. This informant was too important to risk with someone else. Unlike Ewen, Robert listened to reason.

But even so, she hated the idea of leaving like this. She might have refused to go if she hadn't been fairly certain the hard-headed brute would toss her over his shoulder like some Viking barbarian and carry her away.

When it came to doing his duty as a soldier, Janet suspected there was nothing that would get in his way. Yes, that was Ewen: the perfect soldier. He didn't make trouble, did his job, followed orders, no questions asked—or tolerated, she thought angrily. Arguing with him was like trying to argue with a stone wall.

What she didn't understand was why she cared. She'd like to think it was because he was interfering with her duty, but she knew that wasn't what was making her heart squeeze when he walked away as if she didn't matter to him at all. As if the air had not just been crackling between them.

And blast him for bringing up her sister! He didn't understand anything.

She didn't know whether she was more annoyed with him or with herself. *Him*, she decided with certainty as she watched his back grow smaller. He didn't turn around— not once. Not even to see if she was following.

Her gaze narrowed, her frown deepening as she noticed

something and marched over to where he stood with the horses.

"What's wrong with your leg?"

The slight tensing in his shoulders was barely noticeable, but it was there. "Nothing."

Without warning, he circled his hands around her waist, picked her up, and unceremoniously plopped her down on her horse. It happened so fast that had she blinked, she might have missed it. She felt a little bit like an iron pot taken straight from the oven.

She gritted her teeth, refusing to be put off. She'd had enough of running into stone walls. She was going to find a way to break him down, one way or another.

"You were favoring your left leg climbing up the rocks." She'd noticed it as he picked his way up the rocks that surrounded the edge of the loch. Rather than moving with a natural stride, he paused in between each step to lead with his right foot.

As if to prove her wrong, he mounted his horse from the opposite side than he usually did, slipping his left foot in the stirrup first. His movements were smooth and there was no indication that it had caused him pain, but she suspected that it had.

He turned to face her. "As I said, it is nothing."

Annoyance turned to something else as the ramifications hit her. Her eyes widened with alarm. "You're hurt!"

He edged his horse away, as if he sensed she might reach for him. "I took an arrow in the leg a few weeks ago."

She felt as if all the color had been leached out of her in one squeeze. "You were injured in the war?"

Of all the things she'd thought of during the past months, his lying in pain was not one of them. He loomed so large in her mind, seemed so big and indestructible, that she'd never considered . . .

Stone walls didn't get hurt!

Oh God, what if . . . ?

Reading her expression, his softened. "A small injury, to be sure."

But she didn't believe him. An arrow could leave a path of destruction far wider than its pointed head if it was deep. If the person who pulled it out didn't have skill. If the wound didn't heal. If it putrified. If he caught fever.

She looked down at his leg. Was it her imagination or was that a large dark circle in the leather along the side of his thigh?

Her gut checked. "Is it still bleeding?"

"Nay."

He lied.

Before she could question him further, he flicked the reins and started forward.

Fear forgotten and furious once again, she rode up beside him. "Someone should look at it."

He didn't bother turning to look at her, but his jaw clenched. "Someone has. I will have her look at it again when we return."

Her? "I can look at it, if you like." Over the past few years of pretending to be a nun, she'd done quite a bit of nursing.

He glanced over at her. "That won't be necessary."

"But I've nursed—"

"Helen isn't a nurse. She's one of the best healers I've ever seen. She could be a physician, if she wanted."

If it were true, it would be an extraordinary achievement. She'd never heard of a female physician. Janet felt a hard sting in her chest. The admiration in his voice when he spoke of the woman's skill couldn't be ignored—and neither could his lack of regard for hers. She'd thought he was a man like her father and brother who could not approve of a woman in a position other than wife and mother, but apparently she was wrong. It was just her of whom he didn't approve.

But there was something else about how he said the

woman's name. A familiarity. A fondness. "She must be very old to have become so accomplished."

He looked at her oddly, as befit the question. "Helen isn't old. She's younger than you."

This sting was more like a stab. Had she really found his bluntness and frank manner of speech charming? Did he think her so old? She was past the first blush of youth certainly, but she liked the way her face had matured. Was he seeing something she wasn't? "How can you tell beneath all the warts and moles?"

He looked at her as if she were daft, which was exactly how she felt. "You don't have warts and moles."

"Not me," she said, frustration rising inside her and threatening to spill over in a deluge of embarrassing tears. "The healer. Healers are always old and wrinkly, with lots of warts and moles."

He threw his head back and laughed. The sight was so rare and wonderful that for a moment it stole her breath. Her chest squeezed.

Oh God.

Oh no.

He looked so different. So happy and carefree. Not rigid and uncompromising at all. He looked . . . He looked like a man who could steal her heart without even trying.

Then he spoke and ruined it. "Helen is one of the most beautiful women I've ever seen. But I'll make sure to tell her that."

He laughed some more, and Janet wished she could sink into her saddle and disappear.

She felt like a fool, and worse, a jealous fool. The only good thing was that he didn't seem to have any clue as to the reason for her silly questions.

Janet fell into a rare silence as she tried to sort out her tangled emotions.

Not only did he obviously respect this Helen for her skills, he also thought her beautiful. And in that moment, with her heart squeezing and tears stinging her eyes, Janet knew she wanted him to feel that way about her. For some reason, his respect was important to her.

He couldn't be so indifferent to her. The infuriating man had disturbed her thoughts for months! It hadn't been just her, and she intended to prove it. But how?

She had plenty of time to consider her options as they rode north for miles, not retracing their path along the road, but circling back through the hills and forests. It was dusk when he finally stopped in a dense patch of trees near a river, which she assumed was the Tweed, which they'd tried to cross on the way to Berwick before. She looked around for a bridge or ford to cross but didn't see anything.

He dismounted and then moved to help her do the same. "We'll rest here until it's dark."

"I thought we were going to meet the others?"

One side of his mouth curved. "We are. They're here."

He whistled, and an instant later three figures stepped out of the shadows like ghosts. Big, fearsome ghosts dressed from head to foot in black. Even their helms were blackened. They'd been only a few feet from her, but she hadn't seen them. They seemed to blend into the night.

She took a step back, unconsciously seeking his protection. His hand slid around her waist to steady her, as if it belonged there. She sank against him, letting the hard strength of his body surround her and envelop her in its heat.

The fear dissipated, and she felt herself relax.

Then she smiled. It wasn't because she recognized MacLean. She was glad enough to see the warrior whom she'd last seen escorting Marguerite back to Melrose Abbey, but that wasn't the cause of her happiness. Nay, the cause of her happiness was pressing hard against her backside.

Whatever else he might want her to think, Ewen Lamont was *not* indifferent. And he'd just showed her how to prove it.

Eleven

❦

Ewen had spent years of training, learning to listen to and follow his instincts, but in this case they'd let him down. It was instinct that made him reach for her when he realized she was scared, but having the bottom that he could remember every curve and contour of pressed against him was harkening other instincts. Very primitive and powerful instincts.

He thought he'd tamed the wild beast inside him, but it was roaring again. Blood surged through him, hot and pounding, concentrating in one particularly painful area. Hell, he didn't need a war hammer, he had one banging against his stomach.

He hoped to hell she thought a weapon was exactly what she was feeling, but the wool of the farmer's clothes didn't hide his body's reaction nearly as well as the leather of his armor.

He let his hand slip from her waist and stepped away, snapping his frustration at his friends. "Bloody hell, take off the helms! You're scaring her."

MacLean did so first, and then stepped farther out of the shadows into the dusky light. He gave her a short bow. "My lady."

Janet recovered quickly. The manners, grace, and elegance befitting the daughter of an earl emerged so effortlessly, Ewen wondered how he hadn't recognized it right away. "Janet," she corrected him. "Please. Although I fear we were not introduced properly before."

MacLean smiled, a rare feat for his dark facade. "Under the circumstances, it was understandable, Lady Janet."

Ewen didn't miss the grateful smile she threw in Mac-Lean's direction for his understanding of her deception—or the "see that" one she threw in his.

The other introductions were made, MacKay first and then Sutherland, and Ewen felt his temper heat with every well-mannered word. The ruthless, more-brigand-than-knight warriors he'd fought alongside for months sounded like bloody courtiers out of some bard's tale.

Gallantry skills, he recalled her jibe. What use did a Highland warrior have for those?

None. But never had he felt the lack of them so acutely.

Sutherland kept staring at her, as if he couldn't believe his eyes. For some reason, it made Ewen want to smash his fist through his teeth. The two women were completely different—couldn't he see that?

Janet seemed amused by her brother-in-law's reaction. Or perhaps she was used to it. "Do we look so much alike?"

"I apologize," Sutherland said with a smile. "You do. The resemblance is uncanny."

He shot Ewen a look as if he should have warned him.

"They're twins," Ewen reminded him. What the hell did he expect?

"Actually, we didn't look much alike the last time I saw my sister," Janet said. Her expression clouded, as if the memory caused her pain.

Sutherland shook his head. "Well, you do now."

The way his fellow Guardsman couldn't seem to stop looking at her was beginning to irritate Ewen. "They don't look that much alike. In the light you will see that Janet's eyes are greener. Her hair is shorter and not quite as blond.

Janet also has a freckle right above her lip that Mary doesn't have. Mary's face is rounder, and she's not as slim as Janet."

Ewen realized he'd said too much when all four faces turned toward him—Janet's with a frown and his three friends' with varying levels of surprise and speculation. He didn't have a cowardly bone in his body, but he felt the sudden urge to crawl under a rock and hide.

Sutherland lifted a brow. "Is that so?" he drawled.

Ewen knew what he was thinking, but he was wrong. "It's my job to notice details," he reminded them.

None of the men believed him, but at least Janet didn't appear to understand. She was looking at him, shaking her head. "You'd better not let my sister hear you say that. I don't think she'd appreciate being called 'round.'"

He frowned, perplexed. What was wrong with round?

Sutherland explained. "Women who've just had babies can be sensitive about their weight."

"She didn't just have a baby. William is seven months old already."

There was a collective groan, the four of them giving him pitying looks, apparently having given up on explaining.

"Get changed," MacKay said. "As soon as it's dark, I want to get as far from here as possible." The big Highlander scanned the trees with the same kind of wariness that Ewen felt. "Something doesn't feel right."

So it wasn't just him. He'd wondered whether it was being with Janet that was putting him on edge. It was, but it was something else as well.

He nodded and turned to her. "You'll need to change also. That white veil sticks out like a beacon."

"Actually," Sutherland interrupted, "your sister thought you might be more comfortable and draw less attention in these," he held out a bundle of clothing, "at least until we reach the Highlands."

She smiled as she took it. "That was very thoughtful of her, although I'm not surprised. Mary was always the one to think ahead."

Sutherland gave her an apologetic look that Ewen didn't understand right away. "The clothing belongs to my squire."

What in Hades?

Janet looked as shocked as he at the suggestion that she dress like a lad.

"MacRuairi suggested it," Sutherland said before he could object. "He said it helped when he brought his wife out of England."

Lachlan MacRuairi had slipped Bella MacDuff through the English defenses twice.

"One of Christina's kinsmen?" Janet asked.

"Her brother," Ewen responded.

From her wide eyes, Ewen guessed that she'd met Viper before.

"There is also a gown in there for later," Sutherland said. "Mary said you would not like to arrive at court dressed like a lad."

Janet laughed. "My sister remembers me well." Ewen suspected he was the only one who saw the trepidation mixed with the wistfulness that crossed her face. Why was she anxious about seeing her sister? With what she'd risked for Mary, he'd assumed they were close. But then he remembered her reaction to his barb. Was it guilt? Was that what was driving the lass?

"Is there somewhere I can change?" she asked.

"There's an old fisherman's bothy in the trees there beside the river," MacLean said, pointing through the trees. "I will escort you."

The hell he would! Ewen trusted his partner with his life, but he didn't trust him to have any more self-control than Ewen had had in the same situation. "I'll do it," he said in a voice that brokered no argument. "I have to retrieve my armor anyway."

He'd stashed his belongings in a wide gap between a couple of nearby rocks. It wasn't large enough to serve as a cave, but it had been a perfect place to hide his valuable weapons and armor while he went to fetch her.

He walked away before anyone could argue, and relaxed only when he heard her footsteps behind him. Though it hurt like the devil, Ewen did not break his stride, putting his full weight on his right leg. He hadn't realized he'd been favoring the left until she'd pointed it out.

The warmth of the blood on his thigh told him that the wound had opened again, but Helen would see to it when they returned. The last thing he wanted was Janet fussing over him—or, God forbid, touching him.

He smiled, thinking of the odd conversation he'd had with Janet about MacKay's wife. Old, with warts and moles? Where had the lass come up with that?

He stopped when he reached the old fisherman's bothy. It was a simple stone structure—the flat stones had been set together without lime mortar—that leaned a little to one side, but it appeared sturdy enough. Most of its original turf roof was gone. It wouldn't protect her from the elements, but it would provide all the privacy she needed to change.

"Do you need me to light a torch?"

She gazed up to the sky and shook her head. "There is enough light left for me to change. I won't be long." She shivered. "It's too cold to linger. It feels like it could snow."

He suspected she was right; the next few days wouldn't be comfortable by any measure. But at least the cold would help control his other constant discomfort.

He gave her a short bow of his head and started to move away, when she stopped him.

"Wait!"

He turned around slowly—reluctantly.

She bit her lip, looking embarrassed. There was just enough light left to see the blush high on her pretty cheeks. "I-I," she stammered. "I need someone to help me loosen my kirtle."

Ewen stilled, every muscle in his body tensing. He'd thought about undressing her too many times for the image not to leap immediately to the forefront of his mind, where it would not be dislodged. He pictured the gown sliding down her shoulders, revealing the pale, velvety skin inch by inch. He could see the high, silky roundness of her breasts, the slim back, and the smooth curve of her bottom.

He clenched his fists. God's blood, it was his bloody fantasies coming true!

Which was exactly why he couldn't do it. "I'm not a damned handmaiden."

She lifted one delicate brow. "If you don't think you can manage, I will ask one of the others." She bit her lip, apparently considering. "It's hard to figure out which one would have more experience with ladies' gowns." She gave him a cheeky grin. "They are all rather handsome, don't you think?"

He didn't think anything of the sort. The muscle in his jaw jumped. His veins bulged as fire surged through his blood. If anyone was going to touch her, it would be him. All three of his brethren were married—two of them contentedly—but damned if he would throw that kind of temptation in their path. The lass had a body that could make a man weak. Hell, he was doing them a favor. He was bloody paragon of selflessness.

He stormed over to her, trying to get a rein on the sudden blast of anger. "I'll do it."

She looked up at him with that innocent expression on her face. "If you think you can manage?"

His eyes narrowed. Even through the veil of anger, he realized the lass was trying to provoke him. He met her challenging gaze with his own. "If you'll remember, it's nothing I haven't done *hundreds* of times before."

The purse of her mouth told him his strike had been well placed. He wasn't the only one angry now. "I remember."

She didn't bother waiting for him to open the door and walked inside. He followed her in.

A cold, musty smell filled the air. It was really only the shell of a building, with little in the way of personal belongings left inside. But he found a table with one of its legs broken off, brushed most of the dirt and dust from the top, and propped it up for her to have something to put the pile of clothing on.

Despite the dank bleakness of their surroundings, Ewen was painfully aware of the intimacy of the situation. They were alone in a small, dark building, no more than ten feet square, alone in the dark. He could hear the softness of her breath and smell the faint scent of bluebells.

He needed to get out of here. "What do you need me to do?" he snapped.

She payed no mind to his obvious impatience. "I would think that after so many times you would know."

The lass was provoking him all right, but why? He didn't say anything, but the look he gave her was warning enough.

Ignoring him, she began to pull the pins from her veil and wimple. His heart began to pound as he half-anticipated, half-dreaded the moment that was coming. He didn't think he was breathing when she finally finished. Pulling the last piece of cloth from her hair, she shook her head and made a sound of such pleasure, it sent a surge of heat rushing to his cock that no amount of loyalty and duty could hold back.

"Heavens, that feels good!" She sighed.

It felt more like hell. His entire body was shaking as he fought the urge to sink his hands through the wild, mane of golden curls that bounded down her back in a silken veil. The scent of bluebells intensified, and he wanted to bend his head and sink his nose into the silky warmth.

He didn't realize he'd made a sound until she turned to him. "Is something wrong?"

Other than that he wanted her so badly, he didn't trust himself move? "You can't wear your hair like that."

"Why not?"

"It's the wrong color."

Her eyes widened, and he realized his sharply spoken words had wounded her. "Is there something wrong with blond?"

It wasn't blond, it was honey brown with flecks of silver, copper, and gold. It was a crown fit for a queen. It was beautiful.

But he could hardly tell her that. "It will reflect the moonlight just as much as your veil."

She brightened. "I think I noticed a cap in there. I can tuck it up inside."

She removed her mantle next. He stood stone still, staring at the wall, telling himself not to be affected. It didn't work. She let the black wool drop to the floor in a puddle at her feet and he flinched.

This was too close to his fantasies. Was she trying to torture him? Did she have any idea what she was doing to him?

Despite the guileless expression, he suspected that she did. What the hell game was she playing?

The scapular came next. Belted at the waist, all she had to do was untie the rope cord and lift the rectangular piece of white natural wool over her head.

Finally, when every muscle in his body was tensed with restraint, with the effort it took not to reach out and touch her, she turned around with her back facing him.

Glancing up at him from over her shoulder—far more seductively than any innocent maiden should—she said,

"If you could just loosen the top laces, I will be able to do the rest on my own."

He didn't know if he could do it. He wanted to touch her so desperately, he didn't know if he could stop at just the ties.

His mouth tightened. He clenched his jaw. Duty. Loyalty. Discipline. *It's up to you.* His clan was depending on him.

Ewen tried to picture Walter Stewart's face, but all he could see was hers. The big greenish-blue eyes, the tiny nose and chin, the gracefully carved features, the warm, sensual mouth . . .

His hands shook as he lifted them to her back. He was an elite warrior, damn it. He could do this. He'd survived against the worst odds and the most perilous circumstances. *Just focus. Concentrate on the laces.*

He had done this before. Maybe not hundreds of times as he'd claimed, but enough that his fingers shouldn't feel so big and clumsy. But they wouldn't seem to move right. Even in the snowy mountaintops of the Cuillins during training, they'd never felt so frozen.

He stared at the laces, his hands coming to a sudden stop. Her hair was covering the place where they started. He could just move it to the side . . .

Not a chance.

"Your hair is in the way," he managed tightly.

"Oh, sorry." She tipped her head, scooping the wild mass to tumble to the side, revealing the top of the gown and the milky-white nape of her neck. The invitation was unmistakable. It would be so easy to lower his mouth and press his lips to the soft, warm skin . . .

Focus, damn it!

He pulled one of the ends of the bow at the top and slid his finger behind the laces to loosen them. Methodically, he worked his way down her back, trying not to think about what he was doing. But never had he been more conscious of what he was doing in his life.

It was ridiculous. There was nothing particularly erotic about unlacing a gown. The linen shift she wore underneath the form-fitting natural wool kirtle prevented him from seeing bare skin, but he was more aroused by these loosened laces than he'd ever been by a naked woman. Except for her, but he sure as hell wasn't going to think about her naked right now.

Wrong.

He stepped back, trying to clear the image from his mind. Did he have to remember every detail of her breasts? Of her slim back and stomach? Of the heart-shaped curve of her bottom? "That should suffice," he said, his voice gruff with longing.

"Thank you." She smiled. "One of the nuns at the priory couldn't have done a better job."

For some reason, he didn't like being compared to one of the nuns. His gaze bit into hers. "All that practice, remember?"

Janet remembered, all right. Which was what made his determined resistance all the more frustrating. She knew he was feeling the same way that she was: hot, restless, and breathless with anticipation, as if every one of her senses had been heightened to its peak. Awareness reverberated between them like the crackle of lightning.

She wasn't alone in her desire. She could feel it—had felt it hard against her.

Janet had never gone out of her way to entice a man, but something about him provoked her to naughtiness. As had the three years of hiding her femininity. Part of her wondered whether she was still desirable. She thought her little request to help her with the gown would be enough to shatter his resistance and prove he wasn't indifferent to her. This might be her only chance to experience passion.

Fate had thrown him back into her life; was it for a reason? But he seemed determined to walk away, to ignore whatever it was that was between them.

Why? Was it anger at what she'd done? She decided to hone some of his bluntness. "Why are you acting like this?"

"Like what?"

"Like nothing ever happened between us."

"Maybe because what happened between us made me think I'd be burning in eternal hellfire?"

Janet bit her lip, feeling as guilty as she should. "I'm sorry for lying to you. Perhaps I should have told you I was not a nun, but I was scared."

He seemed honestly perplexed. "Scared of what?"

She lifted her chin, boldly meeting his gaze. "That without a veil between us there was nothing to prevent me from . . . you from . . ."

She struggled with how to tell him she was scared that she might have given him her innocence.

But he understood. "I would never have let it go that far."

She tilted her head, looking up at him. She might not have much experience in such matters, but it hadn't seemed that way to her. "Are you so sure about that?"

He stared at her, his jaw locked.

Her heart clenched. In the semidarkness, the angles of his face seemed even sharper. He looked harder. Rougher. Even more remote. But so handsome he made her knees weak.

He didn't argue with her, which she supposed was agreement enough.

She stepped toward him. He stiffened, but she didn't let it stop her from putting a hand on the front of his plaid. Their eyes locked. "Won't you forgive me?"

She could feel the fierce pounding of his heart under her

palm. It was not unlike the sensation of having her hand on the lid of a pot that was about to boil over.

She could see in the intensity of his gaze that he wanted her. She could feel it straining in his muscles. He wanted her, but something was holding him back. A fierce battle was warring inside him.

She lost.

He captured her wrist in his hand and removed it from his chest. "There is nothing to forgive. You were right. It prevented us from making a mistake that could not be corrected. Because that's what it would be, Janet, a mistake. I'm sorry if the kiss confused you, but it didn't mean anything. It would be best if you forgot it ever happened." He looked her straight in the eye. "I have."

She sucked in her breath at the harsh blow, surprised by how much his frank words stung. Before she could clear the scorching blast of hurt from her chest and throat to respond, he was gone.

By the time Janet had finished putting on the squire's clothing, she'd worked herself into such a temper that she didn't even notice the cold. Still, she'd changed about as quickly as she could recall.

A mistake? She slammed the door of the bothy behind her. How like him to make that determination for them both!

She marched the short distance to where the men waited. It was dark now, but the moonlight was strong enough through the wisps of descending mist to guide her through the trees.

Forgotten about it, had he? Well, she would see about that. He'd dragged her away from Roxburgh; she had two, possibly three, days to prove differently, and she intended to use very minute of them.

How she would do so, she didn't know, but she was certain something would come to her.

Janet didn't think she'd taken much time, but all four men were waiting for her when she broke through the circle of trees and emerged into the small clearing where they'd gathered. They'd retrieved their horses from wherever they'd been hidden, including exchanging the two nags she and Ewen had been riding earlier for a pair of fine and sturdy-looking stallions.

Although the four men were outfitted in strikingly similar (and terrifying) fashion—Ewen had exchanged his farmer's garb for the black leather *cotun,* chausses, plaid, and blackened nasal helm that she'd first seen him in—and they were all uncommonly tall and thick with muscle, she identified him right away.

No one said anything as she approached. Indeed, they all seemed to be standing rather still. Her hand went to her woolen cap. Though she'd braided her hair before she'd tucked it inside, she pushed a few errant tendrils at her temples back underneath for good measure.

But it didn't seem to be her hair that had caught their attention.

Was it her clothing? She frowned, doing a quick once-over of the black leather breeches and doublet. She double-checked to make sure the linen shirt was completely tucked in, but everything looked fine. Actually, she rather thought the ensemble fit quite well. The breeches were perhaps a shade snug, but the short coat might have been made for her.

She glanced back at the men, but all but Ewen had turned away and seemed to be very busy fiddling with their horses.

Ignoring Ewen and his black glare that at one time might have intimidated her—God only knew what she'd done this time—she found her bag, which had been propped against a tree, and bent over to place her habit and the beautiful gown Mary had sent for her inside.

She thought Ewen made some kind of strangled sound

low in his throat, but when she turned he, too, was busy with his horse.

She was surprised at how comfortable it was wearing breeches, and how oddly freeing to be rid of all those heavy skirts. She was, however, cold. The only mantle she'd brought with her was the hooded one that she'd worn earlier. As it didn't seem too feminine, she slipped that on over her squire's ensemble. It wasn't lined, however, and she wished she'd thought to bring along an extra plaid.

The men all wore the same dark plaid Ewen had worn the first time they'd met. It looked black at night, but in the daylight, she'd noticed the subtle shades of dark grays and blues mixed in with the black. She wrinkled her nose, thinking it odd. Was it some kind of uniform, then?

Finished, she picked up the bag, which felt considerably heavier with the extra clothing, and walked over to what she assumed was her horse. She knew Ewen was watching her struggle, but he made no effort to help her, even though he stood the closest to her.

If that was how it was going to be, so be it. He wasn't the only one who could pretend "it" had never happened.

A streak of devilishness that had been buried a long time picked that moment to reemerge. He seemed to have an ability to make her feel very *un*-nunlike. In many different ways.

Janet turned to MacLean, who stood a few feet away with his horse. "Ewen, would you be so kind as to help me up?"

She could see Ewen stiffen out of the corner of her eye and didn't need daylight to see his steely blue eyes harden to flinty gray.

MacLean laughed—at least she thought the sound was a laugh, but coming from such a grim facade she couldn't be sure. He and Ewen were much alike in that regard, but Ewen's grimness seemed born of seriousness, whereas Eoin's had a darker, more angry bent.

"I'd be happy to, Lady Janet. But I'm not Lamont."

She feigned surprise, hoping Ewen could see the blush she forced up her cheeks. "I apologize, but you all look so much alike that I can't tell you apart. With those dark plaids and helms, you could well be Bruce's phantoms."

She laughed, but no one else joined her. Indeed, there seemed to be an odd silence. It reminded her of the times she'd walked into her father's solar when he was talking with his men and he'd just said something he hadn't wanted her to hear.

Out of the corner of her eye she could see Ewen step toward her, but before he could move to help her, she turned sharply to give him her back and held her hand out to MacLean.

The big warrior seemed to be amused, but he came forward to take it. Like Ewen, MacLean wrapped his hands around her waist and lifted her effortlessly into the saddle. He was every bit as strong and far more gentle. But unlike Ewen, when he touched her and she put her hands on his muscular arms to brace herself, her pulse didn't race, her skin didn't flush, and her stomach didn't flip.

Unfortunate, that.

Feeling the weight of Ewen's gaze upon them, Janet forced a gasp of maidenly shock to her lips. It had been a long time since she flirted with a man, but it came back to her so naturally, it might have never been gone. She'd always been the more flirtatious of the sisters, but it was more her natural friendliness than real flirtation, and she'd never taken it seriously. Until now.

She gazed into MacLean's eyes, the startling dark blue just visible beneath the edge of his helm. Beneath that hard, grizzled exterior, he was quite handsome, she realized. And sharp; she could see it in his eyes.

Flirting with him wouldn't be difficult at all.

"My word!" She left the men to contemplate what that exclamation might be about. "Thank you, Eoin. You must have all the women at court fighting for your assistance. Not all men are so gentle." Her gaze flickered over to Ewen for just an instant—but long enough. "You'd be surprised at the lack of gallantry in some."

Her barb found its mark. She could see Ewen's fists clench at his sides. He was furious.

Far too furious for "a mistake."

Far too furious for someone who'd forgotten.

Perhaps she'd found her way to break through to him? She would see how indifferent he was when she "forgot," and turned her interest in another direction.

"Not all ladies are as easy to lift as you, my lady." MacLean paused, as if the gentle, flirtatious banter between a man and a woman had been dormant a long time for him as well. "Or as pleasurable," he said with a wicked smile that she suspected at one time had felled the heart of many a maid before anger had taken over.

"If the *lady* is quite comfortable," Ewen interrupted, "we've wasted enough time. I want to be east of Selkirk before daybreak."

If MacLean noticed Ewen's irritation, he didn't show it. He turned to her. "My lady?"

She gave him a conspiratorial wink. "Comfortable enough for now, but if I decide I need a litter, I will let you know." She let her gaze drop over the wide spans of chest and thick arms. "You seem more than equal to the task." He grinned, and she lowered her voice to a whisper that was loud enough to ensure Ewen would hear. "Is he always so grumpy?"

MacLean shot a surreptitious look to the man in question, who was glaring at them so furiously she was surprised smoke wasn't coming out of his nose.

"I'm afraid so, my lady."

She smiled back at him, thinking that under the circumstances, she was rather enjoying herself.

Twelve

✦

The mission had to come first, damn it. As angry as he was—and Ewen couldn't recall the last time he'd been so angry—he knew the danger ahead of him. Hell, not just ahead of him but everywhere around him. The Borders were rife with it.

They wouldn't be safe until they boarded the *birlinn* waiting just off shore for them in Ayr—assuming Hawk and Viper hadn't been called off on another mission. So he buried his anger beneath the call of duty, reminding himself of all he had to do. But it was there, simmering, getting closer to the breaking point with each mile that they rode over the gentle rolling hills of the Tweedsdale.

Although he would prefer to travel on the north side of the Tweed, the bridges were heavily monitored. This part of the Scottish Marches was a maze of rivers and tributaries. At some point they would have to cross water, but it was safer to wait until they were west of Selkirk, where there were numerous places to cross that didn't require a bridge. They could have tried to cross at the place he'd taken Janet to all those months ago, but that was how he and the other Guardsmen had arrived, and he always tried to use a different route to leave in case someone had tracked them the first time.

With the English controlling the border towns, he supposed it didn't make much difference: everywhere was dangerous. But even traveling at night with only a single torch to light their way, he felt exposed. The low hills and fertile valley of the Tweedsdale provided little natural cover. It wasn't until they neared Selkirk that the hills would rise and the forests would thicken. Ironically, he would be returning to Selkirk in two weeks with Bruce for peace talks.

He hoped to reach as far as Ettrick, deep in those hills and forests about twelve miles southwest of Selkirk, before daybreak. There was a cave in the area where they could rest until nightfall.

But they had hours of dangerous and difficult riding ahead of them. Ewen spent the first few hours circling around behind them to hide their tracks as best he could and ensure no one was following them. The snow seemed to be holding off, which was good. Hiding tracks in freshly fallen snow was difficult, unless it fell quickly and heavily.

Ewen had been chosen by Bruce for the Highland Guard for his extraordinary tracking skills. Man or beast, if there was a trail, he would find it. It was what had given him the war name of Hunter. But the other side of tracking was knowing how to hide your own tracks. And like the ghosts that some thought "Bruce's phantoms," it was Ewen's responsibility to make the Guardsmen disappear.

He still couldn't believe how close Janet had come to the truth with her jest. But thankfully, that was all it had been: a jest.

Not that he was much in the mood for jesting. It seemed as though every time he rejoined the group or they stopped for a short break—as much for Janet as for the horses—she was laughing with one of his brethren.

But especially with MacLean. His partner was lapping it up like a starving pup. Who in the hell knew that Striker could smile? In all the years Ewen had known him, he'd never seen MacLean like this. Not only smiling and jesting, but also *talking*. Hell, he didn't think Striker was capable of carrying on a conversation that wasn't about war or battle strategy.

But the strange ease that Ewen had found with Janet seemed to apply to his partner as well. And something about that set him on edge—on deep edge.

The lad's clothing didn't help, either. MacRuairi should have warned him. Women sure as hell didn't belong in breeches—especially snug leather ones. They molded the womanly curves of her hips and bottom to perfection and emphasized the slim lines of her surprisingly long legs. It was distracting. Damned distracting. And he hadn't been the only one to take notice. MacKay and Sutherland seemed embarrassed, but MacLean . . . he seemed a little too appreciative.

It was after midnight when they stopped for the second time. Ewen had gone back on foot to obscure some of the hoofprints, and intersperse a few signs that he hoped would confuse or delay anyone on their trail, when he heard a soft feminine laugh coming from the direction of the river.

The muscles in his neck and shoulders bunched. *Focus, damn it!* He knew he should ignore it. But the sound grated against every nerve-ending in his body. He couldn't take it anymore.

As soon as he came over the rise he could see her. Janet was seated on a rock, and MacLean stood beside her. He was handing her something.

"Thank you," Janet said, taking what appeared to be a piece of beef. "I'm more hungry than I realized."

MacLean murmured something that Ewen didn't hear, and then said, "You are warm enough?"

Ewen was striding toward them, but the sound she made stopped him mid-step. Squeezing the plaid around her shoulders, she gave a delighted sigh that went straight to his groin.

"Wonderfully warm," she said. "Thank you for letting me borrow it. It was most thoughtful of you."

Thoughtful? MacLean? Ewen had never known him to be so attentive to a woman. *Any* woman. And she was the wrong woman.

MacLean shrugged. If Ewen didn't know him better, he'd think his partner was preening. "I thought I saw you shiver at our last stop."

Ewen had seen the same thing. He'd been about to offer her his own plaid—God knew it would help to cover her up more—when MacLean had walked over to her and handed her his own.

Ewen had had to fight the urge to rip it off her. *It should be mine, damn it.*

Janet glanced over as he approached, but rather than acknowledge him, she turned to MacLean with a roll of the eye in his direction. *That* grated.

Though Ewen knew his partner had heard him earlier, it was only then that MacLean glanced in his direction.

He cocked his brow. "Is something wrong?"

Ewen held his temper by the barest of threads. "Other than the fact that they can probably hear you talking halfway to London? Unless you want the English down on top of us, keep your voices low. And stop all that bloody laughing."

If Ewen hadn't already known how ridiculous he sounded, their expressions would have told him. But nothing was worse than their quick exchange of looks, and Janet whispering "grumpy" under her breath, while trying not to laugh.

"What did you say?"

Janet shook her head, mirth shimmering in her eyes. "Nothing."

MacLean attempted to change the subject. "Did you see anything?"

Ewen glowered at Janet until she finally sobered. Only *then* did he answer. "Nay."

She studied him, her gaze assessing. "You are being very careful. Do you have cause to believe someone is following us or are you always this vigilant?"

"If you haven't noticed, my lady, the Marches are currently occupied by English troops. There is no such thing as too careful or too vigilant when it comes to war. The fact that you don't understand that is exactly why you shouldn't be out here."

She stiffened and gave him a long, scathing stare that made him want to turn away. Without a word, she turned sharply and said to MacLean, "Thank you again. I will see you up by the horses."

Both men watched her walk away, Ewen cursing his harshly spoken words.

MacLean gave a low whistle, shaking his head. "You were a little hard on the lass, don't you think?"

Ewen tried not to sound as defensive as he felt. "It's the truth, and anyone that's been doing what she's been doing needs to hear it. This isn't some game."

"And you believe that she thinks it is?"

"I think she has no idea of the danger she is in." Ewen's eyes narrowed. "Edward's men will not go easy on her if they discover what she is doing. The fact that she is a woman will not make a difference." He didn't need to remind MacLean of what had happened at Lochmaben; he'd been there. "I can't believe you are defending her. Would you allow your wife to do what she's doing?"

A dark shadow crossed MacLean's face. It wasn't often that any of them brought up his wife. But perhaps it was time for him to remember that he had one.

MacLean's mouth fell in a hard, angry line. "Aye, I just might. If it would mean I'd be rid of her sooner." He paused, giving Ewen an appraising look. "Interesting comparison to make though."

Ewen didn't like the way his partner was looking at him, as if he *knew* something. "I only thought to remind you of your own, since you seem to have forgotten."

He shrugged. "I like Lady Janet. She's easy to talk to."

Bloody hell, he knew that. Ewen clenched his fists. "She's not for you."

MacLean gave him a taunting smile. "I didn't realize that you'd staked a claim."

Ewen took a step toward him. They'd been partners for five years and been through hell together. He'd never thought that he would feel so close to striking him. "I haven't. You know very well that the lass is meant for someone else."

Ewen's voice must have revealed more than he intended. MacLean immediately backed off, the taunting smile replaced by his usual dark expression. "Aye, but the lass doesn't know that. She is doing this for you, you know. She's trying to make you jealous."

Ewen was stunned. Was it true? His eyes narrowed at the man he thought was his closest friend. "And you went along with it?"

MacLean shrugged unapologetically. "As I said, I like her—and she is easy to talk to—but I wanted to see if it worked." He gave him a long pitying looking. "By the look on your face the past few hours, I'd say it did."

Much to his disgust, Ewen realized MacLean was right. She'd gotten to him.

"What are you going to do?" MacLean asked somberly.

What *could* he do? "My duty."

"Perhaps you should tell her and give the lass a choice?"

"Women of her station do not have a choice." And neither did he.

"I had one."

Ewen was stunned once again. From the way MacLean acted, Ewen would never have thought he'd wanted to marry his MacDowell wife. "You did?"

Something dark and angry and so full of hatred crossed MacLean's face it almost made Ewen take a step back. "I made the wrong one because I thought . . ." He clenched his jaw. "Perhaps you are right. Deliver the lass to Bruce and don't look back. You'll save yourself a whole hell of a lot of trouble."

His friend walked away, and Ewen wondered whether he was talking about Ewen or himself. Perhaps it didn't matter, because either way MacLean was right: Janet of Mar was a whole hell of a lot of trouble. The kind of trouble that could cost him everything, if he wasn't careful.

Why was Janet going to so much effort for a man who spoke to her as if she were five years old?

She had no idea.

The narrow-minded Highlander had made it perfectly clear that he didn't think she had any part in the war. Fine. But she knew differently, and his opinion wasn't going to change anything. She had every intention of finishing what she'd started. As long as the king needed her, as long as she could be of use, she would put herself in as much danger as she wanted. He had no right to tell her otherwise. He could glower and chastise until he was blue in that obnoxiously good-looking face of his, but she didn't have to heed him. He wasn't her father or her husband.

Thank God.

Was it so difficult to understand that what she did was important to her? For the past few years she'd had a purpose. Something that she not only enjoyed and was good at, but that also made her feel as if she mattered. She didn't have anyone looking over her shoulder telling her she couldn't do something. She'd been able to turn what her father had thought of as a character flaw in a woman—the propensity to make a man see he was wrong—into a useful skill.

And the more she helped, the less she thought about the

past, and the thoughtless young woman who'd tried to be a hero but had only ended up causing so much trouble. She owed it to Mary, but most of all to Cailin. Though she'd never forgive herself for his death at least she could see to it that it meant something. But Ewen wanted to take that away from her.

She would never think to ask him to stop being a soldier. It was what he did. Presumably, and from what she'd seen, he was good at it.

Not that he would ever see the comparison. To him, women were pretty accessories. A wife was someone to birth his children, tend his castles, and never raise her voice in protest.

Well, that wasn't her. And Janet had seen what happened when a woman who had her own opinions married a bull-headed, overprotective man who assumed he knew best. Janet had no interest in following Duncan and Christina's example. Or her mother's, for that matter. Strife or serfdom, neither was appealing.

None of which explained why her heart squeezed when Ewen left the cave not long after they finished eating their second meal of dried beef, ale, and oatcakes.

MacKay, who'd exchanged a few words with Ewen before he left, came over to where she was huddled at the back of the small, rocky cave. There would barely be room for all five of them to lie down, but without a fire, she suspected she would be glad of the warmth provided by their nearness.

"You should get some rest, lass. We have another long night of riding ahead of us, and the terrain won't be as friendly as it was today."

"Where did Ewen go?"

"To the loch. His leg was caked with blood, and I told him to wash it or Helen would have both our hides."

She bristled at the mention of the younger-than-you-are, beautiful healer. "Helen?"

The strapping Highlander smiled. "Aye, my wife. She's a healer. She told Lamont that if he opened that wound one more time, she wasn't going to fix it again." He laughed. "But she will. She can't help it. It's what she does."

His wife? Janet was struck twofold. Not only because she'd been jealous over this man's wife, but also because he was clearly proud of her. "Your wife is a healer?"

"Aye, a very good one."

There was no mistaking the pride in his voice. Good God, a husband who was proud of a wife who worked? Miracles did happen. Too bad his friend didn't feel the same way. But could he? Not likely. Still, the possibility intrigued her more than she wanted to admit. "Perhaps I should see if Ewen needs help. I've done some nursing."

MacKay looked at her appraisingly, rubbing his hand over a week's worth of stubble on his jaw. She thought he might refuse, but eventually he nodded. "Let me get you something first."

Janet made her way down the rocky shoreline with the cloth and ointment Magnus had provided. Dawn was still a half-hour away, but the sun was already making its presence known, casting a soft glow over the misty sky. The promise of snow hung in the frosty air. Without wind, the weather was bearable—just.

Washing in the icy water of the river, however, was another matter. Her hands were still blue from her earlier efforts. So just about the last thing she expected was to see Ewen emerge half-naked from the river like some kind of ancient Norse sea god.

She stopped dead in her tracks, her mouth going dry. She should turn away. Really, she should. But she couldn't. All right, in all honesty, she didn't want to.

She'd seen men without shirts. She'd even seen muscular men without shirts. But never had she seen one who made her want to stand back and stare in admiration.

She was sure there was plenty of good uses for broad shoulders, arms that bulged with strength, and a stomach roped with band after band of muscle, but right now all she could think about was that he was beautiful. That it was a shame to cover such magnificence even with leather and studs of steel. That she would give just about anything to put her hands on him.

Other details shuffled through her frozen brain. The dark triangle of hair at his neck that narrowed to a thin trail beneath his linen braies—the *damp* linen braies that rode low on his waist and clung to thick, muscular thighs.

She shifted her gaze quickly from another big bulge that they clung to. She was bold, but not *that* bold.

She had only a minute before he noticed her, but she made every second count.

He shot her a glare and reached for a drying cloth, furiously scrubbing away all the lucky drops of water that clung to his chest.

For heaven's sake, she was acting like a lovesick thirteen-year-old!

Belatedly, she averted her eyes.

"What do you want?" he growled a few moments later.

To her disappointment when she glanced back, he'd donned a linen shirt and pulled on some breeches.

Ironically, now that he was dressed, she blushed. "I didn't realize . . ." She bit her lip. "I'm sorry to intrude, but Magnus gave me some ointment to tend to your leg."

"I don't need—"

"I know you don't need it, but he said to remind you that Helen will blame him if you catch a fever and die, so you'd 'bloody well better see that you don't.' *Helen*," she stressed the woman's name, "Magnus's wife."

He gave her a puzzled look. "I know who Helen is."

She should be grateful that he had no idea how jealous he'd made her, but for some reason his utter lack of understanding annoyed her.

He held out his hand. "Give it to me. I'll take care of it."

Janet pursed her lips. "I know you think I'm incapable of rational thought, but I do know what I'm doing."

He frowned. "I don't think that."

She made a sharp sound. "That's why every other word out of your mouth is about how stupid and foolish I am—"

He reached out and took her by the arm. "I never said you were stupid or foolish. I said you didn't understand the danger."

"But I do. Just in the same way you do, and yet still choose to do what you do."

His frown deepened. "It's not the same."

Suddenly, Janet felt tired. Too tired to try to make him understand. Too tired of banging her head against a stone wall—no matter how impressively built.

She stared down at him. He still had his hand on her arm, but he let it drop. "Are you going to let me help or not?"

He hesitated.

"What's wrong?"

His gaze shifted uncomfortably. "It isn't . . ." His cheeks darkened. "It wouldn't be proper."

Janet gaped at him. My God, he was blushing! "*You* are modest?"

A flash of annoyance cleared away the blush. "Of course not. I was merely thinking of you."

She tried not to laugh, but she feared the smile showed behind her pursed lips. "I've been pretending to be a nurse for quite a while. I think I can manage not to faint with maidenly shock."

She did. But just barely. It was one thing to tend old men and women, and another to stand inches away from a man who made your heart skip, even when he wasn't sliding his breeches—and then his wet braies—down his hip.

He managed to keep himself covered except for the top of his outer thigh, but good gracious, she felt like she was jumping out of her skin. How was she going to touch him so intimately and not think about . . .

Her gaze flew from the big bulge (where to her horror she'd been looking), and heat flamed her cheeks. Only the sight of the wound prevented her from thrusting the ointment into his hand, babbling some excuse, and racing back to the cave.

But the angry mass of torn flesh brought her back to reality. She gasped in half-horror and half-outrage. Though the dip in the freezing loch had washed most of the blood away, it was still a red, angry mess. The crusted black flesh where the original wound had been burned closed had been ripped open again—shredded, actually—and blood was seeping out. Instead of the small hole she'd hoped to see, the seared wound was nearly two inches long and jagged in shape, as if someone had just pulled the arrow out without thought or care.

Her eyes met his with accusation. "How could you let it get like this and say nothing?"

"It isn't that bad," he said defensively.

She gave him a glare, not bothering to deign that with a response, and went to work.

But even her anger couldn't completely mask the effects of touching him, and her hands shook as she started to apply the ointment.

Thinking to keep her mind on her task, she asked, "Who pulled the arrow out? I assume it wasn't Helen?"

He bit out a harsh laugh. "Hardly. She was furious that I didn't wait for her."

She should have known. "You should have. You made a mess of it."

He shrugged unapologetically. "There wasn't time. I was in the middle of a battle and it was getting in my way. It was deeper than I thought. It hit the bone and stopped."

"You could have bled to death."

One side of his mouth lifted. "It wasn't that bad. It looks

much worse now since it's been opened up a few more times."

"Did you ever think to let it heal?" He shrugged and started to say something, but she stopped him. "Let me guess: there wasn't time, and you were fighting."

He grinned and stopped her heart with a wink. "Smart lass."

Ignoring the hammering in her heart brought on by the rare display of boyishness, she rolled her eyes away and resumed her task. After finishing with the ointment, she started to wrap the clean cloth around his leg, but as soon as her hand dipped toward the inside of his leg, he grabbed her wrist. "I'll do it."

Their eyes met and the hammering started all over again—harder this time and more insistent. She couldn't escape from it. It was in her chest, in her ears, in her throat. It stole her breath.

She needed . . .

Wanted . . .

His eyes pulled her in. Or maybe it was his hand still holding her wrist? She didn't know, but one minute she was staring into his eyes and the next she was in his lap, her other hand was on his shoulder, her lips were on his, and she was warm again. Perhaps warmer than she'd ever been in her life.

It felt so good. *He* felt so good. The heat of his mouth on hers. The velvety softness of his lips. The minty spiciness of his breath, and the fresh scent of the water that still clung to his skin and hair.

She made a soft mewling sound, unconsciously opening her mouth, sinking deeper into the kiss.

He made a low growling sound, opening his mouth over hers, and for one moment she thought he meant to deepen the kiss. Her pulse jumped and warmth spread through her as she anticipated the deep thrust of his tongue claiming her, and the strength of his arms wrapping around her.

Kissing him was like nothing she'd ever imagined. She could get lost in the perfection of the sensations assailing her. It was as if she were floating. Sailing away on a sea of sensation. Soaring up the stairway to heaven. Being transported to a magical land filled with new and wonderful possibilities.

It was new. It was exciting. It was perfect.

And then it was over.

He made a harsh, strangled sound low in his throat, almost as if he were in pain, and thrust her harshly away.

For one moment, Ewen forgot himself. For one moment, her nearness and the feeling of her hands on him proved too much to resist. He could see it in her eyes, feel it in the flutter of her pulse under his hand as he held her wrist, and practically taste it on her lips.

She wanted him, and not all the land in Scotland or all the duty and loyalty in the world to the Stewarts and his clan could stop him from wanting her back. So when her mouth moved toward his, he didn't do anything to stop it. He let her fall, let her slide into his lap, and let their lips come together one more time.

He just hadn't anticipated the blow to the chest that crippled him with longing, the overwhelming desire that crashed over him, the mind-numbing pleasure, or the fierce and nearly irresistible urge to take her into his arms and make her his.

How could a kiss do this to him? How could the simple contact of her lips on his make him so weak? Strip him of almost everything he believed in?

Because it felt good. *Really* good. It felt like nothing he'd ever experienced before. It felt big and powerful and significant. It felt like nothing else mattered except for the two of them. And for that one precious moment in time it felt something else, too. It felt perfect.

It would have been perfect. He knew without a shadow

of a doubt that making love to her would be as close to heaven as he would ever hope to get on this side of the gates. But he had just enough conscious thought, just enough strength, left to put an end to it. Because no matter how desperately he wanted a few minutes of heaven with her, he'd be left with a lifetime of hell and recriminations.

He wasn't his father. He couldn't ignore his duty and responsibilities. Even for her.

But the look on her face tore his resolve to shreds. She looked stunned and dazed, and too damned aroused for any innocent maid.

Hell, he almost wished she'd go back to pretending to be a nun. At least then she'd attempted to hide her desire. But not anymore. It was there, naked, staring at him, daring him to take what she offered.

He clenched his fists so he would not reach for her again, and then turned away. Recalling the state of his clothing, he finished wrapping the clean cloth around the wound and pulled up his breeches. But the thin layers of cloth weren't enough. He'd need a suit of the English mail to arm himself against her—and that probably wouldn't be enough.

She was still standing there, watching him, when he was done. He wished he hadn't looked at her. The stunned look had turned to something else: hurt. And it knifed in his chest like a mangled blade.

"Is there . . . was there . . . is something wrong?"

He steeled himself against the urge to comfort her. To offer her reassurance. To tell her it was too damned perfect—that was the problem.

He couldn't meet her gaze when he said, "You shouldn't have kissed me."

"I didn't . . ." Her protest dropped off when he looked at her. It was nearly dawn, and there was enough sunlight to see the spots of dark pink on her cheeks. "You didn't seem to mind so much last time."

He detected the challenging glint in her eyes and knew he had better put a stop to this. "As I told you before, I am no longer interested."

The glint turned to a full spark. "What has changed? Other than the fact that you do not now think I am a nun."

He ignored the heavy sarcasm. "The fact that you are not a nun doesn't make any difference. You're the king's sister-in-law, and it's my duty to bring you back to Dunstaffnage—that's all."

"So it didn't mean anything to you? The fact that you are here doesn't mean anything?"

"I'm a warrior, Janet; I go where and do what I'm told. I'm here for one reason and one reason only: to do my job. Don't read anything more into it."

She sucked in her breath, her eyes widening. He'd never struck a woman in his life, but somehow it felt as if he'd just done so. The wave of remorse hit him hard. He didn't want to hurt her, damn it.

He didn't even want to have this conversation.

He shouldn't need to explain it to her. It was obvious. This wasn't how it was done. They weren't free to follow their feelings. They weren't free to marry. And she sure as hell wasn't free to do anything else. She should know that.

But if he expected her to run away, he was the one who should have known better. She was Janet of Mar. The sister-in-law of a king, and daughter of an earl. She wasn't sweet and docile but bold and confident. She didn't cower or run from danger, she met it head on with a knife in her hand.

How could she have possibly thought he would think her stupid? The accusation had taken him aback. Christ, if anything, the lass was too intelligent—and too headstrong and stubborn, for that matter. Bold, confident, opinionated— none of the things a woman should be. Which sure as hell didn't explain why he liked her so much.

He was trying to protect her from the horrible things

he'd seen, but she'd taken his concern as criticism, as a lack of intelligence, as *patronizing*. He cringed inwardly, realizing from her perspective that it probably was. But he hadn't meant it that way, damn it. What did she expect, that he would sit back and let her be captured by the English? Tortured? Killed? It was almost as if she wanted him to defer to her judgment. That was crazy, wasn't it?

Stewart was going to have a hell of a time stopping her. What if he couldn't?

The lass was too prone to getting into trouble, as her next step—toward him—proved. "I don't believe you."

His fists clenched. He wanted to pull her back into his arms so much, the physical restraint hurt.

Damn her. Couldn't she see that this was impossible?

He swore, taking a step back (not in retreat, damn it!), and raked his fingers through his hair. He wasn't good at this. He didn't like conflict. He just tried to keep his head down and do his job. But she wouldn't let him. "What the hell do you want from me, Janet?"

She blinked in surprise, staring at him. "I . . ."

She didn't know. She was acting on impulse and feeling, not on thought. He should relish the moment of putting lead on that silvery tongue of hers, but instead he felt sad. Unbearably sad. It was impossible, and when she thought about it, she would see it, too.

"I thought so," he said softly, before turning and walking away.

He hoped for the last time.

Thirteen

✣

It wasn't often that Janet's tongue tied, but Ewen's question had forced her to ask herself a question she hadn't wanted to think about: what did she want from him?

The truth was, she didn't know.

Marriage wasn't an option. Assuming Robert could be persuaded to marry her to an ordinary warrior—even one whom he seemed to value—that certainly wasn't what she wanted.

Was it?

Instead of sleeping as she should, she stared at the dark stone wall of the cave for most of the day, pondering that question. Janet had thought she had her life all planned out. She had thought she was meant to be alone. After the deaths of two fiancés, the loss of her family, and with what had happened with Cailin and her sister Mary, it seemed prudent to avoid entanglements. Frankly, she'd never wanted to marry and was content in the belief that God must agree with her. She would become a nun and continue on as she'd been doing: helping the king for as long as he needed her.

It was certainly preferable to being treated like a serf or a child. Not taken seriously. Coddled and "protected" until she couldn't breathe. Robert would do his best to protect her, but there was always a risk.

But Ewen confused her and made her wonder whether there was something more than the future she had planned.

A nun shouldn't think about—dream about—a man and his kiss for months. And a nun certainly shouldn't find her heart pounding in breathless anticipation for more.

Maybe that was it. Maybe "more" was what she wanted from him. Marriage might not hold any interest for her, but it was clear—at least with him—that what went along with it did.

She wanted him the way a woman wants a man, and no matter what he tried to tell her, he wanted her, too. What was holding him back?

She didn't know, but she intended to find out.

But good gracious, had she really kissed him? Her cheeks grew hot all over again. She supposed she might have. She'd thought he'd pulled her toward him, but maybe she'd just fallen into his lap? There was something different about Ewen. Something that made her act with an unusual boldness—even for her.

If she wanted "more," she suspected it was going to take a lot more boldness on her part to batter down that stone wall. Her mouth curved. As the daughter of an earl, and a woman who was ready to spend the rest of her life as a nun, she really shouldn't be looking forward to it as much as she was.

It seemed as though Janet had just closed her eyes when she was being jostled awake with her brother-in-law staring down at her. He was really quite handsome, in an almost dazzling, hurt-the-eyes way. Perhaps even more so than Mary's first husband had been, and the Earl of Atholl was said to have been one of the most handsome men in the kingdom. She hoped that Kenneth Sutherland was a better husband.

But Mary had always been more pragmatic than Janet. She'd never set unrealistic expectations, and she accepted her fate with more grace than Janet could ever manage.

"It's almost dark, my lady." Seeing that she was about to

correct him, he amended his speech. "Janet. We need to get back on the road."

She forced herself not to groan. The prospect of another long night on horseback, after a short and uncomfortable few hours of sleep, did not sound promising. But knowing she had no choice, she dragged herself out of her makeshift bed, which consisted of Eoin's borrowed plaid and the leather bag that held her clothes as a pillow, grateful once again for the lad's clothing. It really was much more comfortable and easier to move around without layers of cumbersome skirts in her way. Perhaps one day women would be able to wear such clothes without comment or sensation? Ha! And maybe someday men would fly like birds.

She looked around the cave. "Where is Ewen?" she asked her brother-in-law.

The last time she'd seen him was after he'd returned from the loch and exchanged a few words with Magnus. She'd assumed he'd returned while she was asleep.

"Making sure we aren't being followed."

"All day?"

Sir Kenneth shrugged. "He and MacLean had watch. You needn't worry. I'm sure he had a few hours of sleep."

Her cheeks heated. "I wasn't worried, I—"

A commotion outside the cave prevented her from finishing her thought. Ewen was back, and from the urgent tones of his hushed voice, and the clipped exchange with Magnus, she suspected something was wrong. "What is it?"

Her brother-in-law shook his head. "I don't know, but be ready."

He went to join the others who were gathered at the mouth of the cave, while Janet hastily gathered her belongings and tucked her braids back under her cap. She longed to run down to the river and wash, but instead she did the best she could with the water she had in a pouch, washing her face and using a cloth and a mixture of wine, salt, and mint to clean her teeth.

The men were still talking in hushed tones when she approached a few minutes later. She glanced beyond them into the dusky, tree-covered hillside. The first flakes of the long awaited snow had just started to fall.

Unconsciously, her gaze sought out Ewen's. As if feeling its weight, he glanced up. Her heart dropped. She knew before she asked, "What is it?"

She had new appreciation for his direct, matter-of-fact way of speaking when he didn't try to soften or hide the truth. "We are being followed."

She surprised him. Ewen expected tears or panic, or at least some other feminine sign of alarm, but Janet's expression barely changed; her only sign of concern was a slight widening of the eyes that someone who had been watching her very closely—as he'd been doing—would have picked up.

He might not like the idea of women in war, but he had to admit, her cool-under-pressure reaction was as impressive as any battle-hardened warrior's.

She didn't waste time with questions about his certainty. "How close are they?"

"About three miles east, heading this way. I saw them from the top of the mountain," he pointed to the hill above them, "so with the distance and obstacles, I can't be sure, but I'd guess there are at least forty men."

A slight paling of her cheeks told him that she fully understood the danger. "How are they tracking us?"

"They must have gotten lucky." Whether they were the same men as before or new, he didn't know. And he sure as hell wasn't going to ask them. They were the enemy; that was all that mattered.

Ewen had covered their tracks as best he could, but the horses, the speed at which they were traveling, the darkness, and the damp ground made it impossible to hide all traces. A good tracker—a *very* good tracker—who knew what he was looking for, and guessed their general direction, could find them. In the daylight, that is. "The darkness should slow them down."

He glanced at the softly fallen snow blanketing the ground in a thin layer of white. Instead of the beauty, all he could see was disaster. Why the hell couldn't it have snowed while they slept?

He didn't realize he'd frowned until she asked, "But?"

"But the snow will show our path like a map."

Again, she didn't blink, and his estimation of her went up another notch. "What is the plan?"

"We were just discussing that," Magnus interceded.

From the way she looked back and forth between the men, she seemed to have guessed that there was some disagreement. There was. MacLean wanted to head higher into the hills and lure them into a trap, while Ewen and Sutherland didn't want to fight a battle with Janet anywhere nearby. Even though they were ninety-nine percent certain they would win, there was always that one percent chance that something could go wrong.

Fortunately, MacKay agreed with them—to a point. "We'll head into the hills and try to lose them," he said.

The English didn't like venturing into the wild, for good reason. Bruce had taken control of the countryside, using the hills and forests to his advantage for his new pirate style of warfare.

"And if we don't?" she asked.

"We'll get rid of them another way," MacKay answered. They'd try the conservative choice first, but if they couldn't lose their pursuers, they would fight.

Sutherland smiled. "Never fear. One way or another we will get you back to Scotland and your sister safely."

Janet managed a smile at him, but her eyes were for Ewen. "I do not doubt that."

The mission. She knew he would see it done. The display

of faith should feel like a compliment, but instead it felt like a challenge: *Is that all this is?*

Damn it, that's all it could be.

Their eyes held for a tense heartbeat, but then he turned away, the need to leave as quickly as possible taking over.

"Make sure you don't leave anything behind," he warned her. The men didn't need to be told, but she probably wasn't used to taking such precautions. He didn't want to leave any sign of their presence behind or make it easy for anyone to track them.

Not a handful of minutes later, they were mounted and racing as fast as the storm and shrouded moonlight would allow, higher into the hills west of Ettrick. They didn't dare attempt to use a torch; it would be like a beacon blinking up the mountainside. Movement was easier to detect on hillsides as it was, and keeping themselves from being seen was going to be challenge enough. Fortunately, their progress need not be hampered by efforts to conceal their tracks. With the snow, Ewen didn't bother; it wasn't coming down heavily enough to cover them or any efforts to sweep them aside in time.

It was slow going. The horses, although good, all-purpose rouncies, were not the quick, agile, and sure-footed hobby horses preferred by Bruce for the so-called "pirate" warfare of the Highland Guard. But they were bound by what fresh horseflesh was available to them. In the hills, snow, and darkness, it was a constant battle to keep the horses at a quickened pace.

But the rouncies weren't the only problem. Though a capable rider, Janet did not have the experience and stamina of a warrior. MacKay, who had been only a passable horseman when they'd started, through years of experience and that stoic Highland grit and determination had forced an aptitude that nature had not intended. But Janet hadn't had that kind of experience, and it was clear that the long night of riding the day before had taken its toll.

As the night drew on, her struggle to keep her seat and control of the horse increased. A horse needed a strong, confident rider at a time like this, and Janet was faltering with every mile.

But she didn't complain. Even when her mount took a misstep that nearly toppled her off her saddle.

Ewen saw it happen in what seemed like half the normal beat of time. He was watching the steady up and down of her shadow, when all of a sudden the rhythm broke. She lurched to the side—his heart doing the same—and cried out. He saw her slipping, saw the distance to the ground, and realized how hard that ground would be. A couple of inches of snow would not cushion her bones from breaking.

He shot forward to try to catch her, wrenching his leg in the process. If he weren't so focused on her, the burning knife of pain might have concerned him.

Somehow she managed to stay seated.

He grabbed the reins, pulling her to a stop. "Are you all right?" It happened so quickly, he didn't have time to keep the emotion from his voice. She'd scared him, damn it. More than he wanted to think about.

Her face was lost in the shadows and the darkness, but he could see the movement of her nod. "I think so." Her voice shook a little, and he had to fight not to pull her into his arms. *Not yours.* "I'm sorry, I'll try to be more careful."

He could see her readjust the plaid she wore over her head like a hood, which had fallen off as she nearly fell.

His mouth hardened. "It isn't your fault. These are treacherous riding conditions for anyone."

MacKay hadn't seen what had happened, as he'd been riding ahead with Sutherland, but he must have guessed. "We're pushing you too hard."

"No, really, I can do this. I'll pay more attention."

MacKay and Ewen exchanged looks. Despite her protest, they both knew this wasn't working.

When they'd started out from the cave, they had about seventy miles or so to reach the *birlinn* in Ayr, much of that over rough countryside. They weren't using roads—not that many existed through the hills and forests of southwestern Scotland. In the past few hours, going as fast as they dared, they'd probably covered no more than ten miles. Even if they could outpace the English at night, the enemy would catch up with them in a few hours of daylight.

If the English were still following them, that is. And every instinct in his body clamored that they were. Ewen couldn't see them, but he could feel them pressing, a far more ominous force than the snowy darkness around them. The last time he'd felt like this was five years ago, when he and the rest of the Guard were fleeing west with Bruce across the Highlands and the king had been forced to seek refuge in the Isles. Then, as now, it felt like they were being hunted. Used to being the stalker and not the quarry, it was an odd sensation for him—and not one that he enjoyed.

They didn't have a choice. He wasn't going to take any chances with her. His first—his only—objective was to keep her safe. "We need to separate."

Janet's heart dropped. "Separate? We can't separate." What if the English caught up with them? The odds were horribly against them as it was.

It's because of me. Janet hated knowing that she was slowing them down. It wasn't often that she was forced to confront her weaknesses so openly, but she did not hide from them.

She might not have the physical strength or endurance that these men did, but she was every bit as determined and had no intention of giving up. "Please," she looked back and forth between the four shadows, wishing she could see their faces. "I can do this."

From the concern in Ewen's voice before, she thought he might have been worried about her, but there wasn't a hint of concern now when he snapped, "No, you can't. You aren't a strong enough rider."

She flinched. Trust Ewen not to cushion the blow. The worst part, of course, was that he was right.

Sir Kenneth attempted to ease the sting of Ewen's words. "What Lamont means to say—"

She cut him off. "It's all right. He's right. I'm not strong enough. But I don't see how that will change if we split up."

"They won't be following you," Ewen said with his typical lack of explanation. The get-the-job done soldier had taken over. He turned to Magnus. "Take the horses and head north toward Broad Law. With any luck Boyd and Seton will still be there with Douglas, and you can give our English pursuers a nice surprise. I'll head west with the lass and take cover in the forest. As soon as it is safe, I'll find some horses and catch up with you at Ayr."

At least he meant to go with her. She didn't know what she would have done if he'd tried to send her with someone else.

"I'm going with you," Sir Kenneth said. Ewen seemed poised to argue, when her brother-in-law added, "If this doesn't work, you'll need my sword." He paused. "She's my sister."

The show of family loyalty touched her, but she still didn't understand. "But how can you be sure they won't follow our tracks instead?"

She could almost hear Ewen smiling. "We won't have any."

She learned what he meant a few minutes later when she found herself tromping through the icy water of a small burn. They'd led the horses to the water, making it look like the group had stopped to rest, and then with Ewen in the lead and Sir Kenneth behind her, the three of them had taken off on foot through the water, leaving no tracks in the freshly fallen snow (which thankfully had abated), while Magnus and Eoin had ridden off with all five horses.

She was so cold, she almost missed the horses. Almost. Her feet might be freezing, but her aching muscles and sore backside welcomed the change of movement, especially as they seemed to be heading downhill.

Ewen was right; the English would never be able to follow their path now. But when she said so aloud, he corrected her. "Tracks can be followed in shallow water. Can you feel the stones shifting under your feet? A good tracker would see the signs. It isn't easy but if you know what to look for, it's possible. Of course, our pursuers won't know to look for it." He turned around. "Watch your step— there is a large rock ahead."

Janet took note of the shadow sticking out from the few inches of water and stepped around it, drawing her plaid in tight and making sure the bottom stayed clear of the water. She'd rolled up the edges of her leather breeches, trying to contain the discomfort to wet feet and hose.

She wouldn't ask how long. She wouldn't. Even if it killed her. No matter how cold and miserable, she wasn't going to complain. She might not be able to ride a horse as well as they could, but she could certainly walk for long distances. As a courier, she'd walked for miles. Although never this fast, and never through cold water in December. She suspected that if it weren't for her they would be running, even loaded up with weapons and carrying all the bags, including hers. She was determined to impress Ewen, even if it killed her.

"How do you know so much about tracking?" she asked.

"It's what I do."

Why did she feel that was an understatement? She suspected he was good at it—very good at it. "You really are one of Robert's phantoms, aren't you? Moving around like a ghost."

She said it as a jest, but both men fell oddly quiet. Her brother-in-law recovered first, chuckling from behind. "What do you think, Lamont? You want to be a phantom? Maybe we should ask the king if he needs any new *recruits* when we return?"

"I hear they'll take just about anyone nowadays," Ewen replied in way that made Janet feel that she was missing something.

"I must admit I was surprised to hear that Christina's brother is reputed to be one of the illustrious phantoms," she said. "I remember Lachlan MacRuairi as a mean, black-tempered brigand. He must have changed."

Neither man responded. Ewen stopped to help her over a branch that had fallen in the stream. Though he held her hand for only a moment, it was enough to make her heart quicken.

He dropped it the moment she was clear.

"Do either of you know him?" she asked, her voice a little breathless.

She was growing rather used to dead pauses. Ewen finally answered. "A bit."

"Has he changed?"

Another pause. "Nay. You'd do best to stay away from him."

Janet took another step in the frigid water, trying to ignore the soppy feeling in her boots, and frowned. "I won't be there long enough to see much of anyone beyond my sister. I must be back in Roxburgh as soon as possible. I need to be back in time for St. Drostan's."

Sir Kenneth started to say something, but Ewen cut him off sharply. "Assuming you can convince the king to let you return."

He was being far too complacent; she knew how he felt

about her part in this war. "Is there something you aren't telling me?"

"I thought you were sure that once you explained it to the king, he would agree?"

She bristled, knowing he was challenging her but unable to resist. "I am."

"Then you have nothing to worry about."

She pursed her mouth, thinking that it wasn't like him to capitulate so easily.

She was about to question him further, when he said, "Don't bring me into this. It isn't my fight. It's between you and Bruce."

He was right, not that she liked being reminded of how he wasn't interested. "How much longer of a delay do you think this will cost us?"

She couldn't be late. Something important was brewing; what if she missed it?

The dark shadow of his broad shoulders shrugged. "Once I am sure they have taken the bait and followed MacKay and MacLean, we will find some horses. Hopefully by morning, so not more than a half-day, I should think."

She heaved a sigh of relief.

They walked for hours, eventually reaching the end of the stream near a small village. By that time, her feet were no longer cold; they were too numb to feel anything.

Ewen was talking to Sir Kenneth. "There's an old Roman road that runs through the village. We can take that until we catch another river—"

He stopped suddenly, catching a glimpse of her shivering, and muttered an oath that she heard quite distinctly. "Why the hell didn't you tell me you were cold?"

After slogging through the water and snow for hours at a pace she would consider more running than walking, Janet wasn't in the mood for his overprotective male attitude. In spite of what he would like to think, she wasn't going to break like a poppet made out of porcelain. Nor was she going to feel blame for chattering teeth. Jerusalem's temples! Any *normal* person's teeth *should* be chattering.

"Of course, I'm cold," she snapped back. "I've just been walking through a freezing river. Anyone normal human being would feel a little chilly, but it isn't anything I can't handle or haven't done countless times before."

The sky had cleared and there was just enough moonlight to make out Ewen's slightly taken-aback expression.

Her brother by marriage gave a sharp laugh. "I daresay, I'm cold as well, my lady. Despite all appearances, Lamont is quite human, and I imagine he is as well, although I suspect he'd rather eat nails than admit it." He gave her a roguish wink. "Mary told me that you could stand toe-to-toe with anyone and weren't easily cowed. I can see she was right. My friend over there isn't exactly known for his tact—especially around ladies' delicate sensibilities."

"I noticed," Janet said dryly.

"Delicate?" Ewen scoffed under his breath. "The lass doesn't know the meaning of the word."

She knew he hadn't meant it as a compliment, but she took it as one. "Thank you."

He scowled at her with that same why-won't-you-fit-in-the-nice-box-that-you-are-supposed-to look that her brother Duncan used to have.

"Your sister will be happy to have you back," Sir Kenneth said. "She's missed you terribly."

Janet paled, the familiar anxiety gnawing at her. "I-I missed her as well."

"She never gave up looking for you. I think she must have visited every church and hospital between Berwick and Newcastle."

Janet looked at him, startled. "She did?"

He nodded. "Aye, she said she always sensed you were still alive. She said she would have known if you weren't."

Emotion suddenly gripped her throat. Was it true? Had Mary forgiven her? Had she not blamed her for what had happened?

Janet could only nod.

She glanced at Ewen. He was no longer scowling but watching her with a puzzled look on his face. Fearing she'd revealed more than she'd intended, she lifted her chin and said, "Are we going to keep moving?"

She thought he smiled, but no doubt it was a trick of the moonlight. With a bow, he said. "As you wish, my lady. Don't let me slow you down."

She couldn't believe it: he was teasing her. A soft glow spread inside her, warming some of the chill from her bones. "I won't," she teased back, sweeping past him in what she hoped was the right direction.

It didn't take long before they ran into the old road that he'd mentioned. It was odd to imagine Roman legionnaires marching here hundreds of years ago. Though they'd avoided most roads before now, with the number of travelers that used the road even in the snow, Ewen said it would be difficult for anyone still following them to identify their specific tracks.

Despite her previous protestations, by the time they turned off the road and navigated a very dark patch of forest to a small motte upon which sat the ruins of an old fort, she was exhausted and, as the grumbling coming from her stomach suggested, hungry. Needless to say, she didn't argue when Ewen said they would rest here for a while.

Taking shelter in what was left of the stone foundations of the fort, they sat on the rocky floor with their backs against the wall and ate a cold and rather lackluster meal of dried venison and oatcakes, washed down with a choice of whisky or ale—she chose the latter. Her feet were like ice as she took off her hose and boots to warm them by the small fire Ewen had made. It felt like heaven, and slowly some of the chill left her bones.

Ewen didn't sit for more than five minutes before he was up again.

Shaking her head, Janet watched his big, solid form disappear into the darkness. "Does he ever rest?" she said to her brother-in-law.

Sir Kenneth laughed. "Not much when he's on a mission. But don't worry, he's used to it. We all are. He'll get some rest when it is safe."

" 'We'?"

Something flickered in his gaze. "Bruce's army," he said quickly, but she had the feeling that he had been referring to something else.

They were silent for a while, the sounds of the night enveloping them. It was so quiet. Almost eerily so. "Do you think we are safe?"

"Aye, lass. Lamont's the best. It would take more than luck for the English to find us now."

"And Magnus and Eoin?"

He laughed. "Don't worry about them. They can take care of themselves. MacLean probably already has picked out the perfect place for a surprise attack. The English don't stand a chance."

"But forty against two?"

"Hopefully they caught up with Douglas—Sir James," he clarified. But he needn't have. The Black Douglas was well known along the Borders. "But even if they didn't, forty Englishmen aren't enough for two Highlanders."

Janet dismissed his boasting as typical Highland hyperbole. It had to be an exaggeration, didn't it? Then why did he seem genuinely unworried?

Ewen returned a few minutes later, and she heaved a sigh of relief.

"I think they took the bait," he said. "We can rest here

for a few hours. In the morning, I will see about finding some horses in the village."

She nodded and laid her head back against the wall, closing her eyes. The difficulty of the past few days seemed to catch up with her all at once. She didn't notice the hard ground, the stony pillow, or the cold, and didn't even bother to lie down, all she could think about was sleep.

Feeling the weight of his gaze on her, her eyes flickered open just before she was about to doze off. Something fierce and poignant passed between them. Something undeniable. Something that made her feel safe. "Sleep," he said.

And for once in her life, Janet obeyed without argument.

She woke with a start. With a premonition. With a feeling of dread. It was almost dawn, and a quick glance around told her that once again, Ewen was gone. Sir Kenneth had been asleep, but he stirred at her movement.

"What is it?"

Janet shook her head. "I don't know." She squeezed her plaid in tight, as if it would protect her in his absence. But then she heard a sound. A distant sharp, keening howl. "What is that? A wolf?"

Like a wraith summoned by her voice, Ewen appeared in the doorway. "It's not a wolf, it's a hound. We need to move . . . *now*."

Fourteen

❧

Dogs, damn it! How in the hell had they caught their scent?

Ewen didn't have time to think about it. They needed to lose themselves in the forests and hills of Lowther before the English caught up with them. If he could hear the dogs, they had to be close.

The Highland Guard used the countryside as a weapon. The more dense the forest, the steeper and more unfriendly the terrain, the more they could take away the English advantage—both in number and their superior weaponry. The English heavy armor and horses were a liability in the wild, and Bruce had learned to use that to his benefit.

Ewen didn't waste time trying to cover signs of their presence, breaking camp as soon as they could gather their belongings. The old motte and fort had provided shelter, but it would provide little defense. Worse, Janet would be right in the middle of it.

She made him feel vulnerable in a way that he'd never felt before. *Bàs roimh Gèill.* Death before surrender, the motto of the Highland Guard. He'd never thought he would question it. But he would surrender a thousand times before he let anything happen to her.

He didn't know what that meant, but he knew it was significant. In the heat of danger, in the face of an attack, he wasn't thinking about Bruce, Stewart, an unfinished castle or his responsibility to his clan, he was thinking about her—her safety was all that mattered, and it wasn't just because of the mission.

Steeling himself, he turned to face her. But nothing could have prepared him for the fist that wrapped around his heart and tugged when their eyes met. He could see the fear, but also the trust that no matter how desperate it might seem, he would protect her. It moved him. Humbled him. Nearly brought him to his knees with the force of an emotion he'd never felt before. God, he—

He didn't finish the thought.

But nothing could stop him from reaching out to cup her face. She nuzzled her cheek into the leather of his gauntleted hand, burrowing right into his heart.

"We have to run," he said, his voice unrecognizably tender.

She nodded. "I can do this."

He believed her. She was strong and determined. And for the first time, he realized that he wouldn't want it any other way. He'd never thought of a woman as anything more than a bed partner or the keeper of the home and hearth. A delicate, fragile creature whom it was his job to protect. A necessity, but never someone to stand by his side, to talk to and argue with—not to mention drive him crazy. But Janet made him want all those things.

He swept his thumb over her mouth tenderly. "Don't stop, no matter what you hear. I will find you."

The small smile that curved her mouth stole his breath. "I know."

And so they ran. Ran as fast as he could push her into the snow-covered moors and mist-shrouded hilltops that loomed in the distance. Bruce's army had taken refuge in them many times before, but it would be too much to expect to find anyone this near to the village. It was up to him and Sutherland to get them out of this. They wouldn't be able to outrun their pursuers, not on foot, with dogs and horses chasing them.

They didn't have as much time as he'd hoped. The shadow of the fort behind him in the breaking dawn had yet to fade when he caught the first glimpse of horses.

"The river!" he shouted over his shoulder to Janet. "A few hundred feet ahead through the trees. Follow it until you reach the edge of the tree line and then into the hills. Remember what I said. Don't stop. No matter what you hear."

Her face was flushed from the exertion of running, but he thought she paled. "Ewen, I—"

He didn't let her finish. "Go!"

He couldn't hear it. Not now. He waited until she'd disappeared into the forest before turning to Sutherland. But the newest member of the Highland Guard had already anticipated him. "The pass?"

Ewen nodded. The deep, narrow valley of the glen would slow the horses down and give him and Sutherland time to get into position.

But there wasn't time. The enemy was already breathing down his neck. He turned and drew his sword right as the first mailed arm came swinging down toward him. He blocked the blow of the poleaxe with a quick twist of his sword that send the Englishman's weapon flying from his hands. A moment later, Ewen's sword struck down hard on the rider's leg, nearly severing it.

He heard the man's startled cry before he toppled to the ground, his life's blood pouring from him. A quick glance told Ewen what he needed to know: a dozen men-at-arms, one knight, de Beaumont's arms, two dogs barking wildly.

No sooner had he apprised himself of the situation than the next rider was on him. He felt a roar of energy surge through his blood as the rush of battle crashed over him. He held his sword in two hands over his head and brought it down against the other man's blade with enough force to knock him from his saddle.

One by one he and Sutherland struck down the enemy,

working in tandem as they moved the attacking English-men into position in the narrow pass.

Just like that, the battle shifted. The horses couldn't ma-neuver. Instead of the aggressors, the English knight and his men became like herring trapped in a barrel. With Ewen on one side and Sutherland on the other, there was nowhere for them to go. They were forced to abandon their horses or die.

They died anyway.

The loud clash of battle began to dull as the English fell beneath their swords. The barking had stopped. One of the dogs appeared to have been trampled by the fleeing horses, and the other . . .

Ewen swore, shaking off some of the sweat that had gathered beneath his helm to clear his vision. Where was the other dog?

While fending off blows, he scanned the area around them, grazing over the bodies of the men and horses that had fallen alongside them. No second dog.

A chill raced through his blood as he realized there was a man missing as well.

There were still four soldiers left. Three of them had converged on Sutherland, hoping to overpower him, while the other tried to keep Ewen from helping him. Sutherland didn't need help. And neither did Ewen. He exchanged blows with the man-at-arms, a thick-necked, barrel-chested brute, who managed to land a solid blow of his sword on Ewen's shoulder before the edge of Ewen's blade could meet his neck.

Sutherland had realized what had happened. "Go!" he shouted between swings of his sword. "I'll finish them off."

Ewen didn't hesitate. Jumping on one of the remaining horses, he tore off in the direction he'd told Janet to run.

He leaned down low over the courser's neck to avoid the branches and limbs that splayed out in all directions of the forest that circled the base of the hills, and prayed. Prayed he'd counted wrong. Prayed that he reached her in time.

But a moment later he heard a piercing sound that would haunt him for the rest of his life. A shrill, terror-filled scream tore through the misty dawn air, stopping his heart and catapulting him forward into the dark, unfamiliar abyss of fear.

Janet had every intention of following his orders. But when the piercing clash of metal on metal shattered through the air, her head instinctively turned at the sound.

She stopped to look for only a minute, but the sight that had met her eyes was not one she would soon forget. It was battle, in all of its gruesome, horrifying chaos. Twice before she'd seen the violence of warfare—the night at the bridge when she'd tried to rescue her sister and the day in the forest with Marguerite when she'd first met Ewen—but the fierceness, the brutality of it, startled her anew. The sight of swords swirling, dirt flying, blood spurting in a gnarling mass of men and beast struck terror in her heart. As did the sounds. The very loudness of it. The violent clamor of steel and death.

Like a steel-clad plague of locusts, the English swarmed the two Highlanders. By all rights it should have been a slaughter. She couldn't breathe, fearing Ewen would be cut down with the first stroke. But she'd forgotten, or told herself she must have exaggerated, his skill in her mind. The extraordinary strength and deadly intent. The brutally cold purpose by which he went about his task. Sir Kenneth fought the same way, not like a knight but like a barbarian. It wasn't too hard to imagine them striking terror across the seas in a Viking longship.

The two Highlanders might be overmatched in number, but they were far superior in skill. In the first shadowed blink of daylight, in the midst of that chaos and horror, with their blackened helms and dark-colored plaids flaring like ghostly robes, they looked like deadly, menacing beings from another world.

They looked like . . . *phantoms*.

The realization stunned her for a moment, but then, remembering Ewen's admonition, she turned and ran. Ran until her legs ached and her lungs felt as if they would explode, through the trees and underbrush, along the rocky riverbank as it wound through the forest.

She'd gone no more than a mile when she heard barking behind her. Fear tightened her already straining chest. She looked over her shoulder, saw the hound racing up behind her, and against every instinct in her body that screamed danger—*run!*—she forced herself to slow.

The dog was trained to hunt. To pursue. It would not stop, and she could not outrun it.

She would not be its prey. With her hand on the hilt of her blade, she turned to face it. Half-expecting it to leap on her, she was surprised when it stopped about ten feet away. They stared at one another in a silent face-off. Beast and man. Or in this case, woman.

Animals had always liked her. She tried to remember that as she stood perfectly still, except for the heavy rise of her chest sucking in air.

The deerhound was big, its gray head at about the level of her waist. Its mouth was pulled back, letting her see every one of its impressively long teeth, but its black eyes were more curious than angry. Could a dog be curious?

Its shaggy fur was dirty and matted, and it looked to be in need of a good bath, but it was a nice-looking animal, with the long, lean lines of a hunter, if perhaps on the skinny side.

With the hand that was not holding the hilt of her blade, she reached into the leather purse at her waist and dug out a piece of dried beef. Cautiously, she held it out, murmuring soothing sounds as the dog eyed her speculatively. Her heart hammered as the dog slowly made its way over to her. Not wanting to tempt fate, she put the beef down on the ground. The dog pounced on it. Devouring it in seconds, it looked up at her again, giving a little bark of encouragement.

In spite of the circumstances, she laughed. It was a cute little devil, once you looked past the size and teeth.

Tentatively, she held out her hand, letting the dog sniff her, murmuring her apologies. "I'm sorry, that's all I have."

It barked again, and then panted expectantly, sitting at her feet. When she reached out to pet its head, it crooned.

Janet laughed. "Why, you're not so terrifying—"

Suddenly, a horse and rider broke through the trees. A startled gasp stuck in her throat, the gleam of mail identifying him as the enemy. The man reached for her, obviously intending to pull her onto his horse, when suddenly the dog leapt, its teeth clamping onto the mail-clad arm, trying to drag him off. Somehow dog and beast became tangled under the back hooves of the horse, causing the horse to pitch forward.

She heard a hideous snap and the pained howl of the dog. She turned away quickly, but instantly realized what had happened: the dog had been crushed under the horse, the horse had broken its leg, and the rider . . . the rider had been tossed off but was slowly coming to his feet. Swearing, he pulled out his sword and swung it down on the tangled mess of dog and horse.

She screamed and turned away.

"Damned stupid cur," he growled. With one swipe, the pained crying of the dog stopped. He followed it with a second, and the anxious rustling of the horse as it tried to stand stopped.

Knowing he would come after her next, she tried to run, screaming again, when his steely hand caught hold of her arm.

He spun her around, his sword lifted above his head.

"Where do you think you are going, you stupid rebel bitch—"

Janet didn't think, she reacted. She was fortunate he'd grabbed her by her left arm, because it was the right she needed to jerk the blade from its scabbard and thrust it up with all her might between his legs, hoping to find the gap in the mail.

Just as her knife plunged, she heard a horrifying thump. His eyes widened. His hand tightened on her arm, and then released as he fell to her feet, a spear sticking through his neck.

Ewen had never experienced that kind of rage. The sight of Janet clasped in the rough, steely hold of the knight did something to him. She looked like a flower about to be crushed in a steely vise, her delicate bones no match for the strength of the big, mail-clad warrior and the sword that could at any moment take her head.

A black rage came over him. Bloodlust. The urge to kill. His vision narrowed as if he were peering through a dark tunnel with one objective in sight. He adjusted the spear in his hand. He didn't let himself think that if he missed, she would die. He didn't have time.

Forty, thirty, twenty feet away . . . he threw with all his might.

The spear ripped through the air with a whiz, piercing the mail of the knight's coif as if it were butter.

Ewen hit the ground the same moment the soldier did. Janet turned, saw him, and with a soft cry that tore through his heart, raced into his arms.

He held her close as she buried her head against his chest, savoring every bloody sensation that came over him. *She's safe,* he told himself over and over. *Safe.* But his damned heart wouldn't stop pounding.

The emotions clamoring inside him were like nothing he'd ever experienced, and it took him a while to get them under enough control for him to speak. "Are you all right?"

She nodded against his chest, but he needed to see for himself. Carefully he tipped her chin back and looked into wide, tear-filled eyes. The baby-soft skin under his fingertips was so pale it seemed almost translucent. "I was so scared. The dog . . ." She looked up at him, stricken. "It was horrible."

A wave of tenderness rose inside him with chest-crushing intensity. "It's over, sweetheart. It's over."

She nodded obediently—he doubted she'd done that since she was a child, and probably not even then—but the horror of the attack was obviously still weighing on her. She trembled against him, her slender shoulders shaking, and a fierce wave of protectiveness surged over him. It took everything he had not to put his mouth on hers and kiss her until they both forgot.

But he didn't. The danger was over, and with its absence came the reminder of his duty.

Slowly, reluctantly, he let her go.

She blinked up at him, at first surprised, and then with a wounded look that tore at him mercilessly.

He cursed the unfairness of it. The duties, the loyalties, the responsibilities that made it—*them*—impossible.

Suddenly, she gasped, her gaze flying to his arm. "You're hurt!"

He glanced down, realizing the Englishman's sword had sliced through his *cotun* and blood was seeping out. Truth be told, he didn't feel it. Although he couldn't say the same about his leg, which throbbed and burned like someone had thrown whisky on it and then lit it on fire. "I'm fine. It's only a scratch."

She screwed up her mouth in the familiar purse. Who knew annoyed could look so sweet?

"Your arm could be hanging by a string and you would say you were fine."

One corner of his mouth lifted in a half-smile. She was probably right.

"You warriors are all alike—" She stopped and looked around anxiously. "Where is Sir Kenneth?"

"Don't worry. He was finishing up when I came after you. He should be along any minute."

"I can't believe—I wouldn't have believed it if I hadn't seen it for myself. Two men against so many." Her voice held the unmistakable reverence of awe. But he couldn't enjoy it. She was treading too close. Somehow he knew what she was going to say even before her eyes locked on his. "You are part of it, aren't you? You are one of Bruce's phantoms?"

God's blood, the lass courted trouble like a lovesick troubadour! She'd seen too much, and now she was making guesses—dangerous guesses that could put them all at risk. Wasn't what she was doing dangerous enough? Knowledge—even suspicions—like that would have half the English army after her. Identifying and capturing the members of Bruce's secret army was top on the list of the English command.

His expression gave no hint of the storm of emotions her question had unleashed inside him. He feigned unconcerned amusement. "Didn't your parents tell you there is no such thing as ghosts?"

She lifted her chin. "Do you deny being part of the secret army that has wreaked havoc with the English troops—"

He cut her off with an oath, taking her by the arm. "We need to go."

"You didn't answer my question."

But barely had the words left her mouth when she heard it, too. The bark of a dog, and not far behind it, the sound of horses. Her eyes widened, and she dug her heels into the ground, preventing him from pulling her toward the horse. "But what about Sir Kenneth? Don't we need to wait for him?"

His mouth fell in a grim line. "He'll find us."

He hoped. But the sound of approaching horsemen did not bode well. He cursed again—silently, not wanting to add to her concern. But the mission that had started out bad only seemed to be getting worse.

He was about to help her up on the horse, when she pulled away again. "Wait! I forgot my dagger."

Realizing she must have used it to try to defend herself, he stopped her from going after it. "I'll get it."

He approached the body of the dead knight. It didn't take him long to locate the knife.

Well, I'll be damned. If his spear hadn't ended the bloody Englishman's life, her blade, which was wedged deeply in his leg, would have.

He felt an unmistakable swell of pride. The lass was a fighter. His first impression all those months ago of a Valkyrie had not been far off.

Wiping the blood from the blade on his chausses, which were already splattered with any manner of deathly grime, he handed it back to her.

She looked up at him hesitantly. "Did I . . ."

He knew what she was asking. "You defended yourself well, lass. You would have hobbled him for life," he lied.

She sighed, looking visibly relieved. "I wasn't sure."

He had enough death on his soul for both of them. He could protect her from that at least.

Another bark—this one discernibly closer—put an end to the brief delay.

Helping her onto the horse, he mounted behind her and they were off, riding hell-bent for leather along the river-bank toward the hills. They would ride the horse as long as they could—he hoped long enough to break the scent and make it more difficult to follow them. One of the best ways to do that was with another animal. Water would also help. Whenever it was shallow enough to do so, he steered the horse into the river.

They continued at that frantic pace for a few miles, until the sounds of their pursuers grew fainter and fainter, eventually disappearing altogether.

He heaved a sigh of relief. They'd lost them for now, and none too soon. He was forced to slow their pace considerably, as the ground started to rise and the forest and river valley gave way to heather-covered hillsides that beckoned to him like the first sight of land after days at sea. Home. Refuge. Safety.

Though dawn had broken some time ago, a thick blanket of wintry mist hid the barren mountaintops from view. Not only did they look ominous and haunting, they would also provide plenty of cover for them to disappear. Even if the English picked up their trail again, they would think twice about following them into such forbidding terrain.

But he wasn't going to take any chances. Knowing the horse would only hinder them from this point, when he came to a small bridge over the river, he told Janet to wait while he rode it across. Dismounting, he hit the horse on the rump and watched it gallop down the narrow path. With any luck it would do so for some time. Careful to hide his tracks, he retraced his steps to where Janet stood watching him.

She stared down at the dark river with a wrinkled nose. "I assume my feet are going to be getting wet again?"

He grinned at her expression. "Afraid so."

Instructing her to step on rocks or harder ground whenever she could, he helped her down the riverbank and into the water. Unfortunately, unlike the last river, the banks were steep, and the water swirled nearly up to her knees.

They followed the river up the hill until the ground grew too steep and the water became falls. Trudging up the bank, he motioned to a large rock. "We can rest here for a while."

Not needing any more encouragement, she collapsed. Shrugging off the bags he carried, he used one of them as a seat and joined her. Fortunately, along with the bags of their belongings, he was also carrying the food. He tried not to think about Sutherland, telling himself their new recruit could take care of himself. But the attack shouldn't have happened. It was Ewen's job to make sure it didn't. If he felt responsible, it was because he *was* responsible. He'd failed, damn it, and the failure didn't sit well with him.

What had gone wrong? How in the hell had the dogs picked up their scent?

Apparently her thoughts were running in the same direction as his. "Do you think we've lost them?"

"For now," he said. "With the horses and the river, the dogs will have trouble following the scent."

"How did they pick it up in the first place?"

"I don't know. I made damned sure we didn't leave anything—"

He stopped, his gaze catching on a shimmering coil of golden hair that had slipped from its braid. Even in the mist, her golden head shone bright. Her *bare* golden head.

His mouth fell in a hard line, as the explanation for what had happened became clear. He swore. "Where is your cap?"

Fifteen

❧

Janet's hand went to her head reflexively. She was surprised to find smooth strands of hair under her palm instead of wool. "Oh, I didn't realize." She thought back. "It must have fallen off last night, when I slipped from the horse."

He swore again, which was redundant in her opinion, as the look on his face said it all. He was furious. Beyond furious, actually. Irate. Stormy. The forty-days-and-forty-nights kind of stormy.

"That must be how they are tracking us."

"I'm sorry, I didn't realize—"

He stood and hauled her to her feet. She was half-surprised that he didn't take her by the ear like a naughty pup. "Damn it, I told you we needed to be careful. No wonder they were able to follow us so quickly. You led them right to us."

He didn't need to say it; she knew what he was thinking. *This is why a woman doesn't belong here. A woman has no business in war. Go back to your nice little box and stay out of it.*

She'd wanted so much to impress him, to show him that she could help as much as he could—in a different way, perhaps, but in a manner that was also valuable. Instead she'd proved his point. How could she expect him to see her a certain way if she made silly mistakes?

Janet wanted to argue with him. Her instinct was to defend herself, to try to talk her way out of it. But for once she didn't have an excuse or an explanation. He wasn't being unfair, he was only speaking the truth—even if most people wouldn't have spoken it so plainly. But avoiding hurt feelings wasn't Ewen's forte. Nay, he was honest and straightforward to a fault.

Usually she didn't mind. But she was scared and tired, having slept only a few hours in the last couple of days, and feeling unusually vulnerable after what had happened earlier. They'd shared something in the forest: an honesty of emotion that she wasn't going to let him deny. She'd been so sure he was going to kiss her. So certain that he'd put aside whatever reservations he had. But he'd turned away from her again. And now . . .

Her hands twisted, a sick feeling growing in her stomach. "It was an innocent mistake."

"A mistake that could have gotten us all killed."

She flinched as much from the steely hardness in his gaze as from the verbal lash that went along with it. "I've said I'm sorry; I don't know what else I can do."

"Nothing. But next time I tell you something, try to follow orders."

Janet had reached the limits of her passive acceptance of guilt. "I am not one of your men you can order about."

"That is painfully clear. My men are much better disciplined."

Now he wasn't the only one who'd lost his temper; hers sparked like wildfire. Her twisting hands fisted at her side. "Fine. Women have no place on the battlefield—is that what you want me to say?"

His eyes flashed. He leaned closer to her and growled, "It's a bloody good start."

Janet wanted to stomp her foot in outrage. But as that would no doubt give him more fodder for treating her like a bairn, she tossed her head with a loud harrumph.

He was the most infuriating, patronizing, brutish, and blastedly *unreasonable* man she'd ever met!

And yet, even as he stood here taking her to task—which unfortunately in this case was deserved—a silly part of her still hoped that he would take her in his arms and tell her it was all right. Comfort her, as he'd done before. For such a formidably built man, he'd been surprisingly gentle.

But comfort was the last thing on his mind. "You'll have to take off your clothes."

She drew back. "My clothes?"

"Aye, all of them. And get in the river. You reek of bluebells; scrub every last bit of it from your hair and skin. We need to make sure they've lost the scent."

"But . . ." She looked at the small pool below the falls. Even from here it looked freezing. And bluebells didn't reek.

He clenched his jaw as if fighting for patience. "Damn it, can you just follow directions for once?"

Their eyes locked in a silent battle of wills. She'd had just about enough of his brusque commands. A secret smile crept up her lips, as the devil inside her reared its ugly head.

I can follow directions, all right. "As you wish."

She let the plaid drop from her shoulders and fall into a dark puddle at her feet.

He blinked.

Lifting a distinctly challenging brow, she unfastened her doublet, which joined the plaid at her feet a moment later.

He managed to find his voice by the time she'd kicked off her boots and started to shimmy the leather breeches over her hips.

"What are you doing?" he said—rather inanely, in her opinion.

She smiled, removing her hose. "Following orders." She gazed up at him innocently. "Do you need some water?"

"Water? No, why?"

"Your throat sounds a little dry."

And with that, she lifted the shirt over her head.

It must have been the battle. Or perhaps the physical exhaustion of the past few days. But as Ewen stood there, watching her, his limbs turned to lead. He couldn't move. He didn't have the strength to stop her.

Oh God, stop her.

But before some manner of self-preservation could take hold, her shirt landed on the ground.

The world stopped. His heart forgot to beat. His mouth was dry all right. Burning dry. *Searing* dry. His throat was as parched as the deserts of Outremer, and he knew there wasn't enough water in the oceans of Christendom to quench the thirst he had for her.

She was perfect. Long of limb, slender and curved in all the right places, with miles and miles of flawless, creamy skin. The firm, round breasts that had been emblazoned on his memory were even more spectacular than he'd remembered, the nipples smaller, tighter, and darker pink, and the soft, feminine place between her legs . . .

Sweet God in heaven! He groaned. Desire fisted in his groin, hot and aching, pulling and squeezing with need.

Her voice brought him back. "Is this what you wanted?"

The husky challenge of her voice sent a fireball of lust racing down his spine. It gathered at the base, pulsing—nay, quaking—with need.

He looked into her eyes.

Damn her! The lass didn't have a weak or vulnerable bone in her body. Even naked as the day God made her, she was bold and challenging and strong.

Strong enough to break him.

In the spate of two long heartbeats, he had her in his arms, her velvety-soft skin plastered against him.

She gasped at the suddenness of his movement but didn't

resist. Nay, she'd asked for this, and by all that was holy, she would get it.

For one fraction of a heartbeat, Janet felt a flicker of fear and wondered whether she'd pushed him too far. But then she was in his arms, and she knew he would never hurt her. Even out of control, Ewen held her with a gentleness that was belied by the strong, hard-as-a-rock body against her.

The leather and steel of his armor against her naked flesh was a shock, albeit not an unpleasant one. There was something oddly sensual about having all that warm leather and cool metal pressed against her. Or maybe it was just that she'd been so cold before, the heat radiating from his body made any discomfort seem small.

She tilted her head back, looking into his eyes.

The fierceness of his expression sent a thrill shooting through her veins.

"Damn you," he said angrily, his last gasp of protest before surrender.

All thoughts of gentleness were forgotten as his mouth covered hers. He kissed her roughly, his lips moving over hers with a fierce possessiveness that made her gasp. And moan. More than once. Especially when he started to use his tongue. The deep, penetrating strokes definitely elicited lots of moans from her. Low, urgent moans that seemed to start somewhere deep inside—right about the place she could feel him hard against her.

She shuddered, her body responding to the primitive evidence of his desire. She was achingly aware of every thick inch of that evidence.

He pulled her in closer, bending her back, going deeper and deeper. She had to fight to keep up with him, her innocence no match for the raw onslaught of passion.

She knew he was punishing her for forcing him to this, trying to frighten her off with the intensity of his desire.

But Janet met him stroke for stroke. She might be an innocent maid, but the instincts he roused in her were those of a wanton.

She wanted this. Every bit as much as he did, and the raw sensuality of his passion only fired her own.

Aye, she was hot, her skin almost feverish. She seemed to be melting, dissolving into a pool of molten heat.

He'd removed his gauntlets and the feel of his big, callused hands roaming over her bare skin—stroking, caressing, squeezing, leaving no inch untouched—only increased that heat and elicited far more of those little moans.

"God, you feel so good. Your skin is so soft." The warmth of his breath tickled her ear, but it was his words that made her shudder. "I want to touch you all over. Every inch of you, *mo chroí*."

"My heart." The tender endearment made her chest squeeze. Janet couldn't believe it was Ewen speaking to her like this. The silky-smooth words couldn't have been more at odds with the brusque warrior who spoke without thought or care of social graces. It was a heady combination, the fierce, rough passion mixed with the soft, sensual words.

His hands possessed her, sliding down her back, over her bottom, lifting her a little harder against him, rocking . . .

Sweet Mother! She might have jumped, her entire body sparking with an energy not unlike bottled lightning. She forgot to breathe, her body clenched and waiting.

For what?

"God, you're killing me."

Normally, she wouldn't think that was such a good thing, but the way he said it made her think it might be.

His mouth moved down and over her neck hungrily, setting her skin ablaze in its path.

Her heart was pounding. Her knees were wobbling. And the place between her legs . . .

A fresh surge of heat rose to her cheeks. She didn't even want to think about what was happening there. She was hot and achy and . . . wet, with strange little flickers—

Oh! He rocked against her again and those strange little flickers started to pulse. She wanted him there. Right there. The thick column of steel wedged high and tight, riding against her.

"Sweet Jesus, you're driving me wild." His voice was ragged and tight with restraint.

Janet knew the feeling.

"I want to be inside you," he whispered in her ear.

She almost cried out with disappointment when he released his hold on her bottom and the sweet pressure went away. But her disappointment lasted only a moment. His hand skimmed over her stomach to cover a breast.

"So soft," he groaned, squeezing, cupping her gently in his hand. "Your breasts are incredible. I've dreamed of doing this since the first moment I saw you."

He had?

Janet was glad he didn't seem to expect a response, as she was having a difficult enough time breathing. The sensations his hands wreaked on her body were commanding all her attention. Instinctively she arched into his hand, having discovered rather quickly that pressure increased the sensations.

But she hadn't anticipated the feeling of his fingers on her nipple. The rough pad of his thumb over the sensitive, throbbing peak nearly sent her jumping out of her skin again, as another one of those lightning rods sent a flash of energy shooting through what seemed to be every nerve-ending in her body.

He made a harsh sound before his mouth covered hers again.

She sensed he'd reached the end of his rope. His kiss was no longer punishing, but determined. Every stroke of his tongue, every touch of his hands on her body, seemed calculated to increase her passion, to bring her closer and closer to something that hovered just out of her reach.

She shivered with anticipation.

He lifted his head. "Are you cold?"

Aroused beyond measure. She shook her head, managing a breathy, "Hot."

"Good." His eyes darkened. "You're about to be even hotter."

She shuddered again, hearing the sensual promise in his raspy voice.

He was as good as his word. A moment later when his mouth found her breast, she thought she'd fallen to the fiery bowels of hell, for surely it must be a sin to feel this good.

She cried out as his tongue circled her nipple and he began to suck. Gently at first, and then a little harder, as she arched deeper into his mouth.

The heat. The scrape of his chin. The silky brush of his hair on her skin.

It was too much.

It wasn't enough.

She started to squirm in frustration, and he finally gave her the relief she unknowingly sought.

His tongue laved and flicked against her nipple at the same time that his fingers brushed between the juncture of her thighs.

She stilled, instinct telling her what he was about to do. She had a moment of panic. Twenty-seven years of maidenhood, of holding on to her chastity like a holy relic, was not relinquished without a small pang of uncertainty. Was this wrong?

Almost as if he'd heard her unspoken question, he lifted his head. Their eyes met, and any uncertainty she had faded in the intensity of emotion she saw mirrored in his gaze.

And then he touched her. *There*. In the place she'd unknowingly reserved for him for this moment.

Pleasure bloomed from deep inside her like a flower unfurling its velvety petals in the sun, as he held her gaze and stroked her. It was magical. Beautiful. The most natural, perfect thing in the world. How could it be wrong?

The sensations were building faster now, racing at a frantic pace toward a determinable end. And moments later when she looked into his eyes, as he stroked her to the very peak of passion, when her breath caught, her body clenched, and warmth spread over every inch of her, shattering into a blinding light, Janet knew something else: she was very glad she wasn't a nun.

Ewen was lost the moment he looked into her eyes. Seeing her break apart, watching the passion spread over her face in sensual euphoria, swollen lips parted, cheeks flushed and eyes soft with pleasure, unleashed something inside him that could not be held back.

Lust surged through him, unlike any he'd ever experienced. It was more powerful. More intense. Deeper. It filled not just his cock—which was as hard as a pillar of marble—but his bones, his blood, every inch of his body, including a part of him that he wished it didn't: his heart.

His need for her was elemental. Like water and food, and the air he breathed, he had to have her.

The last ebb of her release had yet to fade before he had her on the ground, the discarded plaid underneath her.

He fumbled with his braies. *Next time,* he swore. Next time he would make it perfect. This time he'd be lucky if he lasted a few minutes.

He was out of control, past the point of reason, his body moving on its own command. He didn't want to let himself think. Blood pounded through his body, in his head. Sweat gathered on his brow. He'd never wanted anything so intensely in his life.

Blissfully cold air hit his hot skin as he released himself from the painfully binding braies. He moved himself into position, levering his body over hers, inches—seconds—from sweet relief.

He was hard as a spike, red and throbbing. Painfully throbbing. I-need-to-come-right-now throbbing. A drop escaped in wicked anticipation.

His teeth clenched. A few more seconds . . .

He couldn't wait for that first exquisite moment of contact, when the hot, sensitive tip would meet warm, feminine dampness. He could almost feel her tight and warm around him, a velvety tight glove, gripping . . . squeezing . . . milking. His buttocks clenched.

Her eyes fluttered open. The smile that spread across her face squeezed his chest like a vise, cutting off his already labored breathing. So beautiful . . .

"That was wonderful. I never imagined . . ." She looked up at him. "Is there more?"

Greedy lass! He smiled. "Aye, this is only the beginning. I am going to make you—"

Mine.

He stilled. The word jarring something inside of him, rousing his conscience from its drugged slumber.

"Make me what?" she said gamely. She glanced down, eyes widening as they fell on him. "Oh . . . *Oh!*"

Her eyes shot back to him uncertainly, and with more than a little fear. It wasn't without cause. He was built for a woman's pleasure.

But she wasn't a woman, she was a maid.

Is a maid, he corrected.

Every muscle in his body flexed with restraint. It would be so easy to surge inside. He bowed his head, his body shaking, fighting for control as the need of his body warred with his mind. A mind he wanted to shut off.

Just finish. You can make it good for her. She wanted this. It's too late, damn it.

But it wasn't too late. Not yet.

She isn't yours. But she can be. A few more inches, and you can make it so.

But at what cost? Everything he'd been fighting to achieve? Was he like his father after all?

He swore, not realizing he'd uttered the vile oath aloud until she gasped.

"What's wrong?" She reached up and touched his taut face.

He shrugged her off and pulled away, every instinct in his body roaring in protest.

"I can't do this."

"Why not?"

He was already on his feet, moving away. He couldn't look at her; the emotion in her voice was eating away at him enough. He needed a minute—more than a minute—to get himself under control. "There's some soap and some extra clothes in my bag. Wash off the damned flowers. As soon as you are done we can go."

Walking away was the hardest thing Ewen had ever done. He cursed every step that took him away from her. His honor and loyalty had been pushed to the very breaking point, leaving him nowhere to go.

Sixteen

❧

Janet didn't understand what had just happened. One minute he was there with her, and they were as close as two people could be; the next he was somewhere else. Somewhere she couldn't reach. The fierceness of his expression alarmed her. He looked broken—tortured. She called after him as he walked away, but he acted as if he hadn't heard her and continued on.

Leaving her flat. Literally, on her back. If she weren't so confused, she might have felt like crying. How dare he leave her like this! She'd been ready—eager—to experience it all. She'd given herself to him, and he'd rejected her.

Alone, and without the heat of his body, she shivered. The chill of the misty morning once again seeped into her bones. But it was nothing compared to what was to come. With no choice but to do what he said, she then spent two—perhaps three—of the most unpleasant minutes of her life, bathing in the icy pool of water below the falls.

Forcing her feet off the rocky ledge was no mean feat. Only knowing that she was to blame for the English tracking them compelled her forward. She jumped. To say the water was a shock was an understatement of prodigious proportions. It leached every bit of sensation from her bones, taking her lethargy and any lingering memory of what had just happened with it. But she would never forget. He'd shown her a glimpse of heaven, and nothing could take that away. Not him. Not the water. Nothing.

Sputtering to the surface, she scrubbed her hair and limbs with the sliver of plain soap, attempting not only to erase the "reek" of bluebells, but also to keep the blood moving so she didn't freeze to death.

Getting out didn't provide much relief. Her teeth were still clattering minutes later when he returned. She didn't have to ask where he'd been. From his damp hair, she realized that he, too, had bathed, albeit farther down the river.

His gaze swept over her. If he was pleased to see that she'd done as he bid, she couldn't tell. All evidence of the tortured expression was gone from his face, his features once again schooled into a blank mask.

The lack of emotion rankled. How could he be so unaffected, when she was so *very* affected? Her mouth pursed, anger breaking through some of the confusion.

"Do you need any help?"

Apparently, he'd noticed the difficulty she was having getting dressed. Though she'd managed to don one of his shirts and a pair of wool breeches, the shirt was already half-sopping from her wet hair and her fingers weren't cooperating as she tried to pull on the hose.

She shook her head. As a peace offering—if that's what it was—it wasn't enough. He'd rejected her, leaving her like that, and she wasn't going to let him pretend it had never happened. As if putting *on* her clothes could blot the evidence from memory!

She was just about to wrap herself in the plaid again, when he stopped her. "You can't wear anything you had on before. We'll leave it with the other things."

"But it belongs to Eoin, and it's *warm*."

She thought his mouth pulled a little tighter. "MacLean will understand." Ewen took off his own plaid and handed it to her. "You can wear mine."

Their eyes held for one long heartbeat, as if there were some kind of significance beyond the heat it would offer, but then he looked away, and the moment was gone.

She took the plaid and quickly wrapped it around herself, unable to hold back the sigh of pleasure as warmth
enveloped her frozen limbs. The heat from his body seemed
captured in the intricate weave of the woolen threads. If
she inhaled (which she did), she could just catch a faint
scent of the familiar pine and leather.

After a few minutes she was warm enough to finish
dressing. She gathered the sopping strands of her hair into
a tight braid at the nape of her neck and fastened her boots.
At least he hadn't insisted she go barefoot.

He held out a piece of rope, which she looked at blankly.

"For the breeches," he explained. "The ties don't seem
to be working very well."

Indeed, she had to constantly yank the pants up from
riding down over her hips. Still, they were better than her
other options: her habit or the fine gown Mary had sent
for her to appear in at court.

She tucked the linen shirt into the breeches and bunched
it around her waist, using the rope as a belt. Noticing the
way his eyes fell on her hips, lingering with almost palpa-
ble hunger for a moment until he forced his gaze away, she
made sure to take her time. Petty revenge perhaps, but it
proved surprisingly satisfactory.

The added belt helped, and a few moments later, after
he'd bound her old borrowed clothing around a pile of
rocks and tossed it in the pool, he gathered their belongings to go.

But Janet wasn't ready to leave. Not without an explanation.

She caught his arm before he could walk away. "Why
did you stop like that? Did I do something wrong?"

His jaw clenched, his steel-blue gaze meeting hers. "Not
now, Janet. We need to move higher into the hills. They
will not have given up the hunt."

"Perhaps not, but unless you think they are right behind

us, surely you can spare me a few minutes? Do I not deserve some kind of explanation?"

His expression turned pained. "You did nothing wrong. It was my fault. It never should have happened."

"Why not?"

His eyes flared hot. "Because it's not right. Your innocence belongs to your husband, damn it."

Janet stiffened, trying not to overreact or be disappointed. His reaction was understandable—that was how most men thought. But she didn't want him to think like most men. She wanted him to see her for herself and not as a possession or accessory. Was that too much to ask?

At times she could almost be convinced he was different. That his unreasonableness was just a result of inexperience. That he didn't know any better, but that once he got to know her, he would see her as . . . what? Capable. Certainly not a virgin to be bartered and sold like a prized cow.

"My innocence belongs to me," she said firmly. "It is mine to lose or not."

"I wish that were true. But it isn't that simple, Janet. You are the daughter of an earl and the sister-in-law of the king. Your husband will expect—"

"What husband? I am not married, nor do I ever intend to be."

Her vehemence took him aback. "You sound so certain."

She lifted her chin. "I am."

"You can't seriously be considering becoming a nun?"

After what had just happened, it sounded just as implausible to her. But she would do what she must. "If that is my only alternative to marriage."

"You make marriage sound like a death sentence. Would it really be so horrible?"

She thought of her family. Yes, it would be. How could she explain? How could she make him understand what to him—to most men—must seem unnatural? "I would lose myself."

His brow wrinkled. "How?"

"I would no longer have the ability to control my own actions. Everything—even the smallest decision—would be controlled by my husband. My will would no longer be my own. I have no wish to be treated like chattel."

He frowned. "It's not always like that."

She lifted a brow. "So you know of many men who treat their wives as equals?"

His frown deepened. "A few."

Her heart skipped forward. Did that include him? "And would you allow your wife the power to make her own decisions even if they did not agree with yours?"

"We aren't talking about me."

"No, we aren't," she said quietly, her heart squeezing with unexpected disappointment. She couldn't have been thinking of him as a husband, could she? "But you wished to know my reasons, and you are a perfect example. You've made your feelings about what I'm doing quite clear. By what right could I expect another man to feel differently? Can you imagine a husband permitting me to continue my work?"

His mouth tightened mulishly. "Your work is dangerous."

"So I need to be protected from myself, is that it?" Not surprisingly, he didn't answer. She decided to turn the question back on him. "Why are you so sure I shouldn't be doing this? Why do you have such little regard for women—or is it just me?"

He appeared shocked. "Jesus, Janet, just because I don't think it's safe for you to wander all over Scotland by yourself in the middle of a war, doing something that could get you killed if you are discovered, doesn't mean I think less of you. Bloody hell, you've proved yourself to anyone after today. You've done as well as any man." Her chest lifted at his words. He had no idea how much they meant to her.

"But being a woman makes you vulnerable in different ways. When I think of what could happen to you . . ." His face darkened, and his eyes took on a haunted glaze. "Damn it, do you have any idea what the English would do to you if they found out what you were doing?"

There was something more at work here than simply his view on traditional roles for men and women. Obviously, he was speaking from personal experience. "Tell me what happened."

His jaw clenched so tightly she could see the muscle below it start to tic. "It was a few years ago—not long after we landed in Scotland after being forced to take refuge in the Isles for a few months." She swallowed. It was when her brother Duncan had been killed. "We were being hunted, the tide had not yet turned, and a handful of villagers—mostly women and children—helped to hide us in the hills. The English found out, and when we returned to thank them," his eyes met hers, "there wasn't anyone left to thank. The women had been raped and beaten before they'd had their throats slit. Only one lass survived."

Janet gasped. Though he'd spoken with his usual bluntness, she could hear the emotion in his voice and realized how horrible it must have been. "It wasn't your fault."

"Of course, it was," he snapped. "We asked them for help, never imagining the risk we were asking them to take."

"But they would have done it anyway," she said softly. "Even knowing, they would have helped you."

"How can you possibly know that?"

"Because I would have done the same."

He stared at her, not saying anything for a moment. "Why is being a courier so important to you?"

"The why shouldn't matter. The fact that it is should be enough." Was it too much to hope that a man could understand that? "I do not ask you why you do what you do. Just because I don't wear armor and carry a sword doesn't make what I do any less important." She paused. "This war won't be won by the sword alone, Ewen. How do you think Bruce's phantoms know the right place to attack?" He was watching her intently. "Good intelligence passed by couriers."

She left it at that, not wanting to say more.

He seemed to consider what she'd said, but whether he gave it any weight, she couldn't tell. "Is this about your sister?"

She stiffened. "What are you talking about?"

"You don't have to prove yourself or atone for what happened at the bridge. Mary doesn't blame you. If you only knew how desperate she's been to find you, and how anxious she is to have you back."

Janet's heart devoured every word. Was it true? She wanted to believe him and yearned to question him, but that would mean acknowledging to herself that his words held some truth. "My sister has nothing to do with this. Isn't it enough to want to help? Must there always be a further reason? How about you—why are you here, Ewen? What made you decide to be one of Bruce's phantoms?"

He shot her a glare but didn't take the bait. "I joined Bruce's *army* because my liege lord, and a man I respected above all others, asked me to do so. I've stayed to keep my clan from extinction."

Her eyes widened at the blunt honesty. No patriotic fever or talk of freedom and tyranny from him, just ambition and reward. "Your father?" she asked.

It took him a moment to realize what she meant. When he did, he laughed. "Hardly. My father was not a man to inspire much devotion. Nay, I speak of the former steward—Sir James Stewart."

Janet couldn't hide her surprise. Was that the lord he'd spoken of who'd fostered him? The Stewart Lords of Bute were one of the most important clans in the country. "You are connected to the Stewarts?"

A wry smile turned his mouth, as if he guessed the direction of her thoughts. "Not closely. My mother was Sir James's cousin—his favorite, as it happened." Seeing her confusion, he sighed as if resigning himself to having to say more. "My mother was betrothed to the Chief of Lamont when she met my father—one of his chieftains— and decided to marry him instead. Needless to say, the Lamont chief was not happy. He went to war with my father and would have destroyed him without Sir James's help." He shook his head. "Ironically, it was my father being cut off from the rest of the clan that gave me the ability to save it."

"What do you mean?"

"Like the MacDougalls, the MacDowells, and the Comyns, my cousin—the current chief—and his clansmen stood against Bruce and have been exiled and had the clan lands dispossessed, except for my lands in Ardlamont. Were it not for my connection to the Stewarts, and thus to Bruce, I would be with them. As it stands, I am the last Lamont in Cowal. My clan lives or dies with the skill of my sword, so to speak."

Janet was stunned. No wonder he seemed so stubborn and single-minded about every mission. The future of the once great clan rested on his broad shoulders. But something else he'd said gave her a whisper of possibility. "You are a chieftain?"

He held her gaze. "Do not be too impressed, my lady. It is a minor holding only—with half a castle."

Her brows furrowed, not understanding the sarcasm. "Until the king rewards you with more for your service?"

He shrugged. "If that is his will."

She eyed him speculatively. Though he'd said it with nonchalance, she sensed how much it mattered to him. This was what drove him. Reward and a position for his clan under a Bruce kingship.

It also provided another explanation for why he'd

stopped. Despoiling the king's sister-in-law was hardly likely to ingratiate him to Robert.

But there was no reason Robert should ever find out. Not that she thought that was likely to sway Ewen. He was proving to have an inconveniently steely streak of honor in him.

She bit her lip, wondering if there was another way. Despite his continued rejection and appalling behavior in walking away from her in the middle of lovemaking, she still wanted him and wasn't going to give up.

Why it was so important to her, she didn't know. Either she was a glutton for punishment or there was something truly special between them that was worth the continued blows to her pride. And then there was the passion. The undeniable attraction that sprang up between them like wildfire. She could not discount that.

In any event, "I can't do this" wasn't an answer she intended to accept. It sounded too much like no. If Mary's voice whispered a warning, Janet pushed it aside. She knew what she was doing. Besides, there was no one else around to get hurt.

He scanned the area behind her. "We've rested long enough."

She lifted a brow in question. "Resting" wasn't how she would describe what they'd been doing.

If she wasn't sure that it was impossible for him to blush, she would have sworn his cheeks darkened as he took in her meaning. "Aye, well, you can sleep once I'm sure that we've lost them."

"I think I'd prefer to do some more resting."

He shot her a reproachful glare. "Janet . . ."

He might have been scolding a naughty pup. She blinked up at him innocently. "What?"

"It isn't going to happen. I told you it was a mistake. It's over. *Over*."

She smiled, knowing that neither of them believed him. It wasn't over; it had just begun.

Ewen pushed them mercilessly, as much to put distance between them and the English as to keep her too busy to plot his downfall.

The lass was trouble.

And stubborn.

And too bold by half.

She was also smart.

And achingly sweet.

And far stronger than he'd ever expected.

He couldn't believe she was still on her feet. So far today she'd been hunted by dogs, attacked by an English knight, killed said knight with a well-placed dagger to the leg, trudged for miles knee-deep in an icy river, suffered a bath in that icy water, and hiked for miles over frozen, mist-topped hills. As if that weren't enough, she'd also come within a hair's breadth of ruin.

One orgasm couldn't make up for all that. Though it had been one hell of an orgasm. He didn't think he'd ever forget the look of ecstasy and surprise on her face as her body had shattered under him. The rush of color to her cheeks, the half-lidded eyes hazy with passion, the softly parted lips swollen from his kiss.

Jesus. Heat swelled in his sorely abused groin. The release he'd taken in his hand after leaving her had barely taken the edge off. How was he going to keep his hands off her until they reached the coast, when all he could think about was finishing what they'd started?

The lass had invaded his senses, penetrated his defenses, and slipped under his skin. He wanted her with every fiber of his being. Even exhausted, his leg on fire, cold and hungry, he couldn't look at her without thinking about throwing her down on the ground, wrapping those long, slim legs around his waist, and giving her exactly what she was asking for.

So he did what any fearless warrior would do: he didn't look at her.

But he didn't know how much more of this he could take. *More resting . . .* bloody hell! Was she trying to kill him? God knew why, but the lass had gotten it in her head to give him her innocence. Did she have any idea how hard it was for him to refuse that kind of an offer?

Of course, she didn't, and after hearing her views on marriage, he sure as hell wasn't going to enlighten her. He had no doubt he'd have to drag her kicking and screaming all the way to Dunstaffnage. Bruce was going to have a hell of a battle on his hands when she found out about his plans.

The worst part was that he wasn't sure he blamed her. He'd never considered marriage from a woman's perspective before, but he had to admit, her concerns were not without merit. He'd always taken for granted a man's role of absolute authority. To a woman like Janet who was used to making her own decisions, it would be stifling. She would chafe against those bindings at every turn.

But what was the alternative? Ewen wasn't like MacKay, he couldn't let his wife follow them into battle. He frowned. Although he had been grateful more than once to have a skilled healer at hand.

Helen is different, he told himself.

But wasn't Janet?

They climbed to a small plateau in the hillside, and he stopped. Though it was only a few hours after noon, daylight was already fading.

"Wait here," he said, pointing to a rocky outcrop. As he'd done every few miles, he let her catch her breath while he circled back to attempt to hide their tracks. The snow on the ground had hardened as the temperature dropped the higher they climbed on the mountain, making it easier to do so. But where the ground was too soft, instead of hiding, he set about confusing their pursuers by walking backward, breaking off in other directions for a while, or making a number of footprints in one area.

When he returned a few minutes later, she was seated on one of the rocks, watching him. "Is anyone following?"

He shook his head.

But something made her curious. "Why did you stop to look at the bracken back there?"

He sat down beside her and pulled out his skin. After taking a long swig, he handed it to her. "Some of the stems were broken where we brushed by."

She frowned. "I thought you were hiding our footprints."

"I'm hiding our tracks."

"Isn't it the same thing?"

He shook his head. "I'm looking for any disturbances on the landscape, not just footsteps. Any sign that someone might have passed."

"And you can tell from a few broken twigs that someone has passed."

He shrugged. "It's a sign."

She gave him a long look. "How did you become so good at this?"

"My father's henchman was a tracker. He used to take me out with him when I was young, and later when I returned from fostering. He noticed I had an unusual memory for details and taught me how to use that skill to track. But it's mostly experience." Years and years of learning what to look for.

"What kind of details?"

"Look behind me." He waited a few moments. "Now close your eyes and tell me what you saw."

She looked back at him. "Is that a trick? There is only a flat area of moorland dusted with snow, with a few rocks scattered about."

"Look again." He didn't turn, but called up the image from memory. "The rocks scattered about the moors are graywacke sandstone, but about twenty paces behind me are a few granite rocks stacked in what is probably the beginnings of a summit cairn. Just to the left, you can see the outlines of a narrow path from the north where the grass has been tramped down—probably by mountain hares, if the pile of scat nearby is any indication—and the snow is slightly lower. Near the patches of purple moor grass sticking up through the snow on the west side of the hill are the tracks of a small group of red deer hinds. Directly over my left shoulder about five paces behind me is a small bump in the snow. If you look closely, you can see a few brownish feathers sticking out. I suspect it's the carcass of a grouse brought down by a hen harrier or peregrine falcon."

She gaped at him. "You didn't even look."

"I did earlier. I told you, I have an unusual memory."

"I'll say. And a keen eye for detail." She smiled delightedly. "What else do you look for?"

He wasn't used to such an eager audience, but as the subject clearly interested her, and knowing it would help pass the time, he explained some basic principles, such as how to minimize your imprint on the landscape and make sure no signs were left behind; deception tactics to mislead your pursuers, such as walking backward, looping around, stone hopping, and toe walking; how to move with the wind to hide your scent, how to avoid changing directions at obvious places, and how to break a scent trail as they'd done with the dogs.

She listened to him with rapt attention, clearly fascinated.

"Every time you take a step," he said, "look for stones, hard ground, patches of ice, existing roads or paths, resilient mosses, things like that. Your tracks will be less visible."

"So think hard," she said.

That was one way of putting it, but he tried not to think about "hard" given his problems in a certain area.

She looked up at him. "It seems so obvious now that you point it out, but I never realized."

"Most of what I do is common sense. You just have to think about it."

"You are being modest." She tilted her head to look at him. "No wonder Robert wanted you for his secret army. I can imagine a skill like yours is useful for men who want to appear like ghosts."

He could feel her eyes on him, so he was careful not to react. *Damn it,* the lass was relentless! He should be surprised that she'd figured it out, but he wasn't. She could find trouble without even looking for it.

"Aren't you going to say something?"

He turned to look at her, his eyes boring into hers. "Should I tell you how much danger you could put both of us in by just mentioning the subject, irrespective of whether it is true?"

Her gaze never wavered. "But it is true. I know it is."

Clearly, he wasn't going to dissuade her. He knew he should try. He'd taken an oath, and it wasn't just his own life at stake, but he didn't want to lie to her. So he did the next best thing and said, "Let's go. Rest time is over."

She groaned. "But we just sat down. You're just trying to avoid my questions." He didn't deny it. "The English won't be chasing us forever, Ewen. One of these days you won't be able to avoid answering."

He didn't know; he was pretty damned good at avoiding things. Except with her—which was part of the problem. He didn't answer, simply holding out his hand instead.

He helped her to her feet—with another dramatic groan on her part—and they were off.

Although he was fairly certain they'd lost their pursuers, he wanted to reach the next ridge by nightfall. There was an old stone shieling where they could take shelter. It was too dangerous to wander around these mountains in the dark, especially in the mist. In the morning, he would see about finding horses to take them to Ayr, where he sure as hell hoped MacKay, MacLean, and Sutherland would catch up to them.

Teaching her about tracking proved to be an effective way of passing the time, distracting them both—him from thinking about the pain in his leg and the fate of his friends, and her from asking more questions he couldn't answer about the Highland Guard. She was an eager pupil, surprising him with her interest, as well as with how quickly she seemed to pick it up.

They were able to move at a much quicker pace since she'd become more conscious of the signs she was leaving behind as they climbed, and thus he didn't need to spend as much time backtracking to cover them up.

He should have instructed her earlier. Why didn't he? It was one of the first things he did with men under his command. Had he thought the principles too difficult to grasp, or solely the province of men?

She was right, he realized. He assumed that because she didn't wear armor and carry weapons, she was ill equipped for war. But Janet of Mar seemed to be turning many of his preconceived notions about women on their head.

She wasn't fragile or helpless. She was strong and capable. Too bloody capable, to his mind.

Although he might be willing to admit that he'd underestimated her abilities, he wasn't wrong about the danger. She might have defended herself against the knight today, but without the element of surprise—or if there had been more than one man—she'd be just as dead as those women at Lochmaben. Even if she were the best damned courier in Scotland, it didn't override his instinct to protect her.

But did she need protection?

He thought back to their conversation about the women

at Lochmaben. He'd never believed a woman could understand the danger and still want to be involved. Just like him, she'd pointed out. That was ridiculous, wasn't it?

By the time the shadow of the shieling appeared on the horizon, Ewen had achieved one of his objectives: the lass was exhausted. Too exhausted to do anything more than climb into the folds of the plaid he'd set out for her as a blanket, after cleaning out the debris from the former animal occupants, and sleep.

Her virtue—and his honor—was safe.

For now.

But when he climbed into the small stone hut beside her a few hours later, and she instinctively turned to him, burrowing into his arms, something hard and heavy lodged in his chest. The weight of inevitability? The stony certainty of fate? Because nothing had ever felt more perfect. Alone on a mountain, taking refuge in a stone hut meant for sheep while being hunted by Englishmen, he'd never felt more content.

He tucked his arm under her chest, snuggled her small bottom into his groin, buried his nose in the silky softness of her hair, and savored every minute of holding the woman who wasn't his, but who sure as hell felt like it.

Seventeen

❦

Janet woke with a start. It took her a few panicked heartbeats to remember where she was, but eventually she started to breathe evenly again. The stone shieling on the mountain. With Ewen.

She frowned. Ewen, who was nowhere to be found. She didn't need to look around the small stone hut to see that he was gone; she could tell by the empty chill at her back.

He'd slept beside her. Instinctively, she knew that. Not that she could remember it, blast it. The last thing she recalled was being tucked under the warm folds of his plaid. She'd been so tired, she'd fallen asleep the moment her eyes had closed.

He'd probably counted on that, the blighter. He'd marched her over these hills until she was too tired and cold to do anything but collapse.

All she could recall was a feeling of warmth and contentment. Of being perfectly relaxed and snug in her bed, unburdened by the events of the day.

He'd held her, she realized.

Janet shook her head with mild disgust. The one time he'd taken her in his arms and held her, and she hadn't been awake to enjoy it! If she weren't so sure that there was something special between them, his attempts to avoid her might have been demoralizing.

She'd just finished rolling up the plaid when the blighter in question ducked through the low door of the shieling.

He had to crouch slightly to stand up inside, as the domed turf roof was only about six feet high in the center.

"You're awake? I didn't think you'd be up until midday."

At first she thought he was criticizing her, but then she realized he was teasing. She gave him a knowing look. "I was cold without you beside me."

His face went blank—too blank. "I was outside most of the night, keeping watch." He handed her a skin before she could argue. "You can use this to wash until we reach the burn."

She took the pouch of water gratefully. Her eyes and teeth had a distinctly gritty feel. All she needed was a comb—which should be in one of the bags—and she might even feel human again. She thought about prodding him about their sleeping arrangements, but decided to leave it—for now. Instead, she asked, "What burn?"

"Near the village of Cuingealach. We need a horse. The English seem to have given up the chase, but I want to put as much distance between us as possible."

A wise plan. But something had been bothering her. "Why do you think they were chasing us in the first place?"

He hesitated, seemingly to take care with his words. "We had some trouble on the way to find you in Roxburgh."

"So they were looking for you?"

"Probably."

The knowledge eased her conscience somewhat about the lost cap. It hadn't been all her fault. Moreover, as she expected it was going to be hard to convince Robert to let her return to Roxburgh after what had happened, the fact that the soldiers had been after Ewen and the others and not her, would help. Of course, there was no question of Ewen escorting her back. It was too dangerous for him. But it wouldn't be for Novice Eleanor.

"Shall we be much delayed, do you think? I must be back in Roxburgh within the fortnight."

A strange look crossed his face. He looked away almost uncomfortably. "You will have plenty of time. But we should go."

"What about Sir Kenneth? How will he know how to find us?"

"Don't worry about Sutherland. He'll catch up with us if he can."

If. She caught something in his expression that she'd been too scared and upset to notice before. A slight darkening of the eyes and tightening around the mouth.

Janet stilled, as horror slowly dawned. "You think something has happened to my sister's husband?"

As if Mary didn't have cause to hate her enough already.

She must have looked as stricken as she sounded because he swore, drawing his fingers through his hair. "Damn it, that's not what I meant. I'm sure he's fine."

"And if he's not?"

He took her chin and tipped her face toward his. "If he's not, it has nothing to do with you. This is what he does, and sometimes—most of the time—it's dangerous. Mary knows that."

Janet nodded, but in her heart she couldn't accept it. If anything happened to her sister's husband, Janet would never forgive herself.

A cap. A blasted cap! He couldn't have died over something so insignificant . . . could he?

Tears filled her eyes. Ewen's thumb stroked her cheek, as if he'd wipe them away before they could fall. The gentleness caught in her heart and wouldn't let go.

I could love him.

With the smallest amount of encouragement, she could love him. The realization of how easy that would be rose up and grabbed her by the throat, both awe-inspiring and terrifying. It would change everything.

He looked as if he might say something more, but instead he dropped his hand from her face and stepped away.

"Get ready and have something to eat while I take another look around. The mist isn't as thick this morning, and I want to be off these mountains before it lifts."

He was almost through the entrance when she called out, "Ewen!"

He turned and looked at her over his shoulder. Her heart squeezed. With his dark hair, steely blue eyes, rough-hewn features and stubble-shadowed jaw, he looked so ruggedly handsome it hurt.

Why him? After all these years, why had this one man finally threatened into her heart?

"Thank you."

"For what?"

She blushed. For being here with her. For keeping her safe and warm. For holding her in his arms. For bringing her the water to wash this morning. For not blaming her, and trying to make her feel better.

"For everything," she said softly.

Confused, his brows furrowed slightly, but he nodded.

A short while later they were climbing more hills, continuing on their way east. Although rested, her legs were still sore from the day before, and she was glad that he'd eased up on the pace a little.

She frowned, wondering if his leg was bothering him. But after watching him for a while, she didn't detect any sign of the injury or pain and concluded that the ointment must have worked.

He was right about the mist. It did not linger, lifting by mid-morning, about the same time they reached the burn of which he'd spoken. The stream was about three feet wide, flowing through a deep ravine. It was beautiful, set in the landscape of moss, rock, and a light dusting of snow—patches of snow, more accurately, as the warm sun was already melting winter's icy breath.

She took her time, washing her face and hands and enjoying the moment of peace. She should have known it wouldn't last.

Ewen gritted his teeth for the battle ahead. He should have known she wasn't going to like his plan. God, did all women have so many *opinions*? Thinking of his fellow Guardsmen's wives, he suspected they did.

Bloody hell, what was happening to him? It had been so much easier when he didn't think about what a lass thought or wanted.

Her gaze slid over him in a silent scoff that sure as hell shouldn't make him hot, but his cock didn't seem to notice her flashing eyes.

"A change of clothes does not hide what you are, Ewen. Anyone who looks at you will see that you are a warrior." The observation pleased him far more than it should. As did the way her eyes lingered appreciatively on his shoulders and arms. "Let me go with you—I can help. You will be less obvious with a wife by your side."

Remembering how well that had gone the first time, he declined. "I'm buying a horse, Janet. I've done this hundreds of times before. There is nothing to worry about. I will be back before you even realize I'm gone."

She shook her head. "But what if there are soldiers about?"

"There won't be. As you can see," he pointed down into the valley at the dozen or so holdings and small church nestled into the hillside, "it's a small village. No castle means no English."

"I can help you. Remember what happened in the inn? I'm good at talking with people."

And he wasn't. But he could bloody well bargain for a horse. Knowing that they'd be standing here forever if he didn't do something, Ewen tried a different tack. One that held more truth than he wanted to admit. "That's not why

I don't want you to go. I know you could help, but having you with me would put us both in danger."

"Why?"

"I'd be worrying about you. Focusing on you. You make me . . ."

He didn't know how to explain. Weak. Vulnerable. Words he'd never used to describe himself before.

Christ!

If she noticed his discomfort, it didn't stop her from asking, "Make you what?"

He settled on, "Distracted."

His answer didn't appear to satisfy her. She wrinkled her delicately turned nose. "I'll stay out of the way; you won't even know I'm there."

As if that were bloody possible. "I *always* know you're there."

"Why?"

"Why?" he repeated, not having anticipated the question.

"Aye, why do you always know I'm there? Why am I so different?"

His jaw hardened. "You know why."

She lifted her chin in a manner that told him that she intended to be difficult about this. "No, I'm afraid I don't."

He knew what she was trying to do, damn it. But if it meant keeping her safe, he'd say whatever the hell she wanted him to. "Because I care about you. Because the thought of something happening to you makes me lose my damned mind. That's why I don't want you going with me."

She smiled, and he swore it was as if the sun had just come out. "All right."

The acquiescence had come so easily, he didn't think he'd heard her right. "All right?"

She nodded. "And just so you know, you distract me,

too." She gave him a small smile. "I had no idea you were so romantic."

Romantic? Him? *Bloody hell!* She was reading too much into this. "Janet, you don't understand—"

She waved him off—actually waved him off. He didn't think anyone had done that since the cook had shooed him away from the kitchen—and the freshly baked tarts—when he was a lad.

"I understand quite well. You'd better go now, before I reconsider, while I'm still agog over the poetry of 'lose my damned mind.'"

His mouth twisted. She was teasing him. It was still difficult for him to believe how natural it seemed.

He should correct her and make sure she understood that this didn't change anything, but she was right: he didn't want to give her the opportunity to change her mind. It would have to wait. "Aye, well don't get used to it. I'm afraid I've a limited supply of poetic words. I can't think of anything that rhymes with 'bloody.'"

She laughed, and the sweet sound reverberated in his chest.

"How about 'study'? Or maybe 'muddy'?"

He gave a sharp laugh. He should have known she'd think of something. "I'll work on it." He sobered, and the wry smile slid from his face. "I won't be long. Stay out of sight. If anyone approaches, you can slip behind those rocks."

It wasn't a cave, but the space between the big boulders was large enough to slide between. He wished he didn't have to leave her alone, but it couldn't be helped. If they were going to reach the coast anytime soon, they needed a horse. He would have preferred two, but that would be much harder to explain.

His first priority—his *only* priority—was getting Janet to safety as quickly as possible. But he would also concede a twinge of uncertainty about his leg. Something didn't feel right. All the climbing yesterday must have aggravated it. Unfortunately, he hadn't thought to take the ointment from MacKay before they separated. Nothing appeared wrong when he'd looked at it earlier while bathing— actually, if anything the bleeding seemed to have lessened— but it had hurt like hell every time he took a step. The pain was sharp and deep—biting. And he was tired. More than he should be. The sooner Helen could look at it, the better.

"I'll be fine," she assured him. "If anything goes wrong, I have my dagger."

Although he knew better than she did how well she could use it, it didn't exactly ease his mind to think about her needing to do so.

He nodded. "I'll be back before you know it."

Their eyes met. His feet didn't want to move. She looked so sweet and trusting. So beautiful and strong. He wanted to reach for her with every fiber of his being, as if it were the most natural thing to do. But he didn't. He forced his feet to walk away.

"Ewen." He turned. "I . . ." He could see some kind of turmoil on her face, and an emotion he couldn't name. "Be careful."

He nodded, wondering what she'd been about to say. Indeed, he seemed to be thinking about it the entire way down the hill to the village. She'd been about to tell him something. Something he suspected he didn't want to hear, but longed to hear at the same time. His chest burned. Knowing he would only drive himself mad thinking about things that could not be, he forced his mind to the task at hand. *Focus.*

His plan was simple: he would offer enough money to avoid any questions. Normally when the Highland Guard needed horses in the Borders, they made use of the network of Bruce supporters in the area. Unfortunately, the loyalties of this village tucked away high in the hills of Galloway were unknown. They had supporters in Douglas, Lanarkshire, about fifteen miles away, but as that was also where they'd run into trouble earlier, he wanted to avoid the area.

As the village did not have an inn, he started with the nearest holding and worked his way across, getting more and more frustrated with each stop.

There didn't appear to be a single horse for sale in the entire village, let alone one that was suitable. Hell, at this point he would welcome an old field nag.

After a half-dozen stops, his frustration was showing. But when he approached the next croft, he caught sight of something roaming in the field that would make it go away: a beautiful, sturdy, and agile-looking courser.

Unfortunately, the owner was proving difficult.

"Where did you say you were from?" he asked.

Ewen eyed the old farmer, whose weather-beaten face hid an agile and shrewd mind. "Roxburgh," he answered curtly. "Are you willing to sell the horse? I'll offer you ten pounds."

Even for the fine animal it was a generous offer. The old man should have jumped at it. Instead, he stroked his long, gray beard assessingly. "'Tis a lot of silver. You must really have need of it."

Ewen's temper was running thin. The farmer obviously suspected something, and Ewen didn't like the way he was putting him off with questions, but he wanted that damned horse. He gave him a hard look. "Will you sell me the horse or not?"

"He isn't for sale."

Ewen clenched his teeth and counted to five. "Why not?"

"He isn't mine to sell. I'm caring for him. I was a stable-master in King John's army." *Ah hell, Balliol!* Definitely not a friend of Bruce's, then. "I still take in ailing horses when I can. This one belongs to the captain to the guard at Sanquhar." *Damn.* This just kept getting better and better. Sanquhar was one of James Douglas's castles now garri-

soned by the English. The old man's eyes gleamed devi-
ously. "Perhaps you can put your request to him?"

Ewen didn't need to ask what he meant. He could just
hear the clop of approaching horses now. He looked over
his shoulder, catching the glint of mail in the sunlight as a
half-dozen English soldiers entered the outskirts of the village from the pass to the west. Although they were still a
good distance away, they were closing in fast.

He wouldn't be able to flee without being seen. When he
wasn't hobbled by injury, he ran fast—but not faster than
a horse. In these wide-open hills, with no mist to hide his
direction, he couldn't be sure that he could find cover fast
enough to lose them.

And then there was Janet. What if in hunting for him,
they found her instead? He couldn't risk it.

He swore over and over again in his mind, but there was
only one thing he could do: come up with a good story or
best six mounted, mailed knights with no more than his
dagger.

As he didn't have Janet's facile tongue, he suspected it
was going to be the latter, and even for one of the elite
warriors of the Highland Guard that was no mean feat.

God's blood, could this get any worse?

A few minutes later, when the sound of a voice calling
out his name that sent a blast of ice through his veins to
chill every last bone in his body, he had his answer: Aye,
this could get a hell of a lot worse.

"Ewen!" Janet didn't let his death glare stop her. She'd
known he would be furious, but the moment she'd seen the
banner flying in the distance from her hillside perch, she
wasn't going to let anything stop her from trying to warn
him. Unfortunately, it had taken her a long time to find
him, and now it was too late. She approached the croft at
the same time as the soldiers. "There you are! I'd begun to
think you'd forgotten all about me."

She saw his eyes widen as he took in her appearance. With one hand at her hip, as if supporting her back from exhaustion, she patted her softly rounded belly with the other. "Have you found a horse for us to ride yet?"

His face was as dark and brooding as a storm cloud, but after a moment's pause, he realized his part and came forward to help her. His eyes bored into hers, promising retribution, as he slid his arm around her waist protectively. "I thought I told you to wait for me," he said, adding after a pause he hoped didn't sound awkward, "*mo chroí.*"

She laughed, as if used to his masculine bluster, which surprisingly she was. He would no doubt bellow and growl like an angry lion when this was over, but she didn't care. He needed her help, whether he wanted to admit it or not.

He was practically unarmed. She wasn't going to watch him being thrown in irons and dragged away from here.

Lifting to her tiptoes, she placed a soft kiss on his cheek, as if soothing him with a placative balm. The grip around her waist instinctively tightened. She felt a shiver of awareness as their bodies melded together. "I grew tired of waiting," she said, a little flustered by the contact. "Both the babe and I are restless."

The part of the loving, soon-to-be father apparently wasn't one with which he was familiar. It took him a moment to feign concern. He put his hand on her rounded belly—or in this case, the pillow of clothes she'd stuffed under the cotte Mary had sent her to wear. The undergown was still too fine for whatever he was pretending to be, but the plain brown wool was better than the gold embroidered silk surcoat that went over it.

"The babe is all right?" he asked.

Aware of their interested audience, she mirrored his concern in her own eyes and sighed with weariness that she did not need to feign. "I hope so. I didn't realize how tiring it would be. I'm just so exhausted. I shall be glad when our journey is done."

"What is going on here?" an authoritative voice boomed. One of the soldiers—the leader, she suspected—had come forward, putting himself between Ewen and the old man, who stood at the doorway of his rectangular stone croft with its crucked turf roof.

"I am seeking a horse for my, uh, wife," Ewen explained. "She is weary and cannot walk any farther."

"You didn't tell me it was for a lass," the old man said with a surprised frown on his face.

From her position tucked against his body, it was easy for Janet to look up and give Ewen a reproachful shake of her head. Then she glanced over to the old man with another weary sigh. "Sometimes I think he forgets he has a wife. He didn't want me to come, but I insisted, and now I fear I've caused all sorts of problems."

The old man gallantly jumped to her defense. "A wee, bonnie lass like you, what kind of problems could you cause?"

"You'd be surprised," Ewen said under his breath, but loud enough for them to hear.

Janet jabbed him in the side with her elbow and shot him a glare. "I told you I was sorry." She turned to the old man for help. "He blames me."

"For what?" the soldier interjected.

"For losing our horse in the first place." She twisted her hands anxiously. "It was all my fault. I didn't tie the reins well enough, and it wandered away in the storm. Now we must use the coin that we'd planned to give to the abbey to buy another one." When the men looked at her in confusion, she added, "He did not tell you we are on our way to Whithorn to pray for the birth of the child?"

The old man shook his head.

For some reason the tears weren't difficult to produce. The though of carrying Ewen's child filled her with all kinds of strange emotions. Deep emotions. Tender emotions. "We've lost so many," she said softly. "I just want to give him a son."

Ewen seemed caught up in the emotion as well. He tucked her under his arm again and soothed her with gentle strokes of her head. "Don't fret, sweeting, all will be well."

Janet rested her cheek on the solid wall of his chest and took a shuddering breath. Good heavens, he felt good. With the strength of his arms around her, it was easy to believe him.

"This horse is not for sale," Ewen added, "but we will find another. Come, love."

He started to lead her away, but a voice stopped them. An irritated, nasally *English* voice. "Wait. Someone will explain to me what is going on here, *now*."

Janet muttered one of Ewen's favorite curse words under her breath and looked up at the big Englishman looming over them in the saddle. Surprisingly, it wasn't the heavy armor and numerous weapons shimmering in the sunlight that worried her, but the sharpness of his gaze. Beneath the steel helm, she could tell that the blue-eyed captain with the dark hair and neatly trimmed beard was no fool.

And it was very clear that he wasn't going to let them just walk away.

Eighteen

✿

The way the soldier was looking at Ewen sent chills racing up and down Janet's spine. And Ewen—blast it—wasn't making any effort to deflect suspicion. He was acting every inch the fierce and formidable warrior, using his war-honed, muscular body to shield her.

Jerusalem's temples! He might as well have shouted his occupation. He looked like a man who was born with a sword in his hand and would fight to the death to protect what was his. In this case, her.

It would be rather sweet, if it weren't going to get them killed.

"My wife and I are making our way to Whithorn Abbey to pray for the child," he said curtly, the authority of a Highland chieftain booming in his voice. Good gracious, could he not at least attempt to fake deference? "We lost our horse, and I was trying to buy this one from the farmer." He motioned to the horse in the yard. "I was not aware it did not belong to him. If you would be interested in selling—"

"I am not," the captain interrupted. "Is this true?" he asked the farmer.

The old man nodded. "Aye, he offered me ten pounds for the animal."

From behind Ewen's broad shoulder—which was impressive, she had to admit—Janet didn't like the way the soldier's eyes narrowed. He took in Ewen's simply garbed appearance. "What kind of peasant walks around with that much coin?"

Janet could practically hear Ewen grinding his teeth. He truly was horrible at this. Mild-mannered, unassuming, and politic didn't seem to be in his nature. 'Twas a good thing he was such a good warrior; he wouldn't last two days as a courier.

"The kind who is going to an abbey to pray for an unborn child," he snapped.

Janet groaned at the unmistakable sarcasm in his voice. Why didn't he just draw his sword? The effect was the same.

This had gone on long enough. It was clear she needed to do something, and fast. Drawing the soldier's attention away from Ewen, for starters.

She hoped this would work. She'd been pretending to be a nun for so long, she was a bit out of practice. Fortunately, with nothing better to do while she'd been waiting earlier, she'd taken some pains with her appearance. With a toss of her freshly combed hair over her shoulder, she tugged the dress down a bit over her chest and stepped out from behind her "husband."

She smiled sweetly at the irate soldier (Ewen's tone had obviously not gone unnoticed). "My husband is not a peasant, my lord," she said, walking toward him. She thought Ewen growled something, but she ignored his warning. "He is a master builder. For the last two years, he has been working on improvements to the castle at Roxburgh." That ought to explain the heavily muscled physique as well as the calluses on his hands, were the captain to look.

She was rather fond of those calluses . . .

Her skin tingled, and she had to force her mind away from *why.*

Before the Englishman could ask more questions, she heaved a weary sigh, not missing the way his gaze fell to the tight bodice of her gown. She looked up at him tearily, giving him her best helpless, maiden-in-distress look. It took some effort. "My husband . . . he is worried about me and the child," she said by way of apology for Ewen's manners. "It has been a difficult journey." Her voice went higher and faster with her increasing distress. "The storm came, and then I lost the horse, and you see he was so angry—rightly so, I'm sure you'll agree."

The soldier shot Ewen a look as if he didn't agree at all. Janet regretted having to cast him in the role of bully, but it was necessary to bring out the soldier's chivalrous nature. "I had to keep stopping every mile, and then I said I couldn't go on—not until we found another horse. I'm sure it is horrible of me, but the thought of taking one more step across those mountains . . . I'm too heavy to carry, you see. And then he called me *round*?" The men gasped in understanding. A single tear slipped down her cheek. "I just couldn't do it." She blinked up at him, pleased to see that he seemed to have forgotten all about Ewen. "I'm just so very . . ." She swayed dramatically, as if she might swoon. "Tired."

Barely was the word out of her mouth than the soldier had jumped down to take her arm and steady her. "Do not distress yourself, dear lady." He shot a glare to the old farmer. "Why are you just standing there? Quick, get the lady something to drink." He led her over to a stool that sat by the door. "Rest here; you should not stand for so long in your condition." Janet smiled as she looked up into the soldier's concerned gaze, knowing she had him.

Ewen didn't know whether to throttle her or stand and cheer. By the time they rode out of the village a few hours later, they not only had a horse but full bellies as well.

Watching her had been something of a revelation. No actor upon the stage could have performed better. She spun her story with such ease and confidence, even he had started to believe it. He'd actually found himself telling the old man and his wife that the child would be named James if it was a laddie, after the man who'd taught him everything he knew. James Stewart had indeed taught him everything. Of course, the farmer didn't realize that Ewen wasn't talking about building, but about being a warrior and a chieftain.

Aye, she'd done well, but he could never forget the heart-stopping moment when he'd first seen her. It had been a shock. Not just that she'd disobeyed him and put herself in danger, but also how she'd looked. She didn't look anything like a nun or a lad. Dressed like a lady for the first time since he'd known her, he'd been riveted by the sheer feminine sensuality of her long golden hair tumbling over her shoulders in loose ringlets, and the sweetness of the curves revealed by her form-fitting gown. Her breasts were spectacular. The gown seemed to have been constructed to make a man think they were being presented just to him, like some kind of bounteous offering to the gods. Jesus, he'd wanted to toss his plaid around her shoulders and bury his head in them at the same time!

Of course, one large curve had been rather a surprise. *Pregnant*. It felt like a boulder had slammed into his chest. It squeezed. Tightened. Burned with an emotion he'd never felt before. A kind of fierce possessiveness came over him that dwarfed anything that had come before.

He wasn't as skilled as Raider or Saint in hand-to-hand combat, but he would have taken on every one of those soldiers bare-handed to protect her. Hell, he would have taken them on bare-arsed naked, as his father had done with the wolves, to protect her.

He'd been nearly out of his mind with anger—and probably jealousy, damn it—when she'd purposefully started to ploy the English captain with the feminine charms he hadn't yet finished admiring.

Only the realization that it was working had stayed his hand. But it had taken every ounce of self-restraint that he had (and some he did not have) not to go over there and smash his fist through the bastard's appreciative gaze. The fact that the captain knew exactly how angry Ewen was only seemed to fit the part she'd cast for him as the harsh, overprotective, short-tempered husband.

Who in the hell could mistake him for that?

So he fumed silently, if not invisibly, as Janet went about dispelling the soldier's suspicions, enlisting the farmer's help to find a villager who might have a horse for sale, charming the farmer's dour wife into cooking them a hot meal, and somehow getting them out of there without a blade drawn. He wasn't foolish enough to wish differently, but right now, with the way his body was teeming with restless energy, he would have welcomed the fight.

Once he was certain they were not being followed, he circled back to collect his armor and weapons from where he'd left them by the burn. The detour was regrettable, but even with the weight of two on the horse, they should be able to reach Sundrum just outside of Ayr by nightfall. There was a safe house there for them to spend the night, where he hoped the others would catch up with them.

Though he was holding her securely about the waist in front of him, and his body was painfully aware of her, he hadn't said a word since they left the village. With all the strange emotions twisting inside him, he wasn't sure he trusted himself.

They'd been riding for about an hour when she finally broke the silence. "Go ahead. I know you're angry. Just get it over with. But before you start yelling, I just want it noted that I only left the burn because I saw the banners and was trying to warn you." He opened his mouth to respond, but she cut him off. "I also want it noted that you weren't exactly making friends in the village." This time his mouth didn't even open before she cut him off again. "You only had a dagger. I know you are an exceptionally skilled warrior, but you would have to have been a *real* phantom to fight your way out of that."

He quirked a brow. Thought he was an exceptional warrior, did she? He rather liked hearing her say that. "May I speak now, or do you have anything else to say?"

She lifted her chin, meeting his gaze. "I'm done. For now."

She looked like a penitent waiting for the lash. He was sorry to disappoint her. "You did well, lass. Thank you."

He'd seemingly done the impossible: rendered her speechless. She could catch flies with her mouth open like that.

" 'Thank you'?"

He shrugged. "The babe was a stroke of brilliance."

"Brilliance?" she repeated dumbly.

"I see why you have made such a good courier. I can't decide whether you missed your calling as a lawman or as a performer on the stage."

"You mean you're not angry?"

He gave her a sidelong look while navigating the horse through a narrow clearing of brush. "I didn't say that. You took five years off my life when I saw you coming down that hill—and another five when you started flirting with the captain."

"I wasn't flirting, I was distracting."

He gave her protest all the attention it was worth—in other words, none. " 'Tis a dangerous game toying with a man like that, but I have to admit, you sized him up well. He had a heavy streak of English chivalry in him. Not that I wasn't about ready to take his head off for looking at you like that."

She blinked up at him in the sunlight, looking so beautiful that he would have cut off a limb to be able to kiss her again.

He cleared his throat and forced himself to look away.

She was so quiet for a moment, he could almost hear her thinking. "You really think I'm good at what I do?"

The happiness in her voice made his chest squeeze. And the way she was looking at him . . . It was as if he'd just plucked the sun from the sky and handed it to her. He could get used to that look.

"After what just happened, I can hardly deny it."

She shook her head, bemused. "I can't believe you aren't going to yell at me."

"Aye, well, don't make a habit of doing something like that. Not all men are as honorable as Sir Ranulf." That, as it turned out, was the captain's name. A bit of his anger returned. "Some might see fluttering lashes and a healthy display of cleavage as an invitation."

She gave him a sly look over her shoulder. "You were jealous."

"Jealous?" he blasted, outraged. "I wasn't jealous."

"It's quite understandable—Sir Ranulf is quite a handsome man."

If he'd been able to see straight, he might have noticed the wicked twinkle in her eye. But he was too furious. "Handsome? That pretty popinjay? I wonder how much time he spent staring into the looking glass to trim that beard of his. There wasn't a damned hair out of place!"

Only when she burst out laughing did the haze clear his eyes. His eyes narrowed, realizing she'd teased him into revealing far more than was wise.

The minx fluttered her eyes and leaned forward, giving him a bird's-eye view of that spectacular cleavage. "And what of you, Ewen? Are you the type of man to view it as an invitation?"

For one foolish moment he let himself look. He let his eyes plunge the wicked depths between her breasts. He gorged himself on the fullness, the roundness, the silky softness of the creamy white skin. He could almost taste her . . .

He sucked in his breath at the force of the heat that gripped him. At the knife-edge of lust that roared through his blood. As if guessing his pain, she slid her bottom back in the saddle against him. Nudging.

It took everything he had not to grab her hips and rub her harder against him. Only the cool challenge in her eyes stayed his hands.

"It's not an invitation I am free to accept, damn it. And you know very well why. How do you think the king would react—or Stewart would react—to discover that I'd taken your innocence?"

She frowned. "Stewart? Do you mean young Walter Stewart? Why should he care?"

Ah hell! Ewen clamped his mouth shut, realizing his mistake. "He is my liege lord. His father vouched for my loyalty, and I will not see that repaid by embarrassing the son."

She appeared chastened, his explanation seemingly satisfying her. "So it is Robert's reaction that worries you? You think he would punish you for being with me?"

Think? Ewen gave her a hard stare. "I *know* he would. And he would have every right to. You are his sister-in-law, for Christ's sake. I am the chieftain of a disfavored clan with one finger of land left of a once great lordship. My clan is hanging on by a thread, Janet. Any hope I have of recovering that land rests with the king."

Janet could see the conflicting emotions warring on his face and almost felt bad for pressing him. Almost.

She understood the source of his dilemma; she just didn't see it as an insurmountable problem. Not after what he'd said.

She still couldn't believe it: he'd not only thanked her, but also had admitted that she was good at what she did. He'd seen what she could do and recognized how she could be useful. *"Brilliant."* The admiration in his voice had nearly made her weep.

After days of wondering whether all she was doing was banging her head against a stone wall, she'd finally gotten through to him. He wasn't like her father or Duncan—or most of the other men she'd met. He *was* different. She was right: his apparent lack of regard for women had been a consequence of ignorance and inexperience rather than true belief. He didn't see her as a helpless accessory or as a serf, but as someone capable, valued, and worthy of respect—like Magnus's wife, Helen, the healer he'd mentioned.

It was what she'd always wanted from a man but never dreamed of finding. She was more certain than ever that this was right. How could he hold her in his arms like this, with their bodies pressed together intimately, and deny it? She wanted him to touch her. To make love to her. She wanted to feel his body connected to hers and know what it was to experience passion.

The problem was convincing him.

It was disheartening to think that she'd held so tightly to something for twenty-seven years, and then when she finally was ready to let go, was having to persuade a man to take it.

"This is between you and me, Ewen. I see no reason for Robert to be involved at all. If you want me, and I want you, why should anything else matter?"

He gave a harsh laugh, devoid of even the illusion of amusement. "You can't be that naive. You know that isn't the way it is done. Sharing a bed is not that simple."

She lifted her chin, not liking his tone. "It should be."

"Perhaps, but until that day, a noblewoman is not free to give her innocence wherever she wishes."

Janet knew he spoke the truth, but it didn't mean she had to agree with it—or abide by it. "There is no reason Robert needs to know."

He stiffened. "*I* would know. I would not dishonor you like that."

Janet glanced up at him sitting behind her, seeing the steely expression set on his face. That infernal nobility of his was proving problematic again. "Because we are not to be married?"

The look he gave her was fierce, searing in its intensity. His jaw clenched even tighter. "Because we *cannot* be married."

His vehemence took her aback. She was silent for a moment, absorbing the implications. He must have taken her protestations against marriage to heart. Or was it something else? *Cannot* . . . Perhaps he was alluding to their differences in station?

But somehow it felt as if he'd just thrown down the gauntlet. And despite his recent epiphany, she wasn't sure she wanted to pick it up. Sharing a bed, as he'd put it, was one thing, but trusting a man to put her fate in his hands was another. Did she want to marry him?

Nineteen

After days of being hunted, the ride from Cuingealach, the little village in the hills, to Ayrshire proved disconcertingly uneventful.

They crossed the hills between Douglas and Sanquhar, and continued west through the Airds Moss. By late afternoon, they neared their destination.

Though the English presence was still heavily felt, this was William Wallace country, and many of the martyred patriot's followers had come over to Bruce. A number of Wallace's relatives lived in Sundrum, including a cousin who the Highland Guard used for occasions such as this.

Ewen should be relieved. His mission was all but complete—or would be in the morning, when they met Hawk and Chief in Ayr with the *birlinn*. He would return Janet to her family, and he would go back to his duties with the Guard, tracking the next enemy or missing ally. Bruce would be grateful, and Ewen would be one step closer to restoring the name of Lamont—and, he hoped, the lands as well.

It was exactly what he wanted. Exactly what he'd been fighting for.

Then why was he trying to eke out every minute on this horse? Why did it feel like the moment he let go of her, this would all be over?

But there was no "this." There never had been. She couldn't be his. He'd made that clear. He'd told her he couldn't marry her, and from her silence since, it seemed she finally understood.

It was what he wanted.

So why was he disappointed that she hadn't protested? Why had a tiny part of him hoped the idea of marriage to him wasn't so inconceivable?

He stopped at a small burn in the Broad Wood to water the horse for the last time before reaching Sundrum. His leg was much improved since acquiring the mount, but it grew tight without movement, and it felt good to move about.

He wasn't delaying.

Janet returned from tending her needs and sat on a rock by the stream, nibbling on a piece of dried beef, while he held the horse to water.

"Tell me about Helen."

He glanced over at her in surprise. Not exactly the conversation he was expecting after their last. He stiffened slightly, wondering if she'd noticed something about his leg. He was careful not to favor the other, but the lass was too damned observant. "What do you want to know?"

She shrugged. "She's good at what she does?"

"She's one of the best."

"You said she could be a physician? How could that be? She is a woman."

"It's rare, but not impossible. Your brother-in-law's brother, the Earl of Sutherland, is married to a woman who trained in Edinburgh for a while at one of the guilds until she married. Helen might have as well."

"But then she married Magnus?"

Ewen wasn't sure where she was going with this. "Aye, but Helen never wanted the guilds. She's happy doing what she's doing."

"And what exactly is that?"

Ewen finished letting the horse drink and then led it from the burn, tying the rein around a tree. He crossed his arms and looked at her, knowing he was treading dangerous ground. She was no doubt trying to trick him into revealing something about the Guard or confirm his place in it. "She tends to the ill; what else would she do?"

"Does she go into battle with you?"

"No."

"But she is nearby?"

"Why are you so interested in this?"

She shrugged. "I just am. It's not usual, you must admit, for a gently born lady to take on such a role."

"Helen is unusual."

"As is her husband. He is a rare man to permit his wife to put herself in such danger."

He laughed. "MacKay hates every bloody minute of it."

She looked genuinely perplexed. "Then why does he go along with it?"

"Because he knows she is needed. And—"

He stopped.

"And?"

He shrugged uncomfortably. "And because he loves her."

"Oh." It obviously wasn't the answer she expected.

His mouth twisted in a smile. "Surely you've heard of it?"

Their eyes met, and a sharp frisson of awareness passed between them.

She blushed, lowering her gaze. "Aye, just not in marriage."

The wry tone did not hide the sadness underneath. "Your parents did not have a happy marriage?"

She made a sharp sound. "My father gave my mother as much consideration as he would have given a serf. Most of the time he forgot she was there. When she did find the courage to speak, he would cut her down so cruelly, she eventually began to believe that she was as stupid as he made her feel."

He winced, having seen more than his share of similar marriages. "Not all marriages are like that, lass."

Her mouth twisted with cynicism. "Aye—some, like my sister Mary's, are full of misery, heartbreak, and infidelity, and others, like my brother Duncan's, are constant battle-grounds of strife and discord. He and Christina would fight for hours. He was constantly dragging her off to their chamber to do God-knows-what to the poor woman."

Realizing she was serious, Ewen burst out laughing.

She bristled. "I don't see what is funny."

Seeing the hurt on her face, he sobered. "I'm sorry, lass. I can't speak to your sister Mary's first marriage. I knew the Earl of Atholl, and though he was a hell of a warrior, I didn't pay much mind to his relations with women who were not his wife. I've known Sutherland for a while, though, and to my knowledge he has been faithful to your sister since he first set eyes on her." He left out how amused they'd all been by it, given that Mary had rejected him as a suitor. "It was your comment about Duncan that made me laugh. His passion for his wife was well known—both in and out of the bedchamber. I suspect they made up just as passionately as they argued."

Janet's eyes widened, her cheeks reddening as she took in his meaning.

Her brows drew together. "How do you know so much about my brother?"

Damn. This wasn't exactly a subject he wanted to be discussing with her. "I fought with him for a while."

She looked stunned. "You did? Why did you not tell me before?" She seemed to realize something even as the words left her mouth. "You were with him at Loch Ryan, weren't you?"

He nodded.

She let out a slow breath. The way it hitched painfully made his chest squeeze. He wanted to reach for her, but forced his hands to his side.

She was quiet for a moment, as if steadying her emotions. "How did he die?"

Ewen saw the blade flashing in the sunlight before it came down upon Duncan's neck and forced the hideous image away. She didn't need to know the details. "Bravely, lass. Like the fierce Highland warrior that he was. I was proud to fight alongside him."

She knew he wasn't telling her all of it, but for once she didn't press. "It must have been horrible," she said. "All those men who died." She shuddered. "You were fortunate to make it out alive."

"Aye."

It had been a bloodbath. The MacDowells had been told of their arrival and had been waiting for them. Ewen had been in one of only two *birlinns* that had managed to escape. Whoever had betrayed them had cost almost seven hundred men their lives. One day that person would pay.

Janet saw the dark emotions cross his face and regretted invoking the painful memories. But somehow it made her feel better to know that Ewen was with Duncan when he died. Though the loss of her brother would always be a painful hole in her heart, Ewen had soothed the hurt just a little bit.

Was it true what he'd said about Duncan and Christina? Had she so misinterpreted the feelings between them? What went on behind those closed doors?

Apparently more than she'd realized.

Suddenly, all those long hours in the bedchamber took on a very different meaning—one sensual rather than sinister. Her brother had always seemed so subdued afterward. She'd taken it for regret, but what if it was something else?

It was disconcerting to realize how little she knew about something that had been going on right before her.

She arched a brow, watching as Ewen fiddled with a bag

tied to the horse, eventually removing a skin. How did he know so much?

After taking a long swig, he sat down beside her. It was nice, this, sitting here with him without a cloud of danger hanging over them. Apparently, in no hurry to continue their journey, she decided to ask him. "Did your parents love each other?"

He tensed almost imperceptibly. She sensed right away that the subject was not a welcome one. But he answered her question. "Aye, though they shouldn't have."

"What do you mean?"

"When my father abducted my mother—with her approval—away from the Chief of Lamont, it nearly destroyed my father and our clan. Had it not been for James Stewart, it would have."

"Yet there is something undeniably romantic about it. Your father must have truly loved her to be willing to risk so much."

Ewen's face hardened. "My father was an irresponsible ruffian who did whatever the hell he wanted, without any sense of the consequences. He fought hard, drank hard, and apparently loved hard. Duty and loyalty didn't mean a damned thing to him. He stole his chief's bride, for Christ's sake, knowing full well there would be war."

Hearing him speak of his father explained so much. It seemed Ewen had done everything he could to distance himself from the type of man his father had been. His discipline, his sense of honor and responsibility, were the opposite of his father. Where his father had been wild and irresponsible, Ewen was the model soldier, doing exactly what was expected of him.

"What about your mother?"

His fingers clenched on the skin he still held in his hand. "His irresponsibility killed her."

She gasped. "What happened?"

"He couldn't keep his bloody hands off her. She'd barely

given birth to me before he got her pregnant again. She died in the birthing chamber ten months after my saint's day. The child—a little girl—was stillborn."

The way he said "little girl" made something in her heart catch. "Oh Ewen, I'm sorry. That is horrible. Growing up without a mother . . . It couldn't have been easy."

He shrugged. "I didn't know any differently. Fortunately, the Stewarts took me in to foster or I might have ended up every bit as wild and disreputable as my father. When he wasn't fighting or drinking, he was trying to kill himself with some fool challenge. That's actually how he died. The Lamont chief finally had his revenge, daring my father to climb a cliffside near Dundonald Castle in the rain."

"He must have been devastated after your mother's death."

"He was building her a castle when she died. For years, all he would talk about was finishing that castle. But, of course, he never did. As a boy, it came so that I hated even the bloody sight of those half-constructed walls."

Her heart squeezed. It must have been a painful reminder of his father's failures.

He shook his head. "But you know what the worst part is? He somehow managed to get me to do it for him. So now, on top of trying to regain some of the Lamont lands, I also need to earn enough coin to finish the blasted thing."

Emotion lodged in her chest and for the first time she admitted to herself what it was: she loved him. With every fiber of her being, she loved him. How strange after all these years to have finally lost her heart.

He was staring off into the distance, lost in his memories, the strong lines of his handsome face cast ablaze by the orange hues of the fading sunlight. Nay, lost was wrong. She'd *found* it. Her heart had always belonged to him.

"You are a good man, Ewen Lamont," she said softly.

He turned to look at her and something strange flashed in his eyes. It looked almost like guilt. But then he smiled wistfully. "I'm a sentimental fool, and I think you've spent too many nights on this hard ground." He stood and held out his hand. "Come. You've a warm bath, a hot meal, and a comfortable bed waiting for you."

She sighed dreamily, slipping her hand into his and allowing him to help her up. "It sounds divine. But Ewen . . ." Steel-blue eyes met hers. "None of that will change my mind."

He held her gaze for a long pause. And then he said something that she didn't understand, but that held the vague sense of a warning. "I hope you'll feel the same in a few days."

The sight of the lime-washed walls of the wattle-and-daub farmhouse, nestled against a small hill on the banks of Lochend Loch, should have been cause for celebration. It was the first stop on the end of their journey. They would be safe here.

But to Ewen it represented a bitter return to reality. Free from the narrowed vision of danger, where getting Janet to safety and staying one step ahead of the English who stalked them was all that mattered, he could see clearly what the guilt, which had been building since he'd first realized how important her place in the king's network was to her, had been trying to tell him.

She was going to hate him for not telling her the truth. For allowing her to believe she could actually be returning to Roxburgh in a few days. For not telling her about the betrothal.

What had seemed prudent and not-his-place at the outset now felt like a betrayal. It *was* a betrayal. He couldn't pretend otherwise. Their relationship had changed. The sinful attraction he'd felt for "Sister Genna" had transformed into something deeper, something more intense, as he grew to know—and care about—Janet. Somewhere in there, the right thing to do had switched, and if he'd ever had an opportunity to correct the mistake, he'd missed it.

Finishing this mission was going to exact a personal cost that he'd never imagined. He'd known she'd be angry; he just hadn't realized how much it would matter to him.

Part of him wanted to tell her the truth, but he knew it would probably be better this way.

Maybe if she hated him it wouldn't be so hard for him to walk away? Maybe it would stop him from thinking of things that couldn't be? Maybe it would make it less hard to see her marry someone else?

His chest burned. The very thought of it ate like acid in his gut.

His hand clenched the reins, and unconsciously his arm drew tighter around her waist.

What the hell choice did he have? The king wasn't going to very well set aside the betrothal with Stewart to let her marry one of his Guardsmen—not to mention a Lamont—even if Ewen could convince *her,* which he wasn't sure he could. The only option open to him was one he wouldn't consider. He wasn't his damned father. He wouldn't "abduct" his liege lord's bride. He wouldn't risk everything for one woman. No matter how much he wanted her.

And God, how he wanted her! After so many hours with her in his arms, every inch of his body burned with need. The scent of her hair, the slimness of her waist, the heaviness of her breasts, the curve of her bottom, had infused his senses, imprinted on his consciousness, invaded his soul.

He didn't want to let her go.

She turned to look up at him. "Is something wrong?"

He startled. "Nay, why?"

"Aren't you going to get down? I assume this is our destination?"

He cursed under his breath, trying to cover his embarrassment. How long had they been standing there?

He pried his arm from around her waist and jumped

down. After helping her to dismount, he tied the reins to a post. "Wait here, while I make sure we are welcome." She nodded, but then he thought of something else. "It is important that you only call me by my first name."

She frowned. "Why?"

"Lamont is not exactly a welcome name in these parts. There are some who still believe that my kinsmen had a hand in killing William Wallace's father." Not to mention that his cousin, the exiled Lamont chief, was a vassal of the Earl of Menteith, the man who was responsible for turning Wallace himself over to the English.

Normally, he would simply use his war name of Hunter. But with Janet here that wasn't an option. She knew too much already.

Fortunately, the answer seemed to satisfy her. "Very well. And who am I?"

He knew what she was asking, but there was no way in Hades that he was going to pretend to be married to her again. He couldn't stand another night of sleeping beside her. "Janet. That is all they need to know. I would not make them uncomfortable by learning that they serve the king's sister-in-law in their humble abode."

"I would not make anyone uncomfortable, but it has been many years since I've been served by anyone. I do not expect it, nor do I wish it. I assure you, this humble abode will seem like a castle compared to some of the places I've stayed."

He didn't miss the soft rebuke. If she was also trying to tell him that their difference in station didn't matter to her, he pretended not to understand. It might not matter to her, but it would to the king. Of that he was damned well sure.

With one last look that felt suspiciously like goodbye, Ewen went to find the farmer.

Once Janet realized the truth of her feelings for Ewen, everything seemed to fall into place. If she had any doubts about what she wanted, they were soon put aside upon arriving at the small farmstead.

She sat at the table set out before the softly glowing peat fire, enjoying the warmth that enveloped her. It wasn't just the heat from the flames or the satisfaction of a good meal, but also the company. The Wallaces were gracious hosts, and their happiness was contagious.

Ewen was right; not all marriages were horrible. The Wallaces were proof of that. Their fond banter, subtle loving glances, and unconscious touches spoke of possibility.

Robert Wallace was a distant cousin of William Wallace. He'd fought alongside his illustrious relative until six years before, when Robert lost a hand at a skirmish in Earnside. Margaret was considerably younger than her husband, and far prettier. The dainty, dark-haired lass with her elfin features and slim build seemed utterly wrong beside the grizzled warrior of around forty years, who had the towering height of his famous relative and the imposing bulk of a smith. But somehow they went together perfectly. Her bright laughter and open, sunny nature complemented her husband's gruff, taciturn disposition. It was clear he doted on his young wife. His young *pregnant* wife.

The odd pang Janet had felt in her chest when she'd first realized Margaret was with child had become more identifiable as the evening wore on. It was longing. Sharp, aching longing.

On the heels of her own "pregnancy," Janet had never felt the absence of children in her life so acutely. Of course, there were times over the years when she'd thought of a child—of what she would be giving up by taking the veil—but given that a child required a husband, and considering the importance of the work she was doing, it seemed a small price to pay. In the abstract, perhaps it was. But it didn't feel so small right now, sitting with a beaming pregnant woman on one side and the man she'd just realized she loved on the other.

It felt like something she wanted. With him. Children. Cozy nights before the fire. Loving glances and tender touches. She wanted what the Wallaces had.

She knew what that meant. *Marriage.*

She waited for a few seconds to react to the word, but the usual bad taste did not rise to the back of her mouth. It *must* be love, she thought with a wry smile. With Ewen, a happy marriage seemed possible.

She knew there were complications. The king for one, her work for another. Robert was probably the easier of the two. If Ewen was indeed in his secret guard as she suspected, that would help. Ewen wouldn't like the idea of her continuing her work, but he understood how important it was to her. He wasn't like her father and brother—he wouldn't try to stick her in some box. He valued her—he'd told her as much. If he loved her, they would find a way to make it work—like Magnus and Helen.

She'd finally met a man who was strong enough to let her be herself. His force of will might be a lot quieter than hers, but it was just as strong. There would be battles between them, aye, but she was looking forward to them.

Of course, she wasn't the only one who needed to be convinced that it was a good idea. He wanted her, of that she had no doubt, and he cared for her—he'd admitted as much. But did he want to *marry* her? He'd said it was impossible, but what if it wasn't?

Her gaze slid to the man in question. He was locked in a quiet conversation with Robert Wallace about the war, while Janet and Margaret finished their meal—the latter pretending not to listen to the men's discussion.

"Are we talking loud enough for you, wife? I wouldn't want you to miss any of our private conversation," Robert said, looking up. His expression was chastising, but his eyes were soft as they fell upon his wife.

Margaret didn't miss a beat. "That is quite considerate of you, Robert. I'm sure it is all beyond my poor woman's understanding, but if you could speak a little louder that might help."

Her eyes danced as she leaned down and whispered to Janet, "Although I'd hardly qualify the exchange of a few words and the occasional grunt a conversation. I don't know which of them is worse."

Janet burst out laughing.

Robert's eyes narrowed on his wife. "What is so funny?"

Margaret smiled and gave Janet a wink as she stood from the table. "I'm afraid it is private."

Robert shook his head, but Janet didn't miss the small smile as he turned back to his conversation with Ewen.

Margaret started clearing the platters from their meal. When Janet rose to help, she ordered her back to her seat. "You are a guest," she said, and then in a whisper, "Besides, you must tell me if they say anything interesting."

Janet smiled conspiratorially. "I shall do my best. But 'interesting' is probably more than we can hope for."

Margaret chuckled. "You're probably right. How about this: try not to fall asleep."

"I make no promises," Janet said. "I can't remember the last time I've felt so comfortable. You have a lovely home, Margaret."

She could see how much the comment pleased the other woman. "I think you saw the apple tart."

Janet laughed. "I may have, at that."

Margaret moved to the other side of the long room, while Janet relaxed. She eyed the two men at the end of the table surreptitiously. She must not be as adept at overhearing as Margaret, because she could make out very little of what was being said. Although she was used to Ewen's sparse conversation, even for him, he seemed unusually subdued tonight.

Something was wrong.

Was he more worried than he'd let on that his friends

had not arrived? He'd seemed confident that they would arrive soon. Or was something else bothering him?

She frowned as he refilled his goblet again. He seemed to be drinking more than usual tonight. His face looked a little flushed.

She waited for a break in the men's conversation. "Is your leg feeling all right, Ewen?"

He looked over at her. "It feels fine. Why do you ask?"

She blushed, not wanting to admit that she'd been watching his intake of ale. "You had not mentioned it for a while, and I was just wondering how it was healing."

"It's fine."

"You are injured?" Margaret asked, approaching the table.

"Some time ago," he answered.

"But it has not healed properly," Janet interjected.

Ewen shot her a glare. She smiled.

Margaret frowned. "I have some ointment—"

"Really," Ewen said. "It's fine."

"Leave the lad alone, Margaret," Robert said. "He's old enough to decide for himself whether he needs help."

Margaret and Janet looked at each other with a roll of the eyes. There was no age old enough for men to admit they needed help.

"I am rather tired, though," Ewen said, pushing back from the table. "I think I shall retire."

"Already?" Janet said, not hiding her disappointment. "But what about the tart?"

She wasn't ready for the night to end—or for the journey to end, for that matter. She knew very well that Ewen could be called away for another mission as soon as they returned, and she would have to leave almost immediately as well, to make it back to Roxburgh in time for St. Drostan's Day.

The complications with the English they'd faced on their journey were certainly going to make persuading Robert more difficult, but given the importance of her contact's information, and the fact that Ewen and the other phantoms wouldn't be with her to draw the attention of the English, she was confident he would see the necessity.

And then there was the other matter. The *them* matter.

Ewen looked at Margaret. "I will look forward to a slice in the morning." His gaze finally fell on her. "You should get some rest as well. We will leave early and will have a long day ahead of us."

Janet nodded and let him go. For now. She would rest, but only *after* she said what she wanted to say. He needed to know how she felt. As what she had to say needed to be said in private, however, she would bide her time. But before this night was done, Ewen would know what was in her heart.

Twenty

✤

Ewen sat on a stool before the iron brazier that Margaret had thoughtfully provided for his warmth in the barn, drawing the edge of his blade over the oiled whetstone with long, slow, deliberate strokes. It was something he did before battle, to calm himself and keep his mind off what was ahead. A ritual, he supposed. They all had them. Most of the Guardsmen tended their weapons, but MacSorley liked to take a short swim, and Striker read from a small leather-bound folio he carried around with him like a talisman. There were always a few prayers—and a few long drinks of whisky.

But tonight, like the ale and the swim in the loch that had come before it, the ritual wasn't helping. Nothing was helping to keep his mind off Janet and what lay ahead. And it sure as hell wasn't helping to ease the restless energy teeming inside him. He felt as on edge as this damned sword.

He wished he could say it was just lust. God knew, he'd been pushed well past the limit that any hot-blooded man should be expected to endure. He wanted her so intensely his teeth hurt just to look at her. But although a hard cock was a part of it—a large, painful part of it—it wasn't all of it.

Lust wasn't what made his chest burn every time their eyes had met tonight. He hadn't missed her reaction to

Margaret's condition and the longing on her face, just as he hadn't missed the way she'd looked at him afterward.

It wasn't possible, damn it. Why was she tormenting him with things that couldn't be?

Because she didn't know they couldn't be.

One more day. One more day and this would all be over. He could be damned sure she wouldn't be looking at him like that after tomorrow, and what he wanted would no longer make a difference. But he could find little joy in knowing that she would hate him, even if it was for the best.

Doing the right thing shouldn't be this hard, damn it.

He swore as his hand slipped and his thumb met the edge of the blade. A line of blood gushed from his fingertip, a few drops landing on the whetstone before he could draw it away.

Bloody hell! Good thing he didn't put much store in omens. If he did, that was a bad one.

The door burst open just as he got to his feet. Even in the shadows he recognized her. "What happened, are you all—" Janet stopped, her eyes widening as she took in his bloody finger. "Your hand!"

She took a step into the barn, but he stopped her. "It's nothing." He picked up a piece of the bandage left over from wrapping his leg, and wrapped it around his thumb. "I nicked myself on the blade. I happens all the time," he lied, although it was true that the cut was merely a nuisance.

Unlike his leg. That hurt like the blazes, which was odd as it didn't appear any worse. What little blood there was seemed thin—watery-looking, actually—but it was alarming. After going for his icy swim in the loch earlier, he'd wrapped the wound in a fresh linen, and it felt a little better. But he had to admit he was concerned. Not concerned enough, however, to have her touching him. If that was why she was here—although he didn't see any ointment or linens in her hands. Whatever the reason for her appearance, it wasn't a good idea.

"What are you doing here, Janet? It must be after midnight. You should be sleeping. Get back to the house."

She ignored him. "We need to talk." Closing the door softly, she walked toward him. As she drew closer, she came into the light.

God's blood! He felt as though someone had just landed a fist in his gut. A fist of temptation. She was a walking fantasy. A siren sent to lead him straight to Hades. She looked like she'd just rolled from bed. Her golden hair tumbled around her shoulders in a mass of slightly mussed—*sensually* mussed—waves that caught the flickering candlelight in a silvery halo. His plaid was wrapped around her shoulders and clutched together at the front, but he could still make out the thin linen chemise that she wore underneath. *All* that she wore underneath. Below the edge he could see a hint of bare leg and feet that she'd hastily shoved in her shoes without hose.

She stopped a few feet from him and he tried to breathe, but the air in his lungs seemed to have turned solid.

For the first time in his life, the hunter experienced what it was like to be caught. Like a deer in the bowman's gaze, he couldn't move.

He watched her gaze flicker back toward the darkened stalls, where their horse and a few other animals were housed, and then to the small corner where a comfortable-looking pallet had been laid out for his use. In addition to the brazier and the stool, there was a small table with an oil lamp. The smell was earthy from the peat rather than pungent, and the air was sultry and warm.

Coupled with the way she looked, it made him think of . . .

Hell, everything about her made him think of that. He was balancing on a sword's edge. He clenched his fists, one hand balling around the bandage. "You need to leave,

Janet, *now*. Whatever you have to say can wait until morning. This isn't right. You shouldn't be here with me alone
like this. What if the Wallaces wake and notice you are
gone?"

The fierceness of his tone didn't seem to make any impression on her. She lifted her chin to meet his gaze. "We've
been alone for almost two days. The Wallaces are fast
asleep, and even if they do wake, I suspect they will know
exactly where I have gone—Margaret especially." She
took another step toward him, and he had to force himself
not to take a retreating step back. But his skin drew tight
over his bones. His blood pounded through his veins, and
his heart was hammering like a drum. "What I have to say
is important and cannot wait."

He frowned, a prickle of concern piercing through his
anger at her invasion and the urgency to just get her the
hell out of here. "Is something wrong?"

She shook her head.

"Then what is it?"

She bit her lip, as if she didn't know what to say. Given
that she *always* knew what to say, his concern grew.

"I've changed my mind."

"About what?"

"I do not think that I wish to be a nun."

Some of his anger returned. "And this is so important
that you sneak out of your bed in the middle of the night
to come to find me?"

She shot him a glare, her mouth pursing. "It means that
in the right circumstances, I *might* consider marriage."

He stilled. The air seemed to have left his lungs. Actually
the air, the blood, the bones, and pretty much everything
else seemed to have left him as well.

Was she trying to say that she would consider marrying
him?

From the way she lowered her gaze and the soft pink

blush on her cheeks, he suspected that was exactly what she meant.

Jesus! Though he was wearing only a tunic and a thin pair of wool breeches, he felt a sheen of sweat gathering on his brow. What the hell was he supposed to say?

"Janet, you know that the right circumstances will be decided by the king. If it is your wish to marry, Bruce will be the one to find a husband for you—a *suitable* husband."

Her mouth tightened distastefully. "Robert isn't like that. He will consider my wishes."

Ewen swore under his breath. How could he tell her that "Robert" had already found a husband without considering her wishes at all? Not to mention that the king had warned Ewen to stay away from her.

He shuffled uncomfortably, suddenly feeling as if he were walking through a garden of Sutherland's black powder bags—with sparks on his boots. "He will find you a husband who has more than a finger of land and a half-built castle."

Rather than discourage her, his words seemed to embolden her. "But what if he could be persuaded? Don't you see, I could help you. If you were to marry me, it would improve your position with Robert. He would be sure to return some of your land to you, and—"

"Stop!" He took her by the shoulders and shook her, not realizing what he was doing. "What you are saying is impossible. Damn it, do you ever hear the word 'no'? It isn't going to happen."

She drew in a hard breath, staring at him with a hundred questions in her eyes. "Why not? I thought you . . ." Her eyes turned to his, tearing at him. "I thought you cared about me. Don't you want me?"

Bloody hell! He let her go as suddenly as he'd grabbed her, not trusting himself. He wanted her with every fiber of his being. He wanted her so desperately, it took everything he had not to pull her into his arms right now. "It isn't that simple, Janet."

"Why not?"

The hurt in her voice nearly broke him. He knew there would be tears in her eyes if he looked, so instead he dragged his fingers through his hair and paced a few steps before the iron brazier. "It just isn't."

"But I love you."

His feet stopped. His heart stopped. Everything seemed to stop. It took a few moments for the words to sink in. For one instant he felt a burst of something akin to pure happiness—happiness like he'd never experienced before. But then it was tamped down under the bitter weight of duty and loyalty. People were counting on him, damn it. She belonged to another man.

He wasn't going to be like his father, even if it bloody killed him. He would not do this. *Discipline.*

He turned and forced himself to look at her, every muscle in his body drawn as tight as a bow. His jaw was clenched, his fists were tight, and the pain in his chest doused whatever he'd been feeling in his leg.

She stared at him with round eyes, looking more vulnerable than he'd ever seen her. "Aren't you going to say something?"

"What would you like me to say?" He hadn't meant it to sound as harsh as it did, but he'd never been good with words. He'd never been good with any of this. As the mess he'd made of everything proved.

She flinched, her fingers turning white as she squeezed the plaid tighter. "I thought. . . ." She stopped, choking on a silent sob. "I thought you might feel the same way. But I can see I was wrong." The first tears slid from her eyes, each one a lance of pain through his heart. "I should not have bothered you. I'm s-sorry."

He could barely hear the last word through the tiny sob. He could see her shoulders shaking as she turned to leave.

He couldn't do this. He couldn't let her leave like this. "Janet, wait."

And that's when he made his mistake. He reached for her.

Janet was too hurt to be humiliated, although she was sure that would come later. Heaven's Gates, she'd practically asked him to marry her! She'd given him her heart, and he hadn't wanted it. Her chest felt as if it had been crushed by an enormous boulder—or ground under a heavy boot.

She couldn't breathe—didn't dare breathe—for fear the hot rush of emotion constricting her throat and chest would pour out in a flood of torrential sobs.

Do you ever hear the word 'no'?

Aye, she'd heard it. Loudly. Dear God, how could she have been so mistaken? Was this just another example of her barreling down the mountain like a rolling stone? Had she imagined something that wasn't there?

Her lower lip trembled. Her shoulders shook. The tears began to flow. Oh God, she had to get out of there!

She heard him call after her and would have ignored him if he hadn't caught her arm.

"Let go of me!" She tried to shrug him off, not wanting him to see her cry. Not wanting him to see how badly he'd hurt her. Could he not leave her one shred of pride?

Apparently not. He wouldn't let her go; his big warrior's hand closed around her upper arm like a steel manacle. He spun her around so she was facing him, but she wouldn't look up. She kept her gaze pinned to the embroidered neck of his linen tunic. But even that hurt. It tied at the neck, and she found herself staring at the dark patch of skin underneath. Skin that she still wanted to touch.

The heat of his body enveloped her. Cruelly. Teasingly. Taunting her with memories of things that would not be.

"I don't want to hurt you."

She gave a sharp laugh that came out as more of a broken sob. It was rather late for that. "Then what do you want, Ewen?" She looked up into his eyes, a flash of reckless anger restoring some of her boldness. "Oh, wait. I know what you want." She leaned her body into his, her nerve-endings sizzling at the contact. But desire wasn't love. "How could I have confused this for anything else?"

He made a harsh groan, twisting her arm around to cinch her in even tighter against him, although she didn't think he was aware of what he'd done. "Stop it, Janet. That isn't true."

His face was a dark, tortured mask. His mouth a hard line, his eyes chips of steel, his jaw clenched.

Her heart seized. She hated him for making her want him so much. For every one of the hard muscles pressed against her that made her body heat, even now. For being so handsome it made her heart ache to look at him. For making her lose sight of her plan and believe even for a moment in faerie tales. And most of all for not loving her back.

"What isn't true?" she taunted. "That you don't want me?" She pressed her hips against him. "I'd say your body disagrees." Her eyes bored into his. She was shaking with anger, frustration, and hurt. She wanted to lash out. She wanted to hurt him just as badly as he'd hurt her. "But you know what, Ewen? That is no longer enough for me. I no longer want you. So let me go!"

Panic rose hard and hot inside him. She meant it. Ewen could see it in her eyes. She didn't want him anymore. He'd pushed her away one too many times. It was what he wanted, wasn't it? He'd thought so. But as they stood there pinned together, sparks of anger and desire clashing between them in a fierce battle of wills, he knew he couldn't let her go. If he let her walk away now, it would be too late. He would lose her. She would never come back. It would be over.

He could fight desire—he might have even been able to win—but he couldn't fight the fear wrought by thoughts of a future without her. She'd battered down his defenses until he just couldn't fight it anymore.

To hell with it. His mouth covered hers in a hot, possessive kiss meant to leave her no doubt of his intentions. He was going to make her belong to him, in the only way he could. For the first time, Ewen didn't hold anything back, giving his desire free rein.

He proved her a liar with his lips and tongue, entreating—nay, demanding—with each deft stroke, until she was returning his kiss with as much heat and passion as burned inside him. She did want him.

The plaid she was clutching—his plaid—fell into a pool at their feet as her arms circled around his neck. Her tiny body stretched out against his and he sank into her, breathing her in in hot, heavy draws.

It was incredible. Her warmth. Her softness. The heady scent of her hair. He delved deeper, fitting her body into his, digging his hand through the silky golden strands to cup her head, and sinking his tongue deeper and deeper into the sweet, warm cavern of her mouth.

He couldn't get enough. His mouth was ravenous for her taste, his hands eager to roam every inch of her, and his body aching for more pressure.

She moaned and shuddered, her tiny fingers clutching—digging—into his shoulders, visceral proof of how much she wanted him.

A bolt of heat struck hard in his groin, filling him. Making him swell. Throb. Bead.

He wasn't going to last.

Sweeping her into his arms, he carried her over to the pallet. He broke the kiss only long enough to set her down and tear off his shirt before coming down beside her.

Her eyes widened, traveling over the spans of bare skin. Nay, "traveling" wasn't quite right. "Feasting on" was perhaps more accurate. He was not unaccustomed to women admiring the effects of warfare on his body, but with her it was different. With her, it mattered.

"My God, you're beautiful," she blurted.

He smiled. "Warriors aren't beautiful, lass. I thought you were good with words?"

She blushed, even though she knew he was teasing her. "Very well, 'perfect' then." Her eyes went to the cut he'd suffered in the battle with the English the previous morning. "The wound does not hurt?" He shook his head. As he'd told her, it was no more than a scratch. "What is this?" she asked, outlining the mark that bound the Highland Guard on his other arm with her finger.

Ah hell. "Nothing."

She ignored him. "It's the Lion Rampant with some kind of band and inscription." She squinted in the candlelight. "*Or inveniam viam.* 'I shall find a way,' she translated. "Fitting for a tracker. It sounds like the inscription for a sword."

"It is," he said. He had the same mark on his sword. The Lion Rampant tattoo, encircled with the torque-like band of a spiderweb, was the mark used to identify each member of the Highland Guard. But many of the warriors had personalized it with weaponry or mottos. Ewen had done both. He had two pikes crossed behind the lion and the inscription on his sword below.

His arm flexed under her fingertips, and thankfully she moved on. She reached out and spread her hands over his chest and arms. "You look as if you are made of steel." She lifted her gaze to his shyly. "You know, I never liked muscles before, but I think they've rather grown on me." Her palm spread over the bulge of muscle on his upper arm and squeezed. "Aye," she said, her voice growing a little huskier, "I am quite appreciative."

Another blast of heat rushed over him. He swore and

kissed her again before her words could drive him any crazier.

He had every intention to take it slow. To savor every minute of what might be the only time—

He stopped. *Don't think about it.*

Instead he concentrated on how good she felt, tucked in under him. He held her cradled against his side, half-propped over her, so as not to crush her with his weight. It also left his hand free to explore, and he made damned sure to leave no part of her untouched. He cupped her breast through the thin fabric of the chemise, brushing his thumb over the taut peak, before sliding his hand back over her waist and hips, and then her bottom, lifting her against him until her leg wrapped around his hip.

Their groans and moans blurred together when he started to rock gently against her. Slowly he increased the pace, mimicking the rhythm with his tongue, as the slow, gentle circles became a fast, hard grind. He let her get used to his size. Let her feel every inch of his length as he moved his body over hers.

But the playacting separated by a few layers of linen and wool wasn't enough for either of them. The frantic race of her heartbeat and quickening breath, between increasingly urgent gasps and moans, matched his own.

Tension pounded through his body. He was so damned hot. Fevered. His body an inferno of need. Sweat gathered on his brow as he fought the instincts pressing inside him. Every one of his muscles was flexed hard, shaking with the effort to find restraint. To find control. To make it last.

But it wasn't going to last. Not this time. It felt too good, and he wanted her too intensely. From the first moment he'd seen her in the forest, half-naked and fierce as a Valkyrie, he'd been waiting for this moment. He hadn't wanted to acknowledge that even to himself, but the truth had finally caught up to him. Or maybe it was fate that had caught up to him.

He knew it was too hurried. Too rushed. But he had to be inside her. *Now.*

With one hand, he unfastened the ties of his breeches and slid them over his hips. The cool blast of air over turgid skin made him groan with relief.

Finesse was beyond him. His hand felt big and clumsy as he reached for the hem of her chemise, easing it just enough to give him access. He forced himself to tease it out. To let his hand rest on her thigh a moment before he touched her. But she wouldn't let him. She started to squirm, to moan, to lift her hips to meet him.

So he gave her what they both wanted, sweeping his fingers over her dampness, before sliding into the tight feminine heat. He groaned. So wet. So damned hot.

A sharp squeeze of desire fisted at the base of his spine. He wanted to be inside her so desperately, it took everything he had not to lever his body over hers and thrust up hard inside. The knowledge of how good it would feel crashed over him in a hot wave, nearly dragging him under.

But he had to make her ready for him. She was an innocent, damn it, and he was going to make this good for her, even if it killed him.

And it bloody well might.

Lifting his head, he broke the kiss to watch her face as he pleasured her.

He felt something squeeze hard in his chest. She was so beautiful. Locked in the throes of passion, her cheeks flushed with pleasure, her golden hair splayed out behind her head in wild disarray, her eyes half-lidded and her kiss-swollen lips gently parted, she looked like some kind of sensual goddess. Knowing that he was doing this to her humbled him. It was his kiss that had swollen her lips, his week's worth of stubble that had reddened the sensitive skin around her chin, and his touch that was making her wild.

But not quite wild enough.

Janet felt as if she were caught up in a whirlwind. A hot, frantic, devastating whirlwind. She'd gone from utter despair to ecstasy in a matter of minutes.

Whatever had been holding him back was gone. When he'd kissed her, she knew he'd made his decision: he'd chosen her. Her chest swelled with happiness. She hadn't been wrong to give him her heart.

Swept up in the heat of his embrace, she gave herself over to the passion. She gave herself over to him. Surrender had never felt so good. The feeling of his fingers inside her—stroking her, bringing her to the very peak of pleasure . . .

Oh God, she couldn't stand it! She moaned, writhed, felt the overwhelming urge to press her hips against his hand. An echo of the memory of what he'd done to her taunted, as the sensation flickered just out of her reach.

"Not yet, *mo chroí*," he whispered in her ear with a wicked chuckle. "I want to taste you first."

Janet didn't want to try to tell him what to do, but she rather preferred this right now to kissing.

She gave a little mewl of protest when he slowed his stroke, and tried not to get irritated when he chuckled. "I promise you'll like this, lass."

She felt her first flicker of premonition when he scooted down, not up. My God, his face was right between her . . .

A sudden flood of embarrassment cooled some of the heat. Instinct brought her legs together hard. "No! Don't! You can't."

He looked up at her, a wicked gleam in his steel-blue eyes. One thick chunk of dark hair slung over his brow, giving him a distinctly roguish edge. He buried his mouth right at the apex of her closed legs, the warmth of his breath making her gasp. He smiled. "I assure you, I can."

He nuzzled her again, gently nudging her legs apart. "You're going to like this, love. Just let me have one little taste."

Oh God! She shuddered—and not with mortification—when he nuzzled her again, this time giving her a flick of his tongue that sent ripple after ripple of sensation right to her toes. Her legs relaxed even more, opening a little wider as embarrassment quickly gave way to the wicked cravings of her body.

When he kissed her *there,* pressing his warm, firm lips to the most intimate part of her, she cried out in shock and pleasure so acute it set every nerve-ending on edge. Or rather, turned every nerve-ending inside out. She was a ball of raw, inside-out nerve-endings. Hot, sensitive, and poised for his touch.

He teased her with gentle flicks of his tongue and soft kisses until she couldn't stand it anymore. She started to lift her hips against him, wanting more pressure.

"Do you like it, love?"

Like it? Good heavens, she'd never imagined liking anything quite so much. She hoped he wasn't expecting her to speak; all she could manage was a breathy gasp.

She forgot to be embarrassed and didn't offer a single protest when he settled himself firmly between her legs, looped her legs over his shoulder, and cupped her bottom to lift her more fully to his wicked, wonderful mouth.

The first loving stroke of his tongue sent every one of those inside-out nerve-endings to tingling. But it was the pressure of his mouth and the grate of his stubbled jaw against the tender skin between her thighs that made her lose all shame.

She started to shake. Started to arch her back and lift her hips harder and harder against his lips and tongue. She told him not to stop. She begged him to make it stop. Faster. Deeper. Harder.

Oh God, yes . . . yes! A rush of heat surged from between her legs to the warm suction of his mouth. He held her there, drinking her in, as she catapulted into a different realm, as her body came apart in wave after wave of hot, undulating pleasure.

Through the mindless haze, she heard him swear. "I can't wait any longer . . . have to be inside you . . . sorry."

His voice sounded almost strangled.

Why was he apologizing?

It didn't take her long to find out.

Twenty-one

❧

Ewen had reached the end of his restraint. Whatever control he thought he had vanished in the wake of her release. He'd wanted to drive her crazy and make her ready for him; he just hadn't anticipated what it would do to him.

It was the most erotic experience of his life. He'd never tasted a woman so fully before. Never had his mouth on her as she broke apart. Never felt so connected as the spasms of pleasure reverberated through her body. She gave herself so freely and completely.

He couldn't wait another minute.

Mumbling some kind of apology, he levered his body over hers. The muscles in his arms and shoulders flexed hard in anticipation as he fought to hold himself steady. To go slow.

Her eyes lifted to his. He felt a click. It was as if something shifted in his chest and locked into place.

Her eyes flickered down and widened. He followed the line of her gaze and saw what she did: a very intimidating-sized erection. He wanted to give her some kind of reassurance, to tell her it was going to be okay, but truth be told, even if he could manage to grunt a few words right now, he wasn't sure how much this was going to hurt. Even soft and wet from her release, she was still small and tight, and he was big and hard. *Very* big and very hard.

Just thinking about it made him pulse. He fought the urge to throw his head back and surge inside.

But it was a battle he lost. His cock was too hard, her slick, warm entrance too inviting, and whatever control he'd had fled the moment he rubbed his sensitive head against her silky dampness. Holding her gaze, he started to press inside, inch by inch, but the intimacy was too intense, the emotions too powerful. It was too much. The gentle nudge became a quick plunge as he possessed her fully, binding her to him in a way that could not be undone.

He let out a groan of pure, primitive satisfaction, overwhelmed by a sensation of relief and something else. The only way to describe it was utter rightness. As if he was where he belonged. As if he'd found his destiny.

Her soft cry of pain broke through some of his haze. But it was too late. Too late for recriminations. Too late to change his mind. Too late to take it back—he'd gone too far, he couldn't pull back now even if he wanted to. She was his.

At least for the moment.

He clenched his teeth, holding himself stone still, wanting to give her time to adjust to the feel of him. But it felt too good. She was tight and hot, gripping him like a damned glove, and every instinct in his body screamed to move.

He stole a glance down at her, surprised to see her eyes not squeezed shut, but looking at him with the emotion that she'd forced him to acknowledge.

Love. His chest squeezed. A wave of tenderness crashed over him. He leaned down and gave her a soft kiss. "I'm sorry."

She smiled. "For what?"

For so many things. "I hurt you."

"It isn't so bad . . . now."

As if to prove her words, she moved, sending a hot swell

of pleasure surging to the tip of him. He groaned, unable to resist the primitive instinct to respond with a movement of his own. A tight, quick nudge.

She winced.

He cursed. "Damn it. I'm sorry. I'm trying not to move, but you just feel so good, it's killing me."

Given how much pain he was in at the moment, the smile that spread across her face wasn't exactly appreciated. "I do? I am?"

He gave her a sharp glare, his teeth clenched tightly. "You don't need to be so pleased about it."

Her smile became even broader.

He leaned down to kiss her again, the movement making him sink deeper.

She gasped, but this time not with pain. Their eyes met. "Oh! That felt . . ."

He knew how it felt. It felt incredible. He moved again, drawing out just a little bit and sinking back in. Her eyes widened. "Oh . . ." Again. "Oh!"

When she circled her arms around his neck to hold on tighter, it was all the invitation he needed. Holding her gaze, he thrust again—and again. Watching for any sign of pain. But it wasn't pain that brought a soft pink blush to her cheeks.

When her hips rose to meet him, he couldn't hold back. His strokes lengthened. Deepened. Went faster and harder, her gasping moans urging him on.

The pleasure was intense. Overwhelming. Like nothing he'd ever imagined. She was . . . everything. And more.

So tight. So hot. Sweat poured off him, the frantic thrusts taking their toll. Pressure built at the base of his spine, stronger and more powerful than anything he'd ever felt before. Her body gripped him, milked him, pulled him over the edge.

And he took her with him. Holding her hips, he thrust in

hard and deep, grinding out her pleasure in slow, hard circles as his own roared in his ears.

He came with a white-hot intensity that shook him to his core. For a moment, the pleasure was so acute his mind went black. Again and again the spasms wracked him. Gripping. Squeezing. Wringing him dry.

"I love you so much." Her words echoed over and over again in his head, in his heart.

When the last ebb had faded from his loins, he collapsed, spent and exhausted, on the bed beside her, reveling in the sensations and strange feelings running through him. He still felt like he was flying. He felt light-headed, his mind a little soft and fuzzy. Almost as if he'd had more of that whisky than he'd realized. *Jesus!* He'd never realized it could be like . . . *that.*

Incredible. Amazing. Like nothing he'd ever experienced before. They'd been . . . connected. Not just joined, but connected. He'd never felt closer to anyone in his life as he had at the moment he was inside her, looking deep into her eyes. When they'd found release together, it wasn't just his body that was sated but his soul. And the euphoria hadn't ended with release. He felt—the feeling was so foreign to him, it took him a moment to put a name to it—*happy.* As if he could lie here with her forever.

She was so damned sweet. So giving. And she loved him? How had he gotten so lucky?

He was about to reach over and tuck her under his arm, when she spoke. "If this is what marriage has to offer, I think I shall be quite content."

She might have doused him with a bucket of cold water, the shock of her words was the same. The fuzziness disappeared. The euphoria and happiness turned to an icy chill as the reality of what he'd done hit him quick and hard.

Fuck.

The oath was well placed. That was exactly what he'd

done—both literally and figuratively. Not just her, but himself as well.

Instead of tucking her against him, he stared at the wooden roof of the barn in stunned disbelief as the ramifications battered down on him relentlessly.

God's blood, what the hell had he done?

In taking her innocence, he'd violated the trust of both his king and his liege lord, and put his future, as well as that of his clan, at risk. One finger of land? Hell, he wouldn't have a fist of dirt to his name when Bruce found out. The half-finished castle—a monument to his father's rashness—would be a blight on the landscape forever. But none of that would matter, because Ewen would be dead. The king was going to kill him.

Ewen had been trying to keep his head down, do his job, distance himself from his "wild" father and rebellious cousin, and not bring attention to himself. Well, Bruce was sure as hell going to notice this. He was almost glad Sir James was dead, so he wouldn't have to see this.

Meant to be. Rightness. Fate. Destiny. Had he really used such fanciful excuses for justifying the inexcusable and losing sight of his honor? For forgetting what mattered? What about duty, loyalty, and discipline? Those were what he was supposed to think about. He wanted to blame it on the whisky, but he knew it wasn't that. He'd been scared of losing her and he'd reacted without thought. He'd let emotion control him. Damn it, he didn't get emotional. This wasn't supposed to happen to him.

He was as bad as his damned father! His whole life he'd been fighting to make sure he didn't end up like Wild Fynlay, and in a matter of minutes, he'd undone it all.

The Lamonts in Cowal would be no more. *Up to you.* God, he felt ill.

At first Janet didn't realize anything was wrong. Still tingling and weak with pleasure, still feeling as if she were soaring through the clouds, she was so caught up in the wonder of what had just happened that she assumed Ewen was feeling the same way.

She wasn't even worried when he didn't respond to her jest. He was probably just as overwhelmed as she was.

It was only when he sat up, swung his legs over the edge of the pallet (giving her a nice view of his broad, well-muscled back), tugged up his breeches, and put his head in his hands that she realized something was wrong.

She realized just how wrong when he muttered a vile oath that she'd never heard from him before.

Her chest squeezed, but she tried not to overreact. So what if this wasn't exactly how she'd pictured the moment? It didn't matter that he hadn't pulled her into his arms, stroked her hair, and told her how wonderful it was. How much he loved her. Really it didn't.

The squeeze tightened to a pang. She wasn't an eighteen-year-old virgin. She was a mature woman. She didn't need such reassurances, even though they would have been nice. She pushed back the hot wave of emotion that rose to her eyes.

Ignoring the silly, girlish disappointment swelling in her chest, she tried to think rationally. His reaction was understandable. Of course, it was. She knew Ewen, and no doubt he would see taking her virginity as some kind of violation of his man's code.

She might think it was ridiculous, but he didn't.

Sitting up behind him, she reached out and put her hand on his shoulder. His muscles tensed under her palm. Another splinter of hurt tried to make its way through the happiness she'd wrapped around herself like a plaid, but she wouldn't let it.

"Please don't be upset. Truly, there is nothing to worry about. We've done nothing wrong." She smiled. "Or nothing that cannot soon be corrected. I will go to Robert as soon as we arrive and explain—well, perhaps not everything." Robert could be just as knightly about these kinds of things as Ewen. "But he will understand. He will be happy to see me finally wed, and marrying me will help your clan—you'll see."

Nothing could have prevented the stab of hurt when he jerked away from her touch. "You don't understand a damned thing—the king is going to be furious!"

Janet blinked back at him in shock, stunned by the force of his vehemence. She didn't think of herself as possessing tender feelings, but he'd managed to find some with his typically blunt and razor-sharp words. "Perhaps it is not an ideal match, but I'm sure Robert can be persuaded—"

He grabbed her by the arm and forced her to face him. "Damn it, Janet! Not everything can be handled with a deft tongue and a few pretty smiles. When the hell are you going to learn that? You have no idea what I've done."

She stopped telling herself to dismiss his reaction. Whatever it was that was causing him to act like this was serious.

He dropped his hand and put his head back in his hands. Suddenly chilled, she gathered the plaid left by Margaret from the bottom of the pallet, wrapped it around her shoulders, and shifted into position beside him. "Then why don't you tell me," she said softly.

She thought he was going to ignore her request. But after a few minutes of grappling, he seemed to reach some kind of decision. "The king has already arranged a betrothal for you."

She sucked in her breath, staring at him in absolute horror and disbelief. She couldn't seem to remember how to breathe. Her mind was busy racing in thousands of directions. It was the last thing she'd expected. Robert had never given any indication that he planned . . .

Betrayal ripped through her, tearing that plaid of happiness into tiny little shreds. But it wasn't just from Robert.

She stared at Ewen, looking for the man she thought she knew. Who she thought knew *her*.

He lied to me.

"Who?" she asked numbly.

"Walter Stewart." The blow took every last bit of air from her chest. Of course! Ewen had let his name slip once. Now she understood the significance. She wanted to laugh, but feared she would cry. Walter Stewart was barely old enough to have earned his spurs. "My liege lord, and the son of the man I owe everything to," he added.

She might have tried to understand his guilt, the depths of the dishonor he must be feeling for his disloyalty and broken trust, but she was too wrapped up in her own pain and broken trust. She stared at his face, searching for something to hold on to. Something to change the inevitable conclusion staring down at her.

She looked away, turning her gaze to her bare toes. At some point she must have kicked off her boots. A sharp pang sliced through her heart. Was it only minutes ago that she thought he was the one for her? "You did not tell me."

It wasn't a question. She didn't care about his reasons why, but he told her anyway. "The king suspected you would not be as . . . uh, amenable to returning if you knew."

The shock was beginning to fade, and anger surged inside her. She looked back up at him, her mouth twisted in a sneer. "How well he knows me. And you went along with it, of course. It was probably easier for you. 'Not your battle,' isn't that what you said? Why should you get involved?"

His mouth thinned at her sarcasm. "By time I realized I *was* involved it, was too late. I knew you'd be angry, and I know it's no excuse, but at the time I was more worried about keeping us both alive."

His admission that he was involved was also too late—and too little.

"You could have told me tonight. You *should* have told me tonight."

"Aye, well I didn't exactly intend for this to happen. I thought it would be easier if the king explained. I thought it would make our parting less . . . complicated."

"If I hated you?"

He stared at her, unblinking.

Dear God! The color washed from her face; that was exactly what he thought. He would have just handed her over to another man and not looked back. Her heart shattered like glass thrown upon the floor. He might as well have done exactly that to it.

Suddenly another truth hit her. Another betrayal. "This is not a temporary stay in Scotland. The king has no intention of letting me return to Roxburgh, does he?"

He didn't shirk from the cold accusation in her gaze. "He does not."

"But you let me think I might persuade him. You *knew* how important this was to me, and still let me believe I would be returning!"

She saw him flinch, but his guilt wasn't good enough.

He shrugged his shoulders. His naked shoulders that even now taunted her with memories. She could see the tiny imprints of her nails. Proof of her stupidity.

"It seemed easier at the time. I thought you might refuse to go, and I didn't want to have to go chasing after you again. What you were doing was dangerous—"

"And, of course, it couldn't be as important as what *you* are doing."

She thought he couldn't hurt her any more than he had by lying to her. She was wrong. *He never believed in me at all.*

She might have tried to understand his attempt to avoid conflict, but not the lack of regard for her. He'd known how much what she was doing meant to her, and in humoring her, in letting her believe her mission was only being delayed, he'd shown just how little he valued her. How little he thought of her. He would never give her what she wanted from a husband.

She stood to leave, but he caught her arm, stopping her. "Just because you can talk your way out of a situation doesn't mean you should. You are overconfident to the point of recklessness. With what happened with the priest in Roxburgh . . . It was only a matter of time before you were discovered. I'm not going to apologize for not wanting to see you in danger."

"How about for lying to me?" *And making me love you?*

His eyes softened. But she felt strangely indifferent to it. An hour ago, she might have seen it as a sign of feeling. Now, she knew better. "I'm deeply sorry for that. I was just trying to do my job."

A sharp scoffing sound erupted from her tightly wound chest. "And the mission always comes first, isn't that right?" He didn't say anything. She looked at his handsome face, seeing the silent plea for understanding. Part of her wanted to give it to him. Part of her wanted to think there was still some way this wouldn't end up so horribly. "And what now, Ewen? What happens to your mission now?"

Surely she couldn't have been so wrong. He didn't deserve a choice, but she was going to give him one.

Ewen had bungled this badly. Which was exactly the reason he'd wanted to avoid it. He couldn't stand the way she was looking at him. Seeing the shattered trust in her eyes. The betrayal. The broken heart.

It tore at him.

He didn't want to lose her. But what the hell could he do? He would try his damnedest to make it right, to salvage what he could of his honor and his place in Bruce's army, but he held no illusions.

"I will explain everything to Bruce when we return. If he agrees, we will be married as soon as the banns are read."

She stared at him, forcing his gaze to meet hers. "You don't really think you can get him to agree?"

He didn't think there was a chance in hell. His jaw clenched. "I thought you were confident you could persuade him?"

"That was before I was apprised of the betrothal. Robert will not 'reward' you for interfering with his plans."

"I will tell him there is no other choice. It is too late." He'd taken her innocence, damn it.

"Then you should prepare to defend yourself with your sword, because he will want to kill you. Robert will not look kindly on your cheapening the worth of his prize."

"Do not speak of it like that," he snapped angrily. "That is not how I feel."

"How *do* you feel, Ewen?"

Like he was trying to find traction on a hill of ice? Confused? Torn? Like a man who'd just lost everything and failed an entire clan? "How can you ask after what just happened? Surely you must realize how much you mean to me?"

He could tell by the flash of disappointment that crossed her face that it was not the declaration she wanted to hear. But it must have been enough. She put her hand on his arm, turning those big sea-green eyes to his imploringly. "Then run away with me. We will find a priest somewhere to marry us. You know it is the only way. Robert will never grant us permission to marry."

Every muscle in his body turned as rigid as steel, his rejection of her words bone deep.

Was fate playing some kind of hideous joke on him, forcing him to face the same choice as his father? Well, he sure as hell wasn't going to make the same mistake. "I am not going to run away."

She watched him, her eyes taking note of his clenched fists and flexed muscles. "Loving me isn't going to make you your father, Ewen."

She gazed up at him with such compassion and understanding that for a moment he wavered. He wanted to pull her into his arms and tell her it would be all right.

But it wouldn't. His feelings for her weren't going to cost him this. "Won't it? Maybe you're right. It wouldn't make me my father. My father had Stewart to help him pick up the pieces; I will have no one."

"You will have me."

As if it could be that simple. "What kind of life would we live? Without the king and Stewart's support, I have nothing to offer you. No money. No castle. Just two hundred people depending on me to provide for them. Should we join my cousin and kinsmen in Ireland with the other 'rebels'?"

She lifted her chin stubbornly, her mouth pursed. "Mary will help. Christina as well."

"You would ask that of them? You would put them at odds with Bruce."

With that, he succeeded in quieting her.

"Running off isn't romantic, Janet, it's irresponsible and foolish. It won't solve our problem; it will make it worse. Nay, there is no other way. We will take our chances with Bruce."

He forced himself not to see the disappointment shimmering in her eyes, but it ate like acid in his chest.

"Then you have made your choice."

"I have."

"Even if it means we cannot be together? Even if it means I must marry another man?"

He took her by the arm, dragging her face to his. "Yes, damn it, yes!"

It was as if he'd blown out a candle; the light in her eyes simply died. He felt the quick stirrings of panic in his chest. Instinctively, he reached for her, but she jerked away.

Her eyes shot sea-green daggers at him, sharp enough to draw blood. "Do not touch me again. You have made your decision; now I have made mine. I will not marry you or Walter Stewart. I will not marry anyone. I will take the veil before anyone tries to force me down the aisle."

His pulse leapt, panic no longer just stirring in his chest but jumping—nay, ricocheting—all over. "You don't mean that."

She didn't say anything. She wouldn't even look at him. Her gaze was pinned on the door behind him. "Contrary to your belief, Ewen, I am capable of knowing my own mind."

He swore, knowing she was slipping away from him but not knowing how to stop her. He stood, swaying from the pain in his leg. But it was nothing to the firestorm of emotions burning in his chest. He hated feeling like this. Out of control. Angry. Panicked. Helpless. She was tearing him apart.

He lashed out blindly, like a cornered beast. "What the hell do you want from me, Janet? Do you realize what this," he jerked his head toward the rumpled bed behind them, "has cost me? Everything I've been fighting for. Is that not enough, or must I cut a vein for you, too?"

She looked stricken; every bit of color slid from her face. Her voice trembled. "I didn't realize there was a price on something that was freely given. I wanted to please you; I'm sorry if it was not enough. But you need not worry. It need not cost you anything. As I will not be marrying anyone, my innocence—or lack thereof—is not important. You offered marriage, and I refused. You did your duty; if there was any damage to your honor, it is assuaged. There is no reason to say anything to Robert at all. Your position in his army need only be in jeopardy if you choose to make it so."

As quickly as the anger had risen, it was doused. He barely heard her words, giving him a way out; all he could see was the hurt his careless words had inflicted. He shouldn't be blaming her. This wasn't her fault. And he sure as hell hadn't meant to make what had happened between them feel like some kind of transaction. "Damn it, I'm sorry. I didn't mean to say that. I never meant any of this to happen. I was just trying to do my job."

"And I got in the way. You were just a simple soldier trying to do your duty, and I was—how did you put it?—a complication." He frowned. That wasn't what he meant . . . was it? She was so much more than that. "I'm sorry for making things difficult for you, Ewen. Had you told me the truth, it might not have happened the way it did. But as you took it upon yourself to make those decisions for us both, I'm afraid now you must live with them. You are a fighter; I'm sure you'll find a way to win everything you desire. It would have been easier—simpler—if we'd never met. And if it's any consolation, right now I wish we never had."

Jesus! What had he done? "You don't mean that."

The look she gave him told him differently. His skin, which had been feeling unusually hot, suddenly felt covered in a layer of ice.

"And that is exactly why I do. You told me once what you wanted in a wife. I should have listened to you. Maybe this is much my fault. I wanted to make you something you were not. You are not Magnus, and I am not Helen. I hope one day you find a woman who will be content to let you cosset and protect her—think for her. But that is not me."

She stood and started to walk toward the door.

He liked it better when she was angry with him. This cold, calm, indifferent stranger scared the hell out him. *I'm losing her. What can I do?*

He felt as if he were falling—flailing—over a mountain without a rope. The hill was steeper, the ice harder and more slippery, and he couldn't dig in his heels to stop from sliding. "Wait."

She turned.

"You can't go."

For one foolish heartbeat, Janet thought he meant to call her back because he'd changed his mind. That he would fight for them, as hard as she was sure he would fight for the king or his clan. But she was wrong—again.

"I can't take the chance that you will try to run," he said.

On the pile of disappointment he'd heaped upon her feet, one more stone shouldn't make a difference. But it did. The mission. Of course, he was thinking about the mission. Not about her.

Although perhaps he did understand her a little after all. For she had no intention of returning with him to Dunstaffnage. She never should have let him take her away from Roxburgh in the first place. She had to get back. She would not take the risk in missing something important. She would deal with her former brother-in-law and his "plans" for her when she was done.

Janet straightened her back, calling on every ounce of her earl's daughter blood. Though he towered over her, even from a few feet away, she still managed to give him a long, regal look down her nose. "So I am to be treated as a prisoner?" She held out her hands, crossed at the wrists. "Will you bind me with chains, or will rope be enough?"

Ewen swore. She saw him shift and wince as he put weight on his leg. It was obviously hurting more than he'd let on, but she bit back the words of concern that leapt to her tongue. He hadn't wanted her help when she'd offered it. He hadn't wanted anything from her. But just like always, she hadn't wanted to hear it. She hadn't wanted to hear "no." She thought she knew what was best.

At least this time, she was the only one hurt. That is, assuming he didn't tell Robert. She hoped he wasn't foolish enough to do so now. There was no reason. He need not lose everything for taking what she'd freely given. She wished she could say the same. For seven and twenty years she didn't know anything was missing. Now she did.

"Jesus, Janet. It's not like that. I just don't want you to do anything . . . rash."

He just kept throwing stone after stone. Eventually she hoped they would stop hurting. "How fortunate I am to have you to look out for me."

"Damn it. I didn't mean it like that. Will you give me your word you won't try to leave?"

"Yes."

He paused, staring at her. "You'll run the moment I turn my back."

She lifted her chin, not denying it. "So I *am* your prisoner?"

His mouth tightened. "You are the woman with whose safety I have been entrusted. I'm not going to let you go."

A shiver ran through her at his words, but she knew it was foolish to attribute anything meaningful to them. Letting go was exactly what he was doing to her.

"I will fight for us, Janet. Just trust me."

She'd done that, and look where it had brought her. He was making it perfectly clear what he thought of her: she was a mission—a duty—nothing more. Her voice shook. "I am not sleeping here with you."

His mouth tightened. "Yes, you are."

"You are going to have to drag me to Dunstaffnage, for I will not go with you willingly."

The muscle below his jaw ticked ominously. "If that's what it takes to keep you safe."

"I will hate you for it."

His eyes held hers, and if he had not cured her of illusions, she might have thought she saw true emotion in them. "I hope you don't."

Janet knew the battle was lost for now. He would not be dissuaded. He was intractable—a stone wall blocking her path. Suddenly the strength left her. It was as if the events of the day caught up with her all at once. Battered and bruised to the depths of her soul, all she wanted to do was roll up into a ball and cry herself to sleep. But he wouldn't even give her that.

She looked to the bed, a stab of pain knifing through her. She could still feel him between her legs, the dull ache a painful reminder of what they had shared. "You cannot expect me to share a bed with you?"

He shook his head, looking sadder than she'd ever seen him. "You can sleep on the pallet. I don't think I'll be doing much sleeping."

"The cost of guard duty."

He didn't respond to her jab but rubbed his leg unconsciously, as if trying to get a knot out, and winced.

She turned away so she wouldn't be tempted to care.

"I'm sorry, Janet. I never meant to hurt you."

But he had. Irreparably.

On her way to the bed, she picked up his shirt and tossed it to him. The naked chest that had only minutes ago given her such pleasure now hurt to look at. He put it on without comment.

She lay down on the bed and he sat before the fire, his back leaning against the wall and his legs stretched out before him. Janet had no intention of sleeping. She crawled under the plaid and watched him from under half-lidded eyes.

He'd retrieved a skin before he sat, and from the long swig he took, she suspected it was whisky.

With any luck, he would drink himself into oblivion.

Twenty-two

❧

Janet woke with a start and shivered. Good God, it was freezing in here!

Here. She blinked into the shadowy darkness, recognizing the rustic wooden walls of the barn. Suddenly everything that had happened came back to her in a wave of hurt and disappointment.

How could he have done this?

She cursed under her breath. She wasn't supposed to fall asleep. Thank goodness for the cold. The brazier must have gone out—

Suddenly, the realization of what that meant hit her. Her eyes shot to where Ewen had positioned himself against the wall. He sat with his head slumped forward like a rag poppet. She didn't need to see his face from behind the silky veil of thick, dark hair to know that he was asleep. Dead asleep. Or rather, passed-out-unconscious asleep, if the discarded skin of whisky by his side was any indication.

She couldn't believe it. The perfect soldier had fallen asleep on duty. It seemed so completely out of character, it gave her pause. Perhaps someone had been listening to her prayers after all. But she quickly told herself not to count her blessings.

Carefully—very carefully—she rose from the makeshift bed. Her heart pounded the entire time, watching him for any signs of movement, but he didn't so much as twitch a single muscle.

She drew in a deep, uneven breath. Less carefully, to test him, she stood. Every tiny sound she made reverberated in her ears like a bell, but still he didn't budge.

Heaven's gates, how much had he drunk? Was he all ri—

She stopped, reminding herself not to count her blessings.

She looked at him. Looked at her boots. Looked at the bag by his side—a bag that she knew held her other gowns, money, and what was left of their food. She looked at the horse in the stall at the back of the barn.

Could she do this?

Her heart lurched, but then continued to pound. Yes. Yes, she could. At least, it was worth a try. She couldn't stay with him.

She didn't know how much time she had, but she hoped she still had a few hours before dawn. Riding the horse would make her easier to track—and she had no doubt he would be tracking her—but it would give her speed that he wouldn't have on foot. And she'd learned some things from him that might help.

She swallowed, thinking of the journey that lay ahead. It would be long and dangerous, but nothing that she hadn't done countless times before. So why did it give her a twinge of fear now? Why did the thought of leaving him suddenly make her uneasy?

Because in the last few short days, she'd grown used to having him by her side. She might not have wanted his protection, but she'd come to appreciate it, and if not to depend on it, then to at least to take comfort in it.

Her heart squeezed. Why did this have to hurt so much? How could he have lied to her like that? Not just about the betrothal but about her returning to Roxburgh. He knew how important this was to her. Yet even with his betrayal, she might have tried to understand—might have tried to forgive him—if he loved her.

But he didn't—or not enough. He would rather see her wed to another man than risk a comparison to his father. The worst part was that she understood. She didn't even blame him. Not really. But she also knew it wasn't good enough for her.

Tears rolled down her cheeks. Damn him for doing this to her! Until he burst into her life like a siege engine, she'd been happy on her own. Content with the life she had planned.

She wiped the tears away with an angry jerk, determined to be so again. Her work was the only thing that mattered now. It was the only thing she had left.

She was better off alone. Hadn't she always known that?

Putting aside whatever reservations she had, Janet made her decision. It took her only a few minutes to gather what she needed. As she led the horse from the stall, she took one last look. Tears blurring her eyes, she left without a backward glance.

Someone was yelling at him. Ewen's head lolled to the left and right. *Stop shaking me.*

"Ewen! Wake up, lad!"

He opened his eyes. It took him a moment to recognize the man before him. Big. Gray haired. Weather-beaten and battle-scarred face. Robert Wallace.

His mind felt like a bog, his thoughts sluggish.

And God, he was hot.

He groaned and would have gone back to sleep if Robert hadn't shaken him again. "The lass, where is she?"

That brought him up quick. Some of the haze cleared from his mind. *Janet.* His gaze shot to the pallet. The *empty* pallet.

He swore, realizing what had happened. He'd fallen asleep, and she'd fled.

How the hell could this have happened? He'd been on duty, damn it! He didn't make mistakes like this.

He tried to get to his feet, but something wasn't right. He couldn't seem to get his limbs to coordinate. Bloody hell, he was as weak as a newborn foal.

"What is the matter with you, lad?" Robert said, giving him a hand. "You're burning as hot as hellfire, and it's cold in here."

"I don't know—"

Ewen's words died in a stab of pain as he tried to put weight on his injured leg.

"It's the leg. Must be worse than you let on." Robert paused to shout for his wife. "Sit," he ordered. "Margaret will take a look at it."

Ewen shook him off, looking around for his things like a man without sight. "I can't. I have to go after her."

"Why would she leave?" Robert asked.

Because he was a blind fool. "To get away from me."

If anything happened to her, he would never forgive himself.

He reached for his sword and nearly fell. God, he felt horrible! He didn't need Helen to tell him that something was very wrong with his leg. How could things get so bad so quickly? He'd thought it was looking better, but it was worse. Much worse.

He bit through the pain and the fog of fever to ready himself. He managed to get most of his armor on before Margaret appeared.

Her soft cry told him that he must look worse than he felt. "You're ill!" she said.

He didn't argue. But a quick glance through the remaining bag told him he was going to need a few things. "I will need some food and drink, and whatever coin you can spare."

Janet had taken it all. He swore again. How could he have been so derelict? He knew she would run. He should have taken better precautions. He should have tied her up, damn it. He should have done whatever was necessary to keep her safe.

He should have done whatever was necessary to keep her with him.

Ah hell! He swore again. Not even the fever could prevent him from seeing the truth.

"You can't go anywhere like this," Margaret said.

"I have to," Ewen said through clenched teeth, fighting the powerful force that seemed to be trying to slow him down. It was up to him. The morning sun was already in full force. "She could have been gone a few hours already." He couldn't lose the tracks while they were fresh.

He picked up the bag and started toward the back of the barn. His leg buckled, and he would have fallen to the ground had Robert not caught him under one arm. "Steady, lad."

"The horse," Ewen said, biting back the wave of nausea that rose inside him. "Just help me to the horse."

"It's gone," Robert said.

The extent of his failure was humiliating. While he was supposed to be on guard, she'd snuck a damned horse past him. "I'll have to go on foot."

"You won't make it to the next village in your condition," Margaret said.

He didn't even make it out of the barn. Darkness rose like a fiery dragon's mouth and swallowed him whole.

Janet didn't stop looking over her shoulder, expecting Ewen to come storming down the road behind her like a demon from hell. Or perhaps, more accurately, a *phantom* from hell.

She remembered how he'd looked the first time she'd seen him. The dark leather armor dotted with rivets of steel, the strangely fashioned plaid wrapped around him, the blackened nasal helm and arsenal of weaponry strapped to his broad, well-muscled chest. Her heart squeezed. She'd been scared for good reason, it turned out. She should have turned and run the first moment she'd seen him.

But either he wasn't coming after her or she was better at hiding her tracks than she thought. She remembered his tips: hard ground, water or rivers when possible, circle back, confuse and obfuscate. She kept to the road, blending and hiding her tracks as best she could. But she knew her best weapon was speed, so she didn't take as much time hiding them as she could have.

Perhaps the misdirection had worked? Recalling what Ewen had done when first taking her from Rutherford, Janet did not retrace their steps east, but rather headed north toward Glasgow, hoping to lose her tracks in the large burgh before turning eastward onto the main road.

But unfortunately, Ewen had the advantage of knowing her destination. Even if she managed to elude him on the road, he would find her soon enough in Roxburgh. Unless she could think of a way of making contact with her source at the castle without returning to Rutherford.

Despite what she'd told Ewen, the idea of donning her habit again did not sit well with her. Having come to the barn in only a chemise—the fine under-gown Mary had thoughtfully provided still in the house—Janet had been forced to choose between the extravagant surcote meant to go over it or "Novice Eleanor's" dark brown wool kirtle. Although she'd chosen the latter—a woman in such a fine gown traveling alone would be much more difficult to explain—she could not bear to put on the white scapular and veil. Instead, she'd wrapped the plaid around herself like a hooded cloak—the one Margaret had left, not Ewen's—and did her best to avoid other travelers on the road.

At this time of year, in the cold, dark days approaching the Nativity, there weren't many. Those that she did come across had any curiosity appeased by her claim of being a midwife, traveling to attend the birth of her sister's first child in whatever village lay ahead.

A few times, she joined another traveling party for a while—including a farmer and his wife taking fowl to market in Glasgow and an old man traveling to Lanark to visit his son—seeking the safety and comfort of numbers. But when questions became too personal, she was forced to part company.

More often than not, she was alone with her thoughts, which as much as she tried to prevent them kept returning to Ewen. It wouldn't always be this horrible, she told herself. But for the first time, she could understand the misery her sister had suffered in her first marriage. How it felt to love someone and not have the person return those feelings. How it felt to be betrayed by the man to whom you'd given your heart.

It was a long, difficult journey. More difficult than it should have been, especially compared to the one that had come before. In addition to not having the English chasing after her, the advantage of staying to the main road was that she avoided the hills that she and Ewen had been forced to traverse. The disadvantage, of course, was the chance of coming upon an English patrol.

For two long days, through Rutherglen, where she'd spent her first night, to Peebles, where she spent her second, Janet managed to avoid such danger. On the third, however, as she and a merchant and his wife with whom she'd been traveling since Innerleithen approached the outskirts of Melrose, where she'd first met Ewen, fate intervened once again. A dozen soldiers appeared on the road ahead of her.

Her blood ran cold. Every instinct urged her to flee, although she knew that was ridiculous. There was no reason for her to run. She hadn't done anything wrong.

She forced air into her lungs in slow, even breaths. How many times had she done this before? Too many to count.

With as much time as she'd spent on the roads as a courier, running into English soldiers was not uncommon. Why was she so nervous?

Taking a cue from the merchant and his wife, she pretended not to notice anything out of the ordinary and continued on the path ahead. If the couple noticed her slight hesitation, they did not remark upon it. However, the merchant, a man old enough to be her father, did let his gaze linger on her face a moment longer than usual. Had he seen her skin pale beneath the makeshift hood of her plaid? His gaze dropped to her hands. Realizing she was clenching the reins, she forced her fingers to loosen. But that, he'd definitely noticed.

As the distance closed between them, the merchant moved his cart over to the side of the path to let the soldiers pass. Janet followed the couple, taking advantage of the opportunity to angle her own mount behind theirs, where she hoped she wouldn't be as visible.

The pounding of her heart in her ears grew louder as the powerful warhorses neared. The ground started to shake, she hoped hiding her own shaking.

The merchant raised his hand in greeting as the first horse rode by.

The pounding in her heart stilled. *Keep going*, she prayed. *Don't stop.*

One . . . two . . . three . . . passed by. Her heart started again. It was going to be all right. But then the pounding stopped—not her heart, the hooves.

"Halt," a hard English voice said. "You there. What is your name? What business do you have on the road?"

No reason to panic, she told herself. *Nothing out of the ordinary.*

"Walter Hende, my lord. I am a merchant on my way to Roxburgh, where my wife and I hope to open a shop."

"What kind of shop?"

The merchant motioned to his cart. "A drapery, my lord.

I've the finest woolen cloth in Edinburgh. Take a look if you like."

Janet ventured a peek at the soldier. Her heart dropped. He wasn't a soldier he was a knight, although she did not recognize the arms of six martlets separated by a thick gold bend. He was an imposing-looking man, and not just because of his heavy armor and mail. He was big—tall and broad-shouldered—with a hard, square jaw and dark, hooded eyes just visible beneath the steel helm.

He motioned to a younger man by his side, whom she assumed must be his squire. The lad jumped down and approached the cart. Lifting back the oiled leather cover, he nodded. "Aye, Sir Thomas. It's filled with cloth."

It was then that disaster struck. The squire glanced in her direction. Because of where he had come to stand by the cart, he had a clear vantage of her face.

He gasped. "Lady Mary! What are you doing here?"

The blood slid from her face. Oh God, this couldn't be happening. The boy thought she was her sister.

"You know this woman, John?" Sir Thomas said.

The lad frowned, staring at her. He must have seen something that made him question his first impression. "It's me, Lady Mary. John Redmayne. I was friends with your son at court. You remember—we met at Bamburgh Castle last year. I came with Lord Clifford."

Sir Robert Clifford was one of Edward's chief commanders in the battle against the Scots. Fear curdled like sour milk in her stomach.

After a moment, Janet finally found her voice. "I'm afraid you have mistaken me with someone else."

The boy's frown went askew.

"Step forward where I can see you," the knight ordered. "If you are not the woman my squire believes, then who are you?"

"Kate, my lord," she said softly, using the name she'd given the merchant.

The knight's eyes narrowed. "Pull back your hood."

She did as he bid, she hoped without showing as much reluctance as she felt. The moment the plaid fell back, a collective silence fell over the knight and his men. They stared at her in shock and unmistakable masculine admiration.

Except for the squire. He smiled broadly. "It *is* her. Lady Mary, the Countess of Atholl."

The lad had obviously not heard of her sister's defection and second marriage. But the knight had. The way his dark eyes gleamed as his mouth curved in a slow smile chilled her to the bone. "And what is the rebel Lady Mary doing in Melrose?"

Janet forced a shy smile to her face. "I'm afraid the boy is mistaken, my lord." She batted her lashes up at him with what she hoped was just the right amount of innocence. But something told her this man wasn't going to be easy to fool. "I am—"

"Our daughter, my lord."

Janet startled and hoped she didn't look as surprised as she felt, when the merchant came up beside her and claimed her by the arm.

Ewen fought the lulling force of darkness, which sought to drag him under. *You can't sleep.* He tried to open his eyes, but the lids were too heavy. Someone had put a weight on them.

Try. You have something to do. He didn't know what it was that he had to do, but he knew it was important. Very important. The most important thing in the world.

Get up. You have to go after her.

Oh God, Janet!

He flailed blindly in the darkness, trying to sit up. But something wrestled him down. Powerful, steely hands clamped his wrists and ankles, pinning him to the bed.

He cried out, writhing in pain and frustration as he tried

to fight his way free. But the steely hands seemed to multiply like some kind of hideous spider.

Have to get up. Danger. She needs me. Oh, God, Janet . . . sorry.

" . . . Tie him down." A soft voice penetrated the edges of his consciousness. A woman's voice. An *angel's* voice. " . . . Getting worse . . . Take leg."

"No!" He lashed out, fighting with everything he had until the pain overwhelmed him and the darkness dragged him under.

Ewen was dreaming again, running through the darkness looking for something—for someone.

Have to find her . . .

He startled and opened his eyes, quickly closing them again as the light stabbed them like a dagger.

He groaned, turning, surprised to feel his arms moving freely at his side.

"He's awake," a familiar voice said.

Oh God, Janet!

He opened his eyes again, blinking up into the face that had haunted his dreams.

He reached up and cradled her cheek in his hand. "You're here," he said, his voice gravelly and weak. She was safe. Janet was safe. "God, I'm sorry."

She smiled, and he felt the first inkling that something wasn't right—a fuzzy prickle nudging the frayed edges of his consciousness.

"How are you feeling?" she asked.

Another face appeared beside hers, also familiar but scowling. Despite the way the man was looking at him, Ewen knew that he should be relieved to see him for some reason.

"I know you almost died," the man said. "But you are going to find yourself close to death again if you don't get your damned hands off my wife."

Sutherland, Ewen realized. *He's alive.*

He dropped his hand from the woman's face. Mary's face, not Janet's.

Mary gave her husband a sharp scowl. "He's been unconscious for nearly four days—do you think you could put aside your primitive male possessiveness for just a few minutes?"

Four days?

Sutherland shrugged unrepentantly. "Not if he's going to look at you like that. Hell, I thought he was going to drag you down on top of him. I was just saving him from a thrashing when he recovers."

Ewen wasn't too groggy to scoff. "That'll be a cold day in hell, Ice."

Mary harrumphed. "Obviously, he thought I was my sister."

"Where is she?" Ewen said, instantly alert. "Where is Janet?"

Sutherland sobered. "We were hoping *you* would tell *us* that."

"You mean she isn't here?" He looked around, suddenly realizing that he didn't know where the hell he was.

Mary seemed to understand his confusion. "Dunstaffnage."

Bruce's headquarters in Argyll, won from the rebel John MacDougall, Lord of Lorn, a couple of years ago.

"We found you not long after you collapsed at the Wallaces," Sutherland said. "I'm sorry for leaving you and the lass alone out there, but it could not be helped. When the English attacked for the second time, I didn't want to take the chance and lead them to you. I caught up with MacKay and MacLean, who had found Douglas. We would have been here sooner, but Douglas had a few problems we needed to take care of." Ewen assumed they were English problems. Sutherland's expression turned grim.

"You were bad. We didn't think you were going to make it. Saint and Hawk got you to Angel just in time."

Angel. That was who had been tending him when he'd woken delirious—

Ewen froze in horror as the rest of the memory returned. He was almost scared to look. Hell, he *was* scared to look. Taking a deep breath, he lowered his gaze to the blanket over him, releasing it only when he saw the lump of his legs—the *two* lumps of his legs.

"You remember?" Mary asked.

He nodded.

"You were fortunate in the location of the wound," Sutherland said. "Angel decided that it would be more dangerous to take your leg because of where the injury was than to let you fight the festering in the bone."

But it wasn't the fact that he'd nearly lost his leg that had turned his blood cold. "Why didn't someone go after her?"

"Striker and I did," Sutherland said. "We only returned last night. We thought we picked up her trail going north on the road to Glasgow, but then we lost it."

"Glasgow? Why the hell would she go there?" But he knew before he'd even finished the question. *Bloody hell!* She'd taken his lessons to heart.

He sat up and would have lost the contents of his stomach had there been anything inside. He swayed as nausea and dizziness fought to take him right back down.

"Wait!" Mary cried, trying to push him back down. "What are you doing? You can't get up."

Ewen gritted his teeth. "I have to find her. It's all my fault."

The door opened and three people burst into the room. "We heard voices . . ." Helen let out a gasp, but she recovered quickly. Her eyes narrowed. "I see it was a mistake to untie you." She shot her husband, who'd come up next to her, an I-told-you-so look.

But it was the third person who'd entered the room that

caused Ewen's heart to sink and a sheen of sickly sweat to gather on his brow.

Robert the Bruce, King of Scotland, fixed his dark, razor-sharp gaze on him. "Where is Janet, and why is it your fault?"

Twenty-three

❧

"Give me one good reason why I shouldn't toss you in a pit prison right now!" the king had demanded.

"Because you need me to find Janet and make sure she is safe," Ewen had answered.

But he couldn't even manage to do that. *Five bloody days!* For five days he'd scoured the countryside, turning over every rock—every leaf—with no sight of her. Janet had proved a better pupil than he could have imagined, using the skills he'd taught her against him.

This was his last lead—hell, it was his only lead. With St. Drostan's approaching, he was back at the priory in Rutherford, hoping that whatever reason she'd had for wanting to return by this time would bring her back.

But from his position in the trees a few dozen yards from the entrance to the priory, he could barely make out the faces of the nuns passing through. He clenched his fists at his side, fighting for patience that had run out days ago. "I can't see a damned thing. I'm going in there."

MacLean stepped in front of him. "You won't do her any good if you are caught. Remember what the king said: stay out of sight, observe, and don't interfere unless necessary. I don't think tearing apart every church between Roxburgh and Berwick counts as necessary."

"Or terrorizing merchants unfortunate enough to sell

sugared nuts," Sutherland quipped dryly from his position behind him.

Ewen grimaced. That had been a mistake. But the merchant had been a provoking bastard, and Ewen had been fed up with his smart-arse answers. Before he knew it, his hand had been wrapped around the man's neck and he had him pinned against the wooden wall of the shop. Not surprisingly, the man had then been far more forthcoming in his responses to Ewen's questions. Inelegant perhaps, but effective.

"This is my last lead," he said through clenched teeth. "I won't take the chance of missing her. Get the hell out of my way."

"Use your head, Hunter," MacLean said.

But Ewen was beyond reason. He stepped around MacLean—rather than push him aside as he was tempted to—but another one of his brethren, or rather his *former* brethren, blocked him.

"You aren't going in there," MacKay said.

"I sure as hell am," Ewen said, muscles flaring with readiness for the fight MacKay was going to get if he didn't move out of his way. Over the other man's shoulder he noticed another handful of nuns emerge from the priory. But none of them was the nun he wanted.

"What the hell do you plan to do?" Mackay challenged. "Walk in there looking like that? The nuns will take one look at you and run screaming. You look as feral and wild as a wolf." He shook his head. "You might want to try to get a few hours of sleep or eat something that doesn't come from a skin. Your leg is far from healed, and you aren't going to do the lass any good if you keel over and die. I'm beginning to think Helen was right. We should have kept you tied up."

Even knowing he spoke the truth, Ewen didn't give a damn. He'd spent his entire life trying to avoid being compared to his father, and right now he was every bit as crazed and unhinged as Wild Fynlay had ever been. "Unless you want to put on a kirtle and have me call you 'Mother,' my sleep and eating habits aren't your concern. I don't have bloody time for this!"

MacLean assumed that he was referring to the king's upcoming journey to Selkirk for the peace parley. "We will only be gone a few days. The negotiations won't last long. Bruce will demand to be recognized as king, Edward's lackeys will refuse, and we will be on our way again. If the lass has not returned by then, we can try again."

Though the parley was held under the sacred banner of truce, Chief wanted them to serve as part of the escort. They were supposed to leave tomorrow to catch up with the others before they reached Selkirk.

Ewen's mouth fell in a thin line, but he didn't say anything. He didn't explain that he wasn't going to Selkirk, and that he was no longer a part of the Highland Guard.

Sutherland had come around to stand next to his brother-in-law. He gave Ewen a hard look. "Why do I get the feeling there is something you aren't telling us? What exactly did you and the king discuss?"

The conversation with the king had gone exactly how Ewen had expected it to go. Once everyone had left the room, he'd explained what had happened. Bruce would have put a blade through his gut—or perhaps an area slightly lower—if Ewen hadn't been on his back, unarmed, and weak from fever. Instead, his worst fears had been realized. The king stripped him of his land, his reward, and his place in the Guard, and he would have taken his freedom as well had Ewen not convinced him to let him find Janet to ensure she was not in danger.

And it had taken some convincing. The king had been inclined to defer to Janet's judgment: if she thought it was important, he didn't want to do anything to jeopardize the informant or the information their contact might pass on. No matter how hard Ewen pressed him the king would not disclose the identity of the informant—except to say that it was someone in Roxburgh highly connected to Edward's lieutenants. Who did Ewen think had been bringing them all the recent intelligence, enabling the Highland Guard to know exactly where to attack?

Ewen had been stunned. Janet was responsible for that? He'd underestimated her importance and knew it. He owed her an apology—one of many—if she would ever listen to him again.

But learning just how in the thick of it Janet was only ratcheted up his concern. Hell, it wasn't concern, it was mind-numbing, bloodcurdling, bone-chilling fear. The stakes would be even higher if the English were to discover her role.

He had just as much faith in her as Bruce did, but Ewen's faith was blinded by something the king's was not. It wasn't until Ewen had lost everything that he could see clearly what duty and loyalty had prevented him from acknowledging. The emotion burning his chest and tearing his gut apart could only be one thing. Nothing else could strike this kind of fear and misery in him. He loved her. And he'd taken her love and thrown it back in her face.

"You will have me."

Her words ate at him. How could he have thought it wouldn't be enough? She was everything. Without her, nothing else mattered.

For the first time in his life, Ewen could see his father not with embarrassment, shame or anger, but with admiration. For he'd done what Ewen had not: he'd had the courage to risk everything and fight for the woman he loved.

And now the woman Ewen loved was God knows where, doing God knows what, because he'd been too much of a fool to do whatever he needed to do to hold on to her. When he thought of how he'd turned away after making love to her, how he'd told her he was going to take her back and hand her over to another man . . .

No wonder she'd run. He would spend the rest of his life making it up to her, if she would let him.

But what if he didn't get a chance to explain? What if something happened to her, and he couldn't tell her how much he loved her?

He had to find her, damn it. He'd tear apart every nunnery on both sides of the Border if he had to.

The danger had finally caused Bruce to relent—but only so far. Hence, Ewen's role as an observer. As for the rest, the Guardsmen would find out soon enough.

"That's between Bruce and me," he told Sutherland.

"Janet is my sister now," Sutherland said, his notoriously hot temper sparking in his eyes. "If you did something to dishonor her . . ."

Ewen's mouth tightened. Sutherland would have to stand in line. "I buggered up, all right. But I'm trying to make it right." He paused, distracted, as another nun emerged from the priory. But even from this distance he could see the build wasn't right. He needed to at least get closer. He turned back to Sutherland impatiently. "I am not going to have this conversation right now. As soon as we find her, I will answer whatever damned questions you want. Now unless you are going to try to stop me, get the hell out of my way."

The challenge was issued to all three of the men blocking his path. They looked at one another and must have recognized the determination in his gaze—or maybe it was the wild, frenzied, just-on-the-edge-of-madness look that convinced them.

MacLean shook his head and sighed, stepping aside first. "You'd better know what the hell you are doing."

Ewen didn't, but he had to do something. He couldn't stand here and wait another minute.

His eyes scanned the area in front of him as he moved through the trees. The river wound to the east side of the priory. From there he would have a closer view of the yard.

He could leave his armor behind and pretend to be a fisher—

Suddenly, he stopped. His gaze flickered back to something he had skimmed over earlier.

"What is it?" MacLean whispered, coming up behind him.

"The lad," Ewen said. "Sitting on the rocks by the river."

"What about him?" MacKay asked.

"I've seen him before." Something prickled at the back of his neck. "The first time I was here, and a few days ago."

Sutherland frowned. "What is suspicious about a local boy fishing?"

"Nothing," Ewen answered. "If that's what he is doing. But look, his line isn't in the water—it's on the edge of the bank—and he isn't watching the fish." He was watching the door to the priory, exactly as Ewen would be doing, albeit far less obviously.

"What do you think he's doing?" MacLean asked.

"I don't know, but I intend to find out."

Ewen kept watch on the door and the boy for the rest of the afternoon. Each time a nun emerged, the lad seemed to study her face every bit as intently as Ewen did. Not once did the boy check the fishing line beside him. Either the lad was the worst fisherman ever or he was watching for someone. But for whom?

If it was a coincidence, it was one that made Ewen uneasy. Damned uneasy. And he didn't think it was a coincidence.

His suspicions were confirmed a short while later, when the door of the priory closed for the night and the lad abandoned his post. Following him was easy, but every step of the way, Ewen's heart jogged a little faster.

The lad wasn't headed to a house nearby, he was headed to Roxburgh. More specifically, he was headed to the castle. Ewen didn't need to follow the lad through the castle gate. From his vantage atop a nearby hill, he could see with bone-tingling clarity directly into the courtyard. Even before the boy approached the building, Ewen had guessed where he was headed. *Ah hell, the chapel!*

His blood went cold, recalling Janet's confrontation with the castle priest at the market.

If the priest was having someone watch the priory, Ewen knew what that meant. The monk found on the road to Berwick had talked before they killed him. Janet's identity had been compromised. That was how the English had followed them so easily from the priory a couple of weeks ago.

It also meant that Ewen wasn't the only one hunting her, and if he didn't find her first, the danger he'd feared would become all too real.

Thanks to the merchant and his wife, Janet had a way to make contact with her source without returning to Rutherford, a place to stay, and a new identity.

Her veil and scapular stayed hidden in her bag. In their stead, she donned a linen cap and became a member of the burgeoning number of tradesmen and merchants who were flocking to the burghs. In the highly structured feudal society, the merchants were somewhere below the nobility and above the rest—not unlike the clergy. As a daughter of a merchant, she enjoyed the same kind of freedom that she had as a nun to walk around largely unnoticed.

Janet didn't know what had provoked the merchant to claim her as his daughter, but it had saved her from what could have been a very difficult—and probably life-threatening—situation. One she very well may not have been able to talk her way out of.

Even with the merchant's claim, Sir Thomas was suspicious. It wasn't until the merchant's wife, Alice, had come forward to scold her for making eyes at the handsome knight when she was nearly betrothed to another, and Janet had broken down in tears, sobbing that she didn't want to marry a man old enough to be her father, that the squire admitted he could be wrong, and Sir Thomas allowed them to move on. Indeed, he seemed to want to escape the family drama and Janet's "rescue me" gaze as quickly as possible.

But her heart hadn't stopped pounding for days, even well after they'd arrived safely in Roxburgh. She'd thanked the Hendes for what they'd done and had been relieved when they hadn't asked her questions, but had simply offered her a place to stay for as long as she needed.

Janet repaid their kindness with hard work, helping them to set up their shop in the lower floor of a building on High Street, which also housed a haberdashery, vintner, and goldsmith.

In retrospect, the run-in with the soldiers near Melrose had proved an unexpected boon. It had given her exactly what she needed: a way of making contact with her informant in the castle that allowed her to avoid places she'd been before. She'd taken Ewen's lessons to heart; she didn't want any way to connect Novice Eleanor or Sister Genna to Kate, the wool merchant's daughter.

On the first Saturday of her return, when the ladies from the castle wound their way through the market booths, Janet was ready. A quick "accidental" bump, a mumbled apology, and a meaningful glance had been all the explanation necessary. Janet had made a point to walk slowly back to the Hendes shop, where she was sure her informant would see her enter.

Janet's guilt for any potential danger she might have put the Hendes in by staying with them was assuaged a bit by the immediate success the couple garnered, after a number of noble men and women from the castle entered their shop and declared their wool the "best in Roxburgh." The Hendes were soon fending more orders than they could fill, including one from the constable of Roxburgh Castle himself, Sir Henry de Beaumont.

On one of these visits, Janet managed a short conversation with her informant while showing her a swathe of fine ruby-colored cloth.

"Is there anything I can help you with, milady?" she'd asked, careful to keep her words innocuous in case they were overheard.

The woman shook her head. "Not as of yet, I'm afraid. But as there are many important celebrations upcoming, I'm sure I will think of some reason for this beautiful wool soon." She smiled. "There is much excitement around the castle with Christmas approaching."

Janet translated the message easily enough: nothing yet, but something big was definitely brewing. "Aye, milady. Even in the village, excitement is in the air. I shall be attending my first St. Drostan's feast tomorrow. I hear it is quite the celebration."

"Aye, there will be a feast at the castle as well," the lady said.

Another lady had come up at that point and interrupted them. The group left soon after, but not before her informant had promised that she would see her on the next Saturday market day a few days hence.

Disappointed that there was still nothing to report and that her sojourn in Roxburgh would extend for at least a few more days, Janet did her best to keep herself occupied.

The hard work kept her mind off her heartbreak and the difficult conversation she would be having with Robert when she finally did return to the Highlands. As much as the prospect of donning a habit again—this time, for real—did not appeal to her, an arranged marriage appealed even less.

Heaven's gates, Walter Stewart? Noble blood or nay, she would not marry a lad barely old enough to have whiskers on his chin. She couldn't bear to think of being with him . . . *intimately*.

For the most part, Janet succeeded in keeping her mind off the passion Ewen had shown her in the barn that night—the way he'd made her feel, how incredible it had felt to have him in her body, the overwhelming emotion that had gripped her—but it went there now.

She would never share that with another man. She knew it with every fiber of her being and from the bottom of her bleeding, ripped-apart, torn-into-shreds heart.

Apparently, however, Janet was not as adept at hiding her heartache as she'd thought.

"The feast will do you good," Alice Hende insisted after returning from the St. Drostan's mass that morning. She eyed Janet knowingly. "Whoever he is, he is not worth working yourself to the bone."

Knowing Alice's shrewdness, Janet did not attempt to deny it. But neither did she want to talk about it. Her feelings were still too raw. "You are kind, but I think it is best if I stay behind. You and Master Walter go and enjoy the mummers. You can tell me all about it."

Alice put her hands on her broad hips. "No."

Janet blinked. "No?"

"Aye, no. You are going to the feast, you will have fun, and that is the end of it."

Thickset and plain of face, the merchant's wife resembled every iron-spined nursemaid that Janet had ever had. Alice had birthed five daughters, all of whom were settled, and there wasn't an excuse or explanation that she hadn't heard. Janet knew she could cajole or entreat until the sun went down and came up again, but Alice Hende would not be swayed.

A swell of emotion filled her chest. What was it about stubborn and domineering that had become so endearing to her?

Blinking back tears, Janet nodded. She knew when she was overmatched.

And in truth, later that evening, she was grateful for Alice Hende's insistence. For the first time in days—weeks?—Janet laughed, and for the first time in years, she danced.

The high street was ablaze in good cheer and firelight. A stage had been set out for the mummers to perform, large trestle tables were laden with food and drink, and musicians had been organized to provide dancing.

Alice had insisted that Janet wear the fine surcote Mary had given her, and the older woman had arranged her hair in a small embroidered cap that left a cascade of golden curls tumbling down her back.

Janet did not lack for partners, and spinning around in the firelight, her cheeks hot and lungs gasping for air, she felt like a girl again. Pretty and alive and, for a moment, carefree.

She didn't realize how much notice she was attracting.

She had snuck away for a moment into the alehouse to use the privy—which was no more than a hole in the wall with a wooden seat over the cesspit—when a cloaked figure stepped into her path as she exited the building.

Her heart stopped. But it took her only a few seconds to recognize the slender, cloaked figure in the torchlight. Good heavens, it was her informant!

Janet immediately glanced about, looking for a place to escape the crowd, and darted into the narrow wynd that ran alongside the alehouse. It was darker there, and there would be less chance of anyone seeing them.

Her heart was pounding, knowing that it must be something important to bring her informant here like this.

"I feared that I would not be able to find you," the lady said. "But then I saw you dancing." The torchlight didn't quite extend into the wynd, and her face was hidden in the dark shadow of the hooded cloak, but Janet could tell from her voice that she was smiling. "I confess I did not recognize you at first. The pretty, smiling merchant's daughter is a far cry from an Italian nun."

Janet was glad the other woman couldn't see her blush. "You have taken a great risk in coming here."

"I had to. This cannot wait." She handed a folded piece of parchment to Janet, which she quickly slid into the purse at her waist. "You must take it to him with all speed. Already it might be too late. The talks are set for the day after next. You must find him before he reaches Selkirk tomorrow."

Janet was just a courier. She was not usually privy to information, so she knew it must be serious for the woman to be telling her this. "Selkirk?"

"Aye, for the peace negotiations." The woman took Janet's arm and drew her closer. Janet could see the panic shimmering in her big eyes. "It's a trap. The English mean to take Bruce."

She wasn't here. Damn, he'd been so sure she would be. *"I have to be back by St. Drostan's Day,"* she'd said.

So where the hell was she? Not at the priory. Nor at the hospital for that matter. Ewen had left Sutherland to watch the priory and followed the group of nuns who'd walked to the hospital after the morning prayers. Orders or nay, his role as an observer had ended last night, the moment he realized the priest was having her watched. Posing as a traveler on the road, he examined every person in that hospital: leper, nun, traveler, the ill or infirm—even the group of ladies from the castle who'd arrived to give alms on the saint's day.

But she wasn't there.

He was running out of rope. Running out of ideas. He'd never felt so damned helpless, never been so lost. The one time he really needed to find someone, his skills had failed him.

Worse, he couldn't escape the feeling that he somehow should have known. How could he not have realized someone was watching her? He should have realized the soldiers from Douglas could not have tracked them that fast. He'd blamed her for carelessness when he'd missed the signs himself.

It was after dark when he left the hospital to rejoin Sutherland at the priory. MacLean and MacKay had left late the night before, after attending to some business in the forest, and not without some argument.

"The king isn't going to like it," MacLean had said. "He ordered all of us back tomorrow. You don't even know that she is here. You can be back by tomorrow night if you ride hard."

Ewen's mouth clenched. He wished to hell she wasn't here, that she was someplace safe and far away. But he knew Janet. If she thought it was important, nothing would keep her away. "She's here," he said flatly. "I don't give a shite about orders." His partner lifted his brow at that, but Ewen ignored him. "You three go and return when you can. I'm not leaving her."

MacKay looked skeptical. "You sure you know what you're doing? If you're wrong, the king won't be happy."

The king wasn't happy now. And Ewen wasn't wrong. "Would you leave your wife?"

MacKay didn't say anything.

"In a heartbeat," MacLean said flatly.

Ewen threw him a disgusted look. "Well, I'm not leaving her."

None of the men stated the obvious: she wasn't his wife, nor was she ever likely to be.

In the end, it was MacKay and MacLean who'd ridden away to join the others and report to the king what had happened. Sutherland had insisted on staying with Ewen. "If I leave and something happens to her, my wife will never forgive me. I think I'll take my chances with Bruce."

Knowing Mary, it was probably a wise decision. But Ewen was glad for the extra sword—and the extra pair of eyes.

He whistled to let Sutherland know he approached. The newest member of the Highland Guard, a man who could fill in just about anywhere and had taken over the dangerous job of working with black powder after the death of one of their brethren, responded with a hoot before jumping down from a tree ahead of him.

"Anything?" Ewen asked.

"Nay. The prioress locked up about an hour ago. I'll assume from your tone that you didn't have much luck either."

Ewen shook his head grimly. "Did the lad show his face?"

A flash of white appeared in the moonlight as Sutherland grinned. "After last night? I don't think he'd step within a mile of this place, even if you weren't paying him to stay away." He chuckled. "I didn't realize we had so many admirers in the ranks of English spies."

"The lad didn't know what the hell he was doing."

Last night, before MacKay and MacLean had left, they'd waited for the lad to leave the castle, followed him, and surrounded him in the forest. There were times that their phantom reputation came into good use. The lad, probably sixteen or seventeen, had been terrified initially. He'd blurted out what he was doing for the priest almost before they'd finished asking the question. For over a month, he'd earned a penny a day to watch the new nun in the priory and report to the priest immediately if she went anywhere or did anything. The boy hadn't understood why he was still watching the place when the nun had left with a man a fortnight earlier, but he was happy collecting his money for as long as the priest wanted to pay.

He'd been stunned to learn he was spying for the English. "I'm not a traitor," he'd insisted. "I'm a Scot."

The lad had been so offended, so ashamed, that Sutherland was right—Ewen probably didn't need to pay him. But he thought it best to ensure the lad didn't have second thoughts.

They'd instructed him to stay away from the priory, but keep reporting to the priest every night as before. Afterward, he was to meet them, and he would be paid a shilling—more than his family probably earned in a week.

Once it was clear they did not mean him any harm, the lad had acted like he was in the presence of demigods, peppering them with questions until they'd been forced to send him away. "Can you really appear out of the mist?" "Do your swords really come from Valhalla?" "Do you have heads under the masks or do your demon eyes glow out of emptiness?" "Where do you go to when you disappear?"

"Perhaps we've found a new recruit?" Sutherland said.

Ewen would have laughed if he weren't thinking that they would be needing one soon. "You never know."

"So what now?"

"We go back to Roxburgh and wait for the lad to report back to us."

"And then?"

Ewen wished to hell he knew. He was out of leads. He didn't realize how much he'd pinned his hopes on today. But one thing was for certain: he wasn't going to give up until he found her.

Janet stared at her informant in stunned disbelief. The English meant to capture Robert at Selkirk under the auspices of a peace negotiation? It defied every notion of honor. It was a breech of a code between soldiers in warfare—by long tradition, parleys were sacred ground under the cover of a truce. "Are you certain?"

"I would not risk this if I were not. It is all there," her informant said, referring to the parchment. "I was only fortunate I found this out earlier this evening. The feast day celebration enabled me to sneak out of the castle. But I must return before anyone notices I am gone. You can get this to him in time?"

Janet's mind was already racing with all she had to do. She would prepare to leave immediately, staying just long enough to say goodbye to the Hendeses, gather her belongings, and with any luck procure a horse. The feast would help in that regard. "I can."

The words had barely left her mouth before they heard footsteps and the sound of voices.

"Where did she go?" a man said angrily.

Janet felt a flash of alarm but told herself it was nothing. Probably her next dance partner looking for her.

The two women's eyes met in the darkness. "Go," Janet said. "Someone is coming."

The woman nodded. "Godspeed," she whispered, and to Janet's surprise, she leaned over to give her a quick hug before turning to go.

But the woman had barely taken a few steps when disaster struck. "There!" a man shouted. "After her! Don't let her get away."

A man came running toward them—a big man. Janet didn't have time to think. She acted on instinct, and her first one was to protect the other woman. Right as the man started to run past her, she stepped in his path.

Her intention was to trip him and sidestep out of the way, but it didn't work out the way she had planned. Her skirt tangled in his foot, and he was able to grab her. They hit the ground together.

The blow jarred the air from her lungs, but she recovered fast and immediately scrambled to her feet. Unfortunately, the big oaf did as well. He was even taller than Ewen, although he didn't smell as nice. This man stank as if he labored with pigs all day.

She would have twisted away, but his hands were like

big, meaty manacles. "What is the meaning of this? Un-hand me!"

Surprisingly, he did. The authority of her tone must have startled him. The man was big and bulky, with a peasant's flat face, blunt features, and a neck that seemed crunched into his shoulders. If it was possible to look thick-headed, he did a fine job of it.

Janet relaxed a little. Talking her way out of this shouldn't be too difficult. "How dare you attack me like that! Look what you've done." She held up her skirt. "You've ripped my gown. Do you realize how much this cost? You can be assured that I will be sending you an ac-counting for the repair."

He backed up a step or two, and she tried not to laugh. "I didn't mean—"

She didn't let him finish, keeping him on the defensive. "Do you make it your business to accost innocent women in dark alleys?"

"Nay, I was told . . . He told me—"

He looked toward the street, and Janet glanced over at the man who was approaching. He was the one who'd is-sued the order.

He was about twenty feet away and looking right at her. "It *is* you," he said. "I thought so but wasn't sure. It's a long way from Italy, Sister Genna."

The blood drained from her face. Oh God, the priest from the market! She wasn't going to be talking her way out of this after all.

But there was one thing she could do. Before the big oaf collected his wits and reached for her again, she ran.

Twenty-four

✖

"After her!" the priest shouted. "Guards! Don't let her get away."

Janet shot down the wynd as fast as her legs would carry her.

One glance over her shoulder sent her pulse jumping through her throat. Figures were shadowed at the mouth of the wynd behind her. A half-dozen soldiers, maybe more. They'd been closer than she realized.

She took some comfort in the knowledge that her source had likely gotten away, but that was dampened by the realization of what was at stake. If she didn't get out of here, if she didn't get to Bruce in time, it could all be over.

Knowing she had only a few minutes to get out of the village before they blocked off the roads, she turned at the first corner and plunged down another dark wynd.

She could hear them chasing behind her, but she didn't think about it. Her lungs were bursting and her legs were weakening, but she didn't slow. She kept her mind focused on getting out of the village. If she could make it to the forest, she had a chance.

But they were fanning out behind her. Closing in.

She needed a horse. But that would have to wait. If she could just make it to Rutherford, she would be able to find something.

And maybe . . .

Her heart squeezed, and it wasn't from the lack of air in

her lungs. She had no reason to think he would be there, but if Ewen had come after her, Rutherford would be her best chance at finding him. *"I will find you."* His words from when they were being hunted came back to her.

"She's heading for the forest!"

Her stomach dropped, hearing the horse and rider close behind her.

But she was almost there. A moment later she plunged into the heavy darkness. It swallowed her like a tomb. A figurative one, she hoped.

She experienced a fresh burst of energy with the knowledge that the trees would slow the horses down and raced through the brush and bracken, pushing limbs out of the way when she could see them, not noticing the scratches that tore through her skin when she could not.

The sounds behind her started to fade. She kept heading in the same direction, praying that it was the right one, but the darkness and trees had taken away her sense of direction.

After another handful of minutes, she had to stop. Bending over, she gulped in air like a starving person. She might be able to walk for days, but running at full speed for twenty minutes had sapped her of every bit of her energy.

Yet she had to keep going.

Slower now, but still running, she threaded her way through the trees. *Please let it be the right direction.*

For so many reasons, she wished she had Ewen with her. He wouldn't get lost, which was more than she could say for herself. With the clouds, there weren't even stars to guide her. She was going on instinct now, looking for any sign of something familiar. It was less than five miles between Roxburgh and Rutherford, with forest between them most of the way. The road was to the north of where she hoped she was.

The sounds were gone now. But she didn't let herself

relax, knowing the forest could absorb sound as efficiently as it did light.

That was why she didn't hear him until it was too late.

A man grabbed her from behind, pinning her arms to her side with his big, steel-clad arm. A leather gauntlet slammed over her mouth before she could scream. Her feet kicked wildly but uselessly in the air. "I have 'er!" he yelled.

Something wasn't right. Ewen's unease had begun to grow about an hour ago. The lad was late.

"He should be here by now," he said.

"Perhaps he was delayed by the feasts?" Sutherland suggested. "It seems to be quite a celebration, if those fires are any indication."

From their vantage on the hill, they could see the main gate and into the castle courtyard. Roxburgh Castle sat on the tip of a small peninsula of land at the juncture of the rivers Tweed and Teviot. The village lay behind and was mostly blocked from view, but they could see the roar of the fires.

By this time of night, the gate to the castle would normally be closed, but due to the feast, people were still flowing freely in and out.

"I'm going in there," Ewen said.

"Are you mad? Roxburgh Castle is one of the most heavily defended castles on the Borders. There are at least five hundred English soldiers garrisoned there right now, waiting to resume the war, where one of their greatest objectives is to kill the members of Bruce's famed secret army. And you are just going to walk right in there without a plan and hope they don't notice you?"

Ewen gritted his teeth. "Aye. I'm sure as hell not just going to keep standing here. With the feast, this might be my best chance to get in there. And I do have a plan. I'll relieve one of the men-at-arms celebrating in the village of his attire."

"That's a plan? It's bloody suicide, that's what it is."

"If her contact is at the castle, Janet could be there right now. The feast would be a perfect opportunity."

"That's a hell of a lot of risk for a possibility."

"Possibilities are all I have right now. Unless you have a better idea," he challenged angrily.

Sutherland's jaw set in a hard line. He stared at him for a long moment. "I'll go with you."

Ewen shook his head. "I need you out here. If something goes wrong, I may need you to use that powder of yours for a distraction."

Sutherland swore. "I sure as hell wish Viper were here."

Ewen couldn't disagree. Lachlan MacRuairi had a unique ability to get in and out of almost anywhere. But right now, Ewen would be grateful for any of his brethren— or former brethren. If something happened, two swords against five hundred wasn't exactly encouraging odds.

Damn, it was hard to believe that he wasn't going to be a part of this anymore. Fighting in this team had been the greatest thing he'd ever done. And these men . . .

They were the closest friends he'd ever had. They were like brothers to him. Leaving this all behind was going to be harder than he wanted to think about.

He and Sutherland had just finished working out the details—there weren't many—of his plan when Sutherland caught a movement coming up the side of the hill. "So much for circumspect," Sutherland said wryly. "The lad isn't exactly trying to hide his eagerness to get here."

Ewen's pulse spiked as the lad drew near enough for him to make out his expression. "It isn't just eagerness— something is wrong."

The lad's eyes were wide as he scrambled over edge of the hill. "Sorry . . . late . . . lady . . ." he gasped, heaved over, between big gulps of air.

Ewen grabbed him by the shoulders and forced him upright at the mention of "lady." "What about the lady? Did you see her?"

The lad's eyes went so wide, Ewen thought they were going to pop out. He was mouthing words, but no sounds were coming out.

"Calm down," Sutherland said at Ewen's side. "You're scaring him."

Ah hell. Ewen let him go, and tried to moderate his tone when he felt like roaring at the top of his lungs. "What happened?"

The lad eyed him warily, still trying to catch his breath. Finally, he uttered the words that sent every drop of blood rushing from Ewen's body.

"The p-priest . . . he found the lady."

Janet fought with everything she had, but the soldier seemed to barely notice as he dragged her through the forest. The road was closer than she'd realized. After about fifty yards, they broke out of the trees and he pushed her forward with enough force to put her on her knees. She gazed up and found herself surrounded by men on horseback. In addition to the priest and the oaf who'd caught her before, she counted a half-dozen soldiers.

But none looked more dangerous than the priest. There was nothing churchly about the menacing gaze fixed on her. "Did you have a nice run, my dear?"

Janet felt a flash of panic but forced it aside. She had to think. She wasn't going to give up without a fight. A handful of different explanations filtered through her mind, but she didn't have time to weigh them all. She went with the first thing that came to mind: pretending that she hadn't known who he was. "You are a priest?" she said, getting to her feet. "Thank goodness! I thought you were with this man who was accosting me." She motioned to the oaf.

The priest shook his head with a tsking sound. "You can

forget the playacting, my dear. I know who you are. Your friend the monk was most forthcoming—with some persuasion, of course." The small smile sent shivers racing up and down her spine. *Poor Thom.* "I know of your transformation from the Italian nun to the novice Eleanor. I suspected you of helping the usurper king to pass messages, but imagine my surprise and pleasure when you led us right to his secret army. I am most interested in learning the names of the men you were traveling with."

"I don't know what you are talking about," she persisted. "You must have me confused with someone else."

His eyes narrowed. The soldiers moved their horses in tighter around her, and she had to fight the overwhelming urge not to try to dart between them and run. The instinct to flee at the danger closing in was primal.

"Do you think removing a veil and putting on a pretty dress will fool me?" the priest demanded. "It took me a moment when I saw you dancing, but I don't forget a face. Especially one as pretty as yours. It's a shame. So much beauty, going to waste."

Janet didn't like the sound of that. She didn't know what to say. Her tongue seemed tangled in her mouth. He wasn't the knight or the squire, and she didn't have the merchant and his wife to help her. She didn't have *anyone* to help her. God, what she wouldn't do for Ewen and his friends right now.

All she had was her wits—which seemed to be failing her right now—and her dagger. She would have to wait for the right time to attempt to get away, which, with all these men surrounding her, clearly wasn't right now.

She tried her luck with the soldiers. "It seems there is some misunderstanding," she said to one of them. "Perhaps it would be best if we returned to town—"

The priest didn't let her finish. "There is no misunderstanding. What were you doing with the woman in the alley? And who is she?"

"Woman?" Janet repeated, as if confused. "Oh, you mean the beggar woman?"

"Do you usually embrace beggar women?" the priest asked, a shrewd glint in his eyes.

Janet cursed her mistake; she'd forgotten about the hug. "I was surprised myself, Father. But she was most grateful for the coin I gave her."

"I do not think so, Genna or Eleanor or whatever name you are going by now. But it isn't your identity that concerns me." Obviously the dead friar hadn't been privy to her real name, or she suspected the priest would be very interested. "We've suspected that someone has been leaking information from the castle, and you are going to tell us who that is. But first things first." Janet didn't like the small smile on his face when he turned to the soldier who'd captured her. "Search her."

His words sent a chill racing down her spine. She knew it wouldn't take them long to find the parchment in the purse at her waist. And if they did . . .

She didn't want to think about it. It wasn't just her life at stake, but also her informant's, the king's, and the future of Scotland itself. If Bruce were captured now, the cause would be lost. Who else would be brave enough to stand up to the most powerful kingdom in Christendom? King Edward would put another puppet on the throne or take it for himself.

She couldn't let them find it; she had to get away.

The time for talk had ended. She reached for her dagger, but she wasn't quick enough. The soldier grabbed her arms in his crushing hold and spun her around to face him.

"Let go of me!" She managed to get one of her hands free and lashed at his face. One of her nails caught his cheek, but it only made him angrier.

In the torchlight she got her first look at him, and she almost wished for darkness. He wasn't exceptionally tall like the man who'd caught her in the alley, but what he

lacked in height he made up for in breadth and bulk. He
was wide as an oak, thick and strong. Beneath the edge of
his helm, all she could see was a squashed-in, crooked nose
that looked like it had healed in the same position in which
it had been punched, a thick, dark beard that covered the
bottom half of his face and a good portion of his neck as
well, and piercing dark eyes that were staring at her with
rage.

"Bitch!" He caught her wrist in his hand and squeezed
so tightly, she thought he meant to snap the bone. He let go
of it long enough to slam his fist into her jaw.

Her head snapped back, and she cried out in pain and
the shock of being struck. He hit her again, this time back-
handing her against the cheek. Blood poured down her
face as tears sprang to her eyes. But still she fought back.
She lashed out wildly—instinctively—but he caught her
blows with ease. He hit her again and again, beating
her into submission. Her jaw . . . her cheek . . . the side of
her ribs. Her head swam; the pain was overwhelming. It
took everything she had just to stay on her feet.

"That's enough," one of the other soldiers said, distaste
evident in his voice. Apparently not all the soldiers were
brutes who enjoyed beating women. "Let's see if she has
something first."

The brutish soldier spun her around again, holding both
her wrists in one vise-like hand, while the other pawed
roughly at her body with obviously relish.

"The purse," the priest said impatiently. "Give me the
purse."

She cried out and made one last frantic effort to protect
the missive, but he snapped the leather girdle from her
waist and tossed it to the priest.

Through tear- and blood-streaked vision, she watched
as the priest removed the parchment from the leather
pouch. A gleam of victory appeared in his gaze as one of
the men held a torch above his head, and he read it.

He folded the damning evidence back up and slid it into his vestments. "I see I was right about you and the lady. I should think with this, Lord de Beaumont should be able to pinpoint the source of his leak. Although that won't be half as much fun as it would be for Randolph here to retrieve the information from you. It's a particular talent of his."

Numb with the pain of his beating, her bruised and battered body still managed to chill. *Torture! Oh God, give me strength.* Though she'd known the danger from the outset—and had known something like this could happen—she had hoped never to face it.

The priest must have read the fear in her eyes because he smiled. "I do hate to deprive him of his fun." He looked at Randolph. "See what you can find out. If she doesn't tell you what you ask, kill her."

Janet's heart leapt to her throat. "Wait. You can't do this. You are a man of God."

"And you are a traitor. The man you call king is a murderer and excommunicated by the pope. God has no mercy for rebels."

Janet turned to the soldier who'd spoken for her before. "Please."

But he turned coldly away, ignoring her pitiful plea. Chivalry had ended with the discovery of the missive.

A moment later, the priest, his oafish minion, and the other soldiers were riding away, leaving her with her torturer and executioner.

"Do not take too long," the priest said over his shoulder right before they disappeared from view.

The brutish soldier started to drag her back into the trees. Janet's heart was slamming against her ribs—her probably broken ribs—and every instinct urged to use what remaining strength she had to fight back. But she had to be patient and wait for the perfect opportunity. She would have only one chance to take him by surprise. So she forced the fight from her muscles, becoming as floppy as a poppet of rags.

When they reached a small clearing, he tossed her unceremoniously on the ground. She looked up at him looming over her and tried to push back the panic crawling up her throat.

Her stomach turned.

He reached up under his habergeon of mail and started to work the ties of his braies. "Don't move, you stupid bitch. I've never fucked someone into telling me what I want to hear, but then again I've never questioned someone as pretty as you. Or as pretty as you used to be. Your face doesn't look too good right now." He laughed.

Janet tried to shut out his words. Tried not to hear what he was saying as she concentrated on the hand reaching slowly for her boot.

Just a few more inches . . .

She gasped when stepped over her. He would have crushed her legs with his foot if she hadn't reacted by separating them. But unknowingly by spreading her legs, he helped her. Her hand found its target.

She grasped the hilt of her dagger in her hand as he knelt down on the ground before her.

All she could see in the moonlight was the cold gleam of his smile. "Aren't you going to fight me? It's much more fun that way."

Her heart was in her throat. She held her breath, waiting for the perfect moment.

He lifted his habergeon. Her eyes went to the protruding mass of flesh, and she shuddered with revulsion.

He saw her reaction. "Aye, it's impressive isn't it." He dropped his gaze and wrapped his hand around himself, giving it a hard stroke.

That was when she struck.

She slid the blade from the scabbard and plunged it into his leg.

He cried out in shock and pain. His eyes widened and then his hands circled around her neck, squeezing . . .

She screamed until she ran out of air.

Ewen took what the boy had told him—that the priest had caught sight of the lady in the village and had sent to the castle for soldiers to arrest her, but the lady had run away before he could catch her—and was able to pick up her tracks at the place the horses had chased her into the forest.

Leaving the boy to watch the road, he and Sutherland followed the tracks through the forest. As it was dark, he had no choice but to use a torch.

He came to the place where another set of tracks appeared from the road, and a dank chill raced through his blood. A few feet later his fears were confirmed: whoever had been following her had caught her. He had just started to follow the tracks where the man had dragged her, when he heard a sound that stopped his heart: a woman's scream.

He didn't hesitate. Even after Sutherland bit out a warning to him to be careful, he plunged into the trees. The sound had been close. Torturously close. He prayed as hard as he'd ever prayed in his life. *Please let me get there in time. Don't let it be too late. Just a few more seconds . . .*

He burst into the clearing, sword raised. When he saw the small figure struggle to her feet from beneath the body of a prone man, everything inside him seemed to come to a sudden halt.

His hand fell. "Janet?"

She looked up at him, and he made a pained sound. The emotions were so fierce and intense, he staggered. His stomach heaved. He'd felt something like this only once before, in the aftermath of his first battle, where the sight of all the blood had sickened him. But it was nothing to the sight of the woman he loved battered and bloody.

"Ewen?" she said softly. "You found me."

She swayed, and he lurched forward, catching her against him. His heart was pounding so hard he couldn't breathe. He cradled her to him like a broken bird. The thought of how close he'd come to losing her made his knees week. "Oh God, are you all right? What happened?"

She buried her head in his chest and grabbed hold of him, clutching him like a frightened kitten. But a glance at the body of the man at her feet told him that his kitten had the heart of a lion. She'd been beaten but not defeated, and through the gut-wrenching emotions wracking him he felt a swell of pride.

He kissed her head, savoring the silky texture of her hair and the scent of bluebells that reminded him of home. She *was* his home. How could he not have known it? "It's all right now," he murmured soothingly. "I have you. Everything is going to be all right. I promise."

Sutherland came up behind them and swore, the torchlight enabling him to see her face. It seemed to break the trance that had enfolded them.

She looked up at him, her bruised and bloody face suddenly intent. "You have to catch them before they reach the castle."

"Who?" he asked.

Before she could respond, the sound of a sharp whistle pierced the night. He and Sutherland exchanged a look. Sutherland responded, and a few moments later, they had company.

Janet was in a state of shock. She could still feel the man's hands squeezing her neck. She had thought he was going to kill her. He would have, too, if her blade hadn't found the perfect spot. Before he could finish her off, he collapsed on top of her, his life's blood still rushing from his body.

Out of this nightmare, Ewen had appeared like an image

from a dream. It had taken her a moment to realize he was real.

He'd found her. He was holding her, and she never wanted to let him go.

But then she remembered the priest. They had to find him before he reached the castle. Her informant's life was at stake.

Her explanation, however, was interrupted by the arrival of three more nasal-helmed phantoms. Under normal circumstances she might have felt a flicker of apprehension, even knowing they were friends, but Ewen was holding her.

"We heard the scream," one of the men said by way of explanation. Magnus, she realized, recognizing his voice.

When she turned from her position pressed against Ewen's chest to look at him, the big Highlander swore.

She bit her lip, tasting blood, and realized her face must look as bad as it felt.

"What happened, lass?" he asked, his voice more gentle than she'd ever heard it.

She must really look bad. "I don't have time to explain. There is a party of five soldiers, a priest, and another man headed back to the castle. You have to catch them before they arrive. They have a missive meant for Bruce. A note that could spell a death warrant for someone inside the castle." She sensed movement from one of the men at Magnus's side and instinctively retreated to the safety of Ewen's chest. Even beneath the darkened nasal helm, he looked meaner than the rest.

"Back off, Viper," Ewen said from behind her. "What the hell is the matter with you?"

The warrior ignored him, his eyes fixed on her—the eeriest eyes she'd ever seen. "When did they leave?"

"A few minutes ago." Janet thought back. "Maybe five?"

"I'll go," the man Ewen called Viper said.

Janet turned to Ewen. "You must go, too. You have to make sure they find them and no one gets away."

Ewen clenched his jaw shut, looking as yielding as a stone wall. "I'm not leaving you."

"Please," she said. "You must do this for me. I beg you."

His eyes searched hers. "Don't ask this of me. You're hurt. Jesus, Janet, you're covered in blood, and your face . . ." His voice caught. The moonlight almost made his eyes look shiny with tears.

She managed a wobbly smile, though it hurt. "My face will heal and the blood is not mine." At least most of it wasn't. "But I need to find Robert as soon as possible, and I cannot do so unless I know the person in the castle is safe."

"Viper will see to it," Ewen said. But he must have read something on her face. "This is important to you?"

She nodded. "The parley in Selkirk is a trap. The English plan to break the truce."

More than one of the men swore at her news. "You are sure?" Ewen asked. "The breaking of the peace at a truce is beyond even the normal course of English treachery."

She nodded. "I am sure. The proof is in that missive."

The mean-looking one with the appropriate name of Viper interrupted. "We need to go if we hope to catch them before they arrive. It isn't far to the castle."

Still, Ewen hesitated. He didn't want to let her go.

Her heart squeezed. "It will be all right," she said softly. "My brother-in-law will keep me safe. Won't you, Sir Kenneth?"

Mary's husband smiled and stepped forward. "As I would my own wife, my lady."

Sir Kenneth held out his hand, and reluctantly, Ewen released her. "I'll hold you to that, Ice," he said fiercely.

Ewen, Viper, and a man she recognized as MacLean started to move off, but Magnus stopped them. "*Bàs roimh Gèill.*" Death before surrender, she translated.

"And Hunter." Ewen turned to look at him. "Hurry back. I think there's something you forgot to tell us."

Ewen's expression turned grim—God, how she'd missed that!—and he nodded. With one last look to her that spoke of things left unsaid, the three men rode off.

Selfishly, Janet wanted to call him back. She wanted his strength around her. She wanted to bury her head in his chest, curl into a ball, and let him make it all go away.

But they both had a job to do.

When it was over . . .

For the first time since she'd left him that night at the stable, Janet had hope.

Twenty-five

❧

Dunstaffnage Castle, Lorn, Scottish Highlands,
Christmas Eve 1310

Janet sat on the trunk at the foot of her bed. The maid-servant had just finished arranging her hair in a circlet of gold when a knock rapped on the door.

She bid the person enter, and her twin sister, Mary, walked into the room. Their eyes met. Mary shook her head in response to her unspoken question, and Janet's shoulders slumped.

The strange, wordless communication that she and her sister had shared as children had come back within hours of their being reunited. Being with her sister again . . .

Emotion swelled in her chest. Janet hadn't realized just how much she'd missed her twin, until Mary had rushed into the room where she'd been brought on arrival to be tended by Lady Helen, Magnus's wife. They'd taken one look at each other and burst into tears. It had been quite some time before Helen had been able to resume her ministrations to Janet's face, ribs, and the broken bone in her wrist.

Janet still could not believe that her sister had forgiven her. Actually, if Mary was to believed, she'd never blamed her. She hadn't realized how much her sister's forgiveness meant to her. It felt as if a great weight had been lifted. To Janet's surprise, talking about what had happened that night—the explosion, Cailin's and the MacRuairi clansmen's deaths, Janet's disappearance—had been strangely cathartic. She would mourn and regret the deaths that night for the rest of her life, but she was ready to put them to rest.

Despite her joy in seeing her sister, however, Mary's shake of the head made her chest squeeze with disappointment. "There is still no sign of him?"

It was less a question than a plea. Not long after Janet had successfully intercepted the king only a few miles before he reached Selkirk, warning him of the treachery that lay ahead, Viper—what she now knew was the *nom de guerre* for Lachlan MacRuairi—and Eoin MacLean had caught up with them. Their mission had been a success. They'd retrieved the missive for the king and ensured the safety of their informant. Ewen, however, had left them at Roxburgh, bound for a destination he would not name. He'd given them a message for her—that he would return as soon as possible—but after more than a week, Janet was beginning to lose hope.

She didn't understand. She thought when he'd found her in the forest, when he'd held her in his arms, when he'd looked in her eyes with such tender, poignant emotion, that he'd changed his mind. That he realized he cared for her and intended to fight for them.

But where was he? Why hadn't he come for her? Had something happened?

Learning about his leg and how close he'd come to death haunted her. She couldn't believe she'd mistaken his fever for drunkenness and left him when he was so ill.

Mary shook her head again. "Kenneth spoke to the king, but no one knows where he is. Not even Robert."

Janet made a face and winced, having forgotten about her injuries. Though Helen said she would heal with little to remind her of her ordeal but a few small scars, the cuts and bruises were still tender.

But Robert, the subject that had provoked her reaction, needed to be dealt with. She hadn't spoken to him since she and the others had relayed the news of the English treachery. He'd been grateful, and furious at what had happened to her, but they'd yet to discuss Ewen or her future.

"I can't believe they just let him leave when he was still recovering," Janet said, hands twisting in her skirts. "What if he's lying out there somewhere . . ."

"The men said he was fine," Mary assured her. "And Bella wasn't too happy with Lachlan either when she found out. But Lachlan pointed out that he wasn't a 'bloody nursemaid' and Ewen had insisted."

"Ewen didn't tell anyone that the king had kicked him out of the Guard?" she asked.

Mary had told her Bruce's secret army—or the phantoms, as she called them—were known as the Highland Guard among the men. Although Janet was not privy to the identities of all of the warriors, she had her suspicions. If King Edward were smart, he would start looking at every Highlander over six feet tall, built like a rock, with an uncommonly handsome face.

"Nay," Mary answered, "but as soon as they found out, the men convinced the king to reconsider the matter."

Knowing how stubborn Robert could be, Janet asked, "How did they do that?"

Mary shrugged. "I don't know, but whatever it was, it must have been persuasive."

"This is ridiculous." Janet threw up her hands and stood. She started for the door.

Mary looked up from where she'd sat on the edge of her bed. "Where are you going?"

"To see that Robert considers correctly."

Even if Ewen didn't want her, he wasn't going to lose everything because of her.

* * *

The years had been hard on Robert the Bruce. He'd changed much from the handsome young knight who'd captured the heart of Janet's eldest sister, Isabella. He was still handsome, but he looked older than his six and thirty years. The war, the difficulty he'd faced after the catastrophic defeat at the Battle of Methven, and his near destruction afterward had taken their toll in the deep lines etched on his face. But it was his expression that had changed the most. The gregarious, lighthearted, chivalrous knight was gone forever, replaced by the serious, formidable, battle-hardened warrior king.

Seated across from him in his private solar, his men leaving at her request, Janet felt a twinge of unexpected apprehension. She might think of him as Robert, but the man before her was undeniably a king. The concern in the dark eyes that met hers, however, gave her courage.

"You are feeling better? Helen has attended to all your needs? I told her that you should have whatever you wished."

She intended to hold him to that. "I feel much better, Sire. Helen has cared for me as if I were her sister. But there is one thing I would ask for."

He smiled, looking relieved. "Whatever it is, you shall have it. I am in your debt, Janet. I know what you went through to get that message to me, and I heard how you protected our informant in the castle by jumping in front of the man in the alley."

Their eyes met, and Janet could see how truly grateful he was. The informant was important to him; it was why he'd trusted her in the first place. But she wondered how he'd heard the specifics of what had happened in Berwick. Someone must have spoken to her informant.

"I still can't believe the English planned treachery in a peace negotiation," he continued. "Both Gloucester and

Cornwall gave me their word. I'd expect it from Gaveston, but not from a son of de Monthermer."

The Earl of Cornwall, Piers Gaveston, was Edward's favorite. The Earl of Gloucester, Gilbert de Clare, was a strong supporter of the king, but he was also the stepson of one of Robert's former close friends, Ralph de Monthermer.

"Yet after Methven, I should no longer be surprised." Robert's face darkened, giving Janet a glimpse of his anger and rage. "From what I read in that missive, they might have succeeded. They planned to surround us with Roxburgh's entire garrison while we slept." He paused for a moment, collecting himself before he looked back up at her. "What is it you want, Janet? If it is in my power, it shall be yours."

Janet held his gaze and did not hesitate. "I want Ewen."

Robert's eyes flashed. "You will not twist my words against me this time, Janet. I already gave my answer to Lamont, when he came to me with his 'request.'"

Janet didn't let his anger deter her. "I am asking for you to reconsider in light of the recent events. I've never asked you for anything before, Robert, but I am asking you now."

He sat back in his throne-like chair, considering her with hard, intent eyes. "What exactly is it that you are asking for?"

"I do not wish Ewen to be punished for what has happened. Return his lands and give him his place back in the Guard, and . . ." Her cheeks grew hot.

"And?" Robert asked.

"And if he still wishes to marry me, give us your permission."

"You would not have me order it?"

Janet shook her head. "I'd no more have him forced into a marriage not of his choosing than I would be forced into one myself."

The king frowned, not having missed her bold reproach. "He took your innocence. I will not reward him for that."

"You don't know me at all if you think he took anything that I did not willingly give him."

"He took advantage of your innocence," Robert said uncomfortably; obviously, he didn't find the subject of such intimate matters with a woman who was like a sister to him a pleasant one.

"I am not a girl, Robert. I am a woman of seven and twenty who has been waiting her entire life for this—for him. I love him."

"Love is not a reason for marriage. He doesn't have land to speak of, or titles, or a fortune."

"Then you can give him more," Janet said. "If what I have done is not deserving of a reward, then what about what *he* has done?" She let him consider that for a moment. "As for love, what of your marriages, Robert? Surely a subject can look no higher than her king for guidance?"

Robert's expression gave no hint that her words had penetrated, but she knew they had. It was well known that Robert had married both his wives for love.

A moment later he shook his head, giving her that exasperated look she recalled from the time she'd spent living with him and Isabella. "You should have been a lawman, Janet. Too bad you were not born a man—I could use you in my privy council."

Janet grinned, recalling Ewen's similar words when she'd first met him. She also remembered something else. Lamont, *lawman*. "Perhaps I shall be, Sire."

Her brows drew together pensively. The kernel of another idea had just taken root when they were interrupted by a hard rap on the door. A moment later, the fierce West Highland chief who rarely left Robert's side, stepped into the room.

Imposing. Formidable. Intimidating. Authoritative. Scary.

None of them came close to describing Tor MacLeod. The leader of the Highland Guard seemed more a peer than a subject, even in the presence of someone as majestic as Robert the Bruce.

"I assume if you are interrupting, it is something important?" Robert asked.

"Aye," Tor said. "There is someone here to see you."

"Tell him to wait."

Tor looked at her, a half-smile turning his mouth. "I think you'll want to see him."

He looked outside the door and waved someone in. Janet gasped, her heart jumping to her throat when Ewen strode through the door.

"You're back!" she cried, and would have run into his arms if she hadn't noticed the man who'd come up behind him.

Her heart, which had been soaring only a moment before, came crashing to the ground. She froze, her mouth falling open in shock.

Though he looked considerably older than the last time she'd seen him, Janet did not have trouble recognizing the lanky new Steward of Scotland, Walter Stewart.

Her gaze shot to Ewen's in mute horror, looking for reassurance. Why had he brought him here?

Ewen wanted to go to Janet the moment he entered the room, but he was very conscious of the man seated in the throne-like chair behind the table. Ewen had gone about this all wrong with the king before; he had to do it right this time.

The relief at seeing her so hale hit him with a powerful blow to the chest. He'd told himself over and over that Helen would care for her, that she was in the best of hands; but she wasn't in *his* hands, and it wasn't until he saw her face-to-face that he could begin to relax.

He took an inventory of her injuries, from the wrapping

around her wrist, the bulky wrappings around her ribs beneath her gown, and the small line of stitches at her cheek. The swelling in her jaw and nose had retreated, leaving the yellowish, black-and-blue remnants of her bruises. The two black half-moons under her eyes suggested that her nose had been broken, although it appeared as straight as before.

Her eyes met his, and the look of uncertainty smashed his good intentions to hell. *To hell with Bruce!* He walked over and held out his hand. She slipped her tiny palm in his, as if it belonged there—which it bloody well did—and he helped her to her feet.

He didn't release her hand, keeping it enfolded in his. With his other, he tipped her head back to better examine her face, tilting it in one direction and then the other. "You are all right?"

She nodded, and he allowed himself one more tender sweep of his thumb along the bruised contour of her chin before he released her and turned to face his king. He didn't trust himself not to kiss her, and with the way the king was looking at him right now, he was already close to walking out of here in chains.

"I thought I ordered you to return on St. Drostan's Day with the others," Bruce said, eyeing him angrily.

Ewen decided not to point out that he'd actually ordered him from his sight. "I had something important that I needed to take care of."

Bruce's gaze flickered to Walter before coming back to him. "You seem to be having trouble following all kinds of orders of late."

Ewen didn't disagree.

The king held his gaze for a moment longer and then turned to Walter. "I assume he has brought you here for a reason?"

"He has, Sire," Walter said, stepping forward with a

bow. "Lamont came to me with a rather unexpected request. He asked to marry my betrothed."

He heard Janet's sharp intake of breath and felt her eyes on him, but he was watching Bruce. The king sat back in his chair, giving nothing away by his expression. "He did, did he? Did he mention that I had refused a similar request?"

"Aye," Walter said. "He mentioned that."

"And what did you tell him?" Bruce asked.

Walter's gaze flickered apologetically to Janet before he answered. "I told him that I would give him my support and break the betrothal, if that was the lady's wish as well."

"It is!" Janet would have rushed forward to assure him, but Bruce held her back with a lift of his hand.

Ewen said a silent prayer of thanks. Until that moment, he hadn't been a hundred percent certain that he hadn't been arguing with Walter Stewart (who despite his youth had proved a formidable opponent) over the past few days for nothing. Ewen had been lucky to walk out of Rothesay Castle without having to promise him his firstborn.

"I assume he told you everything?" Bruce asked.

Stewart, who was obviously very conscious of Janet's presence, blushed. "He did."

The king didn't say anything for a minute, but then he turned to Janet. "MacLeod will take you back to your room. Lady Anna has prepared a feast tonight on the eve of the Nativity. We will speak more later."

Janet started to protest, "But—"

Ewen cut her off, taking her hands in his and giving them a gentle squeeze. "Go now. I will find you." *I will always find you*, he told her silently. "Remember?"

She nodded.

"Trust me," he said softly, holding her gaze. "I won't let you down." Not again.

She wrinkled her ill-treated nose. "I won't always be this biddable."

He smiled. "I shudder to think of it."

He brought one of her hands to his mouth for a kiss before he finally released her, for what he swore would be the last time.

She marched rather huffily toward the door. Looking back over her shoulder, she gave her parting words to Bruce. "Remember your promise, Robert."

"I didn't make any promises," the king protested.

"Aye, but I know you were about to." She gave him a cheeky smile, wincing when it seemed to cause her pain.

Both Ewen and the king lurched toward her with concern. "Are you all right?" they asked in tandem.

Janet's smile deepened. "I will be."

The little minx! That wince had been a reminder. And he wasn't the only one to realize it. When she left the room, Ewen and the king exchanged a look. Ewen suspected he would be wearing an exasperated and slightly defeated look like the one that was on the king's face for a long time. Happily.

Twenty-six

ɣ

Janet had waited long enough. Ewen had left the king's solar over an hour ago. Lady Anna Campbell, the wife of Arthur Campbell, who was the keeper of Dunstaffnage for the king (and also, if his handsome face and muscular physique were any indication, one of the Guardsmen), had been kind enough to inform her of that, as well as where Janet could find him.

She took it as a good sign that he had been given a chamber in the castle, rather than under it in the pit prison. So why hadn't he come to find her?

The castle was abuzz with excitement for the evening's celebration. Janet passed a number of servants on her way down from her third-floor chamber to Ewen's on the first. She frowned, however, when she noticed a young—and quite pretty—serving girl headed to the same door as she with a large bucket of water in her hands.

The girl was about to open the door when Janet stopped her. "I'll take that."

The servant looked horrified. She shook her head. "It wouldn't be right, my lady. The laird is . . ." Her cheeks heated. "Bathing."

"Is he now?" Janet hoped she didn't sound as shrewish as she felt.

The girl nodded. "Lady Helen insists that he soak his leg at least once a day." Janet felt a pang of guilt for her jealousy, but that jealousy was instantly revived when the girl added, "I'm to help him with whatever he needs while Lady Helen attends to little William."

Janet had met her adorable nephew a few days ago. The child was a handful, having just started to crawl. "Is something wrong?"

"The wee laddie bumped his head on the bedpost, but Lady Helen says he'll be fine. Not even a bruise."

Janet nodded, not hiding her relief. "I will take the bucket in to the laird. We are to be married." At least she hoped they were. "But if you wouldn't mind, there is something I would like you to do first."

When Ewen answered the knock at the door, it was the servant girl who replied. "Your water, my lord." But it was Janet who entered the room. She closed the door behind her and walked toward the man sprawled naked in the tub with his back toward her. She was just annoyed enough to look at him without shame, taking in every inch of hard, bronzed skin.

"Shall I wash your back, my lord?" she said in a soft, singsong voice completely unlike her own.

"If you wish," he said indifferently.

The blighter! He should bloody well wash himself! It was with quite a bit of satisfaction that Janet dumped the entire bucket of water on his head. *Cold* water, she'd taken the time to notice.

"What the hell!" He jumped out of the tub and turned on her in shock and anger. Seeing who it was, the anger slipped away. He frowned. "What in Hades are you doing here, Janet?"

She pursed her mouth, crossed her arms, and perused that incredible body slowly, slightly mollified when a rather large part of him started to thicken and rise under her steady gaze.

He swore, grabbed a drying cloth that was lying on the bed, and wrapped it around his waist.

But if he thought to cover himself, he'd miscalculated.

The damp linen clung to every muscle and molded every inch of the thick club. My, it was pleasantly warm and sultry in here.

"Stop looking at me like that, damn it."

Her eyes met his. "Would you rather I called the serving girl back?"

It took him a moment, but something finally clicked. He smiled. Broadly. He looked so handsome it made her chest squeeze. "You're jealous."

She didn't deny it. "You can wash yourself from now on."

He grinned, crossing his arms—probably to distract her. It worked. She sucked in her breath at the impressive display of bulging muscle. Good gracious, she had new appreciation for warfare! "What if I need help?"

"I will help you," she said through gritted teeth, knowing she was being ridiculous.

"I think I should like to see that. Biddable and subservient in one day. I will make a proper wife out of you yet."

Her eyes went to his. The jealousy, the jesting, the muscle admiration, all slipped away. Only one thing mattered. Nothing had ever mattered more. "The king agreed?"

"Aye," he said huskily. In his gaze she could see all the emotion swelling in her heart. "But he did have one condition."

Janet was suddenly wary. "What kind of condition?"

"I must have your agreement."

Tears swelled in her eyes when he dropped to his knee at her feet. He took her hand and looked into her eyes. "I'm sorry for lying to you. I should have told you the truth. I'm sorry for not holding you in my arms after we made love and telling you how much I loved you. I'm sorry for not having enough courage to fight for us, for not doing whatever it took to make you my wife. I thought I'd lost everything, but none of it mattered without you. I know I can't change things or make it up to you, but I promise I will try for the rest of my life if you will agree to be my wife."

Janet stood there in stunned silence. Their roles, it seemed, had been reversed. The man who always said the wrong thing had expressed himself beautifully, and the woman who always knew what to say couldn't seem to find her tongue.

He began to get a little worried, looking up at her uncertainly. "Janet?"

There was one thing she had to know. "What if I wish to continue my work?"

He paused. "You would still do so even after what happened?"

"What if I did?"

"I would try to talk you out of it. The priest may be dead, but there are others who will eventually put it together like he did."

"And if you couldn't convince me?"

He looked as if he would rather be chewing nails. "I would defer—most unwillingly—to your judgment. And I should probably grow just as disagreeable as MacKay when Helen insists on accompanying us."

A broad smile spread over her features. If she ever needed proof of his love, she'd just heard it. "You, disagreeable? It defies belief."

He smacked her on the bottom, and she laughed.

But then she sobered. "I should like to continue to help Robert, but I think my days as a courier are over. You were right; I was overconfident about my abilities and perhaps," she conceded, "even a bit naive about what might happen. I should have exercised more discretion. After two close calls, I think I have overstayed my welcome in the Borders, not to mention run out of identities."

"*Two* close calls?" he boomed.

Oops. "I guess I forgot to mention how I came to be working in a drapery?"

"Aye, I'd say you did."

Janet gave a quick recounting, ignoring the darkening of his expression when she mentioned the squire and knight, and ended with how she's been forced to leave without saying goodbye to the Hendeses. "Do you think there might be a way to get word to them, and see that they are safe?"

"Consider it done," he said.

"Thank you," she said, not realizing how much it had been weighing on her.

"I won't say I'm not glad you won't be insisting on donning your habit again."

Janet smiled. "I wouldn't expect you to. Besides, it would be quite inappropriate under the circumstances."

"What circumstances?"

She wasn't ready to tell him that yet. But it had been her *coup de grâce* if Robert had proved unreasonable. "Don't think I'm finished, though. I have another plan in the works."

He groaned. "I don't even want to ask."

"Don't worry, it is nothing *too* outrageous."

He made a pained face. "What a relief," he said dryly. "Janet, unless you have failed to notice, I am still on my knee." He winced uncomfortably.

Her eyes jumped to his leg. "Oh God, I forgot about your leg." She dragged him to his feet. "Does it hurt horribly? I'm so sorry for leaving you like that—I didn't realize you were ill the night I left. I thought you were drunk."

He smoothed her hair back from the side of her face. "I rarely overindulge in spirits."

She looked at him. "Because of your father?"

He nodded.

"I should have known."

He shook his head. "I didn't want you to know. Hell, I didn't realize how bad it was myself."

"Thank God for Helen," she said.

He returned the sentiment and cupped her chin, lifting her gaze to his. "You haven't answered my question."

She smiled. "Yes . . . Yes!"

"Thank God," he groaned, drawing her into his arms. The tender kiss meant to seal the promise of their future, however, quickly turned into something else. Something hot and demanding. She wrapped her arms around his neck, drawing him closer, plastering her body to his.

The warm stroke of his tongue in her mouth made her shiver. Heat softened her bones, spreading over her in heavy molten waves. God, she loved kissing him.

The circles of his tongue became deeper and hotter, faster and more carnal. His body grew harder, rigid with the force of his desire.

She moaned, and he drew away.

"Ah hell. Did I hurt you?" His finger slid over the cut on her cheek and the bruises on her chin.

She shook her head.

"I wished you hadn't killed him," he said. She looked at him in surprise. But his face was as fierce as she'd ever seen it. "I would have made it much more painful for him for hurting you like this."

She rose on her toes and pressed a kiss on his lips. "It is in the past. And right now I am more concerned with the future—*our* future."

Not so absently, she let her hand fall between them, drawing little circles on his stomach with her fingertips. His skin was so warm and smooth, and the closer she danced to the prominent bulge under the drying cloth, the darker his eyes grew and the harder the bands of muscle across his stomach clenched.

He would have grabbed her wrist to stop her, but she was smart enough to use her injured hand.

"Janet . . ." he warned huskily. "Keep touching me like that, and I might forget my honorable intentions and your injuries."

She smiled and looked up into his eyes. "Good. I'm fine, really I am. Please, I want this. I want you."

Just so there would be no argument, she dropped her hand a little lower, grazing her wrist over the fat tip.

He sucked in his breath. "Jesus, Janet, you don't fight fair."

A wicked smile turned her mouth. "You can be gentle, can't you?"

He scooped her up and carried her over to the bed. "I sure as hell hope so."

With her injured wrist, she needed help to remove her clothes—a duty he was most happy to help with.

"I thought you weren't a 'damned handmaiden,'" she teased him as he unbuttoned her surcote, reminding him of a similar request she'd made in the fisherman's hut not so long ago.

He gave a sharp laugh. "I think I've changed my mind. If you intend to help me with my baths, the least I can do is help you with your clothes."

"Your enlightenment on parity in marriage is truly amazing," she said dryly.

He chuckled. "Not to mention self-serving."

When the last garment was removed, he stood back and looked at her for so long she started to try to cover herself with her hands. But he gently pulled them away. "Don't," he said, his voice rough with emotion. "You are so beautiful." He started to skim his fingers over her bare skin. "I want to touch every inch of you."

It seemed as if he did just that. Janet's breath was already coming fast when he finally leaned over and slid one taut nipple into his mouth, tugging it gently and circling it with his tongue. His silky dark hair slumped over to the side, brushing against her bare skin. She slid her fingers through it, holding him to her. He scooped her breast in his palm, squeezing and plying it between his hands as he took her deeper and deeper into his mouth.

Forgetting all about her injured ribs, she started to arch her back, moaning as the sensations started to build.

He lifted his head. "You are making it hard to go slow."

"And who is to blame for that?"

He grinned, and it made her heart catch.

"I love seeing you smile," she said softly. "You do not do enough of it."

"I haven't had much reason. But I suspect that will change."

She knew it would, especially when he learned—

He leaned over and kissed her, and whatever she'd been about to tell him was lost in the sensual haze that crashed over her with all the subtlety of a tidal wave.

His heat, his scent, the feel of his skin rubbing against hers infused her, drowning out everything but the powerful sensations building inside.

He held his chest over her, careful not to press against her injured ribs, but she pulled him down, wanting to feel the contact. The heat of his bare chest against hers, and the heavy, solid weight of his body on top of her.

He'd removed the drying cloth from around his waist, and she could feel the equally solid length of his erection hot and throbbing against her belly. She pressed and circled her hips, trying to inch him closer.

He groaned, deepening the kiss and the long strokes of his tongue until she couldn't take it anymore. She wanted him inside her. She wanted to feel him filling her.

Her heart was hammering, her breath was quickening, and the place between her legs was quivering with need. "Please," she moaned.

Lifting his head, he looked into her eyes. She could feel him positioning himself between her legs. "Tell me if it hurts," he said tightly, his muscles clenched with restraint.

He pressed into her. Slow and gentle. Inching. Stretching. Filling her. She gasped. Moaned. Opened around him.

It didn't hurt. It didn't hurt at all. It felt incredible. She felt full. Possessed. Loved.

His eyes were dark and hot. "You feel so good."

"So do you," she said huskily.

"I love you, *mo chroí.*"

She smiled, tears of happiness filling her eyes. "And I love you."

Slowly, his body started to move in hers in long, smooth strokes. It was overwhelming, the most beautiful thing she'd ever experienced. He claimed her body even as his eyes claimed her heart. The pleasure was every bit as intense as before, but it was deeper. It wasn't simply the sharing of two bodies, but the sharing of two souls. He made love to her. To every part of her. Slowly, gently, and thoroughly. He was a part of her, and she never wanted to let him go.

Finally, she could take no more. Her soft moans grew more urgent. He heard her silent plea and responded. His strokes started to lengthen. Deepen. Quicken. Become harder. She could feel his body tense under her fingertips even as hers started to break apart. She *had* to break apart. There was nowhere else to go.

She cried out, the pleasure shattering over her in a slow, pulsing wave.

"Oh, God," he groaned, letting himself go. He came into her in a hot rush that melded with her own. It seemed to go on forever. The spasms reverberated through every inch of her, not letting go.

It was just like before, except this time, when it did finally end, he rolled to the side, tucked her up against him, and held her as if he would never let go.

It was a long time later when Ewen found the energy and the words to speak. He was humbled, and a little awed, by what had just happened. He'd never known it could be like that. He'd never felt closer to anyone in his life. He'd swived many women, but he'd only made love to one: the woman who would be his wife. He still couldn't believe it.

As if reading his mind, she asked, "How did you get Robert to agree?"

She was cuddled against him with her cheek on his chest, playing with the spattering of dark hairs in a V at his neck, but to ask her question, she'd propped her chin on the back of her hand to gaze up at him.

"You'd already done most of the work," he said, running his fingers over the bare skin of her arm. "And so had my brethren."

Ewen still couldn't believe they'd refused to go on any missions unless he was brought back. MacLeod had reminded Bruce that he'd given him full authority over the team. The Highland Guard fought for Bruce, but they were MacLeod's men.

"How did you get Walter to come to Dunstaffnage to help you plead your case?"

"It wasn't easy. But I made him see that I was more valuable as his man than not. I also might have given him the idea of an alternative bride."

Walter Stewart might be young, but he was every bit as ambitious as his kinsman James Douglas—and his kinsman Robert the Bruce, for that matter.

She lifted a brow, intrigued. "One more impressive than a daughter of Mar?"

He laughed at her affront. But in this case, yes. "I thought you wanted out of the betrothal, so I thought it better not to argue your finer parts," he squeezed her bottom, "of which there are many."

She made a face, and then ruined the effect by laughing.

He kissed her head and then drew her in closer. "What did you say to the king?" he asked.

She shrugged. "I just reminded him of all we'd done in his service."

"And?"

"And reminded him of his own marriages."

"That's it?"

She shrugged again. "It was enough. But I came well prepared to plead my case and was confident he would see reason. Though I was not forced to use it, I had one argument that would ensure he would see things my way."

He looked at her skeptically. "I thought you were done being overconfident. The king was about as angry as I've ever seen him."

"Ah, but a good lawman always saves the best argument for last."

"And what argument is that?"

Her eyes met his, and he felt something inside him shift even before she spoke. She put her hand over her stomach. "My menses are late."

He stilled. His body had sensed the import of her words, but it took his mind a moment to catch up. "A babe?"

She nodded, tears glistening in her eyes. "I think so. Is . . . is it all right?"

Jesus, how could she ask something like that? A hot wave of emotion crashed over him. It tightened in his chest and throat. He didn't know what to say. He never had. But the difference with Janet was that it didn't matter. She understood him anyway.

But just in case, he told her again. This time with his body.

It was better than all right. It was everything. *She* had given him everything. The hunter had found what he didn't even know he'd been looking for, and he would never let her go again.

Epilogue

❧

Ardlamont, Cowal, Scotland, December 1315

Janet was going to have strong words with that little blue-eyed devil. "James! James Fynlay Lamont, come here right now!" She raced from room to room, coming to a stop when she entered the nursery and saw her husband. He stood a few feet away from her with two bundles tucked under his arms and two thin legs peeking out from behind his.

Even after five years of marriage, her heart still hitched on seeing him, as if part of her still couldn't believe he could be hers. Despite her feelings, however, she'd learned long ago not to let him distract her. She folded her arms across her chest and stared at him. "It's no use trying to hide him. I can see you, James."

A little blond head peeked out from behind Ewen's legs. She didn't buy the innocent look on his face for one moment. "Hand it over, Jamie."

"Hand what over, Mother?"

"The letter you took from my desk." She bent down to the little boy's level, trying to keep her stern expression in the face of a very wobbly lower lip. "It's a very important letter, Jamie. I need it back for the king."

He made a face, reached into his boot, and pulled out the now crumpled piece of parchment. "I don't care about the stupid ol' king. I don't want you to work anymore today. I want you to come play with me."

The mulish, disgruntled look on his face so resembled his father's, she had to look up at Ewen. He just shrugged. "Don't look at *me*."

Janet sighed and drew her four-year-old son onto her lap. Would it ever get any easier? She tried to balance the work she did for the king as his "advisor" and de facto, if not exactly publicly acknowledged, lawman, but there were days—like today—when inevitably that balance tipped.

Now that the war had been won with England, Robert was anxious to have Scotland accepted as an independent kingdom, and she'd been hard at work preparing their arguments for the carefully worded letters that would be sent to the French king and pope, to whom they were also appealing to have the excommunication lifted that had been placed on Robert since he stabbed John "The Red" Comyn at Greyfriar's Church four years ago. The Latin she'd once despaired of had come in handy.

"I thought you were going to play ball outside with Da today?" she said softly, stroking his head.

"We did. But then *they* got in the way. They always get in the way."

Janet tried not to smile and looked at the squirming two-year-old girls tucked under their father's arms. Unlike Jamie, they had dark hair like Ewen's. "What did they do this time?" she asked her son.

"Mary threw the ball in the loch, and then Issy started to cry. I hate when she cries."

Me, too, Janet thought, *and she does an awful lot of it.* She gazed up at Ewen for help.

"I'm trying," he said. "But as you can see, I have my hands full. He slipped away from me."

"I seem to recall someone saying this would be easy."

"I was expecting one, not *two*," he said. "I think it's time for me to go back to war."

"The war is over."

"Don't remind me," he said with an exaggerated roll of the eyes. "I think I hear Stewart calling me."

"Walter can wait," Janet said. "Besides, he has a new bride to think of." She still couldn't believe that the noblewoman whose hand had appeased him was that of her niece Marjory Bruce—Robert and Isabella's daughter. Marjory had been held in England for almost eight years, but had been released last year after the Battle of Bannockburn. "For whatever a man sows, he will also reap," she reminded her husband.

He grinned wickedly. "The sowing was fun, it's just the reaping I'm not so sure about." He belied his words, however, by tickling and kissing the two little cherubs in his arms until they were wild with laughter.

"We were just coming to find you," Ewen said when the girls had finally collapsed on the bed with exhaustion. "If you have a minute, there is something I want to show you."

She looked up at him. After almost five years of marriage, she was attuned to every note in his voice—and she'd heard the thick emotion. "Is it done?" she asked breathily.

Their eyes met, and he nodded.

Wordlessly, she let him take her hand as he led her and their three children outside the old tower house.

"Don't look yet," he said, when she tried to glance up at the nearby hill.

Finally, he stopped. "All right, turn around."

Janet sucked in her breath. The bright late-afternoon sun glistened off the freshly hewn stone, making the castle shimmer and shine like a newly minted jewel. It had four towers, one at each corner, encircled by a formidable wall. It was an impressive fortress by any standard, but that was not what made it important.

She slid her hand into that of the man who had turned her adventurous life as a courier into another kind of adventure. One of laughter and love and joy. "It's beautiful," she said. "She would have loved it."

He looked at her and nodded, the emotion too much for him to speak. He'd finished his mother's castle, and with it, he could at last be at peace with his past. For generations to come, the Lamonts of Ardlamont would fill this castle with love and laughter, giving his mother and father the legacy they deserved.

Hand in hand, with their children around them, Ewen led her into the keep, and into their future.

AUTHOR'S NOTE

Although the "wild" epitaph is my addition, Fynlay Lamont was the head of the Ardlamont branch of the Lamonts during this period. His exact date of death is not known, but it was sometime before 1315. He did indeed have a son named Ewen. Very little is known about the Ardlamont branch of the clan, including from whom they were descended, but it is said that they were vassals of Stewart and "may have fought in Bruce's bodyguard at Bannockburn" (*see* clsna.us/). It's references like this that make me start to believe my own fiction!

The Chief of Lamont at the time, Sir John, supported the MacDougalls against Bruce. As a result the Lamonts, who had been the dominant clan in Cowal in the thirteenth century, saw their fortunes decline, with much of their land going to—surprise!—the Campbells. The resulting feud between the Lamonts and Campbells would last for hundreds of years; as readers of *Highland Warrior* might recall.

Wild Fynlay's abduction of his chief's bride is my fictional explanation for the apparent ill will between the two branches of the clan. Ewen is said to have been killed years later by his relatives and the MacDougalls for his loyalty to Bruce.

Serendipitously, in my research I came across an undated charter from between 1309 and 1325 by John de Menteith (the betrayer of Wallace who later supported his kinsman

Bruce) to Ewen for some land in return for the "service of one bowman in the common army of the King of Scotland" that was witnessed by none other than Arthur Campbell (*The Ranger*). (*See* "An Inventory of Lamont Papers" at archive.org.) I love when things like that happen.

The name of Ewen's wife has not been recorded, but he had a son named James, which, as it doesn't seem to be a popular Lamont name at the time, could conceivably be in honor of the Ardlamont's vassal lord, Sir James Stewart.

As I mentioned in the Author's Note of *The Recruit*, Mary of Mar was alternatively referred to as Mary, Marjory, and Margaret, and as there seem to be some inconsistencies in some of her references, it gave me the idea of having Mary be two people. Thus "Janet," her twin sister, was born.

I knew from the outset of writing the Highland Guard series that I wanted one of the books to emphasize the importance of the church to Bruce's ultimately successful bid for the crown. When I came across a reference in the Calendar of Documents (basically a compilation of primary source documents from the period) to an alleged foiled plot to capture Bruce at a peace negotiation, I knew this was a perfect mission for my "nun" heroine and what I dubbed the couriers of the cloth.

There were actually two peace negotiations held over the winter of 1310–1311. The first was at Selkirk on December 17 (my birthday!), with Sir Robert Clifford and Sir Robert fitz Pain. The second was to be in Melrose in January, with the earls of Cornwall and Gloucester, but Bruce supposedly was warned of treachery and failed to show up. In the interest of my story timeline, I decided to combine the two parleys into one.

This is how one innocuous reference in a letter can inspire a story. From the *Calendar of Documents Relating to Scotland*, Volume III, 1307–1357, page 39, an anonymous letter to the king dated February 19:

> *As to other news—when he was in the North, Sir Robert de Clifford and Sir Robert fitz Pain had by the K.'s leave been at Selkirk 8 days before Christmas, to speak with Robert de Brus, and since then the Earls of Gloucester and Cornwall were to have parleyed with him at a place near Melros, but it was said he had been warned by some he would be taken, and therefore departed, so they have had no parley.*

Note also how Bruce is referred to as simply "Robert de Brus," not Sir Robert or the Earl of Carrick (titles he enjoyed before the "usurping" of the crown) and certainly not "King Robert."

I must admit, as a former lawyer, the character who can talk her way out of anything is particularly close to my heart. When I found out the name Lamont derived from the Norse for "lawman," I knew exactly what Janet was going to have to do with her skills. Alas, I had to make her a legal "advisor," as I wasn't able to find any evidence of female lawyers in this period. Even an advisor is anachronistic, but I like to think Janet would have made it work. The letter she alludes to in the epilogue is a precursor to one of the most famous documents in Scottish history, the Declaration of Arbroath of 1320, the letter to the pope that confirms Scotland as an independent nation.

The family of Mar was one of the most important in Scotland and, as we've seen before, was very well connected. Mar was one of the original eight "Mormaers" of Scotland, which later became known as the Earldom of Mar. "Janet's" father, Domhnall (Donald), was the 6th Earl of Mar; her brother Gartnait, the 7th; and her nephew—another Donald—who was also the son of Bruce's sister, was the 8th. This is the young Donald who appears in *The Viper* and is being raised in Edward II's household along with his cousin the young Earl of Atholl in *The Recruit*. In addition to Isabella, who was Robert the Bruce's first wife, and Duncan, who may have been married to Christina MacRuairi (the Lady of the Isles), there was possibly another brother, Alexander.

Walter Stewart did indeed marry Princess Marjory Bruce, Robert and Isabella of Mar's daughter, after she was released from her eight-year captivity in 1314. Walter's date of birth ranges anywhere from 1292 to 1296. I went with the earlier date, as it fit my plot better. In any event, he was old enough to marry Alice Erskine before he married Marjory in 1315.

Tragically, Marjory died from a riding accident less than two years after her release while heavily pregnant. The child survived and, after the death of Bruce's only son, King David II, would eventually be crowned Robert II, founding the dynasty of Stewart kings who would reign Scotland and later—tons of irony here—England! Readers of *Highlander Untamed* might remember this "Union of the Crowns," which takes place in 1603 at the end of that novel.

Edward II's invasion of Scotland over the summer of 1310, featured in both *The Recruit* and in *The Hunter,* was anticlimactic to say the least. You almost have to feel sorry for poor Edward. Not only did he have the "Hammer of the Scots" legend of his father Edward I to live up to, and the constant problems with his barons, but he put together an army for presumably his triumphant defeat of the Scots and marched into Scotland only to find no one to battle. There were some skirmishes, but for the most part, Bruce engaged in a game of cat-and-mouse and refused to meet him in a pitched battle. As I was writing, I kept picturing Edward looking around yelling, "Come out, come out wherever you are!" Edward II is also the king who was defeated by his wife, imprisoned, forced to abdicate, and possibly killed by having—as legend has it—a hot poker stuck up his bum. Yikes! Sometimes—as Mel Brooks fans may appreciate—it is *not* good to be the king.

When I decided to make "Sister" Janet speak Italian in *The Recruit,* I didn't realize what a can of research worms I was opening for *The Hunter.* What language people would have spoken at the time turned out to be a surprisingly involved question.

In Scotland, Gaelic was certainly spoken in the Highlands and the West, as well as in Galloway, and possible among the peasants in other parts of the country as well. Northern Middle English (which would become the "Scots" tongue) and Norman French would have been prevalent in the towns. The "Greater Lords" probably would have spoken Norman French or Northern Middle English. Robert Bruce is thought to have spoken Gaelic, Norman French, and Northern Middle English and to be literate in classical Latin, as were most of the nobles of his time.

With all this in Scotland, I assumed Italy would be much easier, but it proved surprisingly complicated given the large number of regional dialects and the emergence of Italian as a distinct language from Vulgar Latin. I made it even harder on myself by making Janet a pseudo-nun, as Latin stayed around longest in the church.

The Italian language developed in the early Middle Ages from what is known as Vulgar Latin. The word *vulgar* as used in this context means "common," and Vulgar Latin refers to the Latin that is spoken "of the people." Classical Latin by this time is mostly written. Vulgar Latin was transforming into the various Romance languages certainly by the eighth century, but as Italian is the closest Romance language to Vulgar Latin, it isn't as easy to pinpoint when it became distinct.

It was around the late thirteenth century that the distinction was becoming more evident in the writings of people such as Dante Alighieri. Dante is often referred to as the "Father of the Italian Language," and he wrote the *Divine Comedy* between 1308 and 1321, so you see the problem. I kept waffling on whether to call it "Italian" or "Vulgar Latin" or "Tuscan," being unsure how they would have referred to it at the time. I eventually decided just to go with the familiar "Italian." Believe me, by this time I was wishing I'd made Janet mute!

The meeting at Dundonald Castle between the kinsmen is my invention, but the squabbling among the noblemen is not. It is a precursor to an incident known as the "Capitulation of Irvine." The capitulation, which took place on July 7, is definitely not a high point for Scottish noblemen in the long Wars of Independence, especially as it relates to William Wallace.

Wallace began his famous uprisings in May of 1297 by allegedly killing the Sheriff of Lanark. Very quickly he was joined by William "the Hardy" Douglas. The two had some early success in further attacks and were joined by some other noblemen, including a young Robert Bruce and James Stewart. Apparently, Bruce had been dispatched by Edward I to attack Douglas's holdings for his rebellion and decided instead to join the rebels.

Alas, the confederacy was not a long one. When the nobles were ordered by Edward to appear at Irvine to submit, the English and Scots gathered for a battle. As the probably apocryphal story goes, there was so much fighting on the Scots side that the English simply turned and left! The alternative, that the Scots' squabbling led to their submission, is probably more likely. It is speculated that some of the noblemen had a problem following Wallace, who at the time wasn't even a knight.

This ignominious capitulation by the noblemen was even worse in that it came only a couple of months before Wallace's great victory at Stirling Bridge on September 11, 1297. Many of the Scot noblemen who capitulated at Irvine were on the English side of that battle, including James Stewart, who then supposedly went back to the Scot side when he saw Wallace and Andrew Moray were winning the battle. As I have mentioned before, it's probably easiest just to sum it all by saying that there was a lot of going back and forth by the Scot nobles in the Wallace years (1296–1305).

As I mentioned in the prologue, the families of Stewart, Menteith, Douglas, and Bruce were all descendants of Walter, the 3rd High Steward of Scotland, which probably explains why later both Stewart and Douglas were early supporters of a Bruce kingship. Alan, Earl of Menteith, was as well, but the young earl (his father, Alexander, had died in 1304) was captured at Methven in 1306 and died in prison. His brother and successor, like the young earls of Mar and Atholl, seems to have been held as a hostage in England.

Interestingly, and what influenced the prologue, is that the Lamonts of Ardlamont were Stewart's men and the main branch of Lamonts were Menteiths. There was certainly discord between the two branches of Lamonts, but whether there was discord between Stewart and Menteith, I don't know. I'd like to think so, since the "Lambies," as the Lamonts have been referred to in history, are sometimes held responsible for the death of Wallace's father. Moreover, John "the False" Menteith, Alexander's younger brother, will forever be known in history as the man who turned William Wallace over to Edward I in 1305. If you've seen the movie *Braveheart,* you know the result of that.

St. Drostan's Day was held on December 15 or 16. Drostan was a Celtic monk who lived in Scotland in the sixth century. He was possibly a member of the Irish royal family (or a Welsh prince) and was a disciple of the famous Saint Columba. Drostan founded the monastery of Old Deer in Aberdeenshire. St. Drostan's fairs were known to have been held at Aberlour in Moray for three days and at Old Deer in Aberdeenshire for eight days. Given the strict penitence that was usually observed during Advent, the timing is unusual, but it must have been one of those times when custom won out—at least in those villages. That there would have been a fair in Roxburgh is my conjecture.

A few quick notes. There was indeed a hospital at Rutherford in this period, founded by King David (1124–1152) and dedicated to Saint Mary Magdalene, patron saint of the Knights Templar. And the village of Cuingealach, where Janet and Ewen try to buy a horse and run into English soldiers, is today known as Wanlockhead. It is known as Scotland's highest village, at over 1,500 feet.

For pictures and more information, please visit my website at www.MonicaMccarty.com or www.TheHighland Guard.com.

Coming soon! Look for

THE RAIDER

the next novel in
Monica McCarty's Highland Guard series!

Published by Ballantine Books

ed after the cra-